PENGUIN BOOKS

THE PENGUIN BOOK OF CARIBBEAN SHORT STORIES

E. A. Markham was born in Montserrat in 1939 and, though working in France and Germany in the seventies, has lived mainly in Britain since the 1950s. He has directed the *Caribbean Theatre Workshop*, edited *Artrage* magazine and, in the past decade, has worked in the arts in Papua New Guinea and Ulster. He now heads the creative writing programme at Sheffield Hallam University. He is the editor of *Hinterland* (the Bloodaxe Book of Caribbean Poetry), and has published three books of short stories: *Something Unusual* (1986), *Ten Stories* (1994), and *Taking the Drawing Room through Customs* (1996), and six collections of poetry, including *Misapprehensions* (1995). Among his output are plays and a travel book. Markham edits the literary magazine *Sheffield Thursday*.

THE PENGUIN BOOK OF
Caribbean Short Stories

Edited by E. A. Markham

PENGUIN BOOKS

PENGUIN BOOKS

Published by the Penguin Group
Penguin Books Ltd, 27 Wrights Lane, London w8 5tz, England
Penguin Books USA Inc., 375 Hudson Street, New York, New York 10014, USA
Penguin Books Australia Ltd, Ringwood, Victoria, Australia
Penguin Books Canada Ltd, 10 Alcorn Avenue, Toronto, Ontario, Canada m4v 3b2
Penguin Books (NZ) Ltd, 182–190 Wairau Road, Auckland 10, New Zealand

Penguin Books Ltd, Registered Offices: Harmondsworth, Middlesex, England

First published in Penguin Books 1996
10 9 8 7 6 5 4 3 2

Pages 415–17 constitute an extension to this copyright page

Set in 10/12.5pt Monotype Garamond
Typeset by Rowland Phototypesetting Ltd, Bury St Edmunds, Suffolk
Printed in England by Clays Ltd, St Ives plc

For Andrew Salkey
(And in memory of Sam Selvon)

A Death in the Family
(i.m. Andrew Salkey, 1928–95)

Dear Andrew, I heard of your passing in passing,
tipping it a little in the flow of loss we must wade through
and I apologize, as we do, for not being there;
we expected you back, not like this, to those interrupted
talks in Moscow Road, which would go better now
with the strain of travel and search for allies behind us; we'd be wiser
now – all those Jerusalems desecrated – glossing friendship
with no sparring for advantage, no fear of surrender.

You signed off your letters, *Venceremos*. I'd planned to answer
the last one with a quip, a bit of gossip, tales
of our slippage over here. Forgive me if this sounds like a voice
grown distant; but thank you, Andrew Salkey, anthologist of wastes
and triumphs of our story. Ever frail but renewable, our barrier
against spoilers who make the earth more wretched, holds your text.

E. A. MARKHAM, 1995

Contents

CONTENTS

Preface

In putting together this anthology I'd like to thank the dozens of people who brought so much new and exciting work to my attention. I'd like to acknowledge, particularly, the assistance of Peter Fraser, Jeremy Poynting and Stewart Brown, all of whom had an impact on selection; of Paola Marchionni and Marie Bastiampillai from the Commonwealth Institute Resource Centre and Literature Library for easing my research; of Petronella Breinburg, Lawrence Scott and Ken Ramchand for useful suggestions – and to thank Robert Miles of Sheffield Hallam University, who suggested the project.

Introduction

I

The late, much lamented, Sam Selvon, not long before his death in 1994, was moved to recall 'the wonderment and accolade that greeted the boom of Caribbean literature and art in Britain in the early fifties',[1] and a new book of Caribbean short stories seems timely – yes, as a tribute to Sam, but also because of the current popularity of the short story generally, and the continuing interest in Caribbean writing. What is particularly satisfying is to be able to confirm that the short story has joined the novel and poetry as major forms of literary expression by writers from the region. The short story from Trinidad has long been rich enough to represent a region's literature; and now the Caribbean literary naissance in Toronto is threatening to outstrip even that. But, really, when I'm asked what's special about the Caribbean short story today, I'm tempted to start by dropping five names: Olive Senior, Jamaica Kincaid, Pauline Melville, Alecia McKenzie and Makeda Silvera. And then another five. And another. But enough. Forget the accolade; clearly, something of the wonderment seems to have been sustained. Kenneth Ramchand articulates the general feeling that 'in the last couple of decades women have been the dominant forces in Caribbean literature'.[2] And he links this to the 'return' to the short story form. Others talk of women as the significant, 'new wave', or of women coming out of the *kumbla* – a Jamaican term meaning literary *calabash*, symbolically *enclosed space*, carrying the sense of lack of space, of language, even.[3] The term is used to telling effect in Erna Brodber's novel, *Jane and Louisa Will Soon Come Home* (1980).

We can't simply explain this creative energy away by reference to the marketability of women's writing and the growth of women's presses in a political and critical climate informed by feminism; what is unarguable is that the best of this work has been exceptional. There have been men, too, in this period, writing fine stories. Five names? Garth St Omer, Earl Lovelace, Clyde Hosein, Lawrence Scott, Neil Bissoondath. They, and many more, are represented here.

One effect of new waves is to erase footsteps already in the sand, so we must be more cautious about our discoveries than some non-literary travellers in these regions have been over the last few hundred years. Change the metaphor: the production of so much fine short story writing in a relatively short time serves, at the least, to take the strain off the generation that Selvon referred to, the generation which came to prominence in the 1940s and 1950s – the astonishingly prolific Roger Mais, who died at fifty, Selvon himself, the young V. S. Naipaul, and before them Jean Rhys and (perhaps) Claude McKay – who have had to carry the genre. I'm not attempting to downgrade these prominent names from the past (and they are of the very recent past) but, in Caribbean as in English (British) fiction there tends to be, if not confusion, at least some collusion between what one might call aims and outcomes: the aspiring writer being invited to aim at the short story with, some way down the line towards eventual success, the novel as an outcome. (So the names George Lamming, Wilson Harris, Edgar Mittelholzer, John Herne, Jan Carew and others who populated our early short story collections, have long been assigned to the other art form. The exceptions are V. S. Naipaul, whose stories written early in his career continue to command respect, and Selvon and Jean Rhys, whose success as novelists never quite marginalized their short story work.) The time may be right to move closer to the Irish or American notions of a literary tradition, and to confer major status on short story writers of stature. At the moment a Caribbean Frank O'Connor or Raymond Carver – or, moving further afield, a Borges or a Calvino – would have to rely on more 'substantial' work.

There is a danger and excitement in writing about Caribbean literature: the excitement is obvious in that the work keeps surprising you with its energy. The danger is that an editor faced with so much excellent writing from the Caribbean, and by Caribbean-heritage people living outside the region, has to keep some kind of perspective: how much of this literature belongs to the Caribbean? Does the lightly creolized writing of Lucy Lane Clifford (Barbados/UK, 1853–1929) qualify? And what about a contemporary like Karen Kin-Aribassala of Guyana, whose move to Nigeria – and change of name – fascinates as a West Indian influencing African literature, reversing the literary traffic: can we claim more than that?

The danger is evident in the profusion of recent anthologies of short prose wearing the 'West Indian' or 'Caribbean' label[4] with no editorial overview, the likely result being to irritate the knowledgeable and mislead the inexperienced reader. The terms 'Caribbean' and 'West Indian' as editorial shorthand might have, as many have said, to carry the sort of health warning that 'Commonwealth' (hegemonic connotations) and 'post-colonial' (of a homogenizing tendency, denying countries and regions their particular and distinctive experiences of colonization) already do.

Why am I flirting with this danger, attempting to take in the whole picture of the short story deriving from the Caribbean? Let me backtrack a bit to a survey I conducted – *The Short Story Today* – for a magazine I edit.[5] Writers of short fiction were approached and asked the usual questions: who had influenced them, whom they admired, etc. And what stories by other writers would make it into their own preferred anthology. There weren't many surprises, the usual names coming up again and again: Chekhov, Maupassant, Borges, Raymond Carver, Hemingway. More examples of the good and solid – from Kafka to Joyce to V. S. Pritchett and Somerset Maugham. The relative ignorance, from the response, of the Caribbean achievement in this field seemed a challenge worth rising to.

So, if you're looking for hidden agendas, certain things about the Caribbean short story played on my mind: the under-representation of long-established practitioners (with the exception of Jean Rhys) in general short story collections today; the tendency of Caribbean-heritage writers living abroad to be packaged as the host nation's product;[6] the neglect by critics and scholars of this art form that everyone professes to value – why not make visible a range of stories and the myths informing them! Past collections have tended to assume a different readership for the legends (people, say, fascinated by cultural archaeology) from that of scribal work. And we come back to the question of defining a national literature when its practitioners seem permanently encamped on all five continents. As I suspect we shall soon no longer be able to justify bringing together all this work under one banner – the literary grandparents and grandchildren, so to speak, who might claim to be Caribbean – I thought this might be a last chance.

So there we have it; pre-Columbian legends and myths deriving from India and Africa; something Gothic from the Great House with its history (Collymore, Scott) as well as the still-familiar jumping up in the streets. We include one of Eric Walrond's elemental nightmares from his childhood experiences in the Canal Zone (an early example of 'exile' writing, a persistent feature of Caribbean literature). Probably the short story's special contribution here is in emphasizing the loneliness of exile. (This is true from Jean Rhys to the latest of the new wave washed up in Canada.) What else have we got? A Naipaul who might be unfamiliar to many readers: Seepersad is the father of V. S. and Shiva and great-uncle of Neil Bissoondath, but it's as a member of the Trinidad literary awakening in the late 1920s and early 1930s – and the first Caribbean writer of Indian extraction who could be called professional – that he is included. The Sistren Theatre Collective is included, drawing on some of the myths that empower women. Then, with Makeda Silvera's probing narrative of women who love each other, we seem to be edging to a new freedom of expression in the Caribbean short story. Erna Brodber, in 'One Bubby Susan', seamlessly brings together again the world of myth and story, and Kamau Brathwaite uses modernist techniques of pun, odd layout, misspellings, multiple typeface, etc., perfected over decades as a poet, to contribute now to the post-modernist phase of the story.

What constitutes 'Caribbean'? I'm reminded of the critic Danforth Ross introducing the American short story (1961). He posed two questions. Has the subject kept pace with literary developments in the rest of the world? And has the American short story from Washington Irving, Poe, Hawthorne, Melville and Mark Twain, etc., managed to maintain its American character? These questions are a bit of a challenge when dealing with the Caribbean. Our concern here is with the part of the region usually described as the area stretching from Guyana to Belize and the islands in between – the West Indies. It is said that there are about five million West Indians living 'at home' and about five million living abroad; and it's an interesting question whether giving parity to 'abroad' doesn't in some way legitimize the political condition of division and fragmentation that we complain about in other contexts. Though again, if language separates 'West Indian' from 'Caribbean', it nevertheless performs some sort of bridge between scattered members of the tribe.

Touching on Danforth Ross's other point, we think the subject has kept pace with literary developments in the rest of the world, even though it's still discovering rather than preserving its character.

But to practical matters: what to do about Caribbean writers claimed by other literatures? Is it a parody of imperialism to claim (reclaim) those who don't live in the region? Austin Clarke (Barbados/Canada, b. 1934) and the huge colony of Caribbean writers in Canada[7] are at the moment secure, but as their successors increasingly get involved in pursuing what Stewart Brown calls the Caribbean version of the American Dream, aren't they bound to be lost to our literature? Does it matter? 'Black British' writers, by definition, seem already to have gone elsewhere.

We don't want to be sidetracked into questions about identity, but discussions about where writers belong at least get us thinking about what's distinctive in the literature. Claude McKay was a prominent figure of the Harlem renaissance, as was Eric Walrond, but no one would doubt their essential West Indianness. This is still an important defining characteristic of Rhys (Dominica/UK) and Paule Marshall (Barbados/US), though it seems less so when we come to Rosa Guy (Trinidad/US). Maybe an aesthetic case can be made for people whose work might be presented in more than one national literature on behalf of the literary context which provides the greater resonance. Paule Marshall's 'Barbados' should do better here than in the American 'ethnic' collection where I've seen it languishing.

2 *Anancy and After*

Our Amerindian myths serve, among other things, to remind us – 'arrivists' from Africa, Asia and Europe – of the original inhabitants of the region.

Similarly, the popularity and cultural diversification of major festivals in the Caribbean confirm that genocide (Amerindian) and plantation experience (of Africans) weren't the only traumatic events that shaped the West Indies. The bringing in of East Indians, largely as indentured workers after the abolition of slavery in 1834, was another. (That new form of exploitation started in 1838.) One benefit of all this is the cultural mix we have today. Chinese West Indians, too, had a history of indenture and, like the Chinese everywhere, celebrate Yuan Tan, the Chinese New Year, with shopkeepers and clubs organizing dragon and dance displays, decorating shop windows with great splashes of red and gold, etc. But the myths which inform the great Hindu and Muslim festivals, and have a following and resonance second only to Carnival, have seldom found their way into the literary collections.

That's why Kenneth Parmasad's 1984 collection, *Salt and Roti: Indian Folk Tales of the Caribbean*, is important. These (Hindu) tales survived the crossing and, as Gordon Rohlehr sums it up in his preface to the book, 'introduced us to a legendary world of kings, palaces, functionaries, mandirs, where miracles occur; magic, the supernatural and the wonderful'. Knowledge of these myths is valuable to the appreciation of the Caribbean comic literary tradition. For example, Parmasad's 'Rites of the Dead' (not included here) involves comic misunderstandings surrounding the ritual of mourning the recently dead, acquaintance with which informed my own reading of Neil Bissoondath's story 'Security' from his 1990 collection *On the Eve of Uncertain Tomorrows*. There, Alistair Ramgoolam's discomfiture in Toronto, after having transferred his wealth (though not his belongings), his family and himself from a Trinidad in crisis, might be mildly amusing, a payback for his divided political loyalties (a process which started in an earlier story, 'Insecurity', published in Bissoondath's 1985 collection, *Digging Up the Mountains*) – that, and Ramgoolam's somewhat patriarchal attitudes, warrant the joke against him. But his panic in not wanting to die in a place where the family no longer knows the burial rites isn't just a recognizable immigrant fear but gains resonance from our memory of 'Rites of the Dead'.

Another story from Parmasad, 'Sakchulee and the Rich Gentleman' (included here), is significant in that it introduces from the Indian subcontinent a popular, trickster figure, Sakchulee,[8] not unlike his more famous counterpart, Anancy, from Africa. These Hindu stories – referred to, sometimes, as *kheesas* when they mix the fairy tale with the moral story – would be known to everyone in the community, certainly up to the mid 1950s. They were passed down, generally, by the women, told to the extended family at night sitting round the lighted flambeaux, or at the communal get-together (the *satsang*) where there would be a combination of song, music, the reading of religious texts *and* storytelling. Popular, also, were homilies, drawn mainly from the story of Rama and Sita in the *Ramayana*, where daughters would be encouraged to emulate Sita in the proper duties of womanhood. But it's no surprise that storytelling among Indo-Caribbeans, too, has declined, and for the usual reasons – the growth of public education; the advent of Indian films as a means of transmitting the culture; the drift of rural populations into the towns and cities, etc.

The relative lack of Muslim stories in the written literature probably has something to do with the suspicion that the main Muslim festivals – the Eid-Ul-Fitr (the festival that comes at the end of Ramadan) and the Eid Midad-um-Nabi (which commemorates the birthday of the Prophet) – have successfully withstood secularization, and hence creolization. The exception is probably the festival of Hosein which a guidebook to Trinidad describes as 'marking the anniversary of the massacre of the grandsons of Muhammad . . . celebrated with tassa drumming and papier mâché replicas of the brothers' tombs. These confections, covered in bright paper and tiny mirrors, are carried through the streets by devotees for three nights, followed by drummers and onlookers. On the final night of celebration, huge six-foot or larger versions are brought out, and carried in a final procession to the sea, where they are ceremoniously dipped in the water.'⁹ The Hosein festival is increasingly drawing devotees from non-Muslim Trinidadians. (There is a fine description of the ceremony in Ismith Khan's 1961 novel *The Jumblie Bird*.)

It might be said that the Christian myth is the one that most completely pervades Caribbean literature – as, indeed, it does the lives of Caribbean people. The structure and language, as well as the ethic, of Bible stories come through to us not only in the great novels of Mittelholzer, say, and Roger Mais, but in the short stories that populate leading magazines like *Bim*. It's in recognition of this Christian influence on all things Caribbean that I thought to include here a sermon by Wilfred Wood (b. Barbados, 1936), Bishop of Croydon. But of all the secular myths associated with Caribbean literature Anancy has had the greatest influence on writers.

The tone for Anancy is well set for us by the story of how this most popular of Caribbean traditional tales comes to bear his name. Anancy is the spider-person, a hero originating from Ghana as the Ashanti Spider God. By the time he's translated to the Caribbean Anancy is all trickster, cunning, guile. The story of the naming of the tales is this:

Once upon a time the animals used to come together in the forest for what we might call old-talk. Tiger was king of the forest and, reflecting his status, already had many things named after him – Tiger lilies, Tiger moths, Tiger stories, etc. As the animals sat round in a circle in the evening talking and laughing Snake would ask: Who's the strongest of us all? And Dog would say: Tiger is the strongest; when Tiger whispers, the trees listen; when Tiger is angry and cries out, the trees tremble. And when Snake asks who among them is the weakest, Dog shouts: Anancy the Spider – and they all enjoy the joke.

One day, when the strongest and the weakest meet in the forest, with all the retinue including frogs and parrots and others in attendance, Anancy pays obeisance and asks Tiger a favour. Since you're the strongest, he says, and so many things bear your name, maybe as a generous king, you'd let something be called after the *weakest* in the land. So with the king's permission he would like the *stories* – stories they tell one another in the forest in the evening, stories about Br'er Snake and Br'er Tacumah, Br'er Cow and Br'er Bird, etc. – to be called after himself, Anancy. Now Tiger has every intention of keeping these stories under his own name but thinks he'll play a game with Anancy, humiliate him. Tiger agrees to let the stories be named after Anancy if Anancy goes down to the river and brings him back Mr Snake alive. The joke pleases the listening retinue. Days of stratagems and false starts follow, and finally Anancy manages, with great cunning, to outwit the Snake and brings him back alive; hence, the Anancy stories.

This myth has informed the structure and supplied the ethic for numerous Caribbean stories and many novels. (Anancy has not just informed Afro-Caribbean writers. Willi Chen's game-cock trainer in the parable 'Moro' (included here), would be recognizable to Anancy-watchers. Chen's parents migrated to Trinidad from China.)

The Anancy stories have served us well, shown us that it was possible for the powerless to survive, indeed, that it is possible to overcome forces larger than yourself by employing cunning, patience, wit. This, considering our lack of political, economic and aesthetic status in the world, seemed an appropriate and endlessly recyclable metaphor for people without clear geographical expression, linguistically challenged, drawn irresistibly to this or that foreign centre, where part of the deal seems to be to collude in our own humiliation.

Perhaps it's time to ask certain questions of Anancy: to what extent does a tradition with its mind-set of subterfuge, the self-obsession and maleness of the conceit, the tendency to shirk responsibility because responsibility without power is impossible and power lies elsewhere – to what extent has this way of thinking become something of a burden to us? Is this a caricature whose political force is now spent? Many of the present short story writers – and not only the women – are toying with these notions.

Other traditions, other myths are beginning to shape the stories. Carole Boyce Davies and Elaine Savory Fido's seminal book *Out of the Kumbla: Caribbean Women and Literature* (1990) points to some of these and to things in the culture which still impede expression for women. Davies[10] points out how the oral literature of the Caribbean – proverbs, folk-tales and calypsos – reinforces negative images of women.

A group that's captured the imagination in their effort to recover something of a female-sustaining myth is the Sistren Theatre Collective. Sistren, a Jamaican group, grew out of Michael Manley's emergency employment ('make work') programme (1972–80). In 1977 they produced a play – thirteen black women not trained in these skills, with the help of one Jamaican white woman. They told the invited professional, Honor Ford Smith, 'We want to do plays about how we suffer as women. We want to do plays about how men treat us bad.'[11] Sistren went on to develop skills in screen printing and in publishing (a quarterly magazine), but they started out as something of an encounter group, building up a routine of telling their life stories to one another, then gleaning information, more or less hidden, about Jamaican women of the past who had been prominent in the fight for education and women's rights. They also drew strength from the heroic deeds of women who may or may not have been mythical – Queens of the Maroons[12] – going back to the seventeenth century. The figure who energized them was a female archetype by the name of Ni (Nanny). Ni was as womanly as Anancy was male. She was a warrior, of course, and a priestess; she was leader of the Maroons and, de-mythologized, led them in the mid eighteenth century in their fight against slavery. She was a great military strategist and had the trick of bouncing bullets off her bottom and throwing them back at her attackers. But she also connected with what might be the

Ashanti nurturing tradition; a herbalist, a cultivator able to produce, with her magic powers, fully grown pumpkins from seed to prevent her 'troops' being starved out. Interestingly, in one of the Sistren stories ('Foxy and di Macca Palace War'), Anancy (Anansi) turns up as a slum hoodlum, putting into practice the old ethic of wanting to 'control dat dawta'.

Is this having an effect on portrayal of the trickster who, with all his ingenuity, shows little capacity, in his various exploits, for keeping family together, children fed? (In a few of the stories he is married!) It's interesting that in his latest incarnation, by Andrew Salkey, 'Anancy and Jeffrey Amherst', Anancy claims to be as much female as male.

Andrew Salkey (Jamaica/UK/US, 1928–95) was the perfect bridge between the Anancy myth and contemporary literature, the trickster tradition having informed his novels.[13] His tribute to the Spiderman, *Anancy's Score* (1973) was the culmination of a lifelong interest. Salkey has done as much as anyone to popularize the short story and has won many prizes for his books for children. (Today's writers of popular or children's short stories – Timothy Challender, Earl McKenzie, James Berry – owe a debt to Salkey.) Andrew Salkey was part of the 1950s wave of young writers/students from the Caribbean to England, and over the next twenty-five years he was instrumental in the development of all aspects of Caribbean literature: he was a broadcaster, an editor of anthologies of poems, stories and essays; he wrote radio plays and, in 1966, joined with John La Rose and Kamau (then Edward) Brathwaite to form the Caribbean Artists Movement,[14] one purpose of which was to make artistic talent from the Caribbean visible in Britain. In the mid 1970s Salkey went to America, to Amherst, where he was Professor of Writing at Hampshire College, until his relatively early death.

3 *The Story in Transition (I): The Selvon Phase*

In my 1993 magazine survey referred to earlier, on the short story, many statements were made about the story's brevity and intensity of focus – what one student called its 'packed simplicity'; about its small illuminations affording personal recognition; about its knack of being a microcosm of life – 'like gazing into a rock pool', etc. But I can't resist quoting Frederic Raphael:

> The charm of the short story lies in its density, which is composed principally by a certain (elusive) sense of the author's experience and weight, the richness of his or her knowledge of the world, distilled in narrow confines. Hemingway's over-advertised technique of putting in elements which 'stain' the narrative, even after they have been excised (as a draughtsman rubs out *and* leaves in certain marks), is the key here. I can never wholly believe in the functional genius of a writer who never writes short stories.[15]

Stories have a habit of turning up later as chapters of novels – Claude McKay's 'He Also Loved' had an independent life before being incorporated into the novel *Home to Harlem* (1928) and Sam Selvon used the early 'Johnson and the Cascadura' as the basis of his 1972 book, *Those Who Eat the Cascadura*. Another publishing trick is to hold the collection of stories back until the author publishes a novel. Lawrence Scott was fairly lucky in that *Ballad for the New World and Other Stories* (1994) was shelved for a relatively short time pending the appearance of his first novel, *Witchbroom* (1992). Raphael's mention of technique makes us want to bring things up to date by looking for the sort of tricks – film syntax: jump-cuts, flashbacks, multiple points of view – that make stories look contemporary. But it's true to say that revolution in the Caribbean short story hasn't, on the whole, been overtly concerned with formal experiment – not until now – but with the role of language.

A few words about this: that language is always to be the central issue in any form of writing hardly needs stating, except that its significance might be overlooked here. Part of the excess of privation that Africans suffered after transportation to the New World was the silencing of sophisticated conversation by the separating of people from their own language-groups, making it difficult to repossess the past, to articulate the present. After this experience of linguistic cleansing it was imperative – over the years, over centuries – for survivors who formed the new communities to rebuild speech and eventually get that form of speech recognized as the language of the nation, nation language.[16] Sam Selvon is given credit for being the first West Indian writer to adopt dialect as the narrative voice, to obliterate the (class) difference between the narrator and fictional character. Suddenly, in the novel *The Lonely Londoners* (1956) and stories written around that time (and earlier: Ramchand pinpoints 'Brackley and the Bed') published in *Ways of Sunlight* (1957), the status of the writer as author/teacher putting on a special voice for the reader/pupil is effectively undermined.

Towards the end of his life, when pressed on the point, Selvon admitted that he hoped to revitalize the English language by his use of nation language; and his achievement in this area is clear, though Jeremy Poynting, the publisher of Peepal Tree Books and an authority on Indo-Caribbean literature, has pointed out that Seepersad Naipaul had achieved something similar more than a decade before Selvon.[17] And Vic Reid had, also, pointed the way in his pioneering 'nationalist' novel, *New Day* (1949). Poynting, though, raises a more interesting point, that by focusing on Selvon's use of nation language – playing up the 'folksiness', so to speak – we are not, perhaps, giving weight to Selvon's interest in structural aspects of the narrative, of cultural ideas shaping the story. 'Wartime Activities', an early story, is an example of this. Here, we have a young man fleeing his Indian family in the village to avoid an arranged marriage. He runs off, eventually, to Port of Spain and has a lively, but terrible time. Eventually, he meets an Indian nursemaid and falls in love with her. Of course, she is the young woman that he was to be married to; and she, also, has run away from home. Poynting comments:

> If you actually trace the story, then you can see what Selvon is doing is working out a whole series of kinds of opposition about tensions that he is exploring between the enclosed nature of Indian culture, but its supportiveness and its structuring, and its nurturing aspect. On the other side is the open nature of Creole culture. But also its threatening and very personally challenging aspects. And if you look at the structures there, you find that he works out a whole series of oppositions between these positions: there is a kind of parallel created between things like arranged marriage and prostitution – one existing in one culture, one existing in the other. And it's about somebody who's trying to negotiate a path between the two.[18]

The fascination with Selvon continues because of the sheer fun of his work, the succession of comic types with – in the Caribbean way –

names to match ('Little One', a man about town, 'Dumboy', 'More Lazy', 'Mangohead', 'Small Change'),[19] and because he broke with so many conventions, hinting at new ways in which the short story might develop. He wrote of the newly arrived migrants to London with sympathy and tolerance for the dreams, however impractical, lending their lives eloquence. Also, because his characters have to use the nation's public transport – and service it – and because they do the routine and menial jobs which enable the city to function, we get a sense of concreteness of place (not unlike the feel of Ireland that you get from William Trevor's stories) as if, in one sense, they are a neglected part of the social history. He explored the possibilities of the very short story in many of his 'Christmas' stories published in the *Trinidad Guardian* in the late 1940s. Again, his fiction wasn't ethnocentric, so Indo-Caribbean, Afro-Caribbean and 'other' characters were equally subject to his benign satire.

Among Selvon's most startling achievements is the celebration of London in 'My Girl and the City', published in *Ways of Sunlight*. (This, incidentally, was Selvon's own favourite.) The author (the main character, unusually for Selvon, dons a writer's persona) lights up the city with love, romance; but it's a filmic, exposed-to-the-elements setting for the lovers. It's a romance of constantly interrupted signals, the metonymy of the train wheels destabilizing London; the inability, on the bus, to direct your love-talk to her ears only; the hoardings saying things more simply than you can – all add up to an atmosphere of surrealism welcome in a tradition for which narrative realism is the norm. The lover proceeds to cover vast areas of London by late-night bus and when, occasionally, he meets the Girl, they get drenched, they get lost on their way to the Heath. Is this romantic? True, the Girl has no reality, she generally isn't there. Reel on a couple of decades, replay the scene, it gets more frightening. If Selvon is a transitional figure, in this story he completes the transition.

In the early seventies I was involved in an adaptation for the stage of one of Selvon's best-known stories, 'Obeah in the Grove', where a fifties Labroke Grove landlord encourages a black presence in his house in order to get rid of sitting tenants and sell it. And one of the 'boys', Fiji, decides to work some obeah (magic) to put off potential purchasers. So Fiji invokes something called 'the vengeance of Moko' on the house, gets a parcel from Jamaica containing something ominous, 'cogitates', puts a bottle in a tree outside and achieves his effect. What was interesting in rehearsal was the difficulty of making Fiji credible: he had no background, no track record. Who did he contact in Jamaica? What exactly was in the parcel that we weren't allowed to see? What sort of ritual do you enact to bring off the 'vengeance of Moko'? (Was this obeah as worked by Ma Procop in two of Selvon's Trinidad stories?) It wasn't until these things were addressed, new lines, new scenes, a Caribbean background for Fiji sketched in, that it worked on stage in a way that wasn't folksy. The best of Selvon's Trinidad stories – like those, later, of Clyde Hosein (b. 1940) – have none of this sketchiness.

If Selvon is a transitional figure, Jean Rhys (Dominica/UK, 1894–1979) is another. Rhys's reputation outstrips Selvon's, and her short stories are as accomplished, with most commentators agreeing with Ford Madox Ford (in his preface to Rhys's first collection, *The Left Bank*, 1927) that she has 'very remarkable technical gifts', and commending 'her instinct for form'. If Rhys employed language more along the fault lines of class than did Selvon, she set a standard of accomplishment in these and in her two other collections, *Tigers are Better-Looking* (stories set in England, published, belatedly, in 1968) and *Sleep It Off, Lady* (1976). Like all Caribbean writers she is concerned in evoking the race and colour tensions that threaten everyone's sanity: as a white West Indian she has an intimate view of one side (stories with a West Indian setting) and, as a foreigner in Europe, a woman without means, she experiences the other side, and she does this with a remarkable degree of sophistication. Rhys's stories set in Paris and London have a special sort of challenge: the sensation isn't that of letting a character 'from outside' into your closed world of the story to reveal uncomfortable things there, but more like someone taking the story to you, testing your moral defences.

The tone of her work is thus different from Selvon's. Selvon is usually buoyant; even though his characters are forever dealing with social mishap and the awareness of lack of privilege, they refuse to see themselves as victims. (There is an intellectual resilience here which might derive partly from Anancy/Sakchulee, or it might be that these characters are mainly young men, who are themselves victimizers – of women.) Many of Rhys's protagonists *are* victims, helpless young or very young women. Their tone is often uncompromising, anti-establishment, full of distrust for the adult world; so often there is the threat of suicide, a hint of madness. This connects with the new angry/confident note being struck by many of Rhys's successors.

4 *Beginnings*

It's a matter of convenience to identify, loosely, three phases in the development of the Caribbean short story – writing up to the 1950s, excluding Selvon; Selvon as transitional figure, and the New Phase: contemporary developments.

We begin with the establishment of major literary magazines in the region: *Trinidad* (1929) and *The Beacon* (1931) in Trinidad; *Bim* in Barbados (1942); *Focus* in Jamaica (1943) and, in 1945, *Kyk-Over-All* (named after a Dutch fort) in Guyana. Some writers worked and published abroad, of course, but the emergence of these outlets was important, for, as Ramchand reminds us in *The West Indian Novel and Its Background* (1970), people in the region before, say, 1930 had, among their privations, to endure a 'life without fiction'.

Trinidad's internationally minded, highly politicized angry young men of letters tried to make a difference. Alfred H. Mendes and C. L. R. James (who edited the two issues of *Trinidad*) and a whole movement, which included Ralph de Boissiere and, above all, Albert Gomes, championed realism in the West Indian short story. Gomes, at the age of twenty, edited *The Beacon* (twenty-eight issues between 1931 and 1933, selling between 1,500 and 5,000 copies per issue). In one editorial (*Trinidad*, Easter, 1930) Mendes rails against 'Victorian' hypocrisy; and if it now seems somewhat shrill we might remind ourselves that the previous year's issue of the magazine had brought at least one libel action, visits from the police, denunciation from the pulpit and general establishment accusations of immorality, atheism and communism. A story by C. L. R. James, 'Triumph' (included here) was singled out for its 'obscenity'.

'Triumph' is a 'barrack-room' story, what we could call today an example of 'yard' literature. It shows the desperate position of women living an enforced, semi-communal life, without privacy, relying more or less on stray men for economic survival: their alliances, jealousies, etc., the occasional triumph over the man, the humour and scheming, make them something less than passive, even though they remain victims. If there is 'obscenity' in this 1929 story, then it would relate not to the main characters' limited emotional involvement with their various paramours, but with their playing down the effects of violence and privation, and in the story giving no clue to how this cycle of abuse might be broken. But that's not what the critics had in mind. A version of the 'barracks' is experienced thirty years later by Austin Clarke's Barbadian domestics in 'I Hanging On, Praise God', set in Canada.

The struggle for artistic definition and political independence went together (Gomes was to go on to hold high political office in Trinidad) and helped to energize these literary publications. *Focus*, in Jamaica, was edited by Edna Manley, a sculptor and wife of the lawyer who in 1938 formed the People's National Party and went on to become Chief Minister and Premier; and in Guyana A. J. Seymour used *Kyk-Over-All* as a focus of Guyanese writing. *Bim*, edited by Therold Barnes, then by Frank Collymore (to 1973) and John Wickham, was less fired by nationalism than the others but (with the London-based *Caribbean Voices*[20] programme) has probably had the greatest effect on the development of Caribbean anglophone writing. What's interesting at this distance is that the magazines all tended to promote the sort of social realism in prose fiction (Wilson Harris being the obvious exception) from which the short story is now struggling to free itself.

In his Nobel acceptance speech, in 1992, Derek Walcott wickedly remarks that 'much of our life in the Antilles still seems to be in the rhythm of the last century, *like the West Indian novel*' (my italics).[21] Though we've had spectacular efforts, from Wilson Harris to Erna Brodber and Lawrence Scott, to renew the novel, there is a general feeling that the modernizers are working in other genres, probably poetry. What's interesting to pick up is the sort of debate that has accompanied the production of the short story.

Gomes was scathing about the quality of the stories sent in for his 1932 *The Beacon* competition, and a decade later *Bim* had a go in an editorial (December 1943) at laying down guidelines:

> These [short stories] should be well told in reasonably good English with
> at least a semblance of a plot, sustained interest and something of a
> climax. Do not write merely to express yourself or to mend the world or
> to elevate humanity. Give us something with a wide appeal – and a love
> interest is always welcomed.

This is what editors of popular magazines, including the pulp-fiction
magazines of America, were telling their potential authors.

The work of both main editors of *Bim* reflects this traditional tendency.
Harold Barratt, writing in the joint *Bim/Kyk-Over-All* issue (June 1990)
about Collymore's stories, agrees that such prescriptions for the good
short story tended to trap this writer into a sort of strait-jacket: 'classical
line of exposition, rising action, climax and strong, unambiguous resolution'. And it is true that reading Collymore and Wickham we're always
conscious of a narrative voice that's a little deliberate and distracting,
not fully sensitive to the weight of the story it's charged to narrate, not
fully *in character*. You have a sense less of being lost in the world of
fiction than of enjoying an illustrated lecture. There are exceptions, of
course: Wickham's 'The Old Man in the City', though exhibiting some
of these traits, has a compensating imaginative power, and Collymore's
mildly Gothic strain gives 'The Man Who Loved Attending Funerals'
(included here) and a few of his other stories, a sensation of characters
haunted by the past, struggling to live on.

Even though it's exciting to be moving away from naturalism, we
must recognize that the core of the work falls within those limits; and
the standard set by the best practitioners – Roger Mais in 'Look Out',
for instance – is hard to beat. This superlative story is an indictment of
every man in the West Indies. Here, the unknown woman driven to
distraction stands at the gate, looking out into the night. She's come
from the country to look after her brother's wife and young children,
for the wife is 'a little cracked in the head'. The husband is a petty tyrant
who doesn't have to use physical violence to get his way. Though we're
not sure, because, as the sister reflects, for standing at the gate talking
to a stranger, the brother 'would scold her, inside'. (With later work,
with Silvera, we get the sense that we're being 'taken inside'. And inside
the head, too, of the woman driven mad.)

I've had to omit some social realist writers, with reputations in the genre. Michael Anthony (b. Trinidad, 1930) writes with sincerity and charm, but the stories in *Cricket in the Road* (1973) seem slight, the tone sometimes uncertain; and with the later, more ambitious *The Chieftain's Carnival and Other Stories*, 'based on true events', there is a sense of their being programmatic, externally conceived. Other stories in this tradition that might have got in are Roy Heath's 'Da Costa's Rupununi' and Janis Shinebourne's 'The Maid in Bel Air' (both of which seem one-off triumphs of writers who are fine novelists); Shiva Naipaul's 'The Dolly House' and Dionne Brand's 'Madame Alaird's Breasts' were on the list. Other writers who have a claim include Merle Collins ('Angel'), Cynthia James, Marlene Nourbese Philip, Nicole Craig, Velma Pollard and John Stewart. What I'm presenting is a supplementary or alternative reading-list. Sadly, June Henfrey's stories in *Coming Home* (1994) remain unfinished. Henfrey (Barbados, 1939–92) died before the collection was completed. Three of the six stories are set in the time of slavery, in and around the Great House, and there is something inspirational about her women characters striving for freedom. The work straddles sociological research and fiction.

People used to justify Caribbean naturalistic writing in somewhat predictable ways: that we hadn't suffered debilitating wars on the road to independence (or after); no mass starvation; no recent genocide; no official 'disappearances' on a grand scale. Censorship, yes, but not total or efficient enough to drive writing into symbolism, into allegory. Of course, one answer to that would be to cite the experience of racism and the aesthetic of pigmentocracy; of children suffering neglect and women violence, etc., all of which might be intractable enough to change the shape of the well-made story. As would the surreal experience of perceiving yourself living on the periphery, or *abroad*; or of having to think of home as something possibly mobile, of being victims of what Andrew Salkey memorably calls, in a poem, 'a sea-split marriage'.[22] We don't have to experience *all* of these things – none of us alive has experienced slavery, after all – all you need is to have an imaginative engagement with it.

Neither reader nor writer is in the same place as when the last great natural realist wave of Caribbean writing came along. There has been a shift, and it makes little difference how you identify it; the question is to recognize that it has happened. A shift is anything that leaves you where you weren't. Now you're *post-* instead of *pre-*. It might simply be the experience of having been abroad and returning home. Though this has always happened, it hasn't happened in large enough numbers (post-slavery, post-indenture) till now to be the norm, the common, shared experience – and, therefore, the concept can afford to take wing. (In Pauline Melville's 'Eat Labba and Drink Creek Water', one dream of return is by high-wire act, sixty feet above the Atlantic, lasting twenty-two days, in which time 'only the moon shone'. That character's *imaginative* conceit emphasizes the sketchiness of the Fiji character in 'Obeah in the Grove'.

We're talking about shifts: realizing that there are new accents, and possibly different colours in the family (this time by consent), is a shift outlawing stock response in one area; another shift is having not enough to eat and too much to eat *at the same time* (poverty aligned to vegetarian-ism, say, or health-consciousness); it is television and electronic games at night rather than storytelling on the old porch (still preserved, I'm told, in Miss Welty's Mississippi!); or in changed vocabularies, second marriages and the redefinition of terms like 'independence', 'chief minis-ter', 'president'.

5 The Story in Transition (II): The Third Phase

To talk of the Third Phase in the development of the Caribbean short story seems a less pompous way of recognizing new developments than having to resort too often to terms like post-modernism. New develop-ments might suggest work challenging narrative realist claims to reflect the truth. For me, tell-tale signs are suggestions of turning away from the linear tale with events occurring in strict chronology: with the begin-ning, middle and end proceeding in that order. Or adopting the equally stale variation, the end/beginning followed by flashback, and back again to the beginning/end – that sort of thing. Anything which challenges these pre-modern devices, I'm tempted to place in the Third Phase. There are other requirements, of course: the language must have vitality, the psychology must seem up-to-date, idiom and overall tone (unless the narrative demands otherwise) must be contemporary. (I draw, shame-lessly, on my experience of judging poetry and short story competitions, where it's easy to make an impact on the pile by separating FRESH from

STALE entries, before settling down to the detailed read.) As readers we have our own guide of what is pre-modern: if some critics of the short story locate this (as they did in my 1993 questionnaire) as work not yet affected by Borges or by Calvino and the Italian Gruppo 63, or the American metafictionists – or even the 'pop surrealist', Donald Barthelme – why argue? We're probably talking about the same things.

So what are the signs of new things happening in the Caribbean short story? In an N. D. Williams's story, 'The Great Leap', there is a character called Biswas. 'The Great Leap' appeared in the collection *The Crying of Rainbirds* (1992), and this literary reference to V. S. Naipaul (reminiscent of Nuruddin Farah's extended reference to Chinua Achebe's *Things Fall Apart* at the start of his own 1981 novel, *Sardines*) – one African writer paying literary tribute to another African writer – hints at the sort of playfulness that is both pre- and post-modern. This interest in literary recycling is growing and is reflected by, among those included here, Hazel D. Campbell, and Kamau Brathwaite, in *Dream Stories* (1994), from which 'Dream Chad' comes.

We haven't developed a liking for the short short story even though Selvon hinted at it and Jean Rhys produced some memorable examples ('I Used To Live Here Once', 'Trio', 'A Night'). But where are the complete fables, Aesop-length, New-Testament-like ('The Prodigal Son', 'The Raising of Lazarus') and the miracles of compression that you get in Borges, Kafka and the early James Kelman? (My own favourites are those amazing narratives of the American 'Latina' writer Sandra Cisneros, heavy with male threat, polished and elegant.) The potential for this form of minimalism seems everywhere in the culture, in broadcast homilies that you get on island radio stations (and, indeed, from the pulpits) or in political commentary. Barbara Gloudon's tongue-in-cheek 'Stella' column in the Jamaican *Star* and *Daily News* in the 1970s and 1980s comes to mind. Some think the *Letters Home* are our great untapped wealth of short fiction, early examples, surely, of the 'reader' writing the 'character'. It's the reader's collusion that prevents this work coming to light. But the epistolary form is much used, memorably by Jean Rhys in 'Fishy Waters', 'a *tour de force* of narration' as Ramchand[23] rightly calls it, used also, with utmost delicacy and sophistication, by Alecia McKenzie in 'Full Stop' and, in its telephone idiom, to more comic impact, by Hazel D. Campbell in 'I-Calypso'.

Instead of short shorts, writers have tended to go the other way, threatening to break out of the constraints of the short story. These substantial narratives proliferate, almost constituting a sub-genre: Olive Senior's 'Arrival of the Snake Woman', Velma Pollard's 'Karl'; Hazel D. Campbell's 'Jacob Bubbles' – the shortest of these is forty-five pages – are not unusual. The 'epic' tendency is present in stories by Wilson Harris, N. D. Williams, Merle Collins, Jacob Ross and others. Length might be necessary in dealing with a situation of unusual complexity, or scale, and this reflects a desire of writers to be ambitious within the form. We're accustomed to having great *weight* put upon the short story (Eric Walrond's fascinatingly overwritten narratives are hard to resist), but the wonder of orchestration which is Earl Lovelace's 'A Brief Conversation' suggests new confidence in the – larger – form. 'A Brief Conversation' is a huge comedy of manners (not just because of its length – twenty-nine pages) of family life in the village, one of those timeless, pre-independence communities. But the portrayal of village people in their domestic sophistication is utterly unsentimental. Overt gestures of love are avoided, but the relationships – father with son, wife (belatedly) with partner and mother with her sons discovering more of their humanity – leave us with a sense of delight in the ordinary; the story is both delicate and richly textured; there's something organic about its process, writing following natural contours.

Other things which seem new are risk-taking in subject-matter and a refusal to slip into typecasting. I've referred to the protests which greeted the publication of C. L. R. James's 'Triumph', in *Trinidad*, in 1929. This was essentially a class-based reflex, which work in the Selvon phase effectively challenged. The taboos which are being broken now are sexual and gender ones.

Althea Prince (Antigua/Canada, b. 1945) and Makeda Silvera (b. Jamaica, 1955), whose energetic Sister Vision Press in Toronto publishes Prince, portray women relating to women in new and sometimes uncomfortable ways. When I note the reactions in the Jamaican media to Patricia Powell's 1994 novel *A Small Gathering of Bones*, I wonder if the fact that Prince and Silvera live abroad, in a different cultural environment, hasn't been conducive to their radical literary development. Powell's novel, set in 1970s Jamaica, is about homosexual relationships. Prince's 'Ladies of the Night' (which might have been included here) depicts a harrowing tale of a girl growing up in Antigua, prostituted by her mother, abused by her father (his identity unknown to her), leaving her part-brutalized, part-humanized by the experience. Makeda Silvera, who is included, probes more fully and warmly than any other Caribbean short story writer that I know of, the sexual love of women for women.

The other question raised – reluctance to slip into typecasting – is a difficult one. Chinua Achebe is certainly right when, from time to time, he points out that a Nigerian writer, say, need not portray non-Nigerian subjects and locations in order to be accorded universal significance. Writing about your own place is clearly not typecasting, and there's no need to stray from your village to resonate throughout the world. But it's something of a challenge when, as a writer, you're able to create a world outside yourself so that, at the very least, the reader doesn't make vulgar assumptions about you. That makes stories like Pauline Melville's 'You Left the Door Open' especially appealing. Pauline Melville is an actress; and we *can* see her as the cabaret-artist narrator who specializes in impersonations, taking on the identity of a small-time crook called Charlie, who is too threatening to the audience, who has the same name as a man released from a hospital for the criminally insane, who has the name of the man who invades her house, sexually abuses and terrorizes her, who is a nineteenth-century murderer, who was once a cabaret artist and burglar, and shot a policeman, and attempted suicide, and has taken up residence in her imagination because she has created a character with his name.[24] All of this must reflect something in the author's pysche, and it is a West Indian story to the extent that the author is part-Guyanese and is imaginatively fed by that aspect of her heritage. But it extends the range of the West Indian story. More work of this kind – it connects with Selvon's 'My Girl and the City' – is coming through in this phase.

Talking of fictional shape, it occurs to me that the anthology, itself, is an artefact, a modernist text with its great theme, large structure, its chaotic-seeming detail and (perhaps) an underlying sense of portentousness. But there is something post-modern about it, too – entries by different hands, different styles and textures threatening to undermine the great scheme. I often think that the failure of many group-writing projects is that the participants are too respectful of their brief, they are too determined to write as if they were a single author, whereas the challenge of the single author, often, is to write as if he, as if she, were many.[25]

So there's the great scheme made up of samplers, giving it – we hope – a work-in-progress feel. The creative tension which results has come to be associated, in my mind, with work in the Third Phase that we're talking about. I've hinted that some editors in the past have been cautious, so I'm hoping that this anthology can be loyal to the spirit of the mass of exciting work out there which has escaped us: Opal Palmer Adisa's 'Duppy Get Her', an impressive dramatization of being possessed; John Robert Lee's 'The Coming of Org', Faustin Charles' 'Signpost of the Phoenix' – all represented in Stewart Brown's *Caribbean New Wave* (1990) – are worth investigating.

Pound's injunction for poetry was to make it new; mine, as an anthologist, is to keep it fresh. Casual readers would perhaps know the anthology pieces, and you wouldn't want the table of contents to resemble a rerun of your favourite TV listings for the Bank Holiday. With this in mind Jamaica Kincaid is represented here not by much-praised stories from *At the Bottom of the River* (1983) but by newer work. V. S. Naipaul's 'The Night Watchman's Occurrence Book' and the sketches from *Miguel Street* (1959) lose nothing of their edge, but perhaps 'The Baker's Story' will seem to remind us of ways in which we seek to remake ourselves. Olive Senior's ever-popular 'Do Angels Wear Brassieres?' gives way to a piece which turns the folk-tale on its head; and to another, newer one, where the author takes some risks with form, and is both passionate and unsentimental.

Looking down the Contents list, I'm reminded again of the excitement I felt when I first encountered these stories. Here is Pauline Melville's 'Eat Labba and Drink Creek Water', a complex of literary devices – an expedition (recalling Cortez and Pizarro – and, indeed, Wilson Harris) in search of El Dorado; the history, or at least the decline, of the Great House, an epic of three generations ending with ancient aunts, abandoned, going mad in the collapsing Cooperative Republic (of Guyana); they are obsessed with colour and pigment to the end. The literary devices employed are multiple points of view; first and third person narration; linguistic registers ranging from playground taunts and chants; agenda-type items; stretches of lyricism and a mock-sixteenth-century account of the marvels of distant London. What we have here is frame on top of frame of fragments of experience, not palimpsest-like, because one enriches rather than supersedes the other. (Hemingway's 'staining'?) At the same time the structuring is so appropriate – short, free-floating segments, careful naturalistic detail but no clutter (some characters don't have names, etc.) – that the reader is neither over-whelmed nor confused. The collage-like technique is not unlike that of the great modernist poems ('The Waste Land', 'Hugh Selwyn Mauberley', 'X/Self') – but without their difficulty.

Melville's claims are so insistent that she is represented by two stories. Mervyn Morris has this to say about her prize-winning collection *Shape-shifter* (1990):

> Pauline Melville challenges conventional assumptions about identity, time, and space. Though she is adept at satire – as in 'I Do Not Take Messages from Dead People', 'The Iron and the Radio Have Gone', and 'A Dis-guised Land' – her stories are not content to reinforce the settled illusion of realism; they communicate much by indirection, by symbolic hints; they traffic in intuition; they travel dream and myth.[26]

Enter Lawrence Scott (Trinidad/UK, b. 1943), whose ancestors came from Europe. (Frank Collymore and Jean Rhys also had a European heritage – in Scott's case a mixture of French, Spanish and German.) Scott's 'The House of Funerals' assaults you with its baroque use of language. Here are the opening paragraphs:

> The morning sun blazed down hot on to the small, rusty-roofed houses with filigreed, white, lattice-work verandas, yellowing. Fern baskets, hang-ing from eaves festooned with cobwebs, dripped.
>
> The tumbledown town tumbled down to the wharf in the bay on the gulf and jangled with Indian music. On the High Street loudspeakers blared from the doorways of Ramnarine's Garment Palace and shattered the glass cases in Patel's Jewel Box.
>
> The sea in the bay on the gulf glinted.

It's not hard to pick up the register of the narrating voice but it's impossible to pin it down to any tonal scale. The rhetorical mode of address suggests performance, boulevard theatre, or a TV travelogue of an earlier age. Then, there's the MC's delight in 'naming' with a pedantic precision that draws attention to the one doing the naming, sharing with us the sensuality of choice of words: there's a hint of Dylan Thomas (Llareggub) and the voice of Richard Burton behind it. There is an anapaestic rhythm to the piece which makes us think of verse – and, indeed, we're tempted to see if it will scan. The sea in the bay on the gulf glinted. And the syntax, with the verb coming at the end, brings back memories of Eliot at his most quaint: 'I was neither at the hot gates/Nor fought in the warm rain/Nor knee deep in the salt marsh, heaving a cutlass,/Bitten by flies, fought.'[27]

The point? Scott's language accurately reflects a world which refuses to slip easily into any of the received notions of West-Indianness. We're in a Great House, yes, but people are assigned slightly different roles from those we remember, or they have different titles, so we're forced all the time to do the double-take. There is the Indian undertaker and the African maid. But *she's* a hundred years old: is this Garcia Marquez territory? The Syrian merchant and Portuguese wholesaler have off-stage parts. The family are descended from an 'old French family united with an old Spanish family'. Their name is Monagas de los Macajuelos. (Trinidad, remember, had been a Spanish colony until 1797, with a fair proportion of French-speaking inhabitants.) The person recently dead is Cecile Monagas de los Macajuelos. Scott resists the temptation to play the name for laughs. A rogue element is the grandson who forgets he's to be a pall-bearer, parks his car downtown in the narrow street outside Teresa's Hairdressing Salon where he gets his thrills: this slows the traffic, delays the funeral so that the ceremony has to be speeded up so that the body could be buried before nightfall. The restraint with this relatively minor character, and with other like temptations, shows the author to have excellent artistic manners.

It's a telling mix. The tensions between the European and the Spanish/ Latin American tauten the prose; different worlds are empowered here and Scott reconnects us with the work of Marquez and Jean Rhys. This sensation of retuning linguistic strings alerts us to a new sound in Caribbean prose.

But it's not all literary fireworks: some of these stories excel almost by stealth. The literary sophistication of Garth St Omer's 'The Departure' might easily be missed. A woman and her young son are at the wharf, about to travel; it's evening and they're preparing to board the ferry, which is late. Albert, her thirty-five-year-old brother comes to see them off. Albert has left his drinking pals so that he can perform this service for his sister. There is deep affection, we soon see, between brother and sister, but it doesn't flow naturally; there's a sense that they're both hanging on to something, their pride. The brother is a small man, easily abused (and he invites abuse, as he does at the end of the story when we see him being ritually beaten by the police). Albert is not a seaman, but because of his evident literacy, he is Secretary of the Seaman Waterfront Union. Buoyed with status, he can forget for a few hours his home life with seven young children and a wife whose compensation is to gossip about her husband's drinking. Albert's way of rising above all this, of defeating it, is to don a language of extreme and comic formality, no elisions, no concessions to the idiomatic.

The sister matches Albert well enough in this dockside/drawing-room dialogue, reasserting status (probably mindful of her child born outside wedlock) but also as a way of *giving* to her brother. The dialogue has the feel of a love-duet; then again, like two people translating too literally from another language. (We don't have to break into their thoughts to know that they can sense what's going on.) This isn't the usual parody that you get in some earlier Caribbean writing, where the joke is lost on the speaker. That's why this story breaks through farce and into comedy: Albert's cruelty is both protected and revealed by his cloak of language. When he uses it to frighten the sister's boy, we can't help thinking of his own seven children, and his wife, not brought into the story. It's by the use of this (Standard English, or, with stresses, West Indian Standard) language that brother and sister fill the gaps between their self-image and the parts they're forced to play. Standard English here is being rescued from being the source of easy irony/parody of much earlier fiction, and contributes to the pathos of the story.

Olive Senior (Jamaica/Canada, b. 1941) and Jamaica Kincaid (Antigua/US, b. 1949) have had more critical attention than any of the 'newer' short story writers. Critics rightly talk of Kincaid's 'resistance to canons'; her 'apocalyptic imagery'; her ability to see the magical in the ordinary; and the vibrancy and sensuality of her language which draws on an inherited income of folk-tale, baby-talk and Bible-speak. But it's limiting to see Kincaid as someone who writes poetic prose, or prose poetry. Kincaid's story 'Song of Roland', included here, *is* an astonishing love poem, shot through with lyricism. But this story of a stevedore and the women in his life, in particular the young woman who is a servant, manages to be magical and achingly concrete. It's a disciplined and well-structured story, pinned down to a specific place – it sounds less like Kincaid's 'dry' Antigua than Dominica with its 'three hundred and sixty-five small streams'. In its sensuality, it reminds me of Mario Vargas Llosa's erotic masterpiece *In Praise of the Stepmother*.

In her earlier story 'Country of the One Eye God' (published in *Summer Lightning and Other Stories*, 1986), Olive Senior explodes the myth that there's something benign and cosy about traditional village society, where the young tearaway can return to health, sanity and contrition in the arms of his traditional protector, the grandmother. Here, our man has a gun in his hand, and we're not prepared to bet on his not using it on the grandmother. Senior's 'You Think I Mad, Miss?' is a departure from the linear development of her early stories. The forward thrust of what we might call the Frank O'Connor model, juggling 'exposition, development and drama', has given way to something more open, circular. The implications are exciting: the possibility of a more regular and even distribution of energy along the story, a sharing of responsibility between reader and subject for maintaining that energy, etc. One effect is to empower the subject, another of those women thought mad (recalling Jean Binta Breeze's celebrated poem, 'Ryddhm Ravings').

In this collection, another example of the sense of the new is N. D. Williams's 'Cats in the Eyes of the Pig'. Both in that story and in 'The Inside Child' we encounter Williams's trick of undermining the confidence of the reader, who gets to the end of the story and is suddenly uncertain whose the narrating voice is. This unexpectedly enlarges the frame of reference, and opens up again the story you have just completed.

6 'Abroad'

These thoughts, more or less random, are prompted by the discovery that so many Caribbean stories return to the scene of the Great House, or to versions of it, usually as a form of indictment (Henfrey); sometimes as a way of making sense of the current dystopia (Campbell/Scott/Melville) and sometimes to indicate the collapse of the old order (Hosein in 'Her House'/Collymore/Melville). Here are Melville's old aunts mirroring the house:

> 'Where's Auntie Florence?' I ask timidly.
> 'We had to send her up to Canada to your Uncle Bertie's. She livin' in the past. She talkin' to the dead. She thinks they're still alive. She anxious and upset all the time. She thought everything in the house was on fire. Even us, her sisters. She saw us burnin' up burnin' up like paper, black with a red edge. Paper sisters. She's turned into a screwball.'
>
> ('Eat Labba and Drink Creek Water')

Then there are the stages of distancing yourself from the Great House, one way – not surprisingly – being to become the owner of the House, in whatever manifestation proves feasible, to reverse the shame and humiliation associated with its memory. The seventy-year-old Mr Watford in Paule Marshall's 'Barbados', returning from America after fifty years (where he worked in the boiler-room of a Boston hotel), comes over, as so many have done in real life, as a figure of some pathos. What's the point, you may ask, of the House, when Watford has no family, past or future: he's the only one of ten children to survive, and he has neither partner nor child. So the House is left, appropriately, unfinished. What Watford brings back are somewhat reactionary attitudes, in the way of returnees.

But the usual way of distancing yourself from the Great House is to go abroad – even though going 'abroad' to literal or surrogate 'Mother Countries' is in itself a way of trying to enter the House. Not surprisingly, the door is often slammed in your face (no coloureds), or set up anew at the immigration offices. Then there are those families lured into abandoning, if not Great, at least large houses, for the uncertainty of abroad.

Let's skip a generation. Two generations. Here is someone born in Toronto, in London. That person grows up with talk in the family of the House abandoned, say, in the fifties (I'm thinking of a specific example, close to home). Important this House, because not tainted by slavery, built for a great-grandmother to be born in. A responsibility to maintain by those alive to history. But what proved enabling for one generation might be a burden to the next. The point is that the prospect of self-government and independence stimulated literary activity in the West Indies (and led to the formation of literary magazines between 1929 and 1945). The radicalized sixties and awareness of a black aesthetic – writers renaming themselves, 'Edward' becoming 'Kamau'; Linton slipping 'Kwesi' in before Johnson – produced works that reorientated the literature – works like Brathwaite's *Arrivants*. Now, it's tempting to ask what West Indian reality will drive the expatriate writer to contribute to the next phase of the literature. (Mr Ramgoolam's Canadianized children – 'Security' – are not going to want to inherit, or repair, or add to Mr Biswas' house.)

For Kenyans fighting for independence in the fifties, land was more than a metaphor. The question of working on the land has been one of ambivalence (for Indo-Caribbeans) and reluctance or resentment for the rest. (We must remember that even Selvon's people are largely urban!)

There is a dilemma for Caribbean migrants of a certain age, who wish to stay where they are and enjoy the benefits they've come to take for granted, or even the proximity of supermarkets and health services. After decades abroad they are now in a position to bequeath a Caribbean house to children or grandchildren. But these have usually declined the offer, as they too feel themselves rooted elsewhere.

On the island, the ex-maid in Clyde Hosein's 'Her House' tries to ensure continuity in a house that has changed its function, the family long fled. To what end, when we see the condition of the returnees? They come over as comic or disturbed figures, unable or unwilling to fit in (Senior's 'Real Old Time T'ing', Lorna Goodison's 'Bella Makes Life', Dionne Brand's 'Photograph' – perhaps even 'President Horace the Second, Howe', by E. A. Markham – all make that point).

The same dichotomy affects the writers themselves: Caribbean-born writers abroad who spent their formative years in the Caribbean might be in danger of freezing the Caribbean into memory; Caribbean-heritage people with no experience of living in the Caribbean must resort to *imagining* it. True, they might continue to experiment with form, to 'stain' the narrative.

But this brings us back to the question of nation language. Academics who argue for the use of nation language tend to do so in the most traditional idiom – with the celebrated exception of Carolyn Cooper talking about Sistren.[28] In a sense, this emphasizes the dilemma of having to make use of the 'master tongue' even as you seek to subvert it. Denied the lecture theatre and the authority of the literary essay, nation language will not break free of its associations with class. (Its portrayal as academic discourse in fiction would resist Selvon's revitalization.)

Nation language must grow to mean one thing to people living in the Caribbean and another to people living outside. In the Caribbean it's part of a continuous process of nation-building, a determination that people do not sound foreign in their own place. Abroad, it's a recognition of 'root', yes; but at the same time Caribbean peoples living in Toronto or London or Sydney also strive to speak their respective dialects – the one which identifies them with place and non-Caribbean members of their class. These groups preserve Caribbeanness out of a psychological need (or political calculation) not to be overwhelmed by 'otherness', and in that respect they can contribute a sort of linguistic remittance to 'home'. (It's as if they have become the poor cousins of the family made good, *outside* children acknowledging the legitimate.)

The Caribbeanness of Caribbean-heritage writers living abroad will become increasingly hard to detect; then a national literature might begin to conform to sensible physical boundaries.

7 Further Reading

I've hinted at a reading list. Here's another sort of list to help us identify the updated old stories, and stories soon to be *re*-covered – stories in search of an author, sort of thing – the moment they're written up. Five suggestions:

1 (a) *There's that couple, hitching, somewhere in Europe. It's the early seventies. Cold, laden with bags; they're desperate for a lift. Finally, someone stops. The driver is smoking, the car reeks. Without needing to consult each other, they decline. The story is told, alternately, by two voices, separated by time and circumstance, twenty years apart. It's called* 'Illusions'. (Oh, yes, one of them is not in the best of health.)

(b) *A drawing-room scene somewhere in the islands; 1950s. A pioneer returns home without booty; he is silent throughout the drawing-room conversation, he no longer speaks the family's language. He's been to Panama, to Cuba. The story will dredge for Spanish remains – like panning for gold – before assessing the cost of the expedition all round. Call it* 'Uncle George's Story'.

2 *This one creates a new island for the setting of the story, which is not a replica of our own, but justifies its creation by its political, cultural and social difference from those we know. Release familiar characters into the new environment, and see if they challenge old assumptions. Give it a name and history which myth-makers will find credible.*

Is this, in fact, the island of the cowpeople – the guinea*cow*, the pig*cow* and the horse*cow*, all of which are animal people, different from the guineafowl and the goat goat and the pig pig and the horse horse, which were just things that the family owned to lay eggs and to provide the Sunday roast or milk or meat, or kept – where the horse horse was concerned – as a status symbol? It is known that the *cow*people can fly and are invisible, criss-crossing the world wherever there are people from the island, taking messages, bringing back reports. This story is called 'The Tenth Messenger'.

3 *Treading dangerously, this is the story of the eye-rape. Not the old American South story of eye-rape, but a Caribbean story written by a 'new' man, nostalgic for the bad old days when you could abuse women with impunity. There are many versions of this story, the writer insisting that each one has been misunderstood. It's called* 'Allies'. (Writing is now becoming a dangerous activity.)

4 *Updating the old ones – like the woman abroad, imprisoned in the house of her sons, deciding at last not to repress her sexuality; or that household where the parents forbid the child the chance to run and jump and be hit in the face (for she's a young diva, a soil chemist; or, if a boy, will right the family's wrongs in a non-macho way, etc).*

5 *There* is *something exciting coming through. My term for it is* EPIC REALISM *in the short story. We've had Magical Realism (Central/South America) and Dirty Realism (Raymond Carver, Andre Dubus, Richard Ford and others from the US). Now Epic Realism. What are the characteristics? Non-linear structure (often fragmented and episodic); historical (or current affairs) frame of reference; political parody/satire; literary recycling and in-jokes, I'm afraid (captions, subheadings and the occasional footnote); research: familiarity with the esoteric (but undermined by being worn lightly, or presented as newspaper or encyclopedia inserts); surface sparkle; lack of solemnity – and, with an upbeat tone assuming the collusion of the reader. The non-Caribbean writer who most daringly inhabits this space is the American*

T. Coraghessan Boyle. This tendency will be well represented in the next Caribbean 'new wave'.

Now, for another five stories.

But to look at what's actually there. It's obvious that many writers included here could be represented, without loss, by a different story. For example: 'Insecurity' (Neil Bissoondath), 'The Spirit Thief' (Erna Brodber), 'Bring on the Trumpeters' (Wayne Brown), 'Jacob Bubbles' (Hazel D. Campbell), 'The Stickfighter' (Willi Chen), 'Her House' (Clyde Hosein), 'My Mother' (Jamaica Kincaid), 'Gravel in Your Shoe' (Roger Mais), 'Natasha' (Alecia McKenzie), 'The Iron and the Radio Have Gone' (Pauline Melville), 'The Night Watchman's Occurrence Book' (V. S. Naipaul), 'Let Them Call It Jazz' (Jean Rhys), 'King Sailor One J'Ouvert Morning' (Lawrence Scott), 'Do Angels Wear Brassieres?' (Olive Senior), 'Her Head A Village' (Makeda Silvera), 'Life Sentence' (N. D. Williams), etc.

What says more about the strength of the Caribbean short story is the recognition of work by those not included here: Opal Palmer Adisa's 'Duppy Get Her', Dionne Brand's 'Madame Alaird's Breasts', Faustin Charles's 'Signpost of the Phoenix', Merle Collins's 'Angel', Cyril Dabydeen's 'Mammita's Garden Cove', Roy Heath's 'Da Costa's Rupununi', John Robert Lee's 'The Coming of Org – A Prologue', Ian McDonald's 'Pot o' Rice Horowitz's House of Solace', Shiva Naipaul's 'The Dolly House', Geoffrey Philip's 'The River', Althea Prince's 'Ladies of the Night', Jan Shinebourne's 'The Maid in Bel Air', John Stewart's 'After the Rain', Edgar White's 'The Mark', John Wickham's 'Old Man in the City', etc.

INDIVIDUAL COLLECTIONS OF WRITERS NOT IN THIS ANTHOLOGY
(For those in the anthology, see the Notes on Authors)

Opal Palmer Adisa, *Bake-Face and Other Guava Stories*, Kelsey Street Press, 1986

Michael Anthony, *Cricket in the Road and Other Stories*, André Deutsch, 1973; *The Chieftain's Carnival*, Longman, 1993

Dionne Brand, *Sans Souci and Other Stories*, Toronto, Williams-Wallace International, 1988

Timothy Callender, *It So Happen*, Belfast, Christian Journals, 1975
Jan Carew, *Save the Last Dance for Me*, Longman, 1976
Merle Collins, *Rain Darling*, Women's Press, 1990
Christine Craig, *Mint Tea and Other Stories*, Heinemann, 1993
Cyril Dabydeen, *Still Close to the Island*, Ottawa, Commoner's Publishing,
    1980; *Berbice Crossing*, Peepal Tree, 1994
Zoila Ellis, *On Heroes, Lizards and Passions*, Belize, Cubola Productions,
    1988
Beryl Gilroy, *Sunlight On Sweet Water*, Peepal Tree, 1994
June Henfrey, *Coming Home*, Peepal Tree, 1994
Janet Jagan, *When Grandpa Cheddi Was a Boy*, Peepal Tree, 1994
Ismith Khan, *A Day in the Country and Other Stories*, Peepal Tree, 1994
Earl McKenzie, *Two Roads to Mount Joyful and Other Stories*, Longman, 1992
Roplall Monar, *Backdam People*, 1985; *High House and Radio*, Peepal Tree,
    1993
Velma Pollard, *Considering Women*, Women's Press, 1989
Joan Riley, *The Waiting Room*, 1989
Jacob Ross, *Song For Simone and Other Stories*, Karia Press, 1986
Bob Shacochis, *Easy in the Islands*, NY, Crown Publishers, Inc., 1985
John Wickham, *Casuarina Row*, Belfast, Christian Journals, 1974

USEFUL ANTHOLOGIES

Caribbean Anthology of Short Stories, Pioneer Press, 1953
Stories from the Caribbean, ed. Andrew Salkey, Elek Books, 1965
The Short Story – an Introduction, ed. Kenneth Ramchand, Nelson, 1982
Her True-True Name, ed. Pamela Mordecai and Betty Wilson, Heinemann,
    1989
Caribbean New Wave, ed. Stewart Brown, Heinemann, 1990
The Faber Book of Caribbean Short Stories, ed. Mervyn Morris, 1990
New Writing from the Caribbean, ed. Erika J. Waters, Macmillan, 1994

Notes to Introduction

1 *Ariel*, vol. 24, no. 1, Jan. 1993, review of Ann Walmsley's *The Caribbean
Artists' Movement 1966–1972: A Literary and Cultural History*, p. 181.

2 *Ariel*, vol. 24, no. 1, Jan. 1993, 'New Voices in Caribbean Literature', p. 8.

3 *Out of the Kumbla: Caribbean Women and Literature*, Davies and Fido, Africa World Press Inc., 1990.

4 *Ariel*, vol. 24, no. 1, Jan. 1993, 'New Voices in Caribbean Literature'; *CRNLE Reviews Journal (Special West Indian Issue)*, no. 1, 1994; Tamarack Review's *The West Indies*, 1960; *Pacific Quarterly Moana*, 1983.

5 *Sheffield Thursday*, no. 3, 1993.

6 Jean Rhys is represented by 'Mannequin' in Susan Hill's *The Parchment Moon* (1990); 'Let Them Call It Jazz' is in the *Everyman 1995 Short Stories by Women*; 'The Lotus' in Malcolm Bradbury's *The Penguin Book of British Short Stories*, etc. Examples of being coopted in other literatures include: Jamaica Kincaid's 'The Circling Hand' in Richard Ford's *The Granta Book of the American Short Story*, London, 1992; Austin Clarke's 'Leaving This Island Place' and Dionne Brand's 'Photograph' in Michael Ondatje's *The Penguin Book of Canadian Short Stories*, etc.

7 Difficult to know where to start. But outside the Caribbean, the 'West Indian Literary Capital' has shifted from London to Canada. Present residents include Lillian Allen, Louise Bennett, Neil Bissoondath, Dionne Brand, Austin Clarke, Madeline Coopsammy, Cyril Dabydeen, Horace Goddard, Karl Gordon, Claire Harris, Abdul-Rahman Slade Hopkinson, Arnold Itwaru, Marlene Nourbese Philip, Charles Roach, the late Sam Selvon, Lionel Seepaul, Olive Senior, Roderick Walcott, Edward Watson, etc.

8 Sakchulee may well have derived from the Sheikh Chilli character who appears in the folk-tales of Uttar Pradesh – one of the areas which supplied indentured servants to the Caribbean.

9 *Dwight Guide to the Caribbean*, p. 313.

10 ' "Women is a Nation . . ." Women in Caribbean Literature', *Out of the Kumbla: Caribbean Women and Literature*, Davies and Fido, Africa World Press Inc., 1990.

11 The story of Sistren is told in *Lionheart Gal*, 'edited' by Honor Ford Smith, London, The Women's Press, 1986.

12 *Maroon*: A word derived from the Spanish *cimarron*, applied to African slaves who had run away and managed to live free, avoiding capture. There were Maroons throughout the region, from the sixteenth century. Many were absorbed by the indigenous peoples, and there are few com-

munities today, one in Jamaica, where they fought British invasion in 1655 – on the Spanish losing side. They were later involved in the Maroon Wars. There is a large community in Suriname, once 'Bush Negroes', now the Saramacca, with their own language.

13 *In the Trickster Tradition: The Novels of Andrew Salkey, Francis Ebejar and Ishmael Reed*, Peter Nazareth, Bogle-L'Ouverture Press Ltd, 1994.

14 *The Caribbean Artists Movement, 1966–1972: A Literary and Cultural History*, Ann Walmsley, New Beacon Books, London, 1992.

15 *Sheffield Thursday*, no. 3, 1993.

16 Nation language: a term coined by Kamau Brathwaite to replace the pejorative 'dialect' and the inaccurate *patois*.

17 *The New Voices* (ed. Anson Gonzales, Trinidad and Tobago) vol. 14, nos. 7 and 8, 1976, p. 14.

18 In conversation.

19 This wasn't artistic licence. To the end of their lives Andrew Salkey called Selvon Sam Sam and Selvon referred to Salkey as Sun Sun.

20 Initiated by the Jamaican poet Una Marson and continued by Henry Swanzy.

21 *The Antilles: Fragments of Epic Memory*, Faber, 1993, p. 19.

22 'Two', from *Away*, Andrew Salkey, Allison & Busby, 1980.

23 Introduction to *Tales of the Wide Caribbean*, Heinemann. 'Here Rhys conveys a wide range of social perspectives not just from the substance of what the characters say or think but through the exploitation of a number of ironically juxtaposed linguistic perspectives and styles: a prisoner's statement, defending council's plea, a magistrate's summing up, and a dialogue between a husband and wife.'

24 This is Melvin Morris's excellent reading of it in *Ariel*, vol. 24, no. 1, Jan. 1993.

25 I was thinking of the 1906 novel, *The Whole Family*, involving twelve American authors, including Henry James, each writing a chapter; the novel 'edited' by William Dean Howells.

26 *Ariel*, vol. 24, no. 1, Jan. 1993.

27 'Gerontion'.

28 'Writing Oral History: Sistren Theatre Collective's *Lionheart Gal*', *Kunapipi*, vol. xi, no. 1, 1989. Even Honor Ford Smith's introduction to *Lionheart Gal* is carefully modulated standard.

PART ONE

Folk-Tales, Legends, etc.

WILSON HARRIS

From *The Laughter of the Wapishanas*

In 1948 – when surveying in the upper Potaro Kaieteuran area of Guiana – I came upon a group of Wapishanas who are reputed to be a 'laughter-loving' people unlike the fatalistically inclined Macusis and Arekunas.

The Wapishanas are neighbours of the Macusis and though they are said to be different in temperament they possess equally a certain decorum or ritual stiffness akin to a decoy of fate. At the time I remember making notes on the theme of laughter as the decoy of fate or vice versa.

Events within the past decade bear out the necessity for an imaginative relativizing agency within neighbouring though separate peoples whose promise lies in gateway conceptions of community.

The predicament of the Indian continues to deepen with new uncertainties as to the authority which governs him. Such authority has been at stake for centuries within the decimation of the tribes. And a political scale is still lacking: the land under his feet is disputed by economic interests and national interests. It is within this background that the theme of the decoy seems to me pertinent to the whole continent of South America. For not only does it reflect the ruses of imperialism which make game of men's lives, but it occupies a curious ground of primitive oracle as well, whose horizons of sensibility we may need at this time to unravel within ourselves as an original creation.

Sermon of the Leaf

Somewhere on the staircase of the earth-race laughter was born in the sermon of the leaf. It was a curious inexplicable birth because there were years of drought when the source of laughter itself appeared to wither on the lips of the Wapishanas. A young girl of the tribe (herself called Wapishana) dreamt one day that she now cradled the dry mourning leaf of the elder tree of laughter.

She set out with it on the staircase of drought in search of the colour and nature of laughter – the source of laughter – which she was determined to restore to the lips of her people.

It was an ancient staircase which at that moment looked as dry and brown and wooden as the mourning leaf of the elder tree of laughter. It even had branches that seemed to issue in all directions as though to simulate the age of Wapishana's people: one branch for the elder tree of bird perched faraway in the dazzling reaches of the sky, one branch for the elder tree of fish swimming faraway in the dazzling bed of sky, one branch for the elder tree of animal concealed within bird and fish, one branch for the elder tree of god . . .

These, amongst many other branches, seemed to quiver almost as if they knew intimately the leaf of mission Wapishana bore as she knew her own tongue against her teeth. As if to whisper (one breath to another breathlessness, one flesh to another cage or prison) that that leaf she now carried in her head, in the markings of each palm or hand, sole or foot, had sprung from them – the walking tree or limbs of laughter – in the beginning of age when the people of Wapishana came along the elder branches of fate – along the branches of hunted bird and fish, animal and god.

Wapishana held their flesh or leaf, stamped irresistibly into the root of her senses, to her lips afresh and blew along its stiff razor-like edge as if to share something of the mingling of the sharpest blow of sorrow in the strings of laughter. It was as if the withered sliced lips of her people had become the sculpture of a song – an ancient feast of the bone which sometimes turned the tables of the tree on hunter by hunted in order to memorialize a silent debt of creation – creature to creature.

Wapishana decided to take the first leg of her journey back to the source of laughter along the elder tree of bird which stretched faraway into the dazzling reaches of the sky . . .

ELDER TREE OF GOD

And thus Wapishana came through a veil that was no veil to stand on the last leg of her journey to the source of laughter – elder tree of god – cloud or model of original extremity unfleshed by night or day.

It stood there (that cloud) at the heart of antithesis – contradictory species of darkness – contradictory species of light. Wapishana attempted to grasp it as the assembly of yellow beak, crest, claws, feathers advancing into a single creature upon her – or departing, each at a tangent to the other, into the non-existent mate of heaven.

She attempted in the same token to visualize it as a hollow shower or mint – maiden juice of extinction – comedy of the ironic bridegroom of the soul.

But however she looked at it it became senseless and faint except as the source of laughter – the first or the last model of man made in advance of the woman of the soil – in advance of bog or bed. As such it seemed to possess no authentic subsidence which could be verified – no sunrise, no sunset, no blood – but merely an unconscious plea that in its extremity it was the enduring laughter of the tribe which all would come to wear in death standing against drought – within another folded maiden light as veil or sap out of which the first stitch of rain would fall from the elder tree of god to tie a leaf to unfleshed wood.

JAMES BERRY

Time When Tiger Did Go Sick

As you know, both of them is the oldis enemies. An, today now, Tiger swear him goin crack up all the Anancy bone them once an for all.

Tiger go to bed, man. Him lie down in a bed all still an stiff stiff. Him say to himself: I know Anancy will come an look at me. The brute will wahn to make sure I dead. Him will wahn see how I look dead. Thas when I really goin collar him. Oh how I goin collar that Anancy!

Tiger tell him wife she to burse out the loudis mournful-bawlin she good for. She to stan in the yard an put her two han on her head an bawl out till she bring down every big, small and medium smady.* An Mrs Tiger do that. She bawl an bawl like it not jus her husban she say dead sudden but every one of her family.

Nearly the whole village come down, man, all quick quick an brisk. An them crowd up the yard, all worried. Everybody start talkin to one another in a them sad sad voice. Hear them, 'Fancy how Tiger dead, eh!'

'Yeahs, fancy how Tiger dead!'

'Fancy how Tiger gone – dead dead an gone!'

Anancy, too, man, hear the mournful bawlin-out. But when the Anancy hear the bawlin-out hear him to himself. 'Funny Tiger dead! Tiger such a strong an hearty man, an such a good-feedin man. Funny how Tiger dead an I didn even hear him sick!'

Anancy find himself a Tiger yard, an start mix up with the crowd. Straight away Anancy say to Tacoomah, 'Tacoomah, did you happen to hear Tiger sick?'

Tacoomah shake him head sad sad, 'No, no, Mister Anancy.'

* somebody

6

Anancy turn to Dog, 'Dog, did you happen to hear Tiger sick?'

Dog shake him head sad sad, 'No, no, Mister Anancy.'

Anancy turn to Ram-Goat an Jackass an Patoo an ask them the same question. Every one shake him head sad sad an say, 'No, no, Mister Anancy.'

An the whole yardful cluster roun Anancy. 'It all happen sudden, Mister Anancy. It all happen so so sudden!'

Hear Anancy, 'Did anybody call a doctor?'

Them shake them head. 'That would have been no use, Mister Anancy. No use at all.'

'Did Tiger cry out? Did he bawl out at all?'

'No, Mister Anancy, him didn have time. Him didn have time.'

Listen to Anancy now, talking at the top a him voice, 'Didn Tiger know that no man can meet him Blessed Blessed Lawd sudden an dohn shudder an bawl?'

Everybody go silent like them in church at Mister Anancy words. Tiger hear too. Tiger feel stupid. Him know him slip up bad. Him make the stupidis mistake. Him know him mus do somethin quick to prove him dead. Tiger give the loudis roar you can ever hear.

Hear Anancy, 'Friends, hear that? Anybody ever hear a dead man bawl?'

Everybody go dumbstruck. Nobody at all can answer Anancy. An by time Tiger jump out a bed the Anancy gone. Him gone, man – well away.

LOUISE BENNETT

Anancy and Commonsense

Once upon a time, Anancy, feeling very greedy for power and wealth, decided to collect all the commonsense there was in the world. He thought that everyone would then have to come to him with their problems and he would charge dear for his advice. So, he set out to collect all the commonsense in the world.

He collected and he collected, and all that he found, he put in a large calabash. When he could find no more commonsense, he sealed the calabash with a roll of dry leaves. Then, he decided to hide all the commonsense, at the top of a very high tree, so that no one else could get at it.

Anancy tied a rope to the neck of the calabash, tied the two ends of the rope together and put the loop over his head, so that the calabash rested on his stomach.

He started to climb the tree, but found that the calabash was getting in his way. He tried again and again, but all in vain. Suddenly, he heard someone laughing behind him, and looked around to see a little boy.

'Stupid fellow,' cried the little boy, 'if you want to climb the tree, why don't you put the calabash behind you?'

Anancy was so annoyed to hear this little bit of commonsense coming from a little boy, when he, Anancy, thought that he had collected it all, that he flung the calabash at the foot of the tree and broke it.

And so, commonsense was scattered in little pieces, all over the world, and nearly everyone got a bit of it.

Anancy is the cause.

ANDREW SALKEY

From *Island Sketchbook Narratives*

The Intentional Smell of Things

Take coffee, now, Auntie Mavis said, early, early morning coffee, or something like ginger root or Spanish onion or honey-leaf tobacco or stand-pipe jasmine! Directly, you see, that is the intentional smell of things. True as well for Seville orange, June plum, sweet sop, custard-apple, ripe mango, wild thyme, mint, sage, rosemary, pimento . . .

Come to think of it, true, too, for fresh-cut sandalwood, yucca, lignum vitae, balsa, pitch-pine . . .

And we mustn't forget seashore tang, vegetable mould, grassland after rain . . .

I know they call me Auntie Mavis, but fancy, eh, I don't have a sister or a brother for anybody to call me auntie, and besides, I like standing up alone in this suffocating island world, but I suppose it's out of some sort of good, old-time respect for grey hair and straight ace plain talk that mostly everybody calling me Auntie Mavis. You could ever reckon a nice thing like that?

And as for bauxite red dirt and luscious white sea sand and banana walk and sugar-cane field, which foreign grab from us, long ages: now, that is the intentional smell of once-own-it-and-then-lose-it, in this merry-go-round-and-drop-off-it-like-breadfruit island, the same intentional and detrimental deep hole, gone like wood smoke after breeze blow and rain fall sideways.

So, this miscall auntie, you see here, in the long run, can say to herself, 'There's *the* real intentional smell of things: smoke, breeze and slanting rain, mostly things you can't hold on to and build a world with.'

Anancy, Come Up Trumps, Nuh!

Anancy Spider-man-an-woman, is why dem downgradin you name, an laughin after you so, eh? Ow come dem treatin you as if you was foreign import dem rejec now dat dem clingin to a nex language an culture ways?

I mean to say, de older generations never use to, you know. As you stan up on Tacuma shoulder, bigger and taller an bolder dan istory epaulette, Anancy as spider direc an livin, de cestors never use to downgrade you an you rightful place in dem life eritage, no time at all.

Dis generation doin so, now, all de same. It makin you into trickster widouten tricks dem can learn from an benefit by, in de quiet conscience dem got lap up in dem inside mine.

Maybe, is de deep poetry I got lap up in me own inside mine why dem considerin dat I come light as confetti, easy to brush off after weddin ceremony.

You consider so? You really an truly consider so, after all wha dem downgrade you and you ol-time tory wid?

Know so, yes. Still, wha dem don know is dat dem well an done married to me. When de bed mek up, nex oneymoon mawnin, don is confetti dem find plait up in de sheet an pillow case?

ANDREW SALKEY

Anancy and Jeffrey Amherst

> He knew that the essence of war is violence, and that moderation in war is imbecility.
>
> Thomas Babington Macaulay,
> *Lord Nugent's Memorials of Hampden*

Admirable Caribbea, prehistoric sea, close relative of Sargasso and Atlantic, hushed home of doubloons and pistoles, highway of pirates' atrocities, keel-slashed water stained with the blood of jettisoned slaves, thought it was time for Brother Anancy to drop in, retro, on Jeffrey Amherst, belated by the nightfall of generations though it was.

She badly wanted to have a conscience-report of an English crime that had taken place in colonial America, and there was only one traveller to whom she could entrust the clammy task, extra-physical as all get-out, as it would turn out to be.

It was so Sunday-still on Jeffrey Amherst's Monday morning front veranda that you could hear the fluting hum of distant bees. And Brother Anancy, the ancient African and Caribbean spider-man, who was also a woman, was standing under a nearby maple and watching the military behemoth sitting in his white wicker rocking chair. Amherst took out his English gold watch-and-chain from the fob pocket of his cavalry-twill trousers, inclined his tactics-laden head and looked planet-weary at the face of the watch. He sighed history and closed his eyes. Behind his tired, crinkly eyelids, he imagined vistas of victory flags flapping in a windy sun that would, some day soon, set, regrettably for him.

Brother Anancy walked slow inches towards the veranda steps and asked Jeffrey Amherst, straight out, as was Brother Anancy's brass-face way: 'Why did you send those smallpox-infected blankets to the Indians, eh?'

'And who wants to know?' Amherst's English ruling-class clip didn't unnerve Anancy in the slightest; as an African and Caribbean spider-man—woman, he had been well accustomed to that sort of Albion ambush, ever since the gimlet years of the Middle Passage.

'*I* want to know,' Anancy said, abruptly as a slammed door.

'And who are you?'

'A spider-man who is also a woman.'

'An unusual fusion?'

'Only because the universal ancestors have kept the two quite separate, for ages.'

'Still, absolutely extraordinary that you should claim such a duality.'

'Two heads, two souls, always better than one of anything,' Anancy said, beginning to sag under the drag of Amherst's understatement and patronizing dodge. He leant against the veranda hand-rail and instantly imagined he had got a hold of Amherst's scrawny and squalid reputation.

'So, you want to know why I sent those blankets to the Indians? Well, because I had no recourse to other more salubrious gifts. And isn't accurate aggression of the essence?'

'Essence of what?' Anancy bit back.

'Survival.'

Brother Anancy found it difficult, wholly uneven-Stephen, to grapple with Amherst's sprawling lack of compassion, in brave New England. Fact is, all over the bulldog colony, bravado, brute spite, greed and murder had spliced hunger, disease and loneliness into the lands of the Indian nations, leaving behind not only dispossession but also a grinding solitude as even deserts have no record of, in the criss-crossing layers of their unstoppable sands.

'Would you have sent those infected blankets to Europeans?'

'If the Europeans were alien, aggressive and inimical to the English way of life, yes, certainly. We sent as much and much more so to the Germans, French and others of that kidney, time and time again.'

The man is an everlasting disaster, a conscienceless marauder, a marathon murderer, Anancy said to himself, while tightening his grip on the veranda hand-rail and trying to will away his raw need for gut revenge. *The man is totally without earthly shame is a brazen Briton of wholesale badness is a paragon of elephantine evil is a direct descendant of Beelzebub is a . . .*

'I think you're as uncivilized as a herd of bucking Visigoths!'

'And, my dear Anancy, you are so green, unutterably so.'

'Green is hope is looking forward to change is optimism itself.'

'But, Sonny Jim, I am hopeful. I do look forward to changing times. I most certainly am optimistic. But not on behalf of the Indians.'

Brother Anancy felt the angina-press of history thumping in his chest as he walked away from Jeffrey Amherst's veranda and all he could do, at that moment, was breathe in the noxious military memory and quickly breathe it out in a massive expulsion of miasma and malevolence.

For the umpteenth time, historically, Anancy's male side had suffered great shame, a crater in the intricate balance of his male and female selves.

As inconsolable as a fallen autumn leaf, he left New England and went back home to Caribbea, his head ringing with the death-gasps of the Amherst-disposable Indians and with Amherst's '. . . of the essence' clinking like a cold cliché in his mind's-eye.

The bruising noises continued, all the way, on the return journey, as Anancy's flight across the cloudless, southern sky sliced the ether like a streak of idealism through a hemisphere of injustice and distress.

When he reached home, he said to Caribbea: 'Riddle me a riddle of a world without cruelty and I'll give you a puzzle without an answer, yes?' He paused and closed his man—woman selves, tight shut, so that he would be able to heal the terrible crater. 'Riddle me a riddle of the very first families of America without a country and I'll give you a puzzle with a clear and calamitous answer, yes?' He sat down on a branch of a sea-grape tree, full face with Caribbea, hugged the melded selves and stitched the remaining fissures in the crater, seamlessly.

Caribbea leapt up, gently, and playfully splashed Anancy's face with a filigree of sea-spray, and smiled at his job, well done, albeit painfully.

WILFRED WOOD, BISHOP OF CROYDON

God's Special Mark

Easter sermon preached at St Andrew's Parish Church, Half Way Tree, Kingston, Jamaica, Easter Day, 1988

> With such a hope as this we speak out boldly . . .
> 2 Corinthians 3:12 (NEB)

St Paul, in that beautiful and familiar chapter of 1 Corinthians 13, says that there are three things that will last as long as the world lasts – faith, hope and love. We are called Christians because we believe Jesus to be the Christ, and we believe this through faith. Jesus taught that God is love, so understandably in our worship there is much reference to faith and love. But what about hope? The Church's great festival of Easter, which we are celebrating today, is essentially a festival of hope.

On British television there is a programme called *The Antiques Roadshow*, where specialists are asked to identify various objects, so you see them examining these objects very closely, looking for the maker's special mark. That mark – the maker's mark – will identify the object as the genuine article. In all the events of history, and in all the goings-on in the world around us, God has a special mark. God's mark is *bringing life out of death*.

Sometimes that mark is to be seen in the affairs of a whole nation. For example, the Hebrew people lived as slaves in Egypt, where they were cruelly ruled and badly treated by the Egyptians. They were allowed to live only in the poorest areas; they did the most menial and the dirtiest jobs, and they were paid little or no wages. Their women-folk had no time to be mothers to their own children, because they had to leave them in the poor areas where they lived, while they went to look after the children of the rich Egyptian women. When the Hebrews complained, they were beaten with whips and driven back to work by fully armed Egyptian soldiers and policemen.

You may think that I am describing the plight of black people in South Africa today. In fact, what I am giving you is a biblical description of God's people in Egypt hundreds of years before the birth of Christ. Then, when things were at their worst, and there was no sign of change, God sent a message to his oppressed people: 'Leave Egypt and head towards the Red Sea. Trust me, and leave the rest to me.' They did so, and God brought them through the Red Sea to freedom and nationhood. *New life out of death – God's mark.*

One of the loveliest stories to come out of the 1939–45 war is of a church in London, which one Saturday had been made ready for the Harvest Thanksgiving Service next day. Among the harvest gifts of fruit and flowers, someone had brought a sheaf of corn. That night, Hitler's bombers came, and the entire church was reduced to a pile of rubble: stones, broken glass, burnt-out timber. Months passed and spring came. And there, out of all that devastation and rubble, appeared tiny green shoots of corn. *Out of death, new life – God's mark.*

As with nations, as with nature, so also with individuals. And the greatest example, of course, Our Lord Jesus Christ. He was killed in the most horrible way – as a criminal, when he was innocent of any crime. He was nailed to a cross and a spear was stuck into his ribs. He died painfully and horribly. But God raised him from the dead, and he could show himself to his friends. Still bearing the marks of the nails in his hands and feet. Still with the wound made by the spear in his side. But now full of new life. *Life out of death – God's mark.*

So even people who do not share our faith can see why, for us Christians, Easter is not only a festival of joy. It is a festival of hope. And the resurrection of Jesus, at the heart of our Christian religion, makes Christianity a religion of hope. There is no situation, however grim, however bleak, that is beyond God's power to redeem. We can all go down to the grave, and even in the grave we'll make our song: Alleluia, Alleluia! For we are an Easter people, and Alleluia is our song.

As Christians we are not ignorant of the grimness of the world we live in, and we do not take this lightly. We know, for example, that there exists a stockpile of nuclear weapons capable of destroying all human life within a matter of minutes. We know that we live under the shadow of possible nuclear accidents, or the malfunctioning of some device which could trigger a world war – as could evil or incompetent men in positions of power.

We know the power of human sin whenever we see children starving to death in fly-infested camps in Ethiopia; or see the victims of civil war in Angola, Lebanon and Northern Ireland or the dehumanization of people by racial oppression in South Africa, Namibia and elsewhere. So we are not naïve.

And it isn't only what goes on outside ourselves or on a national or international scale. In our individual lives, and on a personal scale, we can have moments of near despair when our personal relationships, our health, our hopes for the future, all seem to be in ruins. What we thought had been built with concrete is but a heap of smouldering debris, and we must stand exposed to the gaze and comment of open enemy and false friends alike.

As if that isn't bad enough, we find ourselves *at odds with the society we live in*, especially if we are hurt by the greed, the selfishness and material-ism which others have made their way of life, and we see them rewarded with success.

To make matters worse, we are *at odds with those who are nearest and dearest to us*, especially if we are parents, when their need for independence and self-discovery makes them distant at just the time we need them most to support us in our own insecurity.

And worst of all, we are *at odds with ourselves* because of the great, great gap between the kind of lovable and successful persons we would like to be, and the kind of fallible persons we actually are. When these things descend upon us, our depression can be like the darkness of a tomb. And it was out of a tomb that God brought new life on Easter day.

Around three weeks ago I received a letter from a friend in prison. This is part of what he wrote to me: 'It was when I hit the bottom – stripped of clothes, dignity, individuality and status – that God spoke directly to my soul. There is no place that God is not. To paraphrase a piece I came across three days ago: God shattered my plate-glass life, and now we will take the broken pieces and make wind-chimes. Lent is a special time to be in prison. Resurrection is a *promise*, not a maybe.'

As with individuals, so with nature. And here in Jamaica you have the *poui* tree to remind you that, plain and dull as it may be for many months, the time will come when it will burst into the brightest blooms.

As with individuals and with nature, so also with nations. Last week I received a letter from another friend in Britain. She had been reading the autobiography of a well-known churchman, and she found his final theological position unacceptable in that he suggests that it matters little to faith whether anything in the Gospels is history or not. 'But,' she writes (and I agree with her), 'there ought, for the health of the human mind, to be some point where the mythopoeic and the historical faculties engage simultaneously and with divine sanction. And I can't quite believe, although I am aware that it is at present fashionable to think so, that a human being in the first century was so unconcerned to know if a thing really happened. If anyone had told *me* that a man had risen from the dead, I think I would at least have said: "Are you *sure*?" rather than, "What wonderful spiritual reverberations that statement arouses!"'

That caused me to reflect that whatever means God had chosen to give this well-known churchman his faith, it could not have been the same means by which most of us in the Caribbean and elsewhere, with a background of slavery and colonial oppression, had experienced it. Certainly, speaking out of their experiences, my grandparents in Barbados had made it clear to me that whatever injustices the children of God suffered at the hands of human beings were like the sufferings of Christ on the cross, and as surely as he had suffered the worst that wicked men could do to him and had been raised from the dead, as surely would God's children be vindicated and the freedom they enjoyed in the sight of God would one day also be recognized by those who were presently denying it. That was a promise and fact because of the resurrection.

So then we can understand the exchange that took place in the South African Treason Trials in 1956 between the trial judge and that great Zulu leader and Nobel Peace Prize winner, Albert Luthuli (after whom, incidentally, I felt it a privilege to be able to name one of our three sons). Albert Luthuli had described the great lengths that the ANC had gone to in peaceful protests against the unjust apartheid system – the many petitions, delegations, letters, and representations, all to no avail. 'So there was no hope of change, then?' asked the trial judge. 'There was no *sign* of change, My Lord,' replied Luthuli, 'but always there is *hope*.'

And it was not bravado that put into the mouth of that other Nobel Peace Prize winner, Bishop Desmond Tutu, his defiant words to the Eloff Commission: 'The South African Government are not God. They are but men. Other tyrants before them have bitten the dust. They may get rid of a Tutu, but the Church of God will be here long after they are no more than a footnote on the pages of history.'

The faith of the Church is the faith in the risen Christ on whom our *hope* is founded.

So those of us who work and pray for a just, participatory and sustainable community of women and men round the world will not be discouraged by the seeming triumph of evil over good. Every Easter reminds us that the life in Christ which we share with Peter, James, John and the first apostles; with Stephen, Paul and other saints down the ages; with the millions who came after them from every nation and people under the sun; with the thousands who, through the years, sat in these same pews, knelt at this same altar rail and now rejoice in a great light and on another shore – this life was brought out of death by God who now offers to do the same in every generation of those whom he has called.

So we renew our baptismal vows to show that we humbly and gratefully accept this offer, and pray that he will keep us firm in the hope that he has set before us, so that we and all his children shall be free, and the whole earth live to praise his name.

Alleluia – Christ is risen!

KENNETH VIDIA PARMASAD

Sakchulee and the Rich Gentleman

People called him Sakchulee. There was no better name for him, they said. He was wayward. He was a bundle of mischief. He was cunning but seemed always to be such a fool. He tried always to be so honest but many people wished that he were not. He was so simple and so innocent yet he always seemed to be doing wrong. In trying to be too kind, he was often unkind. The more he tried to do good, the more it seemed that he did bad. No one understood him and, try as he might, he never seemed to understand anyone.

Poor Sakchulee! Both his parents had died when he was still a little boy. He was therefore left in the care of his elder brother. This brother had to get a job to support Sakchulee and himself. After he had looked many places, he finally met a rich gentleman who was willing to give him a job. Everyday when his brother went to work, Sakchulee remained at home.

Sakchulee's brother's job was very simple. All he had to do was to fill a barrel with water during the day. All day long, Sakchulee's brother dutifully poured water into the barrel. But he noticed that no matter how much water he poured into the barrel, the barrel would never fill up.

As time went on, Sakchulee's brother became more and more dissatisfied with this job. He longed to leave the job. But there was one problem. When he got the job, Sakchulee's brother had made an agreement with the rich gentleman. He had agreed that he would cut off the gentleman's nose and ears if the gentleman were to dismiss him from the job. However, if he were to leave the job on his own, then the gentleman would have the right to cut off Sakchulee's brother's nose and ears.

This is why Sakchulee's brother was afraid to leave the job even though he was having such a hard time. Many days passed. Every morning, Sakchulee's brother would set out for work with a heavy heart, anxious for this day to come to an end, wishing that the next day would never come. Finally he could stand it no longer. One evening, Sakchulee's brother went up to the rich gentleman. He told the gentleman that he no longer wanted to work there. He had come to keep his side of the agreement. That evening, Sakchulee's brother returned home with both his nose and ears cut off.

Sakchulee was very unhappy to see what had happened to his brother. Now it was his turn to find a job and to take care of his brother. He decided to go and work for the rich gentleman in his brother's place. He told his brother to remain at home and he left for the gentleman's house. When he got there, Sakchulee was given the same job that his brother had been doing. And the very same agreement was made between Sakchulee and the rich gentleman.

Early the next morning, Sakchulee began his new job. He brought buckets and buckets of water to fill the barrel. But, just like his brother, he noticed that the barrel would not get full at all. After this had continued for some time, Sakchulee became quite angry. He kicked the barrel in disgust. Such a vicious kick it was, the barrel fell over on its side. To his surprise, Sakchulee noticed that there were many tiny holes at the bottom of the barrel. The water he was so diligently pouring into the barrel was flowing out through an underground canal and watering the neighbouring fields.

Sakchulee took some mud and some leaves and blocked the holes at the bottom of the barrel. He then put the barrel upright again. This time when he poured water inside, none leaked out and he was able to fill the barrel very quickly.

The rich gentleman looked quite puzzled when he saw that Sakchulee was able to fill the barrel. He then gave Sakchulee another task. Sakchulee's new job was to take care of the gentleman's horse. Soon after he was given charge of the horse, Sakchulee went to the market and sold the horse. However, before he sold the horse, he cut off the end of its tail and kept it for himself. When Sakchulee returned from the market, he took the end of the horse's tail, pushed it into an ant's hole and left it there.

A few days afterwards, the gentleman asked Sakchulee if he was taking good care of the horse.

'Master, has no one told you?' asked Sakchulee.

'Told me what?' the rich gentleman replied.

'The horse got away from me and went into an ant's hole. I tried to get him out but he refused to come out.'

The rich gentleman was both puzzled and worried by this news. He went to the ant's hole and pulled at the piece of tail. Out it came in his hands.

'Look what you've done!' exclaimed Sakchulee. 'You've broken off the tail of the horse. Now he will never be able to come out.'

The gentleman was angry that he had lost such a good horse. But he was afraid to dismiss Sakchulee. He knew that Sakchulee was just waiting for the chance to cut off his ears and nose. He was forced to give Sakchulee another job. He asked Sakchulee to look after his cattle. 'And be sure that, everyday, you take the cattle to the waterhole,' he warned Sakchulee.

Every morning, Sakchulee took the cattle to a field of tobacco to graze. There was not much grass for them to eat so the cattle became thinner and thinner. In the evening, Sakchulee would take them to the waterhole and say to them, 'All right, there is the waterhole. The master said that I should take you to the waterhole. I have done as he has instructed. Now come on, let's get going.' And before the cattle had time to drink any water, Sakchulee would lead them back home.

Sakchulee continued this practice for a few days. He gave the cattle hardly any grass to eat and no water at all to drink. Soon all the cattle died of hunger and thirst.

By this time, the rich gentleman was really anxious to send Sakchulee away but he still feared having his ears and nose cut off. He was again forced to offer Sakchulee another job. This time Sakchulee was told to take care of the goats. Instead of doing this, Sakchulee would kill one goat every day and stuff himself with the goat's meat. When all the goats had been killed and eaten, Sakchulee went to his master with this story, 'Oh master, last night while I was fast asleep, a robber came and drove off all the goats. I heard nothing. Only when I woke up this morning, did I find the goats gone.'

The gentleman could stand it no longer. He shouted at Sakchulee, 'Why don't you go away? You're nothing but a pest! Go away!'

And Sakchulee replied, 'As soon as you are ready to give me your nose and ears, I shall leave.'

Sakchulee remained. A few weeks passed. Then one day, the gentleman employed some women to grind his grain for him. The women came to his house to use his *jhata* (a handmill of stone for grinding). While the women were busy grinding, they made their task lighter by singing out loudly. On this day, the gentleman was somewhat worried and could not bear to hear their happy singing. He called Sakchulee and asked him to tell the women that their singing did not please him. 'Tell them that I can't hear their singing today,' he said to Sakchulee.

Sakchulee approached the women and said to them, 'My master is not pleased with your singing. He cannot hear you well. Could you please sing louder?'

The women were only too happy to please the gentleman. They did as Sakchulee advised. They raised their voices and sang as loudly as they could. The gentleman called Sakchulee again and asked him to give the same instructions to the women. Sakchulee told the women just what he had told them before. And again the women tried to sing as loudly as they could. A few more times this happened until finally the gentleman told Sakchulee in disgust, 'Please tell them to stop!'

'Of course, master,' replied Sakchulee, 'I shall do as you say.'

Sakchulee then hurried back to the women and told them to stop grinding the wheat. The women stopped right away. They left the gentleman's grain undone and went their way. Once more, Sakchulee had got the better of the rich gentleman.

'Please leave and go,' he begged Sakchulee.

'Are you ready to give me your ears and nose?' asked Sakchulee.

The gentleman was not willing. Once more he allowed Sakchulee to remain.

That night, the gentleman and his wife planned to leave secretly for a distant town. Everyone went to bed at the same time. Very late in the night, when Sakchulee was asleep, the gentleman and his wife got up to make ready for the trip. They began to prepare all kinds of foods and sweetmeats to take with them on their long journey. While they were busily packing the food into a large box, Sakchulee got up and overheard them talking.

'We must be sure to leave very early before he gets up,' he heard the gentleman saying to his wife.

'Once and for all, we shall be rid of him,' the wife whispered with relief.

At once, Sakchulee guessed what they were planning. As soon as they went back to bed, Sakchulee got up. He took a bunch of bananas, placed it in his bed and covered it with his blanket. Then he went and hid himself in their box of food.

Early the next morning, the gentleman and his wife got up. They peeped at Sakchulee's bed to make sure that he was under the blanket. Then the gentleman placed the box of food on his head and he and his wife left the house very quietly.

The gentleman and his wife walked slowly along the road. The sun got hotter and hotter. After they had walked some distance in the blazing sun, the gentleman felt something warm dripping all down the side of his face.

'Why did you put so much ghee (butter) in the food?' he asked his wife. 'This hot sun is causing it to melt and drain all over me.'

'But I did not put any more than I always do,' his wife told him.

'You must have. And not only that. I think you've cooked too much food. This box is getting heavier by the minute.'

The wife became a little annoyed when she heard this. She felt that her husband was complaining too much.

'Well, why don't you dash the box on the ground if you find it too heavy?' she muttered angrily.

Sakchulee heard her angry muttering. Terrified that he would be dashed to the ground, he called out from inside the box, 'If you're dashing down the box, please let it fall gently.'

Both the gentleman and his wife were astonished to hear Sakchulee's voice. It sounded so near to them and yet he was nowhere to be seen.

'Here I am, on top of your head,' Sakchulee shouted. 'Please put me down gently, then you can let me out.'

The gentleman was so amazed, he followed Sakchulee's instructions without even realizing what he was doing. He put the box gently on the ground, opened the lid and came face to face with Sakchulee, smiling broadly at them. Sakchulee climbed out of the box and stood before them, a mischievous grin on his face. Now, with Sakchulee standing there before them, they understood not only why the box was heavy but also what was leaking down the gentleman's face. Sakchulee's trousers were dripping wet! The gentleman hastily rushed to a nearby pond to wash his face. His wife took all the food she had spent so much time preparing and flung it away as far as she could.

'What are you doing here?' the gentleman asked when he returned, still not quite able to believe his eyes.

'I have to be where you are,' Sakchulee replied cheerfully. 'If you want me to leave, just give me your ears and nose.'

Since the gentleman was still not willing to part with his ears and nose, Sakchulee was allowed to continue the journey with them.

Night came and they decided to spend the night on the bank of a river. The gentleman arranged the sleeping so that Sakchulee would sleep nearest the river. His wife would sleep between himself and Sakchulee. The plan was to push Sakchulee into the river when he was asleep.

When morning came, the gentleman's wife was no longer lying in the spot where she had fallen asleep the night before. In her place Sakchulee was sleeping quite comfortably.

'Where is my wife? What are you doing there? What have you done with her?' the gentleman shook Sakchulee awake.

'I changed places with your wife last night,' Sakchulee yawned sleepily. 'It was very cold so near to the river. I got up and warmed myself between you and your wife.'

'But where is my wife?' the gentleman persisted.

'Last night, you whispered in my ear that I should push her into the river. That's what I did,' answered Sakchulee.

'What a fool I am!' the gentleman sobbed. 'And what a bigger fool you are!'

'I simply obey what you tell me, oh master!' Sakchulee replied, sounding as innocent as a baby.

So now the rich gentleman was without a wife. Because of Sakchulee, he had lost his horse, his cattle, his goats. His grain was still in the granary waiting to be ground. So many misfortunes had befallen him but this last one was the worst of all. His heart was filled with grief. He felt that he had to make a final attempt to rid himself of Sakchulee.

The rich gentleman decided to visit his mother-in-law. He asked Sakchulee to go with him. He felt that his wife's brothers would make Sakchulee pay dearly for causing the death of their sister. In this way he would not break the agreement and yet he would not have to put up with Sakchulee. On their way, the gentleman bought a bunch of ripe bananas which he asked Sakchulee to carry. Just before they arrived at the mother-in-law's home, the gentleman sent Sakchulee ahead to let them know that he was coming.

As soon as Sakchulee arrived, he went straight to the gentleman's father-in-law and said, 'Sir, I have very sad news for you. Your daughter has died a most tragic death. My master is overcome with grief. He says that I must stop him even if he himself tries to talk about her. He just cannot bear to remember how she died. Please be sure that no one mentions her death.'

'Of course, I'll make sure of that,' replied the father-in-law. He was very concerned that his son-in-law should overcome his grief.

Sakchulee was pleased, knowing that no one would find out how the gentleman's wife had died. Then Sakchulee went to the gentleman's mother-in-law and gave her the bananas, saying, 'I bring these bananas as a gift to you from my master. But I must tell you a secret. My master does not eat bananas but he does enjoy a meal of cooked banana skins.'

The mother-in-law wanted to make her son-in-law as comfortable as possible. The very first meal she prepared for him was a meal of cooked banana skins. Meanwhile Sakchulee had told his master, 'I overheard your mother-in-law talking. She said that the family was so poor, she didn't know what special food she could prepare for you. But I did hear her say that she would prepare the very best she could afford.'

And so, when the meal was offered to the gentleman, he felt obliged to accept it. And to show the family how much he appreciated their kindness, he ate every single piece of banana skin.

That night, when everybody had gone to bed, the gentleman awakened Sakchulee and told him that he had a terrible gripe. He asked Sakchulee to accompany him to the outhouse. Sakchulee got up and brought a clay pot for the master, telling him that the family had provided this for his use. He promised the gentleman that he would get up early the next morning and remove it from the house. Since the family had been so kind, the gentleman felt obliged to use the pot even though he was reluctant.

When morning came and the gentleman got up he saw that Sakchulee was still fast asleep. He tried to awaken Sakchulee but Sakchulee refused to get up. Finally, the gentleman covered himself with his blanket, took the pot in his hands and started to walk towards the door. At this point, Sakchulee, who had not been sleeping, began to shout, 'Look, look, my master is running away!'

Sakchulee shouted so loudly that he awakened the entire household. When they came running to see what was taking place, Sakchulee continued, 'My master is angry. He doesn't like how you treated him. He's going away!'

The mother-in-law, anxious that her son-in-law should not leave in this manner, ran up to him. She held on to his arm, pleading with him to remain. As soon as she did this, the clay pot fell from the gentleman's hands and smashed into a thousand pieces before the eyes of everyone standing there. All that was inside it splashed on to the people standing around. The gentleman was so embarrassed and ashamed, he crouched on the floor, crying.

'Sakchulee,' he groaned, 'please, I beg you. Take my nose. Take my ears. Just take them and get out of my life. I never want to lay eyes on you again.'

Once more, Sakchulee obeyed his master's instructions. Then, very pleased with himself, Sakchulee returned to his home to meet his brother and tell him the good news.

SEEPERSAD NAIPAUL

My Uncle Dalloo

My Uncle Dalloo was, without doubt, the cutest as well as the cleverest man in our village. He was held to be the light not only of my grandfather Gangaram's household, but he was regarded as the light of the whole village. The qualities that raised him to this pinnacle were multiple. He was perspicacious, conniving, and versatile. He was, for instance, the only person in the village who could read and write. And my Uncle Dalloo could read and write not only Hindi – and some Sanskrit – which alone would have been sufficient to raise him high above the rest of our microscopic community, but he could read and write English too. And it was this *Angrezi* qualification of his, to begin with, that quite dazzled and benumbed the villagers. Many I knew who literally prostrated themselves before him in those days, pleading Babaji this, Babaji that.

But his being bilingual was not all the magic. More potent than his being bilingual was the fact that my Uncle Dalloo was a Brahmin of the first water – a most uncompromising member of the priestly caste, tenaciously, inexorably, fantastically and fanatically orthodox. Catch him eating so much as a grain of *channa* with his boots on! Or let him catch *you* calling yourself a Brahmin, or a Maharaj, or a Singh, and not keeping the *churki* – the tuft of hair, long, knotted, and conspicuous – on the crown of the head! Literally and otherwise, Uncle Dalloo would make you *ku-jat* or outcaste on the spot. He was like that.

If by some chance you could hit upon the truth, that my Uncle Dalloo's brand of English was no better than that of a baboo's, you would take good care not to let him know what you thought of it, or of him; otherwise you would soon discover that existence could be a devilishly hazardous business; or, as young Dookhoo the grass-cutter put it, 'Living would become water more than flour for you.' But no fear; in our cul-de-sac of a village there appeared to be none with either so much sense or so much rashness. So Uncle Dalloo reigned unchallenged – a kind of an intellectual superman, Babaji and Maharaj of all he surveyed. His word was law.

For all this Uncle Dalloo was neither very formidable-looking nor a very prepossessing person. He was just cute, about thirty-five when I knew him; small and spare, cherubic and tender. He was singularly and pathetically bald-pated; indeed, he gave you the impression that he was born that way. How else could you explain that tight, shiny scalp of his, with just a straggling fringe of hair above the ears, fine and anaemic things, like sun-starved grass around a gleaming pond?

He never worked with his hands. Certainly I had never seen him grace a cutlass or a hoe. He said he was not born for that kind of life. He said he was a Brahmin. No one could quarrel with him for that – least of all my Aunt Leela. Her he kept in place by a variety of Brahminic subtleties, such as, if she did not obey him in this or that matter she was sure to be reborn into a beetle or into a snake or even into a scorpion. And my Aunt Leela, being herself a Brahmini, albeit Trinidad-born, and having heard nothing to the contrary all her life, quite believed all this. So she obeyed.

I can well guess what kind of life Uncle Dalloo must have led in India. It was plain he came from an impoverished middle-class family who had fallen on hard times in the wake of the Mutiny. I have a strong suspicion that even at the age of eighteen or twenty he must have led a rather grim sort of life; possibly he was well on the way to living on his wits. Uncle Dalloo prided himself on his being Cawnpore-born and bred, and the grand way in which he expatiated on the exploits of the Cawnpore-*wallahs* made all other human beings outside Cawnpore seem insipid and third-rate.

He had attended a government school where, in addition to Hindi, the sirdar also taught the boys some English. In his gay moods he often recited with great feeling and in that peculiar Indian English of his the whole of 'Rule, Britannia'. It was the only poem he ever recited in English. I doubt whether he knew another; but with it he at once charmed and confounded the villagers. They listened open-mouthed, in dumb amazement, not understanding a word of it. But Uncle Dalloo took this as a great compliment. He knew he had established himself in their opinion as a brilliant *Angrezi* scholar.

How a *pukka shaharia* – a rank city man – like my Uncle Dalloo came to dwell in a bowl of a place like Chandernagore was for a long time a wonder to me. When I came to know him better it was clear that that was just the move *he* would be very likely to make in the circumstances. You see, my grandfather Gangaram was not a poor man. A third of the length and breadth of Chandernagore was his; a lovely patch of cocoa plantation on the other side of the settlement was his too; his long pen was never without at least a dozen head of cattle; and, though he himself was chary of admitting the fact, it was somehow known that he had money in the Post Office savings bank up in Chaguanas, the market town, three miles away. Add to this the fact that my Aunt Leela, hard on marriageable age, slight and small like Uncle Dalloo himself, with long black hair and limpid dark eyes, was uncomplainingly attractive. What wonder, then, that soon enough Uncle Dalloo had not only married my Aunt Leela, but, as much as my grandfather himself, became adviser and man in authority.

Most surviving India-born Indians in Trinidad recount tall tales how they were fooled by wily recruiters into coming to the *tapu* to work on sugar and cocoa plantations. But Uncle Dalloo had no such tales to recount of himself. *He* was not fooled into his being recruited by anybody. He was himself a recruiter. Scores of the thousand and one men and women who found themselves on board the good ship *Mutla* bound for Trinidad *tapu* were recruited by him, he claimed. In virtue of this he was automatically made a sirdar over his fellow-emigrants the very day he set foot on board the ship. In virtue of the same fact he continued being a sirdar on Tortuga Estate, to which he was indentured. Thereafter, his indentureship period over, he kept being a sirdar on one plantation or another till he moved in with my grandfather Gangaram to become house son-in-law. And this explains why, in typical sirdar fashion, he habitually clad himself in khaki trousers and tunic, never ventured out unless he was well-booted, and never handled a cutlass or a hoe. Once a sirdar always a sirdar, seemed to be *his* way.

This, his being neatly clad in khaki from neck to ankle, and his going about in boots, made my Uncle Dalloo appear quite a phenomenon to the villagers. They respected him all the more for it. The fact is nobody else in Chandernagore wore boots, and few wore trousers. They couldn't. Chandernagore was not a town. Far, far from it. Chandernagore was a lagoon – for half the year at any rate. It contained, among other animate and inanimate phenomena, about a dozen huts, mostly primitive grass-thatched habitations, planted anywhere and anyhow in the lowlands.

From a quarter of a mile these huts made you think of some gargantuan, prehistoric monsters that had rambled in the slime and slush of the lagoon and then, no longer able to carry themselves, had died, greyed, become fossilized, and remained rooted and inert for ever. For six months of the year the place abounded in flood and mud; often enough the mud reached to the very doors of the huts; floods inundated the earthen floors. The villagers did not mind all this. They were in their element. Mud and they were kin. They welcomed rain, they delighted in floods. These things, they gleefully told one another, were a godsend for the paddy crops. Outsiders looked upon the Chandernagorean as a kind of amphibian; the Chandernagoreans on their part looked upon outsiders as extraordinary people, in that they wore far too much clothes.

Therefore was my Uncle Dalloo looked upon as an extraordinary man. He was so unlike the Chandernagoreans. In that watery, paddy-begetting expanse who but he would want to be in khaki trousers and tunic! And who but he would want to wear boots! Not trousers but mostly short dhotis were what the other menfolk wore. As for boots ... some of the more fastidious villagers, like my grandfather Gangaram, permitted themselves the luxury of a pair of sabots – not when there was mud though, but when there was little or no mud at all.

Uncle Dalloo was a kind of Dr Know-All too. There was no problem he could not solve, no enigma he could not unravel, no ailment he could not get rid of. Hardly a day passed but a villager or two would come to him, wanting to know this and to know that. Nothing was too big for him to tackle; nothing was too little.

Except when he was voluntarily made a gift of a shilling or two, he did not as a rule exact payments for his services. He could not make himself so obviously mean. But indirectly he benefited enormously. In the rice-planting season, for example, he got acre upon acre of my grandfather Gangaram's part of the lagoon planted in rice without paying a cent for labour. At reaping time, too, he got all the paddy reaped, threshed, bagged and toted much in the same gratis kind of way.

He was seldom refused a loan; none dared refuse him a favour. If one did he was likely to find, not long after, all his young rice seedlings mysteriously eaten up at the top by cattle or nipped off under water by crabs. Nobody would know whose cattle ate the seedlings nor how crabs came into the rice patch. It would surprise no one if the sufferer came to Uncle Dalloo and begged him to solve yet another enigma.

Uncle Dalloo had a way with him when put to these tasks. First he would ask some questions. Then he would squat upon his heels, jam his elbows upon his knees, prop his chin upon his hands. As though his brain could not function well enough otherwise. Then he would meditate. He would meditate in a hard, gruelling sort of stare, forehead creased, gaze on ground. If anybody, not knowing he was far gone in thought, interrupted him, he would snap out, 'Shut up!' and none would dare break into his thoughts a second time. If his questions, the answers thereto, and the meditations that followed, did not fetch him a ready solution, he would call for his *Yotish*, which is a kind of Indian *Napoleon's Book of Fate*, but with a deal of religious tang about it; or he would call for his Bible, an ancient, musty, mutilated copy of the Authorized Version which he had kept for years, though I doubt whether he really appreciated or understood the contents of that great book.

One short incident, and I shall be through with this sketch of my Uncle Dalloo.

One evening old Ramdat came to him. This Ramdat was a gnarled, bow-backed, swarthy fellow of about forty or forty-five. Always you saw him in a short cotton dhoti and in a merino, or shirt of some sort, mostly made out of a floursack. The grey house against which fluttered from tall bamboo staffs half a dozen red flags put up to Hanuman, the Monkey God, was his.

'Babaji!' moaned Ramdat, slouching down on his heels, for he would not dare to squat on a level with my Uncle Dalloo, who at the moment was reclining on his stringed bed in the gallery. 'Babaji,' repeated Ramdat, 'I find myself in a great trouble. I come to you in a great distress . . . She . . . she has run away.'

Uncle Dalloo sat up. 'She who?'

'My Joogni . . . the last daughter. She is gone!'

Uncle Dalloo went on his heels now, put his hands around his knees so as to brace his posture. 'Gone where?' he asked.

'That is what I want *you* to tell me, Babaji.'

'Hm!' exclaimed Uncle Dalloo; and you could sense there was plenty in that 'hm'. 'How old is the girl?' he asked.

'Going fifteen this year, Babaji.'

Uncle Dalloo was suddenly visibly annoyed. 'You are a fool of a man,' he said. 'You are a slack fellow. You ought to have had the girl married at least a year ago. It is the law. All the Shastras say so. You could be punished for your slackness.'

Old Ramdat trembled. 'I know; I do not deny it, Babaji. I would have had the child married last marriage season; it was not easy to find a suitable match for her.'

Uncle Dalloo waved aside the excuse. 'There are suitable people right in this village. One match is enough; two would be one too many . . . Where and when was the girl last seen?'

'At about nine yesterday morning. She pushed her clothes in a bucket and went to wash at Chirkut's pond.'

Uncle Dalloo called for his Bible, key and string. The moment I heard him call for these things, I knew he had already had his answer. I knew he had solved the mystery of Joogni's disappearance. If he had not, he would have called for his *Yotish*; for then, whatever the answer, right or wrong, it would be the *Yotish* to praise or blame, not Uncle Dalloo.

My Aunt Leela brought the Bible, the long key and the string. Then, still squatting on his stringed bed, Uncle Dalloo went to work. He opened the book in the middle, placed the key perpendicularly between the pages, with the knob-end sticking out. Then he shut the book and bound it tightly with the string, so that the knob-end of the key kept sticking out.

'Come now,' he said, meaning me.

I knew what he wanted me to do. The Bible would hang on the key; the key would hang from the tip of Uncle Dalloo's forefinger on the one side, and from the tip of my own forefinger on the other side. We would squat facing each other, with the Bible suspended precariously between us.

We did this.

It was a dramatic moment. On whoever's name the Bible turned, that person would be the man who had made away with Joogni. Everybody's eyes were on that Bible. There were my Aunt Leela and my Cousin Rampat looking on too. Old Ramdat watched the Bible as though his life depended on it.

'Steady now!' said Uncle Dalloo. Then he began: 'By Saint Peter, by Saint Paul, *Ramu* has run away with Joogni.'

I said my end of the formula: 'By Saint Peter, by Saint Paul, Ramu *ain't* run away with Joogni.'

The Bible remained steady.

'By Saint Peter, by Saint Paul,' recited Uncle Dalloo, '*Arjun* has run away with Joogni.'

It was my turn now. 'By Saint Peter, by Saint Paul, Arjun *ain't* run away with Joogni.'

Still the Bible remained steady.

'By Saint Peter, by Saint Paul . . .'

Within five minutes Uncle Dalloo and I had repeated the lullaby on the names of almost every youngster in the village – married and unmarried. The book didn't spin. Uncle Dalloo pondered, tried to recall the names of other young gallants. We all had our eyes glued, so to speak, on the Bible. Who could be the culprit? It wasn't Ramu, it wasn't Arjun, it wasn't –

'Perhaps,' cut in my Aunt Leela, 'perhaps the girl hasn't run away at all. Perhaps she is drowned in Chirkut's pond. Perhaps . . .'

'Shut up!' snapped Uncle Dalloo. 'Let me think.'

We kept mum.

'Ah!' exclaimed Uncle Dalloo. 'Steady now! By Saint Peter, by Saint Paul, *Jagna* has run away with Joogni.'

'By Saint Peter, by . . .'

Suddenly old Ramdat drew a long breath . . . The Bible was turning; I am dead sure I didn't see Uncle Dalloo's finger shake; nor did mine. But the Bible *was* turning. It described almost a circle, the key slipped from Uncle Dalloo's finger; the book fell with a thud.

'There!' exclaimed Uncle Dalloo triumphantly. 'There's your answer. It is Jagna who has run away with Joogni.'

Old Ramdat, dumb with rage and shame, groaned and gnashed his teeth, but said nothing.

When he was gone, my Aunt Leela said to my Uncle Dalloo: 'But how did you hit so unerringly on Jagna? Is it true?'

Uncle Dalloo said: 'It is very true. All parties to a row or an argument in this village come to me for advice. If you had been home earlier today, you would have seen when Jagna's father came to me. *His* son, too, is not at home since yesterday.'

'Where is he, then?'

'Hiding with Joogni in Nanaan's hut in the next village,' said Uncle Dalloo.

A Working Woman

Di first ting ah going tell yuh is what really mek me conscious of how dis life do me. Ah been working from ah was seventeen years old until now and all di lickle money dat ah work only go fi food and rent. Ah don't have none save. Di lickle money is too small to save.

Di first job ah ever do was a domestic servant. Ah do it fi three years. Ah was living in Alexandria in di country wid me family. A Big Man in di district had a big property. His son grow up and come to town and was working at Hanna's shops as one of Hanna's big supervisor. After him get married, him wanted a helper, so him come down and ask me faada if him can let me come and me faada say 'Yes.' Dat was how ah come to Kingston.

Ah was di washer and do di cleaning and tidying of di house. Dem have anodder lady who cook. It was stop pon premises. Three of us, di cook, di gardener and me, stop pon premises. Di gardener deh one side by himself inna one room wid only a lickle bed and one table in deh. Me and di cook share a room. Inna it we have two lickle single bed fi me and she and one lickle table inna di middle, to put anyting we had. We suitcase was put down at di odder side pon di floor or pon one box. Di table was di place weh we eat.

A bell connect from fi-dem room to fi-we room. Every morning at five o'clock dat lady ring dat bell. Breakfast have to ready, for Mr Iris have to be on di road by six thirty to reach work by seven. Him a di manager so him carry home most of di key dem and him open di shop in di morning. Ah had to get up and go in di kitchen and get di breakfast. Dem had a big breakfast. Green banana and mackerel or egg and bacon and tea and toast and cornflakes different. As di breakfast finish and him go tru di gate, me start tidy di house and mek up di bed. It was him and him wife and him madda in a two bedroom house. Me mek up di bed and sweep out di house. Di cook start look after whatsoever she cooking for lunch or she do lickle ironing.

By eight o'clock, ah finish tidy out di house. Ah had to wash and iron every day for di man change a white shirt every morning and every evening. Every week yuh have fourteen shirt fi wash fi him, fourteen underpant, fourteen marina, fourteen pair a socks. When him come in from work in di evening, him tidy and put on one. When him go a him bed, him tek off dat and put on him pyjama. In di morning, him wake up and put on one clean suit fi go a work, so ah have dat amount of clothes to look after fi di man plus her clothes and de madda's. By twelve o'clock yuh have to put di clothes on di line. When him come for lunch, it was a small lunch. We have to find our own lunch. She never give we lunch. She only give us breakfast and dinner. We buy banana and mackerel or saltfish and we cook dumpling. Sometimes we used to buy bread or biscuit and dat last we fi di week.

At two, yuh start pick up di clothes to iron dem. She never allow di clothes dem to dry on di line. She just make dem half quail up and den yuh pick dem up, fold dem, damp dem and start press dem.

Yuh iron till four thirty. At dat time she say, 'Yuh can stop iron now and go tidy yuhself.' Yuh put way di clothes and by five yuh go to bathe and change yuh clothes.

Six o'clock is dem dinner time – table set and dey have a big dinner – steak or chicken, vegetable. Dey don't eat much starchy food. Di cook finish dinner and dish it out. My duty was to go round di table wid it in di waiter. Yuh serve di meat first, den di rice, den di vegetable. Dem only tek out a small amount each time. Yuh put di rest pon a side table and stand up beside it. If somebody want anodder piece of someting dem say 'Can you bring whatever-it-is?' and yuh tek it up and yuh serve and yuh go back go stand up side a di food again. If a next somebody want a piece of meat, dem say 'Can you bring the meat?' And yuh bring it. It go on like dat until everybody's stomach is filled. When yuh see everybody close dem knife and fork yuh know dem finish eat and yuh can clear di table. If dey want coffee, dey ask. Den when dey finish and everybody get up from di table yuh go in go tidy di kitchen.

It end up dat is a whole lot of dishes since everyting dat cook have to go into a separate dish. All dose dishes have to wash and pack up and all di pots. Yuh sweep di kitchen. At eight thirty yuh finish work fi di night – dat is if dey don't have visitors. Sometimes dey have visitors dat come before dinner and mek dinner an hour late. So instead dey have dinner at six, it might not be until seven thirty. Den yuh finish work nine or nine thirty. Di pay was twenty five shillings per week. Yuh got one evening off a week and one Sunday a month.

After ah worked deh for a long time, Jill, same country gal like me, came to work next door. Both of us never know anywhere in town, but since me and she get di same evening off we used to go out togedder. Di evening off start twelve o'clock. After yuh finish yuh lickle washing, yuh go Cross Roads to a matinee. Yuh come home by eight because dem don't want people coming in dem yard late.

Me and dem get on all right. Di lickle wife did kind a miserable. She push yuh round and sometimes when she see di tings dem done and notten no deh fi we do, she find work give we. We must come wipe down di wall or come dust out some ole big cupboard dem have all bout inna di housetop.

Dem did have a dog name Champ. Dat poor dog could a get some licks when dem no deh-deh. She no want see no dog mess pon di lawn. It never matter to her where di dog do-do. She just no want see it pon di lawn. Dat mean di gardener must clean it up. Every morning yuh see dis poor gardener man round di yard wid him hose a scrape up dog shit. Di gardener, him swear seh him no supposed to clean up dog shit, so when dem go way him collar and beat di dog. Him couldn't argue wid dem bout it. A work him a work wid dem and dem give di order.

To tell di truth di job was very boring, but in dose days we just accept di fact. We, di young people, wasn't so crazy like di young ones now. Everyting was quieter. Yuh stay in dat job for months before yuh find a friend yuh could change thoughts wid. After serving dinner some a di helpers dem in our area don't stop pon premises, dem go home and have their domestic work to do. Dey have to come out by seven di next morning. It change a little now, because during di seventies di government pass di minimum wage law. It say yuh must only do eight hours a day and it fix di wage; but some a dem who stop pon premises still have it hard.

After ah was working deh three years, ah find out seh me pregnant. As ah reach five months pregnant, me lef di work. Dem never even know seh me pregnant. Ah stay in town wid Amy, di helper from next door who never stop pon premises. Di baby faada never did a help me. When me lef di work, me leave deh wid nine pound save out a di twenty-five shilling a week and das what me use and live till me go back a work. Me never tell me faada seh me pregnant for him would a quarrel. And him did quarrel when him hear, after di baby born.

One day, when me lickle boy was a baby, me was outside washing him clothes and me hear him inside crying. When me go inside and look pon him, di navel was bleeding. Di blood was spurting up to di sky. Me carry him down to Jubilee and dem give him an injection. After him get di injection di whole a di hip was tough-tough-tough. Me had was to carry him back down deh. Dem give him some more injection to clear it up.

Around dat time di nine pound finish and ah had was to look for anodder job. Ah wrote to me faada and ask him if him could tek di baby. (Is him give all di orders, so asking yuh madda wouldn't make no sense, even though is she going look after it.) Him write and trace me and den me madda come fi di baby. Me feel sad sending him way to country, but ah had to work and ah couldn't tek him work wid me. Ah believe me madda would tek better care of him dan if ah leave him wid odder people in di tenant yard.

Ah went to stay wid me bredda who was working as a fireman. Ah pay five shillings to register wid a private employment bureau. Dey seek job fi yuh. When yuh get a job yuh have to give dem half of di first week's pay.

One morning somebody from Milk Products Restaurant phone and say dem want some girls fi work as waitresses. Di lady send me and four more girls. Ah was nervous dat ah might not get di job, but di lady pick three of us out a di five and say we is to buy our uniforms. Dat time dem was wearing white blouse, red skirt and apron. She say ah was to come out to work Monday morning.

Ah work deh fi seventeen years. It was a chain of restaurants all over Kingston. Di owner did name Mr Bent. He was an Englishman. At least, if he wasn't even English, his wife was English. He was a white man. Di business had a milk department and an ice cream and patty factory. Di men work in di factory and did di delivery. Di women only work in di restaurant as waitress, cashier and supervisor. Di men get more wages dan we. Di waitresses get three pounds a week and di cashiers get five. Cheap pay, but it was a lickle better dan domestic work.

Dem no have no union. When ah went dere first time, if yuh say yuh going join a union, Mr Bent fire yuh. Of course, yuh couldn't prove di reason why him fire yuh; dem only fire yuh and yuh and di odder workers suspect di reason.

For twelve years ah did night shifts most of di time. Three in di evening till eleven at night (one week); den eleven at night till seven in di morning (di next week). We never got no extra for night shift.

Ah got a room in Jones Town. Ah was paying just three pound a month for rent. Dat time, it was a quiet area. It was me and one more single woman, Miss Grey, living in di yard. We became good friends.

Inna dem days, tings was more peaceful. Ah was working on East Queen Street. Dat time bus put up by nine o'clock and ah had to go to work at eleven in di night. So ah generally just walk it. Nobody trouble yuh; yuh just walk go on bout yuh business. But later on when di violence start in di sixties yuh couldn't do dose tings anymore. Yuh get timid and start say, 'Lawd, ah wonder if dem going hold me up tonight.'

When he was almost two years old, my lickle boy took sick in di country. Me madda say abscess come out pon him bottom. When yuh down a country and yuh feel sick, dem just have di idea seh a mussy boil and dem putting what dem know good fi boil on it. Is when dem really see him gone bad and get weak dem tek him to doctor. He couldn't survive. After him dead and buried, dem send and call me.

Me go down and me cry and me ask dem how dem could a mek him sick and never send and tell me. She say is within a week him dead. Ah just ask. Ah couldn't quarrel. If yuh quarrel dem box yuh down. Dem time di grandparents feel dem have all di authority over di child. Di grandchildren a fi-dem. Unless yuh married and live wid yuh husband, yuh have no talk over yuh own child inna di house. Dem time deh ah never know where di baby faada deh. Ah just few years ago me see him fi tell him di child dead.

Ah feel sad bout it. Like a spite ah never have anodder one. Dat time ah was young so ah didn't feel it so much because ah feel ah would have anodder one. Like bad luck ah never have anymore. Is now, at dis age, ah really feel it more.

Ah went back to work, so ah didn't have much time to even tink about it cause ah go to work in di nights and in di days ah so tired ah just sleep. Me never have time for notten more.

After several years dem promote me and ah start do cashier work. One morning ah was inna di cage and a man come in di restaurant. Him say to me 'Lady, ah sleep out and ah just going home. Ah want a quart of grapenut cream to carry fi me wife fi mek up back wid her. If me no carry grapenut she nah go tek it.' Me laugh and get up and search fi di ice cream box meself. On one side it have di name of di flavour written. Dat was how we know what cream was in di box. Me tek up one of di box weh mark 'grapenut' and give it to di man. Him tek it and go on.

Lickle later me deh-deh a mind me own business when me only hear, 'Ay! Yuh woman!' As me spin round, someting just go so, 'Whap!' Ah deh so frighten di first ting me catch was me glasses. Me no know who it be nor notten.

'After me deliberately ask di woman fi a grapenut ice cream, she gimme chocolate.' As him say dat now, me member him. Him mussy did go way and open di box and see chocolate cream inna di box. Me no know what him do wid it; mussy throw water inna it dat it soft. Den him come in di restaurant and me and him ketch up.

'Gimme a quart of grapenut,' him say.

'Me not giving yuh notten for yuh don't have no right to throw di ice cream pon me.' Me pick up di cover and show him.

'Don't is "grapenut" write cross di cover here so? All yuh did haffi do is bring it back to me and me would a haffi tek it back and give yuh a grapenut. At dat time, ah would open it and look and mek sure seh yuh get grapenut. But yuh cyaan come gwan like dat.'

Me and him now! One contention di morning. Di man trace! Him trace! Him trace! We fuss and we fuss and we fuss. Him decide seh him a come round di counter and come lick me. Quick time, me close di counter down. One strange customer a siddung deh a try fi drink him tea. But di man strain and swear so-till di stranger haffi intervene. Him and di man start to struggle now, so-till di man haffi drive up some licks pon him fi get fi push him outside. Him come out.

Lickle after, di phone ring. When me answer is Mr Bent. Di man phone him and tell him fi-me man just done beat him up because him ask me fi exchange di cream. Him never tell Mr Bent seh him throw di cream over me. Mr Bent say me fi report a di office. Anytime yuh hear dat now, yuh know seh is not someting good. Is either yuh going get fire or dem going suspend yuh. Sometime dem suspend yuh for two weeks, or three months if customers complain seh yuh rude to dem. Hear dem odder child now. 'Lord, G, me sorry fi yuh. Dem going fire yuh.' Di ting did hurt me till me cry. When di stranger was going away, him write a note wid him name and phone number pon it and say when ah go down ah must give it to di manager and tell him to phone him.

Me go down deh wid brave heart. Me no change nor notten; me go deh cover wid ice cream same way.

Mr Bent must be tell di man what time fi reach dere for when me go in di first office, is him me see siddung deh. Di secretary say, 'Miss G, what yuh and dis gentleman have?'

'We don't have anyting.'

'Well yuh and Mr Bent is going to have it out.' She was trying to pump me before me reach inside.

'A yuh man! A yuh man beat me up!' Mr Bent did have somebody inside, but when him hear di man a cause commotion in di front office, him phone di secretary and say we is to come in right away.

Di man go in wid di idea of telling Mr Bent seh is my man beat him up, but lickle did he know seh me have di man phone number. Me hand Mr Bent di envelope.

'Dis is di man him say is my man. Him just stop, for curiosity's sake, to have a cup of tea and saw di accident.'

Me carry up di cream box wid me and me show him and say, 'Him did deliberately ask for di grapenut cream, but is di box we go by. We not allowed to open di box before we sell di cream, and see di box here.' Ay! Bambah! Ah say di man get off inna di office. Him start swear. Mr Bent say, 'I'm going to charge you.'

'Yuh better no mek di woman dare come back up deh,' him say and him start talk what and what him going to do me.

Mr Bent say, 'She is coming back up there and if ever you put your foot through the door she is to call the police. For she was perfectly right.'

Ay! To deal wid di public is a terrible ting. Dem treat all workers bad, but dem more tek advantage when yuh is a woman. When a di man, dem fraid seh dem will lick dem down back. Tek for instance di bus conductress. Yuh always used to hear dem fussing wid di conductress more dan di conductor. Yuh always hear dem a get under di woman and tell dem weh dem know bout dem and weh dem see dem last night. Dem kind a disgraceful ting which dem don't do wid di man.

Di customer dat did fling di ice cream was a working-class man himself, but yet him still treat me like dat. I tink di working-class people born wid a weight and dem grow wid a weight. Dem have a pressure carrying for dem claim seh dem better off dan di unemployed, but dem not rich. Dem trying to live above dem means and dat mek dem ignorant.

All me life ah live as a single woman. When yuh really working it don't even occur to yuh whether yuh single or double. Yuh working for yuhself so yuh hardly have time to bodder wid man. Me did have one man friend dat was me good good friend till him go a England wid me eighty pounds.

When me was working at Milk Products, me manage fi save eighty pound. Him say him want eighty pound because him get a contract to work on di sidewalk and him need di money fi buy di cement. Me lend him di money. Him say him buy di cement.

A few weeks later him come to me and tell me seh him going to St Mary. Him ask me to wash some shirt fi him. Me wash di shirt dem and when me see him didn't come fi dem, ah decide to carry dem go a him yard one morning when ah finish work. Him did live a Allman Town and me live a Jones Town. Me believe him must be at home since me know him wasn't working dat week. As me reach to Race Course, me meet him sister. She say to me, 'Weh Clerk? Yuh no see Clerk?'

Me say, 'Me no know. Him tell me seh him gone a country.'

She say, 'Dem a how him a go a England today and him gone a country from Monday and no come back yet?' Ah never say a word to her. Ah just pass her. Never say a word, but ah never know a ting bout England.

Dem always leave di key dat if me come deh me know where fi find it. So ah tek it, open di door and put in di shirt dem. Ah notice everyting. Ah read him passport. Ah read all di love letters weh di woman him a go to in England write him. She tell him seh him fi go a St Mary go look pon di children dem before him come up. Ah realize seh she must be his girlfriend for is she him going up to. Ah never do a ting more dan lock back di door quietly. Me go back round a me yard and go straight to me friend Miss Grey room and me say, 'Miss Grey, ah bet yuh no tell me who deh go a England today.' She say, 'No sah!'

'Clerk.'

'How yuh just deh tell me dat now?'

'Because me just deh know.'

'A lie yuh a tell. Yuh never just deh know.'

Me say, 'A Kathleen me meet inna Race Course little while a go a work. A she tell me seh him a go way today.'

She say, 'Cho! Me no believe her. Mind she no have it right.'

So, me bathe, change me clothes and go back round a Allman Town. Me open di room and go in. It was him and Kathleen live deh and him have two cousins in di next room. Me lie down pon di bed and me sleep. Me did tired for me come off work seven o'clock di morning. Me fast asleep when me hear somebody say, 'Weh yuh a do yah?' Me open me eye and same time me just jump up and collar him. 'Gimme me money! Gimme me eighty pounds!' And me and him! Me and him in deh! Him a deh make explain fi dis, explain fi dat. Me say, 'Me no waan hear no explanation. Just gimme me eighty pounds.' And him deh-deh a explain. Dat time me heng on pon di passport and me say, 'If me no get di eighty pounds, me deh go tear it up.' Him fraid fi grab it, for him fraid me tear it. If him want it few more hours fi go way, him couldn't just careless wid it.

Di two cousins come in come hear di commotion and one say, 'What happen Clerk? What happen?' Dat a one big tenant yard. Di landmissis and everybody gather outside a look and a listen. When me tell di two cousins what happen dem say, 'No, a lie yuh a tell. Him must did tell yuh one a di times.'

Me say, 'A Kathleen tell me dis morning.' Him start tell di cousins all sort a someting. Him all swear seh him was going to tell me. Di cousin say, 'Don't say so. If yuh is coming from St Mary now and dis is twelve o'clock and yuh going away five o'clock, what time yuh was going go weh she is fi go tell her?' Dat time a di evening flight dem usually go pon fi go a England. Dem start from Stadium five o'clock and fly inna di night. Whole heap a people was going to England inna dem time deh.

Him find seh dem corner him. Dem deh-deh a trace wid him so-till Kathleen come in. She only do half day work fi come fi follow him go a airport. When she come in and hear, she cry. 'Yuh would a ever like dat to happen me? Yuh wicked; for me would a never want such a ting happen to me.'

One someting in di yard! Till me just get fed up and trace off di whole a dem and fling di passport give dem. Me never tear up di passport for me no feel fi destroy people. If me tear up di passport, it would prevent him from go and since him so wicked normally me wouldn't waan fi have no encounter wid him. If me prevent him from go, him would a haffi go stay till him get anodder passport. Dat mean him deh go tek set pon me. Me no waan have all dat problem. Mek him galang.

Him write di most love letters, but him never send back di eighty pound. Him write and him tell me bout every single ting dat me a do a Jamaica, but him never send back di eighty pound.

Every letter dat ah answer him, me say, 'Send back di eighty pound!' but him never send it back.

One day me say to Miss Grey, 'Me cyaan even bodder write him no more.' Dem day a ben mussy thirty cents yuh pay fi write go a England. 'Me just a waste me money.' And me puddung di letter dem until today me still have dem. Wah day yah, me see one a di cousin on di bus. 'What happen to Clerk?' me ask him. 'Yuh ever hear anyting from Clerk?'

Him say, 'Weh yuh a say G? Clerk almost dead a England fi di woman weh him run way go up deh to. It was a married woman weh have fi her outside children left out yah and she go up deh and married and a she encourage him to come. Me say, G, me hear di husband did have him tru London one whole time deh run him down wid cutlass fi kill him.'

Me say to di cousin, 'Is only a pity him never kill him.'

Him say, 'Ahh G. No so hard. No so hard.'

Me say, 'Den no di same way him did hard to me? So yuh see it work out. Time longer dan rope.'

Ah was working at di Torrington Bridge branch a Milk Products Restaurant for twelve years. Gunman hold me up fi di people dem money and me survive and life just a gwan. Everybody get used to me and everybody on di road know me. One day me reach to work and meet Jenny Brown to change over. She say to me,

'G, yuh no have no job. Mr Bent send letter today say di place a go close down in three months' time.'

'Say wah! Wah reason dem give?'

'No reason at all me child. See di notice yah. It only say fi di company's reasons it is closing down.'

'See yah!'

'Dem say Mrs Bent waan go back a England.' What a someting! Everybody a run up and down. Everybody mad.

'Missis! Yuh should a dch yah today fi hear all di supervisor she. She mussy feel seh she a big official and Mr Bent mussy a go carry her go back a England wid him! When di notice come and we start mek noise, she say she a complain to Mr Bent. "Who don't want to accept what Mr Bent has to say can go, for all dem have is dem years of service."'

'What a someting! Some a di workers have all twenty and thirty years of service.'

'Yuh should a hear di one Robotham a cuss and a trace and gwan bout how much years she a work yah and how she sorry she never go look work for she could a get how-much-how-much job. And me trust furniture and fridge. How me going pay it, G?'

Thank God me never trust more dan one ting at a time. For all me did have was me bed and me dresser. Me start to tink now what me going to do.

Di end a di week Jenny meet me and say, 'G, Miss Bell asking us if we can stay till she come inna di morning. She want to talk to we.' Miss Bell was di manageress at East Queen Street.

'Bout what?'

'Bout union.'

'At dis stage?'

'Dem say might be dem can negotiate fi we.'

We wait and Miss Bell and Mr P, one next worker, come up and talk to we. Dem never keep no big meeting nor notten for we was a small staff. Dem show we all di reasons why we should join di union. Dem say if we pay dues fi di three months dat gone and dues fi di three months ahead, it will come in like di union dah represent we all dat time and dem can fight for we.

Ah never mind paying di five dollars, but ah never really believe it would work. Me wanted was to get whatever compensation we could a get, but we never see how di union could work when we already get di notice and we only have three months to go.

We never used to tek union nor politics serious. We just working and collecting our few shillings. We never understand bout politics. Radio and newspaper never so plentiful dat time and we never understand what cause we problem. Me always used to say di only good ting me see politics do is when Father Manley fight and mek black pickney go a St Hilda's school, where no black pickney couldn't ben go first time. Still ah never listen Busta or Manley and ah never vote. Ah never have no time and when dem tek up census fi election me always deh a work. Dem should a talk bout union in di years before. Dem should a show we all dose reason why it good fi we join in di years before.

Me never go a none a di meeting for me always a work pon night shift and me just feel since Bent dah close down dere was notten we could do bout it. About two months later we get a letter from him. Di letter say who do x years of service getting so many weeks pay. Dat time ah was doing fifteen years wid Mr Bent so me get five weeks pay fi dat. After dat Mr Bent had a meeting wid di senior workers. Him tell dem dat dem can get di restaurant to rent and di business can gradually be theirs. Dey had was to buy di tings in di dairy and di factories. Different workers took over di branches. One of di restaurant manager Mr Phelps ask me if ah want to work wid him. Dat time him was going to tek over Slipe Penn Road. Me was planning seh me going open one restaurant fi meself but since me get di offer of di job, we cut out dat and decide fi go work wid Phelps.

Di Friday was Mr Bent close-down day. Ah stay home di Saturday and Sunday. Di Monday morning me go out to Slipe Road go work wid Phelps. Ah work up deh fi two years and gunman hold me up again up deh. Him only a rent di place and after a time di landlord give him notice and him haffi give up di restaurant.

Me faada tek sick and dead lickle after dat. Di land dat me faada used to farm still deh a country. Me no know if me uncle work it. It just left so. Yuh see, is seven a we. Him left some fi get half acre, some fi get three quarter acre and horse dead, cow fat and jackass mawga. Him did borrow money from bank and di title deh a bank. Anyhow we waan di title fi go share up di land, we haffi go pay di bank di money. All di odder sisters and breddas dem waan me fi do it. Me no have no children so me nah do it for me feel who have children will want it more dan me. So it just abandon.

So yuh see, all me life ah been working and ah don't have a house or a piece of land to show for it. Ah wanted a house of me own because yuh have to have something to bribe di family to tek care of yuh when yuh get old. When yuh don't have anyting dem don't look after yuh and yuh can end up over alms-house. As it is now ah have to be living in me sister's house teking care of it fi her while she is in England.

Ah don't save no money, but ah tink ah get more enlighten and ah learn and understand more as di years go by. Ah get fi find out lickle more bout history and government and di rest of di world. It open me eye and what ah realize is dat di working-class people change a lot even though we still have plenty leave to achieve. In our lickle country Jamaica, history move forward from slavery when we deh-deh a work fi notten and dem usually beat we grandparents.

Dem have maternity leave for women now, which never exist when ah was working first time. On a whole ah tink dis generation tek tings more serious dan we. So a tink dem will achieve more dan we achieve because we achieve more dan our parents. If dem come togedder and keep on demand what dem want to see change and work hard to get it change, dem will get someweh.

ERNA BRODBER

One Bubby Susan

This man here Cundal. Frank. Don't know if you know him. Used to work down at Institute way back when. Now this man now, write a book and say in there say Miss Susan is something some Arawak person carve into a cave. Man even have a photo in this book, of a lady standing in the mouth of this cave and looking for truth like as if is somebody really carve her. But I am here to tell you that nothing don't go so. Them long long time when Cundal writing, where them get camera to go take picture of Miss Susan? You no see something not too quite right? Is just these white people like come to people country, look round two time, take photo, measure this and measure that, no ask nobody no question, no sit down and meditate, and baps – them have answer. Same way. So this man now write it into book that Miss Susan is a Arawak carving and people believe. What in book is gospel so everybody go believe. Well is not so. I am sitting down quiet to myself when my ears start to tingle and I get a strong smell of that flowers that we used to string as beads. The smell so strong, I nearly faint and then the lady start to talk and she tell me.

Well Cundal right bout one thing. The place. Miss Susan really belongs to that place. To be exact, she feel she belong there. I already tell you she don't carve there. Now I telling you, she feel she belong there. So the place is right. Dryland. Near to Woodside. In the parish of St Mary. Now, you know Westmoreland? That is another parish. Now, look at the map of Jamaica. Right. Well you see how Westmoreland chack over the other side of the world from St Mary. Well, forget that. Just them white people and them scribes again. Listen to this now. The world is not flat. Columbus done tell them that long time, so why them must draw the map flat out like a dry-up goat skin with no goat, is something

I can't see. Pay them no mind. Now, if you take that map and roll it a certain way, you will see that Westmoreland nearly to fit into St Mary. Now listen again. If you go outside and take a long pole and push it down into the ground, you see that there is a whole world down there. Sea, earth, river. You can swim the sea and you can swim the river but you can't swim the earth. But the earth have many holes and you can walk upright. No need to swim, for those who never born with fin. You can walk under the earth from one side to the other. Anybody who know how the caves situate that is. Now why I telling you this? For you to know that for those who really know the land, it is nothing to get from Westmoreland to St Mary. Look again in our book and see if the people who really know the land was not doing the same thing in St Mary that the Westmoreland people was doing. Communication knowledge. That's what I call it.

Is a simple matter when you look at it. But simple as it seems to me now and to you now, I didn't find it out for myself. Is Miss Sue tell me. Say it was nothing to swips from Westmoreland to St Mary. She used to do it all the time. Is Westmoreland she rightly come from, but she land up in a cave in St Mary. Not as a carving. And I coming to tell you how now. Miss Sue say, time for her to get married and she never want to married. She did like fly through cave and talk to rat-bat and climb tree and talk to bird and so on. She never want plant no maize and beat up nothing into mortar. Matter of fact all this bammy that her people so proud bout never mean one thing to her. Too dry. She could find fat grass to eat raw any day so why plant cassava and grater it and dry out the milk and cook it? Never make no sense to her and she couldn't bother with it. And that is what a wife suppose to do with all her time. Excuse me. Not true. Not all her time, for them used to play bato. I don't know what that is. Favour like soft ball to me when she describe it. She say big man and woman used to play it too. And regular. So it really wasn't mortar pestle all day long. But what sense thump ball when she coulda swing from tree to tree and whistle to the birds and be by herself. But them insist say everybody must married. So Miss Sue say, she say, run way for her rather than this wife thing. And she do it sudden. Just get a vaps and leave. Tell no one. Now you know that Miss Sue wouldn't really have nothing to pack. The picture on the money is real. Ain't nothing but a little grass around the hips and grass was easy to come by. So she split. In one second.

I don't say she disappear into nothing. That would make it easy and as she tell me, it was not easy the way she reach to Dryland, though it was really close in a way, to her place. What happen now is this. Everybody know everybody. The whole place divide up among chiefs. You leave from one spot to the other, is a new chief. And no fussing or fighting. If they see you at one place long, they say you want to join them and they start same time to find out if you married and if you not married to marry you off and get you into this bammy-making, bato-playing thing all over again for married is all them know bout. No sense in that. So Susan decide she ain't go touch earth except at night when nobody not around to see her. So is pure cave she into all day. Now when she staying in this Dryland cave, a strange thing happen. Hard as she listen she couldn't hear a thing. No mortar pestle, no 'yeow, yeow' and bato playing. She say she say to herself 'Must be just a breed of backless dogs living in this place.' So little by little she start to come out to the cave front. She don't see nobody so she start to make it a habit. Both the staying in that cave and the sitting out at the front from time to time in the day.

Now Susan tell me how she used to sit down still and do this deep breathing, for with all the time she bound herself to spend in the cave, when she get air she did want to take in as much as she could take. Now I don't know if these Arawak Indians is any relative to the Indians in India but I swear to you, what Miss Susan show me that she was doing, was one of those yoga pose that make a person look like Buddha. Now what you would think if you come up to a cave and see a person who you never see yet in the small-small community that you live in, sitting down like a Buddha? Talk the truth. You'd think it was a duppy or a God. Exactly. Well somebody did come and somebody did think so. And this is the beginning of poor Miss Susan's sorrows.

Miss Sue did have it in her head that the quietness of the place was because those who did live there run way leave it and she say to herself 'This is mine. A gwine relax.' But it was not quite so. Man, woman and child – except for that lazy one, playing sick-gone off yes, but only for part day and on shift. Everybody wasn't there one time and when them come home, them so tired, them just drop asleep. Gone make clay pot and make them in abundance. Mr Christopher Columbus come with him red rags and all a-body and them breed of barkless dog now bartering pot for red rag. That's how come the place was so quiet and Miss Sue so alone. But the little boy come and see her and start coming back and seeing her in her Buddha pose and start to have nightmare and to blurt out that him see a god and to have people saying is sick him really sick.

Now you know them always say anybody who say them see God sick, and usually them leave you and your imagination to fight it out. Until they come to need a God. Like how you see AIDS now, it was syphilis that time that come with the tourist rags. People start dropping dead like flies. And the bad treatment was something else. Man used as target practice! It was bad enough that everybody was running off to Agualta Vale to mess around in clay and march down to close to Port Maria where the whitemen be and were in the bargain neglecting them ground and putting life out of kilter. Now married life was mashing up for the whitemen was putting their hands and all, where they should not be put and on top of that beating up the Arawak men and running their swords through them. It was time enough to need a God so when that lazy chap keep on saying that is a god him see, man and man start to make a trek, a few at first, to Miss Susan cave.

Now I have to stop to tell you that the lady's born name was not Susan. Many a time she tell me, but that Arawak name cannot stick in my head and since she don't really object and everybody know who I am talking about, let it remain 'Miss Susan'. Right? Right. So as I was telling you, people now start to come and peep at Miss Susan in her Buddha pose and to nod – 'Is God.' A funny thing was happening too, and to Miss Sue. When she take the pose, is like vibrations would come through her fingers from the air and she would know all sorts of things. When the first man come up and put a problem, Miss Sue find she just give him a answer straight out of her head and that she was right. She turn God now!

Miss Sue say she didn't mind the questions, for is not really she was answering, is just something or someone using her mouth, but what she did mind was the whole heap of thanksgiving. Up to now, she can't get rid of the smell of duppy chain out of her mind. So much garlands come

make out of this thing and put round her neck. No more peace any
more.

Can't even breathe. People cooking racoon and agote as sacrifice to
her. People is something else though! It happens that she could really
get into a deep meditation and she find the meditations getting longer
and that those times she don't even feel like passing her business there,
but it would come by itself all the same. You know the people rush her
push her down, take up this thing, say is gold from the gods, must be
that the whiteman want! Push her away and scrape it up, say they going
pay tribute with it! The thing get so ridiculous with no little bit of space
for herself that Sue start to consider that it was just as cheap she did
married and put up with the bammy-making and the bato. One thought
lead to the other and the other to her usual rebellion and Miss Sue say
to herself 'Not a blast' and decide that she not going to be no God with
no privacy. She decide she gwine form dead and let them leave her.

How she going do this now? She stand up straight now, press herself
against the cave wall and hold her breath yoga style. And people did
believe that she was dead. And it vexed them. At the very time when
the tourists eating out them life and they have no help but from this
God, the God decide to strike! Is stones now. And they start to pelt
her. You could say that they want to get her back to life, if is kind, you
kind. But I know that is plain straightforward disappointment and vexation that make those stones come. Even when she drop, them still
flinging. Even when she so weak, she drop off of the rock face altogether
and long time drop into the sink hole, them still seeing her there and
still stoning. Day after day. Is now them practise to try to see if, like
the whiteman was doing with them, they could use her for target practice!
Now them try to throw stones round what them think is the outline of
her body! Go look at it yourself and see if you can't see how the flying
stones lick the rock face and make the sink that form the image?

So is so the carving come. No man don't sit down and carve it. And
is no real likeness of Miss Sue. Anyway, it is not the habit of that breed
of Indians to carve. They mostly draw. So is just anger make that image.
I don't know why Miss Sue want me to tell this story but I tell it. Perhaps
want to set the record straight. Perhaps want to say something about
freedom but if is that, I can't see the point for I can't see that running

from hole to hole and being a people's God is any kind of freedom. Perhaps she want to say you must be careful how you give or how you stop giving. I don't know. People still flinging stone at that cave. They even lick off one of the breast that those before them make in anger and them now call the image *One Bubby Susan.* I don't know if is something she want to say about this women's lib business like how she is a woman. Perhaps she want to say to women 'Make them call you angel but don't make them make you into no heavenly being, for that is so-so burden-bearing and the day name day you say you tired, them get vex and lick you down kill you.' I don't know but here is the story and I know that the man Cundal shoulda-eh study him head well before him go call Miss Sue this flesh-and-blood woman a carving.

KAMAU BRATHWAITE

Dream Chad: A Story

Dear Reader+
think I ought to xplain or rather share w/you certain strange
circumstances connected w/ the composition of this my perhaps third dream story. It was written, I remember, direct from perhaps a first working ms draft onto a Macintosh that I>
had rented from a Students SelfHelp organization that supplies tvs, radios, computers, & sundry electrical & other applian
ces etc from their office in Haavaad Yaad. It was high summer by the time I came to this story but I recall that it was started at the height of that season, involving, I remember, some
remarkably hot August days, one of which (?Fri 5 August 1988)
closed the University for the very first time in its +750 yr old
history

The first thing to note is that all (now <July 93> **nearly all**) presence
of that HEAT has disappeared down the long spirals of the.
various versions of the story; what took over was the story of
Chad, materializing out of that HEAT from tropical Jamaica
into the summer of Harvard and her relationship w/what wa
(s) ?clearly intended by the dream to be my home at Irish Tn
(IT) where I had left my Eagle Computer which had been such
a wonderful companion for me during & after the dark of my
wife Zea Mexican's sudden unxpected & finally fatal illness &
aftermath and I had left the computer like a kind of emotional
anchor or icon - along w/everything else - all my life w/Mex-
ican my archives my artifacts etc etc etc - up there w/Chad at
IT

What happened as I was about finishing the story was its rejection by the (Harvard) Computer. Okay, you cd say that some thing had gone wrong w/this sturdy rented instrument, which I was using for the first time without any hands-on or knowledge or background - just being told what I needed to know by my friend Frank Dalton, to whom, in fact, I owe what has become a very close relationship w Apple/Mac - in fact in the end I purchased my own Sycorax on which most of the **video style** stories of this collection have been written

But as I was finishing this story - before, in fact, I cd print it out - the machine shall we say *malfunctioned* and I lost nearly all its oratory & I had to reconstruct it all again from scratch & each time I came to the end & was about to run it off, the same strange **deconstruction** occurred - loss of < txt/wiped out of the machine & each time - *is here I remember the* < *HEAT* — I stubbornly construed it again, my memory miraculously working almost like a computer itself (my ART, I felt, vs hear (t)less TECHNOLOGY) though I began vaguely to realize that w/ each re/byte, as it were, I must have been making subtle perhaps changes as if some **spirit in the machine** was willing or trying to prevent me from writing the story or - *since I was per sisting* - punishing me to at least a different, as it now seems > less ?dangerous - even perhaps less **?truthful** version of event (s) that had in fact **not yet taken place(!)**

until there was a moment of the most frightening confrontation when a MESSAGE came up on the computer screen telling me that **there was no way that I cd continue the dream since SOMEBODY ELSE WAS USING IT**

I was stunned, to say the least; went like cold as if I was being personally attacked by some premonition or monitor; while subliminally or whatever, I was wondering or assuming that it was somehow the EAGLE - jealous because I was into a Ma (c)? but in my persistent HEAT + HEART went out &

rented another computer

& ran the story in & off before the spirit cd re/programme itself into the new cinnamon instrument - though of course all this prob meant that the new instrument didnt have the virex or bug that had developed in the first (st)one

But a few days after the printout, I watched Hurricane Gilbert rise up out of the sea south of Vieques, Puerto Rico & head like my dream towards Jamaica. And as soon as I saw it I knew that this was Io & that that was why Sycorax or the Spirit of the Machination had perhaps tried to stop me from writing 'it'. So that when Gilbert hit Jamaica, as I knew it wd, I also knew that my house up there at IT wd be destroyed, the looting & the fire of the dream be/coming instead the wind & water of the hurricane. Though later, after I had, within a few days, got back to Jamaica, I found that somehow that part of the houm that had housed the Eagle & the archives etc had somehow miraculously survived the storm. There had been grievous losses of course, but thanks to Chad, the bulk of my life's work though very much in disarray & hurt & hurl & ruin, had not (?yet) been (totally) destroyed - was still largely *there*, in

fact, and I began to think - to realize - *to fear* – that perhaps

the dream had still to be fulfilled & that there was perhaps some more obscure connection or balance between the Intervening ?Spirit & whatever property or prophecy was embedded in the dream & that the longer the archives etc remain in the house, the more & more chance there is that at some stage the balance might - I don't know how - since I don't even know how or if there *is* or *was* a 'balance' = (re)turn again against me > that if I dont take care and get the archives out of there - as Yale (1991) had <

so generously invited me to do (nobody in the Caribbean being, as far <
as I can see, remotely interested or concerned) - that the story of this <
Dream cd very well eventually come true

PART TWO

Stories

CLAUDE McKAY

Mattie and Her Sweetman

In the neighborhood of 135th Street and Lenox Avenue a parlor social was taking place in the flat of a grass widow called Rosie.

Rosie had sent out invitations to a number of chambermaids, bellhops, waiters, longshoremen, and railroad men whom she knew personally. She asked them to bring their friends and to tell their friends to bring their friends.

The price of admission was twenty-five cents. Soda pop and hard drinks were sold at prices a little more than what was paid in the saloon. At ten o'clock Rosie's place began filling up with guests. It was that type of apartment called railroad flat. The guests put their wraps in Rosie's bedroom and danced in the dining-room and parlor.

Rosie kept the soda pop and beer cold in the ice-box in the kitchen. Whisky, wine, and gin were locked up in a cabinet whose key was secured by a red ribbon suspended from her waist.

The parlor social was good company. There was a fascinating mélange of color: chocolate, cocoa, chestnut, ginger, yellow, and cream. The people for whom these parlor maids and chambermaids worked would have gazed wonder-eyed at them now. Aprons and caps set aside, the maids were radiant in soft shimmering chiffon, crêpe de Chine and satin stuff. How do they do it? those people would have commented, wearing the things they do on their wages?

In that merry crowd was one strange person – a black woman in her fifties. She wore a white dress, long white gloves, black stockings and black shoes, and a deep-fringed purple shawl. She was of average height and very thin. Her neck was extraordinary; it was such a long, excessively skinny neck, a pathetic neck. Her face was much finer than her neck, thin also, but marked by a quiet, dark determination.

She danced with a codfish-complexioned strutter wearing a dress suit. He was tall with a trim ready-to-wear appearance and his hair was plastered down, glistening with brilliantine. His mouth wore a perpetual sneer. The woman danced badly. Her partner was a good dancer and tried to make her look as awkward as he could. The music stopped and they found seats near the piano.

'What youse gwina drink, Jay?' she asked.

'Gin,' he said, casually.

'Rosie!' the woman called.

Rosie bustled over, a marvel of duck-chested amiability. Rosie's complexion was a flat café-au-lait, giving the impression of a bad mixture, coffee over-parched, or burned with skimmed milk, and the generous amount of powder she used did not make the effect any pleasanter.

'Whaz you two agwine to hev, Mattie?' She knew, of course, that Jay was Mattie's sweetman and Mattie did the paying.

'One gin and one beer,' said Mattie.

'Gwine to treat the pianist to something?' Rosie knew how to tease her guests into making her parlor socials things worth giving.

'You throw me a good ball a whisky, sistah,' said the pianist, a slight-built, sharp-featured black, whose eyes were intense, the whites appearing inflamed . . .

Hands waved at Rosie from a group seated at a small table wedged against the mantelpiece, and an impatient young man called:

'Seven whiskies, Rosie, and four bottles a ginger ale jest that cold as you c'n makem.'

'Right away, right away, mah chilluns.' Rosie started a quick-time duck step to the cabinet.

Two girls pushed their way through a jam of men blocking the way between the dining-room and the parlor. The smaller was a satin-skinned chocolate; the other, attractive in a red frock, was cocoa. The cocoa girl saw Jay with Mattie and cried: 'Hello, Jay! Howse you?'

'Hello, you Marita!' said Jay.

'Having a good time?'

'Kinder,' he sneered.

Marita was the waitress at Aunt Hattie's pigs'-feet-and-chittlings joint. Jay went there to eat sometimes. Marita rather liked him, put more food than ordinary in his dish, and chatted with him. She would have liked to keep company with Jay, but he made her realize that he had no desire to go with a girl in the regular way. He never felt that sort of feeling that would urge a fellow on to rent a room for two and live, a good elevator boy, in the Black Belt. For it was easier going with the Matties and grass widows of Harlem. Marita couldn't imagine herself down to the level of Jay's women. Not yet – when she was young and strong and pretty. But she rather admired his casual way of getting along and felt a romantic fascination for the sneer that sharp living had marked him by.

The pianist turned his inflamed eyes to the ceiling and banged the piano. Jay left Mattie alone to jazz with Marita.

'What a scary way she's dressed up!' said Marita as they wiggled past Mattie.

Jay grinned. Marita went liltingly with his movement. He disliked toting a middle-aged black hen round the room. Not that he minded being Mattie's sweetman. He was very proud of his new job. For three months before he met her he had been dogged by hard luck. The bottom had been eaten out of his nigger-brown pants. A flashy silk shirt, the gift of his last lady, had given way around the neck and at the cuffs. For thirteen weeks it had not seen the wash-tub, and when it did it went all to pieces. The toes of his ultra-pointed shoes were turned pathetically heavenward and the pavement had gnawed through his rubber heels down to the base of the leather.

Meeting Mattie at a parlor social in the Belt's Fifth Avenue had materially changed Jay's condition. He had been taken to 125th Street and fitted to a good pair of shoes. Mattie chose also a decent shirt for him. But it was not silk. He hadn't achieved a new suit yet. The choice was between that and an overcoat. Mattie's resources could not cover both at once. One would have to wait until she could put by enough out of their daily living to get it. And so she decided that a heavy, warm overcoat was more necessary, for it was mid-January and in his ruined summer suit Jay had been freezing along the streets of Harlem.

It was not quite a month since Mattie and Jay had come together, and docile as she seemed, she was well worn in experience and carried a smoldering fire in her ugly black body. Years ago she had had a baby for a white man in South Carolina. But being one black woman who did not feel proud having a yellow pickaninny at any price, she had got rid of the thing, strangling it at birth and, quitting relatives and prayer-meeting sisters, made her way up north.

Marita's girl pal discovered friends and went to drink with them. Marita followed, and Jay danced after her and got in with the gang. They were making rapid time with Old Crow whisky. They sent Rosie over to the pianist with a double drink of whisky to spur him on.

'Play that theah "Baby Blues",' she said. 'Them good spenders ovah theah done buys you this drink and ask foh it.'

The pianist tossed off his whisky, turned his eyes to the ceiling, and banged, 'Baby Blues, Baby Blues'.

Mattie stood up and went over to Jay. 'Le's dance,' she said. She loved dancing as a pastime, but it wasn't in her blood, and so she was a bad dancer.

'Not now,' Jay said, angrily. 'Ahm chinning with the gang.'

He was putting away a lot of the boys' good liquor and it was working on him in a bad way for Mattie. Disappointed, she looked round for Rosie. Rosie was bustling about in the kitchen getting new glasses. Mattie gulped down two stiff drinks of gin and returned to her seat by the piano . . .

Baby Blues! Baby Blues!

'Le's do this heah sweet strut, gal.' And before Jay, Marita was on her feet and poised for movement. Her pal was jigging with one of the chocolate boys. The space was filled thick and warm with dancers just shuffling round and round. Hot cheeks, yellow, chestnut, chocolate, each perspiring against each.

'Is that theah thing you' lady now?' Marita asked.

'She ain't a bad ole mammy as she looks,' said Jay. 'She's good giving. Fixed *me* up all right.'

'Did she buy you this heah dress suit? Youse the only one here all dressed up so swell.'

Jay grinned for the compliment.

'No. I hired this off a ole Greenbaum. The other was so bad. But she got me these heah shoes and a swell overcoat. And she's gwina get me a nifty suit.'

'But youse kinder rough on her, though. You ain't treating her right, is you?'

Young and pretty, Marita disapproved of Mattie, old and ugly, having Jay; but she also resented with feminine feeling Jay's nastiness to the older woman.

'I ain't soft and sissified with no womens,' said Jay. 'Them's all cats, always mewing or clawing. The harder a man is with them the better.'

'Think so?' Marita said. Her resentment rose to anger and she wanted to stop wriggling, but Jay's casual manner (which said, I don't care whether you dance or quit) held her tethered to him.

Mattie, sitting alone, had swallowed her sixth glass of gin. Rosie, feeling sympathetic, went and gossiped with her for a while.

'Ain't dancing, honey?'

'No, but I guess I'll take the next one.'

'Don't you sit heah and get too lonely drinking all by you'se'f and that yaller strutter a yourn having such a wicked time.'

'I don't mind him fooling with his own crowd when we goes to a pahty, 'causen Ise pass their age.'

Finished 'Baby Blues'.

Jay went back to the waiters' table. One of his poolroom pals came in and joined the group, greeting Jay with enthusiasm and praising his rig-out.

In the poolroom where Jay loafed and played, he had become the hero of the place since his new affair. Colored boys who washed water-closets and cleaned spittoons for a living, with no hope of ever doing better, envied the way Jay could always get on to some woman to do everything for him. They wished they had Jay's magic. Jay might have his bad days getting by sometimes, but his luck never deserted him. He toted a charm.

The pianist turned his face to the ceiling and began a plaintive 'Blues'. He cast down his eyes for a moment and said to Mattie, 'Ain't you gwina dance, sistah?'

Mattie essayed a smile. 'Guess I will.'

She crossed over to Jay and asked, 'Wanta dance this with me?'

Jay glared at her, 'Wha's scratching you? I don't wanta dance. Ahm having a good time heah.'

The sneer deepened under the influence of the mixed drinks working on his temper. Mattie lingered near the table, but nobody asked her to sit down. Turning to go, she said to Jay hesitatingly, 'Well – any time you feels like dancing with me Ise ready.'

'Oh, foh Gawd's sake,' he exclaimed, 'gimme a chance! Shake a leg, black woman.'

Everybody within hearing turned to look at Mattie, some with suppressed giggling, others with pity, Marita and her pal were ashamed and could not look at Mattie. For there is no greater insult among Aframericans than calling a black person black. That is never done. In Aframerican literature, perhaps, but never in social life. A black person may be called 'nigger' as a joke in Aframerica, but never 'black', which is considered a term of reproach in the mouths of colored people quite as contemptuous as 'nigger' in the mouths of whites. And so Aframericans have invented pretty names such as low-brown, seal-skin brown, chocolate, and even prune as substitutes for black.

Oh, Blues, Blues, Brown-skin Blues: the piano wailed.

'That was a mean one,' said Marita.

'Oh, mean hell. I guess the ole mug likes when you handle her rough. Don't she, Jay?' said his pal.

'Ain't nobody wanting their bad points thrown up to them as nasty as that,' declared Marita.

Her pal agreed. The girls imagined themselves growing old some day and ridden by a special passion like Mattie.

And Mattie by the piano, thinking that everybody was laughing at her, called for another gin. She wanted not to care. She knew she did not belong to a fast parlor-social set where everybody was young or acting young. Rosie with her hostess's tricks looked like a vampire beside her. But although she was ugly and unadjustable, she loved amusement and was always ready to pay for it.

Mattie worked hard doing half-time and piecework, washing and ironing and mending for white people. Her work was finely done and her patrons recommended her to their friends. She earned twenty to thirty and forty dollars a week.

Living for Mattie was harder than working. Having an irresistible penchant for the yellow daddy-boys of the Black Belt, she had realized, when she was much younger, that because she was ugly she would have to pay for them.

She occupied a large rear room on the second floor of a private house, situated in the cheapest section of the Belt. The price was moderate and she was allowed the use of the kitchen and the spacious back yard for laundry work.

Mattie's coming and going quietly through the block was remarked by the good and churchy neighbors of the African Methodist, the Colored Methodist, and the Abyssinian and Cyrenian churches. And they marveled at her, a steady, reliable worker, refusing to be persuaded into membership in a church ...

Mattie brooded. Nevah befoh I been slapped like that by an insult so public. Slam in the face: Black woman! Black woman! Didn't I know I was that and old and no beauty?

Oh, mamma, sweet papa. Blues, Blues, seal-skin, brown-skin Blues. The pianist was gone on a wailing Blues.

Mattie got up to go home. She looked round for Jay. He had hurt her, but her pride had fallen, humbled and broken, under desire. Jay was not in the room. Mattie found him in the kitchen with his poolroom pal and a boozy gang over a bottle of gin.

'I'm gwine along home, Jay,' she said. 'Youse coming?'

Jay was going drunk. 'Why you nosing and smelling after a fellah like that foh?' he demanded.

'Don't get mad, Jay. I ain't bothering you. If you wanta stay –'

'Oh, beat it outa here, you no-'count black bitch.'

Mattie slunk off to Rosie's bedroom and put on her coat. She saw Jay's overcoat and felt it and after a slight hesitation slipped it on over hers. Outside it was snowing. She dove her hands into the deep pockets and said: 'A man's clothes is that much more solid and protecting than a woman's is.' She went home, southward, along Lenox Avenue.

The gang finished the gin. Jay suggested to the waiters they should all go and hunt up a speakeasy. Marita and her pal said they were going home.

'No, you come on along with us,' said Jay.

'Not me. I gotta work tomorrow,' said Marita.

'Me too. That don't make no difference,' said the darkest waiter. The others joined him asking the two girls to change their minds; but the girls went home.

The fellows stood up, arguing just what they should do next, when Rosie elbowed through them and waved a bottle of gin in their faces.

'Le's have another round,' said the mulatto waiter.

'You'd bettah,' said Rosie. 'Wha's this heah talk about you all going when is jest the time to start in on some real fun.'

The boys sat down again, each waiter paying a round of drinks. The waiters had been paying all along. Jay and his friend had not paid for anything. The darkest waiter was soft. He began sifting a pack of cards, crying: 'Coon-can! Coon-can! Le's play coon-can!'

'Ahm feeling high, ahm feeling cocky,' said Jay.

The bottle of gin was finished and they were now ready to leave, but Jay could not find his overcoat.

'Ain't nobody could take it 'cep'n' the one that done buys it.' Rosie grinned maliciously.

Jay was mad and blew Mattie to hell with curses. Just a hussy trick to get me home to bed. Ain't got no shame nor pride, that woman. But I'll punish her some more.

Outside the snow had turned to sleet and a high wind was driving through the shivering naked trees.

'It'll be some sweet skating on the sidewalk tomorrow,' said one of the waiters.

'And bitter cold, too,' said Jay. And the thought of his overcoat gave him a comfortable, warm, and luxurious feeling.

The boys had decided to visit a certain speakeasy. They walked along Fifth Avenue, and Jay stopped before an apartment house.

'It's here, fellahs,' he said.

'All right,' said the chocolate boy. 'Le's go on in and look the fair browns ovah.'

Jay, with his hands in his pockets and his dress suit slightly damp, gleaming in the far-flung flare of the arc-light, was the picture of perfect aplomb.

'But, buddies, I ain't got no money on me,' he announced.

'And I ain't got none, neither,' said Jay's pal.

The waiters exchanged eye-flecks with one another.

'Well,' said the mulatto waiter, 'after Rosie she done ate up so much I ain't none so flush to treat anybody else again 'cep'n' mahself. What about you fellahs?'

His workmates took his cue and said they had just enough each for himself.

'Tell you what, then; we'll call this show off until some other night,' said the mulatto.

The waiters said good night to Jay and his pal. They were unanimous about not treating them in the speakeasy. If Jay hadn't any money to pay in the speakeasy, let him go home to Mattie. They had seen and felt so much as servitors, that they had not wasted any pity on Mattie. There were women whose special problems made them stand for that kind of hoggishness. But, neither had they any servile praise for Jay's attitude.

The waiters saw Jay and his pal out of sight, then entered the apartment house and rang the bell of the speakeasy. They worked. Creatures of service, waiters – that moment serving up a rarebit, this moment a cocktail, next a high-ball; bellhops in livery with ridiculous buttons before and behind, leaping up like rabbits at the touch of a knob. And they were fool spenders having that curious psychology of some servants who never feel life such good living as when they are making a big splurge imitation of their employers . . .

'Come on buddies,' said the mulatto. 'We may be suckers all right in Rosie's joint, but we won't be suckers in a cat dog bite mah laig hear the player piano crying fair chile baby oh boy house.'

Jay said goodbye to his pal and hurried homewards, head bent against the sleety wind, his hands in his trousers pockets, and thinking aloud: Well I was setting for an all-night laying-off, but I guess I'll have to warm up the old black hen tonight, after all.

But Mattie, too, had been thinking hard in the meanwhile. 'I don't know what love is, but I know what's a man!' The cabaret song was singing in her head. She remembered when she first left Dixie and 'went N'oth' to Philadelphia, how she had liked a yellow man and he had laughed in her ugly face and called her 'black giraffe'. She had forgotten the incident, it was so long ago, but Jay made her remember it now. She had hated that man deeply and wanted to do him real hurt. And now she felt the same kind of hatred for Jay.

She lay in bed without sleeping, waiting for Jay, but not in the mood he anticipated. Dawn was creeping along the walls when the bell rang. Mattie raked up a window and craned out her giraffe neck. She had on a white nightcap and looked like a scarifying ghost.

'Who's it?'

'It's me – Jay.'

'Wait a minute.'

Mattie opened the closet where she kept her soiled linen and took out a little bandanna bundle that she had made of Jay's rags of a suit, his old greasy cap, his old shoes, and the remains of his silk shirt.

'Theah's you' stuff. Take a walk.'

The bundle fell against Jay, nearly knocking him over. Mattie raked down the window. The sleet blew in Jay's face and the wind sang round his rump. He turned up his collar and walked shivering toward Lenox Avenue.

FRANK COLLYMORE

The Man Who Loved
Attending Funerals

I have a strange admission to make; but, since I regard myself as already dead, I have no reason to conceal anything: these words of mine are, as far as anything written by mortal hand can be, the truth.

I am fully persuaded that among our manifold emotional interests and activities there is some one or other which, very often unacknowledged, perhaps even unsuspected, is nevertheless the ruling and abiding passion; and this passion may range from those of the crudest and most blatant forms of expression, through an infinity of subtle changes, to others, so unusual, and, at times, so inexplicable, as to evoke from us halting excuses, if not a positive denial.

I make no such excuse or denial: my great passion on earth has been the attending of funerals.

Perhaps this may not be such a strange admission after all: there is something in each and every one of us, especially as we grow older, that tends to receive a sort of satisfaction, a happy consolation, in attending the funeral of some old acquaintance: we are not so much rejoicing that the man whom we knew in his boyhood days is gone from us for ever, but that we, perhaps as the result of our own excellence, or else perhaps safeguarded by some especial providence, have been successful in continuing this business of living, and to observe yet another of our contemporaries fall out of line. This, I think, will be reluctantly admitted by all, especially by those who have their best days behind them, and who, by dint of careful and temperate living, have so far escaped the inevitable end. Each funeral attended is, as it were, a triumphant feather in our cap registering our defiance of fate; and we hold up our heads the bolder, almost convincing ourselves that we shall continue indefinitely to escape the essential condition of mortality.

And, alas, in my particular case, I *had* succeeded in thus convincing myself: until this afternoon I was assured that this matter of dying, of being for ever hidden beneath the green surface of the earth, was not for me; rather, that this procedure, which I had viewed so often, was indeed a performance enacted for my own personal benefit, from which I should always continue to derive an ever-increasing aesthetic delight.

I cannot hope to explain the sources of this delight; my understanding of the nature of the aesthetic response or of the laws of psychology is too superficial to permit me to make any attempt to do so; but of one thing I am quite sure: there was no sadistic strain in my pleasure, no suggestion of deliberate enjoyment in the grief of those left behind to mourn, no relish in the thought that the deceased had met with a final punishment. Very often, on the contrary, mingled with that sense of rapture with which funerals alone could provide me, I experienced a state of profound melancholy and loss, of sympathy with the mourners, of compassion for all suffering humanity.

It was always thus with me. Among the earliest recollections of my childhood years, there stand out boldest those of my disposing by burial of the corpses of such of our household pets or feathered stock as happened to have died from natural causes. I grieved at their deaths, but rejoiced at their inhumation. And, very often when there was no obliging little corpse to hand, I would bury one of my dolls. There was a lovely little cemetery in one corner of our garden which came into being under my devoted hands.

At the age of nine I attended my first real funeral, my father's. I can still recall every moment of that sunny, windswept afternoon.

And, as I grew older, I would pester my mother to allow me to go to the funerals of any of our relatives or friends or important persons in the community of whose deaths I might have heard. And, more often than not, she would allow me to go with one of my uncles.

And how I admired the elegant costumes of the gentlemen: the impressive, fascinating frock coats and top hats, their suave and mysterious blackness, their stateliness, their pageantry, their austerity: proud symbols of the dignity and authority of man! My mother's gift to me on my twenty-first birthday was such an outfit. But, alas, the wearing of the frock coat was a fashion whose days were already numbered. I compromised, later, with the morning coat; during the passing of the years my wardrobe has never been without two or three of these most necessary garments.

In our small community there are few opportunities for one to appear thus formally clad: an infrequent wedding, some official function, perhaps. I could, of course, have continued the old custom of attending church services, but at an early age I had become an agnostic, and therefore not even my vanity would allow me to distress my conscience thus. But there were many other far more important occasions.

You may conclude from the foregoing that my personal vanity was a prime motive for what was fast becoming my overruling passion. But I assure you that this was not so. Always a fine figure of a man, I admit that I derived no small degree of satisfaction on appearing in correct attire at all the funerals I attended: and I must confess, for I wish to conceal not even my most secret offences, that I tended to despise and regard with unmixed contempt those who dared venture into the precincts of death not properly dressed; but all this was purely coincidental, relatively unimportant.

You may think it strange in me, morbid perhaps, that such should have been my chief preoccupation, when other young men, of my own age, were playing games, dancing, drinking, wenching, falling in love, getting married, and making their homes secure for themselves and their children.

I never had any desire to participate in games of any kind: in the tropics the sun works havoc with one's complexion. I had no hobbies beyond a brief excursion in philately, rudely terminated by the dishonesty of a close friend. (And I must confess here in parenthesis that his was one of the very few funerals at which my delight was not unreservedly aesthetic.) Dancing bored me; I had no sense of rhythm. My hesitant experiments in drinking and sexual indulgence left me nauseated. I had no talent for music or for art, and appreciation of them was quite beyond me. I read quite a great deal, biography especially. Poetry I could not understand, and the novel I found distressingly vulgar. I had not the necessary mental equipment to take more than a cursory interest in the scientific discoveries of our times.

I never married. I never met a woman to whom I could accord perfection, and I was determined that nothing short of perfection would entice me to surrender my peace of mind to the exigencies of the marital state; moreover, the financial complexities of such a state dismayed me. I did fall in love once, but of that I shall speak in its proper context. When my dear mother departed this life, there remained my three sisters to whom I could always, until but recently, look for companionship, affection, and consolation. I led a very happy, if uneventful life. I worked hard at the office; I earned the respect and warm regard of my employers; in time I was admitted into partnership in the business. I have never known what it is like to be ill for even a day. A careful observer, unacquainted with me, could never have imagined that I was nearly sixty years of age.

And so, for many years I pursued my methodical, completely satisfying way of living. Indeed, I became something of a local celebrity. I had even heard it said that it could not be claimed for anyone who was someone in our community to have been properly interred unless I was present. And, to my credit, I think, I must state that I allowed no social distinction to influence my attendance. Rich or poor; white or coloured: it was sufficient for me to have known the individual in question, or to be acquainted with one or other of the bereaved relatives – I say nothing, of course, of all those whom I know personally – for me to put in an appearance. I always went alone, for I had discovered at an early age that my friends were not always as meticulous as I in their choice of attire, and I was always conscious, if I may thus express it, of the subtle frisson of admiration, I might almost say, of mental applause, that ran through the gathering on my arrival. Many other faces were almost as familiar as mine on such occasions, for I would not have you think that this passion of mine is an altogether singular one; but I can safely assert, and prove my assertion, that I had outdistanced my nearest rival by ten point five to one. For from my seventeenth year I have kept a careful compilation of these attendances. Over this period of time they average about thirteen a month. If one multiplies this figure by the necessary number of months and years (I have already mentioned that I am nearly sixty: fifty-nine and one month to be quite exact), one will have a pretty fair idea of my performance.

I do not mind admitting that in my early days, before I was in a position to purchase either a carriage or a car, this matter of transport proved a rather expensive item on my budget. But on this score I have no regrets. I was always thrifty, and, as I have stated already, even in those far-off days, I had few vices. No: I always lived quietly, returning home from the office, taking my afternoon stroll, that is, when I was not engaged in my recreation, discussing with my dear sisters (all, alas, now departed: Elspeth, the last to go, died last November) the topics of the day; retiring for the night happy in the knowledge of having committed no misdemeanour, of leaving no duty undone; and awaking next morning, fresh as the proverbial daisy, and, as far as was consonant with my dignity, scampering downstairs to turn with eager expectancy to the obituary notices in the morning newspaper.

And now I must make a further admission, one of far-reaching importance and consequence. As the years went by, some time about my forty-ninth year to be more exact, I made a startling discovery: I was able to foretell the approach of death from a close observation of the faces of those whom I would meet from time to time at funeral gatherings. I cannot hope to explain *how* I knew; all I can say is that it was quite some time before I was consciously aware of this rare gift that had been bestowed upon me; but indeed, I almost refused to credit it, until, as the result of a series of tests, most rigorously conducted, I was under no possible doubt whatsoever. I would note someone or other at a funeral, would perceive some unaccountable and unwonted something in his expression, some unmistakable token, the significance of which could point to but one conclusion. It was indeed as though I had acquired the power of glimpsing, for one fleeting and rewarding moment, the hollow energy of the underlying skull peering through its mask of dissolving flesh. And I would find myself saying to myself, in as matter of fact a way as one might similarly congratulate oneself on being alive on such and such a beautiful day, 'Well, old man, it won't be long for *you* now,' and in a comparatively short while I would find myself reading his obituary notice.

I began to scrutinize the faces of persons more closely, to make more elaborate computations; and I discovered that it became increasingly more simple for me to foretell the death of the person under observation. In fact, during this last year I was seldom off more than a day or two at most.

You will therefore understand that this perusal of the obituary notices in the morning newspapers had become more than a mere matter of information: they contained the confirmation of my judgement; and I see no reason to disguise the fact that this afforded me considerable pride.

I must withdraw the reservation stated at the end of the fourth preceding paragraph: I would literally scamper downstairs.

So it came about that this morning on making my descent I slipped and struck my head against the balustrade. I was stunned for a moment. It left me an ugly bruise on my forehead, and I was annoyed with myself. Such a thing had never happened to me before. And to increase my discomfiture, on turning to the important page in the paper, I read that Mary Ellen Wye was to be buried that afternoon. I was indeed exceedingly hurt that one or other of her brothers had not notified me personally. True, I had not seen the deceased lady for well over twenty years, had not conversed with her for nearly twice as long a time; yet I saw her brothers very often, and, to a certain extent, I still regarded myself as one of the family. For I must tell you that many years ago Mary Ellen and I had almost become engaged to be married. Of all the young women I had ever known, she, and she alone, most closely approached that quality of perfection of which I have spoken. Almost, but not quite attained it, for, despite the fact that we had all grown up together, it was not until I had broached the subject of our impending engagement to my mother and sisters that I learnt with amazement and horror that her grandmother had been the illegitimate child of a garrison officer and a common servant-girl.

She had never married. And now she was dead. Somehow the knowledge that I would be going to her funeral depressed me. This state of depression was a novel experience. It was quite beyond my comprehension.

I went to the office, as usual; I sent a wreath to her home; but I could feel none of that excitement, none of the usual emotions, which such a treat in store usually engendered, flood my being.

I came home early. I was irritated by the unsightly bruise on my forehead. It was very painful to the touch, and I realized it would be quite impossible for me to don my top hat. Very well, I would go (I almost smiled to myself as I realized how I was being forced into doing what I had so long inveighed against) bareheaded. I had a cup of tea. I began to dress.

Then I had a sudden spell of dizziness. I had to recline on my bed for some time before I could complete my toilet. I looked at my watch. It was already eleven minutes past five. I should have to hurry.

It was a bright afternoon. A bank of sullen cloud hung low in the west; there was but little breeze; an unusual coppery glow seemed to pervade everything.

The funeral was, fortunately, at St Moystyn's on the outskirts of the city, only half a mile away. There is little or no traffic at this time of evening, and I was soon there. I parked my car and glanced anxiously at my watch. But, as I entered the quaint little churchyard, I realized how very late I was: the coffin had already been borne to the family vault. The parson was more than halfway through the service. I stood still for a moment, looking at the gathering, and I experienced a sensation of profound disgust. God, I thought, what is our society coming to! Among them all, except for the undertaker in his ill-fitting tubular costume of shiny black, there wasn't another single soul, except one of Mary Ellen's brothers, who wasn't in ordinary everyday wear: tweeds, serges, gaberdines of various shades of blue, grey and brown: a sorry sight to contemplate. They might have been a group of nondescripts chosen haphazardly from a cocktail party. My annoyance and depression were intensified by this shocking spectacle. I shuddered, and involuntarily drawing myself up to my full height, I joined them.

I have already mentioned the strange coppery glow of the evening; in this garish light everything appeared slightly different somehow. And as I blinked my eyes and looked around me, I could hardly give credence to what I saw. At first I thought it might have been some trickery of the weird light, but after a moment's consideration I was positive that it was not; for, as I glanced from one face to another, I became aware, completely and without any shadow of doubt, that the dread impress of imminent dissolution, of which I have already spoken, lay stark upon almost each and every one of those present. It was altogether astonishing, and, needless to say, quite unprecedented. There was standing next to me John Wadell, the accountant. His skin was the colour of that of a man stricken with acute jaundice; the flesh hung in flaccid wattles from his face, his eyes were completely empty of expression or purpose. Indeed, as far as I was concerned, he might have been already dead, as he stood there, his eyes staring into nothingness. Beside him was Dr Hope, for years my sisters' medical practitioner. A ruddy-faced old fellow, he now looked bleached; such colour as remained in his baggy cheeks might have been daubed on by some inexperienced hand at an amateur theatrical performance: you could almost see the blood being slowly drained out of him to coagulate in those two unhealthy splotches. And as I hastily glanced from one face to another near by, at the face of Manley Davis, the dry-goods merchant, at that of Arthur Grimswold of Grimswold Mansions, even at those of the comparatively young King-Lord twins, born on my thirtieth birthday, I could see only leaden faces, saffron faces, waxen faces, livid faces, all of them almost drained of their living essence, all sealed with the sure expectancy of swiftly approaching death.

And as I stood there, speculating on the nature of the oncoming epidemic which was to disperse such wholesale mortality, the full import of what I had seen almost overwhelmed me. Gone were the petty annoyances and depressions of the day; I was caught up in something so stupendous that I could only with difficulty conceal my excitement. I felt myself possessed with a sense of more than physical exhilaration; almost as though, and I hope you will understand what I am trying to express, for I can find no other way of describing it, almost as though I were in process of becoming a god. I state this in all truthfulness, and I venture to say, in all humility. But this is how it appeared to me. Here I was, aware of these petty mortals, clustered in ant-like formation about the grave, aware of their absurd limitation, and so far, far above them in the plenitude of my omniscience. I regarded them with a sense of overweening contempt and scorn; yet, in some strange way, there was in my exalted state of soaring ecstasy, still room for pity.

I note this extenuating circumstance at this moment with some small degree of satisfaction. God knows, I, too, am in dire need of pity, now.

The vault sealed, the wreaths laid on, the mourners moved away in bleak groups. I advanced and shook hands, murmuring a few conventional words of sympathy with the brothers who all, I was surprised to observe, despite the imprint of death on their faces, regarded me somewhat strangely: there was in their attitude not only an ill-designed disapproval of seeing me there, but almost, though I could not understand it at the time, a recoiling such as might have been due to some physical revulsion. Perhaps it was the bruise on my forehead, I thought, for it was, I am compelled to admit, an ugly sight: or was it that I was without my top hat? For I could not, would not, believe that they grudged my paying my last respects to the woman whom they had said often enough I had callously jilted.

But even this ungraciousness on their part could not adversely affect my demeanour towards them. I shook hands with them compassionately, not only on account of their bereavement, but forgiving them their resentment, everything, in the certain knowledge that within three months at most, all three of them, Willy the eminent solicitor, Herbert the MCP, and Arthur, poor shiftless Arthur who had never done an honest day's work in all his life, would be occupying, well, if not the vault with Mary Ellen, some other, or else some cubic feet of space beneath the mould. It was so sad that I could almost have afforded to impart to my words of sympathy a sincerity which I do not often experience. But, infused as I was with this secret knowledge and sense of superhuman power, it was all I could do to prevent myself from shrieking with laughter. Yes, Herbert, the dignified Herbert, one of the few remaining adherents to correct attire for every occasion, would be the first to go. It would be less than a fortnight for him.

The light filtered through the spreading, bare limbs of the flamboyants, gathering, as the evening progressed, more and more intensity; the corpse faces passed me by and departed. I watched them all go. And then I could give way to my laughter, for I knew that for most of them, the next time they attended a funeral ceremony it would be they who would play the all-important role.

The uncanny light flooded the sky. I looked up to it and stretched out arms to it: almost a sacramental gesture, a symbol, as it were, of my apotheosis.

After a few moments I walked out of the churchyard and approached my car. Never have I felt so completely and absolutely at one with everyone and everything. I could have danced my way home. As I drew near the car, I noticed that two little urchins were peeping into it, fingering something. I shouted at them, and they jumped down and ran away.

I got into the car, noticing without surprise that my forehead was aching, had been aching, indeed, all the time. But this was of no consequence. I remember I began to sing. And then I observed that something was wrong. Those two urchins had been fiddling with my rear-view mirror. It was facing the setting sun and the unearthly light appeared to be focused directly upon it. I leaned forward to adjust it.

And, as I did so, I saw, peering into it, a face, such a face as I have never seen, a face which I am determined never to see again. For it was the face of death itself: the remorseless blank eyes, void of every hope or fear known to mortal men, staring from a torn covering of all but putrescent flesh; and, as in an X-ray photograph, through the shadowy open mouth, arrested in an attitude of song, the vacuous grin of the abiding skeleton.

I looked around. Who in God's name, could be playing such a ghastly joke on me? It was quite a little while before I realized I was gazing at my own reflection in the rear-view mirror of my car.

It is now eight minutes past midnight. I have finished with exactly twelve minutes to spare. I have already written Herbert Wye asking him to make all the necessary arrangements. Whom else can I ask? There must be at least one person there suitably attired.

JEAN RHYS

Fishy Waters

THE EDITOR
The Dominica Herald   March 3rd, 189—

Dear Sir,

Yesterday I heard a piece of news that appalled me. It seems that a British workman, Mr Longa by name, who arrived a year ago, has been arrested and is being held by the police. Mr Longa is a carpenter. He is also a socialist, and does not disguise his political opinions. It goes without saying that a certain class of person in this island, who seem to imagine that the colour of their skins enables them to behave like gods, disliked and disapproved of him from the first. He was turned out of Miss Lambton's boarding-house after one night and had the greatest difficulty in finding anywhere to live. Eventually he settled in a predominantly negro quarter – another cause for offence. A determined effort was made to induce him to leave the island. When this failed, with their usual hypocrisy they pretended to ignore him, but they were merely biding their time.

He was found joking roughly with one of the many vagabond children who infest the streets of Roseau, and is to be accused of child-molesting and cruelty, if you please. A trumped-up charge, on the face of it. In this way, they plan to be rid of a long-standing nuisance and to be able to boast about their even-handed justice. The hypocrisy of these people, who bitterly resent that they no longer have the power over the bodies and minds of the blacks they once had (the cruelty of West Indian planters was a byword), making a scapegoat of an honest British workman, is enough to make any decent person's gorge rise. A London barrister, new to this island, has offered to defend Mr Longa without charge. Only one just man among so many?

Yours truly,
Disgusted

THE EDITOR
The Dominica Herald   March 10th, 189—

Dear Sir,

Who is 'Disgusted'? Who is this person (I believe people) who tries to stir up racial hatred whenever possible? Almost invariably with gloating satisfaction, they will drag in the horrors of the slave trade. Who would think, to hear them talk, that slavery was abolished by the English nearly a hundred years ago? They are long on diatribes, but short on facts. The slave trade was an abominable one, but it could not have existed without the help and cooperation of African chiefs. Slavery still exists, and is taken for granted, in Africa, both among negroes and Arabs. Are these facts ever mentioned? The bad is endlessly repeated and insisted upon; the good is ridiculed, forgotten or denied. Who does this, and why?

Yours truly,
Ian J. MacDonald

THE EDITOR
The Dominica Herald   March 17th, 189—

Dear Sir,

It is sometimes said that African chiefs probably had a good deal to do with the slave trade, but I have never heard before that this was proven. In his typical letter I notice that Mr MacDonald places all the blame on these perhaps mythical Africans and says nothing about the greed of white merchants or the abominable cruelty and indifference of white planters. The treatment meted out to Mr Longa shows that their heirs and successors have not changed all that much.

Yours truly,
P. Kelly
Kelly's Universal Stores

THE EDITOR
The Dominica Herald   March 24th, 189—

Dear Sir,

I hate to interfere with the amusement of your readers, but I must point out that according to English law it is highly improper to discuss a case that has not been tried (*sub judice*). In this country the custom seems to be more honoured in the breach than in the observance.

Yours truly,
Fiat Justicia

This correspondence is now closed. *Editor.*

On the same day the editor, who was known as Papa Dom, remarked in a leading article: 'These are fishy waters – very fishy waters.'

6 Cork Street
Roseau, Dominica   March 24th, 189—

My dear Caroline,

Your letter rescued me from a mood of great depression. I am answering it at once – it will be such a relief to tell you about something that I don't care to discuss with people here.

You wouldn't remember a man called Jimmy Longa – he arrived soon after you left. Well, Matt found him trying to saw a little girl in two – can you believe it? – and is to be the main witness for the prosecution. The whole place is buzzing with gossip, arguments, letters to the local newspaper and so on. It is most unpleasant. I've begged Matt to have nothing further to do with it, I'm sure there'll be trouble. He says why should there be, Longa's a white man not a black one. I say 'Jimmy Longa will be an honorary black before this is over, you'll see. They'll twist it somehow.' But he won't even talk about it now. I'm not at all happy about Matt. He doesn't look well and is so unlike what he used to be. I begin to wish I'd never persuaded him to settle here when he retired – a visit to escape the winter is one thing, living here is quite another.

The first scandal about Longa was that Miss Lambton turned him out as he got so drunk every night. He's a jobbing carpenter, quite a good one when he's sober, so he soon found a place to live and got plenty of work. His story is that he's on his way to America and stopped off at Dominica to make some money. I wonder who on earth could have advised him to do that! He gave out that he was a socialist, extreme – the new world must be built on the ashes of the old, that sort of thing. He preached fire and slaughter in the rum-shop and everywhere else so you can imagine he wasn't very popular with the white people. Then he got malaria badly and Miss Lambton, who had him on her conscience, went to the hospital to see how he was. She said he looked very ill and told her that his only wish now was to get back to England, but he couldn't raise the money. She started a subscription for him and headed the list with £10, which she certainly couldn't afford. Nearly everyone chipped in and a good deal was raised. But somehow he managed to persuade Miss Lambton to hand the lot over directly. Then disappeared. There was no case against him – he'd been careful not to promise or sign anything – besides, a lot of people thought it comic. They said 'Poor Mamie Lambton, it seems she's very upset. But what a chap! You have to laugh!' Even when he reappeared, more fanatical than ever, nobody took him seriously – he was the Dominica funny story. And now this.

I've got one piece of pleasant news. Because Matt dislikes the town so much we've bought a small estate in the country where he may be happier. It's called Three Rivers – an old place, and as usual the house is falling to bits. It's being fixed up – but lately I've wondered if we'll ever live there.

No one at home would understand why all this is looming over me so much, but you know the kind of atmosphere we get here sometimes, so I think you will.

I'm so glad you are happy and don't feel the cold too much. Perhaps the next time I write it will all be over and I'll be more cheerful.

> Meanwhile I send you my love,
> Affectionately,
> Maggie

The day after Jimmy Longa's trial there was a long report on the front page of the *Dominica Herald*. The reporter, having remarked on the crowded courtroom, usually empty for assault and battery cases, went on to say that the prosecuting counsel, M. Didier of Roseau, had seemed so nervous at first that he was almost inaudible. His speech was short. He said that it was fortunate that there had been an eyewitness to the attack on the child, Josephine Mary Dent, known as Jojo, for though Mr Longa's activities were common knowledge in Roseau, no one had dared to come forward to accuse him, a white man. 'There are a certain number of children, abandoned and unprotected, roaming the streets. This child was one of them. The accused is a danger to all children, but these are particularly at risk.' M. Didier asked for a sentence heavy enough to deter possible imitators. He then called his first witness, Mr Matthew Penrice.

Mr Penrice said that on the late afternoon of 27 February he was walking up Jetty Street on the way to the Club when he heard a child screaming in a very distressing way. As he approached the house the screams came from, the sound stopped abruptly – no angry voices, complete silence. The house stood well back from the empty street, and there was a fence around it. It occurred to him that a child, left alone there, might have met with an accident, and on an impulse he knocked at the wooden gate. There was no answer so he pushed the gate open. As he did so he heard a man say: 'Now I'm going to saw you in two, like they do in English music-halls.' The yard of the house was quite a large one; there was a tree in the corner, and under the tree a plank raised up on trestles. A naked little negro girl lay on the plank, her head hanging over the end. She was silent, and her face was almost green with fright. The man's back was to him and the saw in his hand was touching the child's waist. Mr Penrice called out 'What the devil's going on here?' The man turned, dropping the saw, and he recognized Mr Longa, who was not in court. Mr Longa said: 'I wasn't going to hurt her – I was only joking.' He had been holding the child on the plank, and when he turned she rolled off and lay on the ground without moving. Mr Longa repeated that it was a joke. When the witness approached the unconscious child he saw that her body was covered with bruises. He did not speak to Mr Longa again, but wrapped the child in his jacket and took her to the house of Madame Octavia Joseph, which was close by. He then sent for the doctor who fortunately was able to come at once. After the doctor had arrived he went to the police station and reported what he had seen.

Cross-examined by counsel for the defence, Mr Penrice was asked if Jetty Street was his usual way to the Club. He answered that it was not, but he was in a hurry to keep an appointment and Jetty Street was a short cut.

Counsel asked him: 'Would it surprise you to know that information from your household reveals that on that particular day you left for the Club very much earlier than usual? The domestic remembers it clearly, as it was her birthday. As your habits are so regular, she wondered why you had left the house on foot on such a hot day, nearly two hours earlier than usual. Why, then, did you have to take a short cut?'

Mr Penrice replied: 'Two hours is an exaggeration. I left my house earlier than usual to go for a walk – I don't mind the heat – and I forgot the time, so I was trying to get to the Club as quickly as I could.'

'When you heard the accused say "Like they do in English music-halls", was he aware that anyone was listening?'

'No, he didn't know that I was there.'

'So he was speaking to the child?'

'I suppose so.'

'Do you know that there is a popular trick on the English music-halls when a girl is supposed to be sawn in two?'

'Yes, I think so.'

'And is anyone ever sawn in two, or hurt in any way?'

'Of course not. It's a trick.'

'Perhaps you were too startled and shocked to realize that when the accused said "As they do in English music-halls" he was really declaring that what he was about to do was not to be taken seriously. It was a joke.'

'It was not a joke.'

'And why are you so sure of that?'

'When the man faced me, I knew that it was not a joke at all.'

'I see. But is there not a certain amount of prejudice against Mr Longa in this island? Are you not very ready to believe the worst of him? Has there not been a great deal of gossip about him?'

'I only know Mr Longa by sight. The gossip here does not interest me.'

'So you are not – shall we say – prejudiced?'

'No, not at all. Not in the way you mean.'

'I am glad to hear it. Now, as you say the child was unconscious and badly hurt, would not the normal thing have been either to take or to send her to the hospital?'

'I didn't think of the hospital. Madame Joseph's house was near by and I knew she would be well looked after so I took her there and sent for the doctor.'

'Mr Penrice, has Madame Joseph ever been in your service?'

'Yes. She was with us for nearly five years, off and on, when we used to winter here before making it our home. That was why I was so sure that she was not only a kind woman, but a perfectly reliable one.'

'When she left your employment, did you give her a large present of money?'

'Not large, no. Both my wife and myself thought she had given us invaluable service. She was no longer in very good health, so we were happy to give her enough money to buy a small house, where she would be comfortable and secure.'

'No doubt she was very grateful?'

'I think she was pleased, yes.'

'As she was so indebted to you, you must have been sure that in an emergency any instructions you gave her would be carried out?'

'In saying that, you only show that you know nothing at all about the people of this island. Madame Joseph is a most independent woman. Even if I – or rather, we – had installed her in a palace instead of a small house, she would not have thought herself bound to follow my instructions. No.'

'And it really seemed to you proper to leave a badly injured child in the care of an ex-servant, however devoted, who had no medical knowledge and no experience of nursing?'

'I did what I thought best for her.'

'And did you tell the doctor that you had taken her there because Madame Joseph was the child's close relative?'

'I did nothing of the sort.'

'But you can imply a thing without actually saying it, can you not?'

'You most certainly can.'

'Thank you, Mr Penrice. You may stand down.'

Mr Penrice was followed in the witness-box by Madame Octavia Joseph, a dignified woman who gave her evidence clearly and obviously made a favourable impression on the magistrate, Mr Somers. When she saw the state the little girl was in, she said, she understood why Mr Penrice was going to the police. 'It was a very wicked person did that.' Soon after the doctor came the child recovered consciousness, but at once began to tremble and scream. Having treated her bruises, the doctor gave her a sedative, said he would call next day, that she was to see nobody, and that she was not to be questioned until she was better. Madame Joseph had done her best to follow the doctor's orders and taken great care of the child, whose condition was much improved. 'But she says she does not remember anything about being attacked. When I told her she ought to try to remember, she only began to cry and shake, so I thought it better for the doctor to speak to her.'

The last witness for the prosecution, Dr Trevor, said that on the evening of 27 February he had been at home when he got a message to come at once to 11 Hill Street to treat a badly injured child. When he first saw the child she had fainted and had obviously been savagely beaten. When she recovered consciousness she was so frightened and hysterical that after treating her he gave her a sedative. She was probably about eleven or twelve years of age, but as she was very thin and undernourished, she may have been a year or two older.

Counsel asked Dr Trevor: 'Have you seen the child since?'

'Yes, on several occasions.'

'When did you see her last?'

'I saw her yesterday.'

'And what did you think of her?'

'I found that her condition had greatly improved. She has been carefully looked after and is well on the way to recovery. Already she seems quite a different child.'

'When you visited this child, did you ever question her or ask her who had attacked her?'

'Yes, after I thought she was better I did question her, of course. She always behaved in the same way. She says she has forgotten. I tried two or three times to question her more closely – the only result is that she becomes frightened, hysterical and quite incoherent.'

'When you questioned the child, was Madame Joseph with you?'

'She was there the first time, but I have often been alone with the child and this is invariably the way she behaves.'

'Did it strike you at all that because of what has happened, she had been mentally affected?'

'No, I saw no signs of that. She'd probably be quite a bright little thing, given a chance.'

'Did you not think it somewhat strange that although she is so much better, she still refuses to say anything about what happened to her?'

'Perhaps it is not as strange as you think. Some people after a great shock or fright will talk volubly, others "clam up" as they say in parts of England. She'll probably talk eventually, but it's impossible to say when.'

'And you find nothing unusual about this "clamming up", as you call it?'

'I have known cases when, after a frightening and harmful experience, the mind has protected itself by forgetting. If you try to force recollection, the patient becomes agitated and resentful.'

'Do you really think that this interesting, but rather complicated theory could apply to a negro child, completely illiterate, only eleven or twelve years of age? Is it not more likely that she remains silent because she has either been persuaded or threatened – probably a bit of both – not to talk?'

'I do not believe that the result of illiteracy is an uncomplicated mind – far from it. And I do not know who you are suggesting could have frightened her. My orders were that she should be kept perfectly quiet and see no one except Madame Joseph, whose house is surrounded by inquisitive neighbours. If anyone else had been there I would have been told, believe me. The child certainly isn't at all afraid of Madame Joseph. On the contrary, she seems to trust her, even be attached to her – in so far as a child like that can trust or be attached at all. However, if you are not satisfied with my evidence, why not question the child? In my opinion you will get nothing at all out of her and may do her harm, but you must decide for yourself.'

Here Mr Somers intervened and said that the child must certainly not be questioned by anyone as long as the doctor thought it might be harmful.

Counsel then asked Dr Trevor: 'Were you led to believe that the child had been taken to Madame Joseph's house because she was a close relative?'

'No. I suppose I took it for granted. In any case, I made no suggestion that she should be moved. I thought she was in very good hands.'

Counsel for the defence, Mr Berkeley, said that his client was too ill to appear in court, but that he would read his statement. This, he submitted, was a complete answer to the charge.

Mr Longa's Statement: 'I had not felt very well that day. It was too hot, so I thought I'd knock off for a bit. But as I might be able to work later on when it was cooler, I left my saw in the yard, with a plank I was working on to make bookshelves. I was very thirsty and had a few drinks, then I fell asleep. I don't know how long I slept before loud screams woke me up, coming from my yard. The noise these children make is very trying and that's putting it mildly. They climb over the fence into the yard to play, and get up to all kinds of mischief. I'd chase them away, but they always came back. They'd follow me in the street, jeering and laughing, and several times I've been stoned. I don't deny I've grown to dislike them very much indeed.

'I got up feeling shaky and in a bad temper, and in my yard I found a little girl lying on the ground, screaming. I asked her what was the matter several times, but she took no notice at all and went on yelling. At last I told her to shut up, get out, and go and scream somewhere else. She wouldn't even look at me, and the noise she was making went through and through my head, so I lost my temper, picked her up and put her on the plank, telling her I was going to saw her in two, but I didn't really mean to hurt her and I told her so. I didn't notice anything wrong with her, or think it strange that she was naked – they very often are, especially on hot days. No, I never meant to hurt her. But I hoped to frighten her a bit, and that she'd tell the others, and then perhaps they'd leave me in peace. These children had made my life a misery, and I wanted to stop them from doing it. I swear that was all I meant – to frighten her. It was just a joke. When Mr Penrice came and accused me I was too confused to say much. I told him I hadn't meant any harm but he wouldn't listen to me, nor would the policemen when they arrested me. I am sorry for what I did and for frightening her, but I had been drinking. I quite lost my temper and was very angry. That is what happened, and that is the truth.'

To this Mr Berkeley added that Mr Longa was now very willing to leave the island. 'He says that even in England he would not be treated with such injustice. As to the rumours about my client, I am surprised that my learned friend has mentioned them, as he has failed to produce a single witness to substantiate them. Without wishing to impugn Mr Penrice's word, I must point out that there is no evidence at all that Mr Longa was the child's attacker. She may have run into the empty yard to hide, or – more likely – she was thrown there by a real attacker who then made off, feeling certain that Mr Longa would be accused. Mr Penrice admits that he heard Mr Longa saying "As they do in English music-halls" before he knew anyone was listening. This seems to me to prove conclusively that Mr Longa's behaviour was a joke – a rough, even a cruel joke if you like, but certainly not deserving of several years imprisonment in a gaol not fit for any human being, Englishman or not.'

Mr Berkeley ended by saying that Mr Longa was a very intelligent man left terribly alone and isolated – also he was not a well man. It was hardly surprising that he turned to rum for consolation, and easy to believe that, woken suddenly, he felt extremely irritable and behaved in a way that was not normal to him.

The Summing-up. The magistrate, Mr Somers, said that this was a very disturbing case. 'There is no direct evidence that it was Mr Longa who first attacked the child, causing the extensive bruising. He denies it strongly, and the child cannot yet be questioned. I find his statement as read by counsel for the defence convincing up to a point. Two things, however, strike me as unlikely. Why should he think that this unfortunate child would know anything about English music-halls or the tricks performed there? Why should his mentioning them reassure her? It probably added to her fright. Also, and more important: however drunk he was, could he have picked up a badly injured naked child and carried her to the plank without noticing the marks on her body? According to Mr Longa he noticed nothing, but proceeded with his savage joke. I find this so unlikely as to be almost incredible. He excuses himself by saying that he had been drinking, but he is a man accustomed to strong drink and there is no report of advanced intoxication from the police who arrested him.

'I am not here to speculate and I cannot accept either hearsay evidence or innuendoes supported by no evidence; but I have not been in my post for twenty years without learning that it is extremely difficult to obtain direct evidence here. Often a criminal is quite well known but the police find it impossible to produce a single witness against him. There is, unfortunately, in these islands a great distrust both of the police and of the law.'

Here a voice interrupted: 'Can you blame them?' and there was hubbub in the court. Several women were in tears. Order was only restored when a threat was made to clear the court.

Mr Somers continued: 'We can only hope that this perhaps natural distrust will diminish with time. In view of my doubts I am glad to hear that Mr Longa is willing to leave the island. I direct that his passage to Southampton be paid by the government. Until he sails he must remain in custody of the police, but must be allowed to receive visitors. He must be able to get food or provisions from outside and care must be taken to restore him to health. I am sure that his able counsel will see that my instructions are carried out.'

The crowd was subdued and less talkative than usual as it left the courtroom, but a group of rowdies shouted at Mr Penrice as he came out. He took no notice of this demonstration, but got into his waiting trap and drove off. A few stones were thrown at him, but the rowdies quickly dispersed when a policeman intervened.

'I bet you anything Mamie Lambton's going to start another subscription,' said Matthew Penrice to his wife when he got home. He added: 'Don't look so gloomy, Maggie. I've one piece of very good news. Octavia tells me that she's been corresponding with an old friend in St Lucia with no children of her own who wishes to adopt Jojo. She's quite sure of this woman and says it'll be the best thing possible. I think so too. She'd get right away from all the gossip and questioning here, and start again. I'll see to it that she gets there as soon as she's well enough. I'll take care of everything, don't worry.'

Maggie Penrice watched the negro maid Janet pile the coffee things on to the tray and walk out, silent, barefooted. When she had said 'What delicious coffee, Janet,' the girl hadn't answered, hadn't even smiled. But they don't smile here, they laugh, they seldom smile. Not smilers with a knife. No? Even when they were alone she didn't speak, but went on folding and unfolding the letter. She reread the last paragraph.

'Thank you for the money you sent. I will keep it faithfully and carefully for her when she grows up and thank you from my heart for giving her to me. You would be pleased to see her. She is getting quite fat and pretty and hardly ever wakes up screaming as she used to do. I now close and say no more from my overflowing heart. Wishing you and your amiable lady all health and prosperity. Anine Dib.'

Maggie said: 'Dib. What a funny name.'

'Syrian, probably,' Matt said. 'Well, that's the last of that, I hope, and now you mustn't worry any more. Much the best thing that could have happened. Surely you agree?'

'Perhaps ... But Matt, do you think it was wise to send her away quite so quickly?'

'The sooner the better, I should have thought. Why not?'

The room was at the back of the house, there was no noise from the street. It was hot and airless and the blinds were half drawn. She folded the letter carefully and put it back into its envelope, then pushed it across to him.

'Because it's all over the place that Octavia's in your pay and that you both sent the child to St Lucia so that there was no chance of her ever talking. They're saying that you did it and pushed it off on to Jimmy Longa. The whole thing is utterly ridiculous, of course, but you ought to stop it.'

'Stop it? What do you want me to do? How can I stop it?'

'Surely that wouldn't be too hard. It's so absurd. How could you have done it — how is it even possible?'

'Do you think these damnable hogs care whether it's possible or not, or how or where or when? They've just got hold of something to grunt about, that's all. If you think I'm going to argue with this lot you must be mad. I've had more than enough of this whole damned place. If you really want to know what I feel, I want to clear out. It's not this particular storm in a teacup that's decided me. I've wanted to leave for some time, and you must have known.'

'They'll say you've run away.'

'God, can't you get it into your head that I don't give a damn what they say here? Oh come on, Maggie, don't look like that. I know how you feel, how you dread the cold, how much better you are here, and its beauty and all that — I only wish I felt like you, but to me it's suffocating.'

'Yes, I know. But I hoped you'd feel better when we left Roseau.'

'The hatred would be exactly the same in the country — suppressed, perhaps. If you don't want to leave you needn't. I won't sell Three Rivers or this house, and the money will be all right — surely you know that?'

'But Matt, you find envy, malice, hatred everywhere. You can't escape.'

'Perhaps, but I'm sick of this particular brand.'

'Do you think I'd want to stay here by myself if you went? Do you really think that?'

He didn't answer but smiled and said: 'Then that's settled.' He patted her shoulder lightly, then he went over to an armchair, took up a book; but Maggie, watching him anxiously, cautiously, saw that he never turned a page. Suddenly she screwed up her eyes tightly and shook her head. She was trying to fight the overwhelming certainty that the man she was looking at was a complete stranger.

ERIC WALROND

The Wharf Rats

I

Among the motley crew recruited to dig the Panama Canal were artisans from the four ends of the earth. Down in the Cut drifted hordes of Italians, Greeks, Chinese, Negroes – a hardy, sun defying set of white, black and yellow men. But the bulk of the actual brawn for the work was supplied by the dusky peons of those coral isles in the Caribbean ruled by Britain, France and Holland.

At the Atlantic end of the Canal the blacks were herded in boxcar huts buried in the jungles of 'Silver City'; in the murky tenements peril-ously poised on the narrow banks of Faulke's River; in the low, smelting cabins of Coco Té. The 'Silver Quarters' harbored the inky ones, their wives and pickaninnies.

As it grew dark the hewers at the Ditch, exhausted, half-asleep, naked but for wormy singlets, would hum queer creole tunes, play on guitar or piccolo, and jig to the rhythm of the *coombia*. It was a *brujerial* chant, for obeah, a heritage of the French colonial, honeycombed the life of the Negro laboring camps. Over smoking pots, on black, death-black nights legends of the bloodiest were recited till they became the essence of a sort of Negro Koran. One refuted them at the price of one's breath. And to question the verity of the obeah, to dismiss or reject it as the ungodly rite of some lurid, crack-brained Islander was to be an accursed pale-face, dog of a white. And the obeah man, in a fury of rage, would throw a machete at the heretic's head or – worse – burn on his doorstep at night a pyre of Maubé bark or green Ganja weed.

On the banks of a river beyond Cristobal, Coco Té sheltered a colony of Negroes enslaved to the obeah. Near a roundhouse, daubed with smoke and coal ash, a river serenely flowed away and into the guava region, at the eastern tip of Monkey Hill. Across the bay from it was a sand bank – a rising out of the sea – where ships stopped for coal.

In the first of the six chinky cabins making up the family quarters of Coco Té lived a stout, pot-bellied St Lucian, black as the coal hills he mended, by the name of Jean Baptiste. Like a host of the native St Lucian emigrants, Jean Baptiste forgot where the French in him ended and the English began. His speech was the petulant patois of the unlettered French black. Still, whenever he lapsed into His Majesty's English, it was with a thick Barbadian bias.

A coal passer at the Dry Dock, Jean Baptiste was a man of intense piety. After work, by the glow of a red, setting sun, he would discard his crusted overalls, get in a starched *crocus bag*, aping the Yankee foreman on the other side of the track in the 'Gold Quarters', and loll on his coffee-vined porch. There, dozing in a bamboo rocker, Celestin, his second wife, a becomingly stout brown beauty from Martinique, chanted gospel hymns to him.

Three sturdy sons Jean Baptiste's first wife had borne him – Philip, the eldest, a good-looking, black fellow; Ernest, shifty, cunning; and Sandel, aged eight. Another boy, said to be wayward and something of a ne'er-do-well, was sometimes spoken of. But Baptiste, a proud, disdainful man, never once referred to him in the presence of his children. No vagabond son of his could eat from his table or sit at his feet unless he went to 'meeting'. In brief, Jean Baptiste was a religious man. It was a thrust at the omnipresent obeah. He went to 'meeting'. He made the boys go, too. All hands went, not to the Catholic Church, where Celestin secretly worshiped, but to the English Plymouth Brethren in the Spanish city of Colon.

Stalking about like a ghost in Jean Baptiste's household was a girl, a black ominous Trinidad girl. Had Jean Baptiste been a man given to curiosity about the nature of women, he would have viewed skeptically Maffi's adoption by Celestin. But Jean Baptiste was a man of lofty unconcern, and so Maffi remained there, shadowy, obdurate.

And Maffi was such a hardworking patois girl. From the break of day she'd be at the sink, brightening the tinware. It was she who did the chores which Madame congenitally shirked. And towards sundown, when the labor trains had emptied, it was she who scoured the beach for cockles for Jean Baptiste's epicurean palate.

And as night fell, Maffi, a long, black figure, would disappear in the dark to dream on top of a canoe hauled up on the mooning beach. An eternity Maffi'd sprawl there, gazing at the frosting of the stars and the glitter of the black sea.

A cabin away lived a family of Tortola mulattoes by the name of Boyce. The father was also a man who piously went to 'meeting' – gaunt and hollow-cheeked. The eldest boy, Esau, had been a journeyman tailor for ten years; the girl next him, Ora, was plump, dark, freckled; others came – a string of ulcered girls until finally a pretty, opaque one, Maura.

Of the Bantu tribe Maura would have been a person to turn and stare at. Crossing the line into Cristobal or Colon – a city of rarefied gaiety – she was often mistaken for a native *señorita* or an urbanized Cholo Indian girl. Her skin was the reddish yellow of old gold and in her eyes there lurked the glint of mother-of-pearl. Her hair, long as a jungle elf's, was jettish, untethered. And her teeth were whiter than the full-blooded black Philip's.

Maura was brought up, like the children of Jean Baptiste, in the Plymouth Brethren. But the Plymouth Brethren was a harsh faith to bring hemmed-in peasant children up in, and Maura, besides, was of a gentle romantic nature. Going to the Yankee commissary at the bottom of Eleventh and Front Streets, she usually wore a leghorn hat. With flowers bedecking it, she'd look in it older, much older than she really was. Which was an impression quite flattering to her. For Maura, unknown to Philip, was in love – in love with San Tie, a Chinese half-breed, son of a wealthy canteen proprietor in Colon. But San Tie liked to go fishing and deer hunting up the Monkey Hill lagoon, and the object of his occasional visits to Coco Té was the eldest son of Jean Baptiste. And thus it was through Philip that Maura kept in touch with the young Chinese Maroon.

One afternoon Maura, at her wits' end, flew to the shed roof to Jean Baptiste's kitchen.

'Maffi,' she cried, the words smoky on her lips, 'Maffi, when Philip come in tonight tell 'im I want fo' see 'im particular, yes?'

'*Sacre gache!* All de time Philip, Philip!' growled the Trinidad girl, as Maura, in heartaching preoccupation, sped towards the lawn. 'Why she no le' 'im alone, yes?' And with a spatter she flecked the hunk of lard on Jean Baptiste's stewing okras.

As the others filed up front after dinner that evening Maffi said to Philip, pointing to the cabin across the way, 'She – she want fo' see yo'.'

Instantly Philip's eyes widened. Ah, he had good news for Maura! San Tie, after an absence of six days, was coming to Coco Té Saturday to hunt on the lagoon. And he'd relish the joy that'd flood Maura's face as she glimpsed the idol of her heart, the hero of her dreams! And Philip, a true son of Jean Baptiste, loved to see others happy, ecstatic.

But Maffi's curious rumination checked him. 'All de time, Maura, Maura, me can't understand it, yes. But no mind, me go stop it, *oui*, me go stop it, so help me –'

He crept up to her, gently holding her by the shoulders.

'Le' me go, *sacre!*' She shook off his hands bitterly. 'Le' me go – yo' go to yo' Maura.' And she fled to her room, locking the door behind her.

Philip sighed. He was a generous, good-natured sort. But it was silly to try to enlighten Maffi. It wasn't any use. He could as well have spoken to the tattered torsos the lazy waves puffed up on the shores of Coco Té.

2

'Philip, come on, a ship is in – let's go.' Ernest, the wharf rat, seized him by the arm.

'Come,' he said, 'let's go before it's too late. I want to get some money, yes.'

Dashing out of the house the two boys made for the wharf. It was dusk. Already the Hindus in the bachelor quarters were mixing their *rotie* and the Negroes in their singlets were smoking and cooling off. Night was rapidly approaching. Sunset, an iridescent bit of molten gold, was enriching the stream with its last faint radiance.

The boys stole across the lawn and made their way to the pier.

'Careful,' cried Philip, as Ernest slid between a prong of oyster-crusted piles to a raft below, 'careful, these shells cut wussah'n a knife.'

On the raft the boys untied a rowboat they kept stowed away under the dock, got into it and pushed off. The liner still had two hours to dock. Tourists crowded its decks. Veering away from the barnacled piles the boys eased out into the churning ocean.

It was dusk. Night would soon be upon them. Philip took the oars while Ernest stripped down to loincloth.

'Come, Philip, let me paddle – ' Ernest took the oars. Afar on the dusky sea a whistle echoed. It was the pilot's signal to the captain of port. The ship would soon dock.

The passengers on deck glimpsed the boys. It piqued their curiosity to see two black boys in a boat amid stream.

'All right, mistah,' cried Ernest, 'a penny, mistah.'

He sprang at the guilder as it twisted and turned through a streak of silver dust to the bottom of the sea. Only the tips of his crimson toes – a sherbet-like foam – and up he came with the coin between his teeth.

Deep-sea gamin, Philip off yonder, his mouth noisy with coppers, gargled, 'This way, sah, as far as yo' like, mistah.'

An old red-bearded Scot, in spats and mufti, presumably a lover of the exotic in sport, held aloft a soveriegn. A sovereign! Already red, and sore by virtue of the leaps and plunges in the briny swirl, Philip's eyes bulged at its yellow gleam.

'Ovah yah, sah – '

Off in a whirlpool the man tossed it. And like a garfish Philip took after it, a falling arrow in the stream. His body, once in the water, tore ahead. For a spell the crowd on the ship held its breath. 'Where is he?' 'Where is the nigger swimmer gone to?' Even Ernest, driven to the boat by the race for such an ornate prize, cold, shivering, his teeth chattering – even he watched with trembling and anxiety. But Ernest's concern was of a deeper kind. For there, where Philip had leaped, was Deathpool – a spawning place for sharks, for barracudas!

But Philip rose – a brief gurgling sputter – a ripple on the sea – and the Negro's crinkled head was above the water.

'Hey!' shouted Ernest, 'there, Philip! Down!'

And down Philip plunged. One – two – minutes. God, how long they seemed! And Ernest anxiously waited. But the bubble on the water boiled, kept on boiling – a sign that life still lasted! It comforted Ernest.

Suddenly Philip, panting, spitting, pawing, dashed through the water like a streak of lightning.

'Shark!' cried a voice aboard ship. 'Shark! There he is, a great big one! Run, boy! Run for your life!'

From the edge of the boat Philip saw the monster as twice, thrice it circled the boat. Several times the shark made a dash for it, endeavoring to strike it with its murderous tail.

The boys quietly made off. But the shark still followed the boat. It was a pale-green monster. In the glittering dusk it seemed black to Philip. Fattened on the swill of the abattoir near by and the beef tossed from the decks of countless ships in port, it had become used to the taste of flesh and the smell of blood.

'Yo' know, Ernest,' said Philip, as he made his boat fast to a raft, 'one time I thought he wuz rubbin' 'gainst me belly. He wuz such a big able one. But it wuz wuth it, Ernie, it wuz wuth it –'

In his palm there was a flicker of gold. Ernest emptied his loincloth and together they counted the money, dressed and trudged back to the cabin.

On the lawn Philip met Maura. Ernest tipped his cap, left his brother, and went into the house. As he entered Maffi, pretending to be scouring a pan, was flushed and mute as a statue. And Ernest, starved, went in the dining-room and for a long time stayed there. Unable to bear it any longer, Maffi sang out, 'Ernest, whey Philip dey?'

'Outside – some whey – ah talk to Maura –'

'Yo' sure yo' no lie, Ernest?' she asked, suspended.

'Yes, up cose, I jes' lef' 'im 'tandin' out dey – why?'

'Nutton –'

He suspected nothing. He went on eating while Maffi tiptoed to the shed roof. Yes, confound it, there he was, near the stand-pipe, talking to Maura!

'Go stop *ee, oui*,' she hissed impishly. 'Go 'top ee, yes.'

3

Low, shadowy, the sky painted Maura's face bronze. The sea, noisy, enraged, sent a blob of wind about her black, wavy hair. And with her back to the sea, her hair blew loosely about her face.

'D'ye think, d'ye think he really likes me, Philip?'

'I'm positive he do, Maura,' vowed the youth.

And an ageing faith shone in Maura's eyes. No longer was she a silly, insipid girl. Something holy, reverent had touched her. And in so doing it could not fail to leave an impress of beauty. It was worshipful. And it mellowed, ripened her.

Weeks she had waited for word of San Tie. And the springs of Maura's life took on a noble ecstasy. Late at night, after the others had retired, she'd sit up in bed, dreaming. Sometimes they were dreams of envy. For Maura began to look with eyes of comparison upon the happiness of the Italian wife of the boss riveter at the Dry Dock – the lady on the other side of the railroad tracks in the 'Gold Quarters' for whom she sewed – who got a fresh baby every year and who danced in a world of silks and satins. Yes, Maura had dreams, love dreams of San Tie, the flashy half-breed, son of a Chinese beer seller and a Jamaica Maroon, who had swept her off her feet by a playful wink of the eye.

'Tell me, Philip, does he work? Or does he play the lottery – what does he do, tell me!'

'I dunno,' Philip replied with mock lassitude, 'I dunno myself – '

'But it doesn't matter, Philip. I don't want to be nosy, see? I'm simply curious about everything that concerns him, see?'

Ah, but Philip wished to cherish Maura, to shield her, be kind to her. And so he lied to her. He did not tell her he had first met San Tie behind the counter of his father's saloon in the Colon tenderloin, for he would have had to tell, besides, why he, Philip, had gone there. And that would have led him, a youth of meager guile, to Celestin Baptiste's mulish regard for anisette which he procured her. He dared not tell her, well-meaning fellow that he was, what San Tie, a fiery comet in the night life of the district, had said to him the day before. 'She sick in de head, yes,' he had said. 'Ah, me no dat saht o' man – don't she know no bettah, egh, Philip?' But Philip desired to be kindly, and hid it from Maura.

'What is today?' she cogitated, aloud, 'Tuesday. You say he's comin'
fo' hunt Saturday, Philip? Wednesday – four more days. I can wait. I
can wait. I'd wait a million years fo' 'im, Philip.'

But Saturday came and Maura, very properly, was shy as a duck. Other
girls, like Hilda Long, a Jamaica brunette, the flower of a bawdy cabin
up by the abattoir, would have been less genteel. Hilda would have
caught San Tie by the lapels of his coat and in no time would have got
him told.

But Maura was lowly, trepid, shy. To her he was a dream – a luxury
to be distantly enjoyed. He was not to be touched. And she'd wait till
he decided to come to her. And there was no fear, either, of his ever
failing to come. Philip had seen to that. Had not he been the intermediary
between them? And all Maura needed now was to sit back, and wait till
San Tie came to her.

And besides, who knows, brooded Maura, San Tie might be a bashful
fellow.

But when, after an exciting hunt, the Chinese mulatto returned from
the lagoon, nodded stiffly to her, said goodbye to Philip and kept on to
the scarlet city, Maura was frantic.

'Maffi,' she said, 'tell Philip to come here quick –'

It was the same as touching a match to the patois girl's dynamite.
'Yo' mek me sick,' she said. 'Go call he yo'self, yo' ole hag, yo' ole fire
hag yo'.' But Maura, flighty in despair, had gone on past the lawn.

'Ah go stop *ee, oui*,' she muttered diabolically, 'Ah go stop it, yes. This
very night.'

Soon as she got through lathering the dishes she tidied up and came
out on the front porch.

It was a humid dusk, and the glowering sky sent a species of fly –
bloody as a tick – buzzing about Jean Baptiste's porch. There he sat,
rotund, and sleepy-eyed, rocking and languidly brushing the darting imps
away.

'Wha' yo' gwine, Maffi?' asked Celestin Baptiste, fearing to wake the
old man.

'Ovah to de Jahn Chinaman shop, mum,' answered Maffi unheeding.

'Fi' what?'

'Fi' buy some wash blue, mum.'

And she kept on down the road past the Hindu kiosk to the Negro mess house.

4

'Oh, Philip,' cried Maura, 'I am so unhappy. Didn't he ask about me at all? Didn't he say he'd like to visit me – didn't he giv' yo' any message fo' me, Philip?'

The boy toyed with a blade of grass. His eyes were downcast. Sighing heavily he at last spoke. 'No, Maura, he didn't ask about you.'

'What, he didn't ask about me? Philip? I don't believe it! Oh, my God!'

She clung to Philip, mutely; her face, her breath coming warm and fast.

'I wish to God I'd never seen either of you,' cried Philip.

'Ah, but wasn't he your friend, Philip? Didn't yo' tell me that?' And the boy bowed his head sadly.

'Answer me!' she screamed, shaking him. 'Weren't you his friend?'

'Yes, Maura –'

'But you lied to me, Philip, you lied to me! You took messages from me – you brought back – lies!' Two *pearls*, large as pigeon's eggs, shone in Maura's burnished face.

'To think,' she cried in a hollow sepulchral voice, 'that I dreamed about a ghost, a man who didn't exist. Oh, God, why should I suffer like this? Why was I ever born? What did I do, what did my people do, to deserve such misery as this?'

She rose, leaving Philip with his head buried in his hands. She went into the night, tearing her hair, scratching her face, raving.

'Oh, how happy I was! I was a happy girl! I was so young and I had such merry dreams! And I wanted so little! I was carefree –'

Down to the shore of the sea she staggered, the wind behind her, the night obscuring her.

'Maura!' cried Philip, running after her. 'Maura! come back!'

Great sheaves of clouds buried the moon, and the wind bearing up from the sea bowed the cypress and palm lining the beach.

'Maura – Maura –'

He bumped into someone, a girl, black, part of the dense pattern of the tropical night.

'Maffi,' cried Philip, 'have you seen Maura down yondah?'

The girl quietly stared at him. Had Philip lost his mind?

'Talk, no!' he cried, exasperated.

And his quick tones sharpened Maffi's vocal anger. Thrusting him aside, she thundered, 'Think I'm she keeper! Go'n look fo' she yo'self. I is not she keeper! Le' me pass, move!'

Towards the end of the track he found Maura, heartrendingly weeping.

'Oh, don't cry, Maura! Never mind, Maura!'

He helped her to her feet, took her to the stand-pipe on the lawn, bathed her temples and sat soothingly, uninterruptingly, beside her.

5

At daybreak the next morning Ernest rose and woke Philip.

He yawned, put on the loincloth, seized a 'cracked licker' skillet and stole cautiously out of the house. Of late Jean Baptiste had put his foot down on his sons' copper-diving proclivities. And he kept at the head of his bed a greased cat-o'-nine-tails which he would use on Philip himself if the occasion warranted.

'Come on, Philip, let's go –'

Yawning and scratching, Philip followed. The grass on the lawn was bright and icy with the dew. On the railroad tracks the six o'clock labor trains were coupling. A rosy mist flooded the dawn. Out in the stream the tug *Exotic* snorted in a heavy fog.

On the wharf Philip led the way to the rafters below.

'Look out fo' that *crapeau*, Ernest, don't step on him, he'll spit on you.'

The frog splashed into the water. Prickle-backed crabs and oysters and myriad other shells spawned on the rotting piles. The boys paddled the boat. Out in the dawn ahead of them the tug puffed a path through the foggy mist. The water was chilly. Mist glistened on top of it. Far out, beyond the buoys, Philip encountered a placid, untroubled sea. The liner, a German tourist boat, was loaded to the bridge. The water was as still as a lake of ice.

'All right, Ernest, let's hurry – '

Philip drew in the oars. The *Kron Prinz Wilhelm* came near. Huddled in thick European coats, the passengers viewed from their lofty estate the spectacle of two naked Negro boys peeping up at them from a wiggly *bateau*.

'Penny, mistah, penny, mistah!'

Somebody dropped a quarter. Ernest, like a shot, flew after it. Half a foot down he caught it as it twisted and turned in the gleaming sea. Vivified by the icy dip, Ernest was a raving wolf and the folk aboard dealt a lavish hand.

'Ovah, yah, mistah,' cried Philip, 'ovah, yah.'

For a Dutch guilder Philip gave an exhibition of 'cork'. Under something of a ledge on the side of the boat he had stuck a piece of cork. Now, after his and Ernest's mouths were full of coins, he could afford to be extravagant and treat the Europeans to a game of West Indian 'cork'.

Roughly ramming the cork down in the water, Philip, after the fifteenth ram or so, let it go, and flew back, upwards, having thus 'lost' it. It was Ernest's turn now, as a sort of end-man, to scramble forward to the spot where Philip had dug it down and 'find' it; the first one to do so, having the prerogative, which he jealously guarded, of raining on the other a series of thundering leg blows. As boys in the West Indies Philip and Ernest had played it. Of a Sunday the Negro fishermen on the Barbados coast made a pagan rite of it. Many a Bluetown dandy got his spine cracked in a game of 'cork'.

With a passive interest the passengers viewed the proceedings. In a game of 'cork', the cork after a succession of 'rammings' is likely to drift many feet away whence it was first 'lost'. One had to be an expert, quick, alert, to spy and promptly seize it as it popped up on the rolling waves. Once Ernest got it and endeavored to make much of the possession. But Philip, besides being two feet taller than he, was slippery as an eel, and Ernest, despite all the artful ingenuity at his command, was able to do no more than ineffectively beat the water about him. Again and again he tried, but to no purpose.

Becoming reckless, he let the cork drift too far away from him and Philip seized it.

He twirled it in the air like a crap shooter, and dug deep down in the water with it, 'lost' it, then leaped back, briskly waiting for it to rise.

About them the water, due to the ramming and beating, grew restive. Billows sprang up; soaring, swelling waves sent the skiff nearer the shore. Anxiously Philip and Ernest watched for the cork to make its ascent.

It was all a bit vague to the whites on the deck, and an amused chuckle floated down to the boys.

And still the cork failed to come up.

'I'll go after it,' said Philip at last, 'I'll go and fetch it.' And, from the edge of the boat he leaped, his body long and resplendent in the rising tropic sun.

It was a suction sea, and down in it Philip plunged. And it was lazy, too, and wilful – the water. Ebony-black, it tugged and mocked. Old brass staves – junk dumped there by the retiring French – thick, yawping mud, barrel hoops, tons of obsolete brass, a wealth of slimy steel faced him. Did a 'rammed' cork ever go that deep?

And the water, stirring, rising, drew a haze over Philip's eyes. Had a cuttlefish, an octopus, a nest of eels been routed? It seemed so to Philip, blindly diving, pawing. And the sea, the tide – touching the roots of Deathpool – tugged and tugged. His gathering hands stuck in mud. Iron staves bruised his shins. It was black down there. Impenetrable.

Suddenly, like a flash of lightning, a vision blew across Philip's brow. It was a soaring shark's belly. Drunk on the nectar of the deep, it soared above Philip – rolling, tumbling, rolling. It had followed the boy's scent with the accuracy of a diver's rope.

Scrambling to the surface, Philip struck out for the boat. But the sea, the depths of it wrested out of an aeon's slumber, had sent it a mile from his diving point. And now, as his strength ebbed, a shark was at his heels.

'Shark! Shark!' was the cry that went up from the ship.

Hewing a lane through the hostile sea Philip forgot the cunning of the doddering beast and swam noisier than he needed to. Faster grew his strokes. His line was a straight, dead one. Fancy strokes and dives – giraffe leaps . . . he summoned into play. He shot out recklessly. One time he suddenly paused – and floated for a stretch. Another time he swam on his back, gazing at the chalky sky. He dived for whole lengths.

But the shark, a bloaty, stone-coloured mankiller, took a shorter cut. Circumnavigating the swimmer, it bore down upon him with the speed of a hurricane. Within adequate reach it turned, showed its gleaming belly, seizing its prey.

A fiendish gargle – the gnashing of bones – as the sea once more closed its jaws on Philip.

Some one aboard ship screamed. Women fainted. There was talk of a gun. Ernest, an oar upraised, capsized the boat as he tried to inflict a blow on the coursing, chop-licking maneater.

And again the fish turned. It scraped the waters with its deadly fins.

At Coco Té, at the fledging of the dawn, Maffi, polishing the tinware, hummed an obeah melody

> 'Trinidad is a damn fine place
> But obeah down dey . . .'

Peace had come to her at last.

C. L. R. JAMES

Triumph

*Where people in England and America say slums, Trinidadians say barrack-yards.
Probably the word is a relic of the days when England relied as much on garrisons
of soldiers as on her fleet to protect her valuable sugar-producing colonies. Every street
in Port-of-Spain proper can show you numerous examples of the type: a narrow
gateway leading into a fairly big yard, on either side of which run long low buildings,
consisting of anything from four to eighteen rooms, each about twelve feet square. In
these live, and have always lived, the porters, prostitutes, carter-men, washerwomen,
and domestic servants of the city.*

*In one corner of the yard is the hopelessly inadequate water-closet, unmistakable
to the nose if not to the eye; sometimes there is a structure with the title of bathroom:
a courtesy title, for he or she who would wash in it with decent privacy must cover
the person as if bathing on the Lido; the kitchen happily presents no difficulty: never
is there one and each barrack-yarder cooks before her door. In the centre of the yard is
a heap of stones. On these the half-laundered clothes are bleached before being finally
spread out to dry on the wire lines which in every yard cross and recross each other
in all directions. Not only to Minerva have these stones been dedicated. Time was
when they would have had an honoured shrine in a local temple to Mars, for they
were the major source of ammunition for the homicidal strife which in times past so
often flared up in barrack-yards. As late as 1915, the local bard, practising his band
for the annual carnival (which still flourishes in Trinidad alone of the British West
Indian islands) – as late as 1915 he could sing:*

> *'When the rumour went round the town*
> *That the Germans was comin' to blow us down,*
> *When the rumour went round the town*
> *That the Germans was comin' to blow us down,*
> *Some like cowards remain at home*

> *Others come forth with bottle and stone*
> *Old lady couldn't bring stone but she come with the pot-chambre.'*

The stones from 'the bleach' were to help even in the repelling of the German invader. A poetic idea, and as is not uncommon with poetry, an anachronism. No longer do the barrack-yarders live the picturesque life of twenty-five years ago. Then, practising for the carnival, rival singers, Willie, Jean, and Freddie, porter, wharf-man, or loafer, in ordinary life, but for that season ennobled by some such striking sobriquet as The Duke of Normandy or The Lord Invincible, and carrying with dignity homage such as young aspirants to literature would pay Mr Kipling or Mr Shaw, thirty years ago. They sang in competition from seven in the evening until far into the early morning, stimulated by the applause of their listeners and the excellence and copiousness of the rum; night after night the stick-men practised their dangerous and skilful game; the 'pierrots', after elaborate preface of complimentary speech, belaboured each other with riding whips; while around the performers the spectators pressed thick and good-humoured, until mimic warfare was transformed into real, and stones from 'the bleach' flew thick. But today that life is dead. All carnival practice must cease at ten o'clock. The policeman is to the stick-fighter and 'pierrot' as the sanitary inspector to mosquito larvae. At nights the streets are bright with electric light, the arm of the law is longer, its grip stronger. Gone are the old lawlessness and picturesqueness. Barrack-yard life has lost its savour. Luckily, prohibition in Trinidad is still but a word. And life, dull and drab as it is in comparison, can still offer its great moments.

On a Sunday morning in one of the rooms of a barrack in Abercromby Street sat Mamitz. Accustomed as is squalid adversity to reign unchallenged in these quarters, yet in this room it was more than usually triumphant, sitting, as it were, high on a throne of royal state, so depressed was the woman and depressing her surroundings.

The only representatives of the brighter side of life were three full-page pictures torn from illustrated periodicals, photographs of Lindbergh, Bernard Shaw, and Sargent's 'Portrait of a Woman', and these owed their presence solely to the fact that no pawnshop would have accepted them. They looked with unseeing eyes upon a room devoid of furniture save for a few bags spread upon the floor to form a bed. Mamitz sat on the doorstep talking to, or rather being talked to, by her friend

Celestine who stood astride the concrete canal which ran in front of the door.

'Somebody do you something,' said Celestine with conviction. 'Nobody goin' to change my mind from that. An' if you do what I tell you, you will t'row off this black spirit that on you. A nice woman like you, and you carn' get a man to keep you! You carn' get nothing to do!'

Mamitz said nothing. Had Celestine said the exact opposite, Mamitz's reply would have been the same.

She was a black woman, too black to be pure negro, probably with some Madrasi East Indian blood in her, a suspicion which was made a certainty by the long thick plaits of her plentiful hair. She was shortish and fat, voluptuously developed, tremendously developed, and as a creole loves development in a woman more than any other extraneous allure, Mamitz (like the rest of her sex in all stations of life) saw to it when she moved that you missed none of her charms. But for the last nine weeks she had been 'in derricks', to use Celestine's phrase. First of all the tram conductor who used to keep her (seven dollars every Saturday night, out of which Mamitz usually got three) had accused her of infidelity and beaten her. Neither the accusation nor the beating had worried Mamitz. To her and her type those were minor incidents of existence; from their knowledge of life and men, the kept woman's inevitable fate. But after a temporary reconciliation he had beaten her once more, very badly indeed, and then left her. Even this was not an irremediable catastrophe. But thenceforward, Mamitz, from being the most prosperous woman in the yard, had sunk gradually to being the most destitute. Despite her very obvious attractions, no man took notice of her. She went out asking for washing or for work as a cook. No success. Luckily, in the days of her prosperity, she had been generous to Celestine, who now kept her from actual starvation. One stroke of luck she had had. The agent for the barracks had suddenly taken a fancy to her, and Mamitz had not found it difficult to persuade him to give her a chance with the rent. But that respite was over; he was pressing for the money, and Mamitz had neither money to pay nor hope of refuge when she was turned out. Celestine would have taken her in, but Celestine's keeper was a policeman who visited her three or four nights a week, and to one in that position a fifteen-foot room does not offer much scope for housing the homeless. Yet Celestine was grieved that she could do nothing to help Mamitz in her troubles, which she attributed to the evil and supernatural machinations of Irene, their common enemy.

'Take it from me, that woman do you something. I's she put Nathan against you. When was the quarrel again?'

'It was two or three days after Nathan gave me the first beating.'

Nathan then had started on his evil courses before the quarrel with Irene took place, but Celestine brushed away that objection.

'She must 'a' had it in her mind for you from before. You didn't see how she fly out at you? ... As long as you livin' here an' I cookin' I wouldn' see you want a cup o' tea an' a spoonful o' rice. But I carn' help with the rent ... An' you ain' have nobody here!'

Mamitz shook her head. She was from Demerara.

'If you could only cross the sea − that will cut any spirit that on you ... Look the animal!'

Irene had come out of her room on the opposite side of the yard. She could not fail to see Celestine and Mamitz and she called loudly to a neighbour lower down the yard:

'Hey Jo-Jo? What is the time? Ten o'clock a'ready? Le' me start to cook me chicken, that me man buy for me − even if 'e have a so' foot ... I don't know how long it will last, before 'e get drunk and kick me out o' here. Then I will have to go dawgin' round other po' people to see if I could pick up what they t'row 'way.'

She fixed a box in front of her door, put her coal-pot on it, and started to attend to her chicken.

Sunday morning in barrack-yards is pot-parade. Of the sixteen tenants in the yard twelve had their pots out, and they lifted the meat with long iron forks to turn it, or threw water into the pot so that it steamed to the heavens and every woman could tell what her neighbour was cooking − beef, or pork, or chicken. It didn't matter what you cooked in the week, it didn't matter if you didn't cook at all. But to cook salt-fish, or ribs, or hog-head, or pig-tail on a Sunday morning was a disgrace. You put your pot inside your house and cooked it there.

Mamitz, fat, easy-going, and cowed by many days of semi-starvation, took little notice of Irene. But Celestine, a thin little whip of a brown-skinned woman, bubbled over with repressed rage.

'By Christ, if it wasn't for one thing I'd rip every piece o' clothes she have on off 'er.'

'Don' bother wid 'er. What is the use o' gettin' you'self in trouble with Jimmy?'

Jimmy was the policeman. He was a steady, reliable man but he believed in discipline, and when he spoke, he spoke. He had made Celestine understand that she was not to fight: he wasn't going to find himself mixed up in court as the keeper of any brawling woman. Celestine's wrath, deprived of its natural outlet, burned none the less implacably.

'I tell you something, Mamitz. I goin' to talk to the agent in the mornin'. I goin' to tell 'im to give you to the end o' the month. I's only five days ... I goin' to give you a bath. Try an' see if you could get some gully-root and so on this afternoon ... Tonight I g'on' give you ... An' I will give you some prayers to read. God stronger than the devil. We g'on' break this t'ing that on you. Cheer up. I g'on' send you a plate with you' chicken an' rice as soon as it finish. Meanwhile, burn you' little candle, say you' little prayers, console you' little mind. I g'on' give you that bath tonight. You ain' kill priest. You ain' cuss you' mudder. So you ain' have cause to 'fraid nothin'.'

Celestine would never trust herself to indulge in abuse with Irene; the chances that it would end in a fight were too great. So she contented herself with casting a look of the most murderous hate and scorn and defiance at her enemy, and then went to her own pot which was calling for attention.

And yet three months before, Mamitz, Celestine, and Irene had been good friends. They shared their rum and their joys and troubles together; and on Sunday afternoons they used to sit before Mamitz's room singing hymns: 'Abide with me', 'Jesu, lover of my soul', 'Onward! Christian soldiers'. Celestine and Irene sang soprano and Irene sang well. Mamitz was a naturally fine contralto and had a fine ear, while Nathan, who was a Barbadian and consequently knew vocal music, used to sing bass whenever he happened to be in. The singing would put him in a good mood and he would send off to buy more rum and everything would be peaceful and happy. But Irene was a jealous woman, not only jealous of her man, but jealous of Mamitz's steady three dollars a week and

Celestine's policeman with his twenty-eight dollars at the end of the month. She lived with a cabman whose income, though good enough, was irregular. And he was a married man, with a wife and children to support. Irene had to do washing to help her out, while Mamitz and Celestine did nothing, merely cooked and washed clothes for their men. So gradually a state of dissatisfaction arose. Then one damp evening, Mamitz passing near the bamboo pole which supported a clothes-line overburdened with Irene's clothes, brought it down with her broad expansive person. The line burst, and nightgowns, sheets, pillowcases, white suits, and tablecloths fluttered to the mud. It had been a rainy week with little sun, and already it would have been difficult to get the clothes ready in time for Saturday morning; after this it was impossible. And hot and fiery was the altercation. Celestine who tried to make peace was drawn into the quarrel by Irene's comprehensive and incendiary invective.

'You comin' to put you' mouth in this. You think because you livin' with a policeman you is a magistrate. Mind you' business, woman, mind you' business. The two o' all you don't do nothing for you' livin'. You only sittin' down an' eatin' out the men all you livin' wid. An' I wo'k so hard an' put out me clo'es on the line. And this one like some blame cab-horse knock it down, and when I tell 'er about it you comin' to meddle! Le' me tell you . . .'

So the wordy warfare raged, Celestine's policeman coming in for rough treatment at the tongue of Irene. Celestine, even though she was keeping herself in check, was a match for any barrack-yard woman Port-of-Spain could produce, but yet it was Mamitz who clinched the victory.

'Don't min' Celestine livin' with a policeman. You will be glad to get 'im for you'self. An' it better than livin' wid any stinkin' so'-foot man.'

For Irene's cabman had a sore on his foot, which he had had for thirty years and would carry with him to the grave even if he lived for thirty years more. Syphilis, congenital and acquired, and his copious boozing would see to it that there was no recovery. Irene had stupidly hoped that nobody in the yard knew. But in Trinidad when His Excellency the Governor and his wife have a quarrel, the street boys speak of it the day after, and Richard's bad foot had long been a secret topic of conversation in the yard. But it was Mamitz who had made it public property, and Irene hated Mamitz with a virulent hatred, and had promised to 'do' for her. Three days before, Nathan, the tram-conductor, had given Mamitz the first beating; but even at the time of the quarrel there was no hint of his swift defection and Mamitz's rapid descent to her present plight. So that Celestine, an errant but staunch religionist, was convinced that Mamitz's troubles were due to Irene's trafficking with the devil, if not personally, at least through one of his numerous agents who ply their profitable trade in every part of Port-of-Spain. Secure of her own immunity from anything that Irene might 'put on her', she daily regretted that she couldn't rip the woman to pieces. 'Oh Jesus! If it wasn't for Jimmy I'd tear the wretch lim' from lim'.' But the energy that she could not put into the destruction of Irene she spent in upholding Mamitz. The fiery Celestine had a real affection for the placid Mamitz, whose quiet ways were so soothing. But, more than this, she was determined not to see Mamitz go down. In the bitter antagonism she nursed against Irene, it would have been a galling defeat if Mamitz went to the wall. Further, her reputation as a woman who knew things and could put crooked people straight was at stake. Once she had seen to Jimmy's food and clothes and creature comforts, she set herself to devise ways and means of supporting the weak, easily crushed Mamitz.

Celestine's policeman being on duty that night, she herself was off duty and free to attend to her own affairs. At midnight with the necessary rites and ceremonies, Ave Marias and Pater Nosters, she bathed Mamitz in a large bath-pan full of water prepared with gully-root, fever-grass, lime leaves, guérir tout, herbe à femmes, and other roots, leaves, and grasses noted for their efficacy (when properly applied), against malign plots and influences. That was at twelve o'clock the Sunday night. On Monday morning at eight o'clock behold Popo des Vignes walking into the yard, with a little bag in his hand.

Popo is a creole of creoles. His name is des Vignes, but do not be misled into thinking that there flows in his veins blood of those aristocrats who found their way to Trinidad after '89. He is a negro, and, as like as not, one of his great-grandfathers (who, it is chronologically certain, began life as a slave) adapted the name from his master. Popo is nearing forty, medium-sized, though large about the stomach, with a longish moustache. He is dressed in a spotless suit of white, with tight-fitting shoes of a particularly yellowish brown (no heavy English brogues or fantastic American shoes for him). On his head he wears his straw hat at a jaunty angle, and his manner of smoking his cigarette and his jacket always flying open (he wears no waistcoat) will give the impression that Popo is a man of pleasure rather than a man of work. And that impression would be right. He has never done a week's honest work in his life. He can get thirty dollars for you if you are in difficulties (at one hundred and twenty per cent, first month's interest and his commission taken out in advance); or three thousand dollars if you have a house or a cocoa-estate. During the cocoa crop he lurks by the railway station with an unerring eye for peasant proprietors who have brought their cocoa into town and are not quite certain where they will get the best price. This is his most profitable business, for he gets commission both from the proprietors and from the big buyers. But he is not fastidious as to how he makes money, and will do anything that does not bind him down, and leaves him free of manual or clerical labour. For the rest, after he has had a good meal at about half-past seven in the evening he can drink rum until six o'clock the next morning without turning a hair; and in his own circle he has a wide reputation for his connoisseurship in matters of love and his catholicity of taste in women.

'Eh Mr des Vignes! How you?' said Celestine. The inhabitants of every barrack-yard, especially the women, knew Popo.

'Keeping fine.'

'Who you lookin' for roun' this way?'

'I came round to see you. How is Jimmy? When you getting married?'

'Married!' said Celestine with fine scorn. 'Me married a police! I wouldn't trust a police further than I could smell him. Police ain' have no regard. A police will lock up 'is mudder to get a stripe. An' besides I ain' want to married nobody. If I married I go'n' have the man in the house all the time, he go'n' want to treat me as 'e like. I go'n' be a perfec' slave. I all right as I be.'

'Anyway, I want you to buy a ring.'

'Rings you sellin' in that bag? I ain' have no money, but le' me see them.'

Popo opened his bag and displayed the rings — beautiful gold of American workmanship, five dollars cash and six dollars on terms. They had cost an Assyrian merchant in Park Street ten dollars the dozen, and Popo was selling them on commission. He was doing good business, especially with those who paid two dollars down and gave promises of monthly or weekly instalments. If later the merchant saw trouble to collect his instalments or to get back his rings, that wouldn't worry Popo much for by that time he would have chucked up this job.

'So you wouldn't take one,' said he, getting ready to put away his treasures again.

'Come roun' at the end o' the month. But don' shut them up yet. I have a friend I want to see them.'

She went to the door.

'Mamitz!' she called. 'Come see some rings Mr des Vignes sellin'.'

Mamitz came into Celestine's room, large, slow-moving, voluptuous, with her thick, smooth hair neatly plaited and her black skin shining. She took Popo's fancy at once.

'But you have a nice friend, Celestine,' said Popo. 'And she has a nice name too: Mamitz! Well, how many rings you are going to buy from me?'

Celestine answered quickly: 'Mamitz can't buy no rings. The man who was keepin' her, they fall out, an' she lookin' for a husband now.'

'A nice woman like you can't stay long without a husband,' said des Vignes. 'Let me give you some luck ... Choose a ring and I will make you a present.'

Mamitz chose a ring and des Vignes put it on her finger himself.

'Excuse me, I comin' back now,' said Celestine. 'The sanitary inspector comin' jest now, an' I want to clean up some rubbish before 'e come.'

When she came back des Vignes was just going.

'I will see you again, Celestine,' he said. 'So long, Mamitz!'

He was hardly out of earshot when Celestine excitedly tackled Mamitz. 'What 'e tell you?'

' 'E say that 'e comin' round here about ten o'clock tonight or little later ... An' 'e give me this.' In her palm reposed a red two-dollar note.

'You see what I tell you?' said Celestine triumphantly. 'That bath. But don' stop. Read the prayers three times a day for nine days ... Buy some stout, Mitz, to nourish up you'self ...'E ain't a man you could depend on. If you dress a broomstick in a petticoat 'e will run after it.

But you goin' to get something out o' 'im for a few weeks or so . . . An' you can see 'e is a nice man.'

Mamitz smiled her lazy smile.

Celestine knew her man. For four weeks Popo was a more or less regular visitor to Mamitz's room. He paid the rent, he gave her money to get her bed and other furniture out of the pawnshop, and every Sunday morning Mamitz was stirring beef or pork or chicken in her pot. More than that, whenever Popo said he was coming to see her, he gave her money to prepare a meal so that sometimes late in the week, on a Thursday night, Mamitz's pot smelt as if it was Sunday morning. Celestine shared in the prosperity and they could afford to take small notice of Irene who prophesied early disaster.

'All you flourishin' now. But wait little bit. I know that Popo des Vignes well. 'E don' knock round a woman no more than a month. Just now all that high livin' go'n' shut down an' I go'n' see you Mamitz eatin' straw.'

But Mamitz grew fatter than ever, and when she walked down the road in a fugi silk dress, tight-fitting and short, which exposed her noble calves to the knee and accentuated the amplitude of her person, she created a sensation among those men who took notice of her.

One Sunday morning she went into the market to buy beef. She was passing along the stalls going to the man she always bought from, when a butcher called out to her:

'Hey, Mamitz! Come this way.'

Mamitz went. She didn't know the man, but she was of an acquiescent nature and she went to see what he wanted.

'But I don't know you,' she said, after looking at him. 'Where you know my name?'

'Ain't was you walkin' down Abercromby Street last Sunday in a white silk dress?'

'Yes,' smiled Mamitz.

'Well, I know a nice woman when I see one. An' I find out where you livin' too. Ain't you livin' in the barrack just below Park Street? . . . Girl, you did look too sweet. You mustn't buy beef from nobody but me. How much you want? A pound? Look a nice piece. Don't worry to pay me for that. You could pay me later. Whenever you want beef, come round this way.'

Mamitz accepted and went. She didn't like the butcher too much, but he liked her. And a pound of beef was a pound of beef. Nicholas came to see her a day or two after and brought two pints of stout as a present. At first Mamitz didn't bother with him. But when Nicholas found out that a dangerous man like Popo des Vignes was his rival, he made Mamitz extravagant presents and promises. What helped him was that Popo now began to slack off. A week could pass and Mamitz would not see him. And no more money was forthcoming. So after a while she accepted Nicholas, and had no cause to regret her bargain. Nicholas made a lot of money as a butcher. He not only paid the rent, but gave her five dollars every Saturday night, and she could always get a dollar or two out of him during the week. Before long he loved her to distraction, and was given to violent fits of jealousy which, however, were always followed by repentance and lavish presents. Still Mamitz hankered after Popo. One day she wrote him a little note telling him that she was sorry she had to accept Nicholas but that she would be glad to see him any time he came round. She sent it to the Miranda Hotel where Popo took his meals. But no answer came and after a while Mamitz ceased actively to wish to see Popo. She was prosperous and pretty happy. She and Celestine were thicker than ever, and were on good terms with the neighbours in the yard. Only Irene, they knew, would do them mischief, and on the mornings when Mamitz got up, on Celestine's advice, she looked carefully before the door lest she should unwittingly set foot on any churchyard bones, deadly powders, or other satanic agencies guaranteed to make the victim go mad, and steal or commit those breaches of good conduct which are punishable by law. But nothing untoward happened. As Celestine pointed out to Mamitz, the power of the bath held good, 'and as for me,' concluded she, 'no powers Irene can handle can touch my little finger'.

Easter Saturday came, and with it came Popo. He walked into the yard early, about seven in the morning, and knocked up Mamitz who was still sleeping.

'I t'ought you had given me up for good,' said Mamitz. 'I write you and you didn't answer.'

'I didn't want any butcher to stick me with his knife,' laughed Popo, 'Anyway, that is all right . . . I was playing baccarat last night and I made a good haul, so I've come to spend Easter with you. Look! Here is five dollars. Buy salt-fish and sweet oil and some greens and tomatoes. Buy about eight pints of rum. And some stout for yourself. I am coming back about nine o'clock. Today is Easter Saturday. Nicholas is going to be in the market the whole day. Don't be afraid for him.'

Mamitz became excited. She gave the five dollars to Celestine and put her in charge of the catering, while she prepared for her lover. At about half-past nine Popo returned. He, Mamitz and Celestine ate in Mamitz's room and, before they got up from the table, much more than a bottle of rum had disappeared. Then Celestine left them and went to the market to Nicholas. She told him that Mamitz wasn't feeling too well and had sent for beef and pork. The willing Nicholas handed over the stuff and sent a shilling for his lady love. He said he was rather short of money but at the end of the day he was going to make a big draw. Celestine cooked, and at about half-past one, she, Popo and Mamitz had breakfast – the midday meal. After breakfast Celestine had to go out again and buy more rum. The other people in the yard didn't take much notice of what was an everyday occurrence, were rather pleased in fact, for after breakfast Celestine had a bottle and a half of rum to herself, and ostentatiously invited all the neighbours to have drinks, all, of course, except Irene.

At about three o'clock Irene felt that she could bear it no longer and that if she didn't take this chance it would be throwing away a gift from God. She put on her shoes, took her basket on her arm, and left the yard. It was the basket that aroused the observant Celestine's suspicions for she knew that Irene had already done all her shopping that morning. She sat thinking for a few seconds, then she knocked at Mamitz's door.

'Look here, Mamitz,' she called. 'It's time for Mr des Vignes to go. Irene just gone out with a basket. I think she gone to the market to tell Nicholas.'

'But he can't get away today,' called Mamitz.

'You know how the man jealous and how 'e bad,' persisted Celestine. 'Since nine o'clock Mr des Vignes been here. He can come back another day ... Mr des Vignes, i's time for you to go.'

Celestine's wise counsel prevailed. Popo dressed himself with his usual scrupulous neatness and cleared off. The rum bottles were put out of the way and Mamitz's room was made tidy. She and Celestine had hardly finished when Irene appeared with the basket empty.

'You see,' said Celestine; 'now, look out!'

Sure enough, it wasn't five minutes after when a cab drew up outside, and Nicholas, still in his bloody butcher's apron, came hot foot into the yard. He went straight up to Mamitz and seized her by the throat.

'Where the hell is that man you had in the room with you – the room I payin' rent for?'

'Don't talk dam foolishness man, le'me go,' said Mamitz.

'I will stick my knife into you as I will stick it in a cow. You had Popo des Vignes in that room for the whole day. Speak the truth, you dog.'

'You' mother, you' sister, you' aunt, you' wife was the dog,' shrieked Mamitz, quoting one of Celestine's most brilliant pieces of repartee.

'It's the wo'se when you meddle with them common low-island people,' said Celestine. Nicholas was from St Vincent, and negroes from St Vincent, Grenada, and the smaller West Indian islands are looked down upon by the Trinidad negro as low-island people.

'You shut you' blasted mouth and don' meddle with what don't concern you. It's you encouragin' the woman. I want the truth, or by Christ I'll make a beef o' one o' you here today.'

'Look here, man. Le'me tell you something.' Mamitz, drunk with love and rum and inspired by Celestine, was showing some spirit. 'That woman over there come and tell you that Mr des Vignes was in this room. The man come in the yard but 'e come to Celestine to sell 'er a ring she did promise to buy from 'im long time. Look in me room,' she flung the half-doors wide; 'you see any signs of any man in there? Me bed look as if any man been lyin' down on it? But I had no right to meddle with a low brute like you. You been botherin' me long enough. Go live with Irene. Go share she wid she so'-foot cabman. I's woman like she men like you want. I sorry the day I ever see you. An' I hope I never see you' face again.'

She stopped, panting, and Celestine who had only been waiting for an opening, took up the tale.

'But look the man! The man leave 'is work this bright Easter Saturday because this nasty woman go and tell you that Mr des Vignes in the room with Mamitz! Next thing you go'n' say that 'e livin' with me. But man, I never see such a' ass as you. Bertha, Olive, Josephine,' she appealed to some of the other inhabitants of the yard. 'Ain't all you been here the whole day an' see Mr des Vignes come here after breakfast? I pay 'im two dollars I had for 'im. 'E sen' an' buy a pint o' rum an' I call Mamitz for the three o' we to fire a little liquor for the Easter. Next thing I see is this one goin' out – to carry news; and now this Vincelonian fool leave 'e wo'k. – But, man, you drunk.'

Bertha, Olive and Josephine, who had shared in the rum, confirmed Celestine's statement. Irene had been sitting at the door of her room cleaning fish and pretending to take no notice, but at this she jumped up.

'Bertha, you ought to be ashame' o' you'self. For a drink o' rum you lyin' like that? Don't believe them Nicholas. Whole day – ' But here occurred an unlooked-for interruption. The cabby, hearing the altercation and not wishing to lose time on a day like Easter Saturday, had put a little boy in charge of his horse and had been listening for a minute or two. He now approached and held Nicholas by the arm.

'Boss,' he said, 'don't listen to that woman. She livin' with Richard the cabman an' 'e tell me that all women does lie but 'e never hear or know none that does lie like she – '

There was a burst of laughter.

'Come go, boss,' said the cabby, pulling the not unwilling Nicholas by the arm.

'I have to go back to my work, but I am comin' back tonight an' I am goin' to lick the stuffin' out o' you.'

'An' my man is a policeman,' said Celestine. 'An' he goin' to be here tonight. An' if you touch this woman you spend you' Easter in the lock-up sure as my name is Celestine an' you are a good-for-nothing Vincelonian fool of a butcher.'

Nicholas drove away, leaving Celestine mistress of the field, but for the rest of the afternoon Mamitz was depressed. She was tired out with the day's excitement; and after all Nicholas had good money. On a night like this he would be drawing quite a lot of money. And now it seemed that she was in danger of losing him. She knew how he hated Popo.

She liked Popo more than Nicholas, much more, but after all people
had to live.

Celestine, however, was undaunted. 'Don't min' what 'e say. 'E comin'
back. 'E comin' back to beg. When you see a man love a woman like
he love you, she could treat 'im how she like, 'e still comin' back, like
a dog to eat 'is vomit. But you listen to me, Mamitz. When 'e come
back cuss 'im a little bit. Cuss 'im plenty. Make 'im see that you ain't
goin' to stand too much nonsense from 'im.'

Mamitz smiled in her sleepy way, but she was not hopeful. And all
the rest of the afternoon Irene worried her by singing ballads appropriate
to the occasion.

> 'Though you belong to somebody else
> Tonight you belong to me.'

> 'Come, come, come to me, Thora,
> Come once again and be . . .'

> 'How can I live without you!
> How can I let you go!'

Her voice soared shrill over the babel of clattering tongues in the
yard. And as the voice rose Mamitz's heart sank.

'Don't forget,' were Celestine's last words before they parted for the
night. 'If 'e come back tonight, don't open the door for 'im straight. Le'
'im knock a little bit.'

'All right,' said Mamitz dully. She was thinking that she had only about
thirty-six cents left over from the money des Vignes had given her. Not
another cent.

But Celestine was right. The enraged Nicholas went back to work and
cut beef and sawed bones with a ferocity that astonished his fellow
butchers and purchasers. But at seven o'clock, with his pocket full of
money and nothing to do he felt miserable. He had made his plans for
the Easter. Saturday night he had decided to spend with Mamitz and all
Easter Sunday after he knocked off at nine in the morning. Easter
Monday he had for himself and he had been thinking of taking Mamitz,
Celestine, and Jimmy down to Carenage in a taxi to bathe. He mooned
about the streets for a time. He took two or three drinks but he didn't

feel in the mood for running a spree and getting drunk. He was tired from the strain of the day and he felt for the restful company of a woman, especially the woman he loved – the good-looking, fat, agreeable Mamitz. At about half-past ten he found his resolution never to look at her again wavering.

'Damn it,' he said to himself. 'That woman Irene is a liar. She see how I am treatin' Mamitz well and she want to break up the livin'.'

He fought the question out with himself.

'But the woman couldn't lie like that. The man must 'a been there.'

He was undecided. He went over the arguments for and against the testimony of Bertha and Olive, the testimony of the cabman. His reason inclined him to believe that Mamitz had been entertaining des Vignes for the whole day in the room he was paying for; while he, the fool, was working hard for money to carry to her. But stronger powers than reason were fighting for Mamitz, and eleven o'clock found him in the yard knocking at the door.

'Mamitz! Mamitz! Open. I's me – Nicholas.' There was a slight pause. Then he heard Mamitz's voice, sounding a little strange.

'What the devil you want! . . . Man, go 'way from me door.'

'I sorry for what happen today. I's that meddlin' woman Irene. She come to the market an' she lie on you. Open the door, Mamitz . . . I have something here for you.'

Celestine next door was listening closely, pleased that Mamitz was proving herself so obedient to instructions.

'Man, I 'fraid you. You have a knife out there an' you come here to cut me up as Gurrie cut up Eva.'

'I have no knife. I brought some money for you.'

'I don't believe you . . . you want to treat me as if I'm a cow.'

'I tell you I have no knife . . . Open the door, woman, or I'll break it in. You carn' treat me like that.'

Nicholas's temper was getting the better of him: he hadn't expected this.

The watchful Celestine here interfered.

'Open the door for the man, Mamitz. 'E say 'e beg pardon. And, after all, i's he payin' the rent.'

So Mamitz very willingly opened the door and Nicholas went in. He left early the next morning to go to work but he promised Mamitz to be back by half-past nine.

Irene, about her daily business in the yard, gathered that Nicholas had come dawgin' back to Mamitz the night before and Mamitz was drivin' 'im dog and lance, but Celestine beg for 'im and Mamitz let 'im come in. Mamitz, she noticed, got up that morning much later than usual. In fact Celestine (who was always up at five o'clock) knocked her up and went into the room before she came out. It was not long before Irene knew that something was afoot. First of all Mamitz never opened her door as usual, but slipped in and out closing it after her. Neither she nor Celestine went to market. They sent out Bertha's little sister who returned with beef and pork and mutton, each piece of which Mamitz held up high in the air and commented upon. Then Bertha's sister went out again and returned with a new coal-pot. Irene could guess where it came from – some little store in Charlotte Street probably, whose owner was not afraid to run the risk of selling on Sundays. In and out the yard went Bertha's little sister, and going and coming she clutched something tightly in her hand. Irene, her senses tuned by resentment and hate to their highest pitch, could not make out what was happening. Meanwhile Celestine was inside Mamitz's room, and Mamitz, outside, had started to cook – in three coal-pots. Every minute or so Mamitz would poke her head inside the room and talk to Celestine. Irene could see Mamitz shaking her fat self with laughter while she could hear Celestine's shrill cackle inside. Then Bertha's sister returned for the last time and after going into the room to deliver whatever her message was, came and stood a few yards away, opposite Mamitz's door, expectantly waiting. Think as she would, Irene could form no idea as to what was going on inside.

Then Mamitz went and stood near to Bertha's sister, and, a second after, the two halves of the door were flung open and Irene saw Celestine standing in the doorway with arms akimbo. But there was nothing to – and then she saw. Both halves of the door were plastered with notes, green five-dollar notes, red two-dollar notes and blue dollar notes, with a pin at the corner of each note to keep it firm. The pin-heads were shining in the sun. Irene was so flabbergasted that for a second or two she stood with her mouth open. Money Nicholas had given Mamitz. Nicholas had come back and begged pardon, and given her all this money. The fool! So that was what Celestine had been doing inside there all the time. Bertha's sister had been running up and down to get some of the notes changed. There must be about forty, no, fifty dollars, more spread out on the door. Mamitz and Bertha's sister were sinking with laughing, and the joke was spreading, for other people in the yard were going up to see what the disturbance was about. What a blind fool that Nicholas was! Tears of rage and mortification rushed to Irene's eyes.

'Hey, Irene, come see a picture what Nicholas bring for Mamitz last night! An' tomorrow we goin' to Carenage. We don't want you, but we will carry you' husband. The sea water will do 'is so' foot good.' Celestine's voice rang across the yard.

Bertha, Josephine, the fat Mamitz and the rest were laughing so that they could hardly hold themselves up. Irene could find neither spirit nor voice to reply. She trembled so that her hands shook. The china bowl in which she was washing rice slipped from her fingers and broke into half a dozen pieces, while the rice streamed into the dirty water of the canal.

Look Out

She was at the gate, resting her arm on the top rail, her chin on her arms, looking out. Out being just any place that wasn't in. The moon rode high in the sky above great banks of clouds. Last night the moon was in eclipse. It was like someone had pulled a red curtain down over the face of the moon. But it was the moon all the same. Come clouds, come eclipse, it was all the same moon.

Somebody was calling to her from the house. That would be her sister-in-law. Her dear brother's wife. But she didn't pay no attention to her. She was a little cracked in the head. It was the moon. The moon made her come out from inside herself where she was locked away; inside her head, behind a smile that was like the double-blank in the box of dominoes. The moon made her come out from behind that dead smile and talk her head off. And shout her head off. But nobody paid no attention to her at all. Her brother's half-crazy wife.

She heard the sound of boots. Someone was coming slowly up the road. She didn't bother to turn her head to look. Just someone coming up the road. No matter.

She said out loud. Just thinking: 'Couldn't be gone ten yet.'

He stopped as though she had spoken to him. He was wearing khaki pants and a blue sports shirt. There was something about him that was lean and hard, and clean. Clean like he'd just come out of the tub. He stopped right under the street lamp that was before the gate and looked at his wrist-watch.

'Ten past,' he said.

She made a little sound with her tongue against her teeth.

But he was still there. Hesitating in his mind. Whether to stop and chat with her, or go on. She didn't give him any encouragement, or otherwise. She just kept on looking out, her chin resting upon her arms, her arms resting on the top of the gate.

'You waiting for someone,' he said. But he wasn't asking. He stood there still hesitating in his mind whether to stop and chat or to go on along his way.

Under the lamp-post there was a diamond-shaped sign that said 'Bus Stop'.

'The bus stops here,' he said. But he wasn't asking. He said it like he was reading the sign aloud, but to himself.

'It's going to rain,' he said. Lifting his face to the moon. 'Did you see the eclipse of the moon last night?' As you might say, 'read any good books lately?'

'Uh-huh,' she said.

Somebody was calling her from the house. Calling in a loud queer voice. He moved just one step. That took him one step nearer to the bus sign, so that he now stood on neutral ground. He might be waiting for the bus at the stop sign, or he might be talking to a girl at her gate, if the bus should come along and he didn't want to take it.

'That's just my sister-in-law,' she said. 'I don't pay no mind to her.' Lifting a foot to the lowest rail of the gate, but without otherwise changing her position.

He lit a cigarette carelessly and looked up at the moon. He stood for a while like that, not saying anything, just looking up.

The clouds were banked up high against the moon, so that she looked wild and stormy tonight, and as though filled with a great unrest.

But cho! It was only the moon. Always the moon. The rest was trimmings. They didn't mean anything.

The man said: 'It's going to rain.' Blowing out a cloud of smoke. To him the trimmings meant nothing.

She wanted to laugh.

'What you are? A weather prophet?'

'Them clouds,' he said. 'See them dark ones underneath like? They say rain!'

'Ain't you smart,' she mocked.

'That's right,' he said, without his face changing.

The man was a fool. She would snub him. She would wait for him to say something to her, and she would take pains to snub him.

Besides it wasn't right she should be here chatting with him. At any moment her brother might ride up on his bicycle. He would scold her, inside. Though who could say she was in fact chatting with anyone? Wasn't her fault there was a bus stop just outside their gate. Wasn't she put it there.

She said: 'Weren't you going for a walk?'

He said without looking at her: 'I was.'

'I changed my mind now,' he said. 'I'm waiting for the bus.'

Her foot on the rail started of itself bouncing her knee up and down. Like she might have been hushing a baby to bye-bye. She was doing that without thinking about it.

But he saw it out of the corner of his eye. Without looking around. Saw her bare knee bouncing. It was a pretty knee – to pass up just like that. She might be waiting for someone, sure. But all the same where he was standing was public thoroughfare. He might be going some place, or not. Wasn't anybody's business. She didn't have to answer back if she didn't want. He could say, it's going to rain, without talking to anyone. Just saying it looked like it was going to rain.

The three children had been put to bed long ago. Her brother's children. Couldn't be anything she could do that her sister-in-law kept calling, calling at her. She just wouldn't pay any mind to her. Let her call. It was the moon. The moon was full tonight. Last night there had been an eclipse, and it looked just like someone had drawn a red blind down over the face of the moon. And bit by bit the blind had lifted. Until the last time she had looked at it, it was just like someone had broken a piece out of the moon somewhere near the top.

A few people passed in the street. She heard them come and go without looking at them. Except when they passed her line of vision looking straight out before her, she didn't see them. Two three bicycles went by, but nothing to make her take her mind off what she was thinking about – nothing.

She wasn't thinking about anything tonight. She wasn't waiting for anyone either. Leastways she didn't know anyone she *could* be waiting for. Except it was that she was waiting for her brother to come home? And why *should* she be waiting for her brother to come home? She was just tired of staying indoors doing nothing. With a crazy woman for company. She was just leaning against the gate, looking out, doing nothing. Thinking about nothing.

Sometimes it got so bad sitting indoors with only her sister-in-law for company, that she wanted to put her hands up to her head and scream!

But she wasn't going to do that. She wasn't going to let it get her that way. The loneliness. The emptiness of everything. Ever since she had left home and come to live with her brother in the city. Because his wife was that way again, bringing them into the world faster than she could look after them.

If she let it get her, someday she would be getting like her sister-in-law. All shut inside her head. Her face blank. Her eyes. That fixed dead smile. All like the double-blank in the box of dominoes.

She hadn't known it was going to be like this in the city. Else she wouldn't have left home in the first place. Short of them hog-tying her and dragging her here. She hadn't known her brother meant to lock her inside a house and not want her to see anyone from outside, and not want her to have any friends or go anywhere. *If* she had known!

Maybe he was just one of those fresh guys. The city, she was warned, was full of them. Or maybe he was a married man himself with a family of three squalling children, and his wife that way again. But cho! That didn't bother her. She wasn't even giving him a thought. That way.

'Ever seen a man climb right up one of them electric-line poles?' he said, looking at her.

'No,' she said. Was he trying to be funny?

Ever seen a man climbing a pole! What was he coming with now. What did he take her for? A fool? What was his line? What was he getting at? Ever seen a man climbing a pole, indeed! What sort of fast one did he think he was pulling out from up his sleeve now? What was he getting around to? What was he coming with now?

Cho! It must be one of those jokes he was trying to tell her. Just one of those fresh guys. Trying to get fresh with her.

'What you talking about, a man climbing a pole?' she said.

'That's me,' he said. 'Linesman.'

'Linesman?' she said.

'Linesman. That's what they call us. Wire-monkeys. We look after the lines.'

So. That was it. He was telling her about himself.

'So what?' she said. Doing her stuff. Pretending she was indifferent.

'You ought to see me going up one of them poles,' he said.

'Why?' she said. Like what.

'With my steel spurs on,' he said.

Steel spurs! What next. What did he take her for, anyway?

'Steel spurs,' he said again. Looking at her.

At the sides of his boots, he said, for gripping the pole. How else could you climb a pole, he said, if you come to think about it?

But she didn't say anything. Just kept on as she was, leaning against the gate looking out. Her bare knee kept on bouncing like all the time she didn't know she was doing it.

So he was a wire-monkey. He climbed poles! He did that for a living. She could see him in her mind's eye climbing up that pole across the way hand over hand – like a monkey – without thinking about it. Wondering how soon her brother might be happening along.

He too was silent. Thinking his own thoughts.

Why didn't he say something? She was suddenly and unaccountably annoyed with him. What did he think he was doing just standing there pulling at his cigarette in a self-satisfied way, like the world and everything in it belonged to him tonight, not saying anything? Just taking it in. Just letting things come to him, and taking it all in. He had a nerve!

She wanted to hear more about him. About this queer occupation of his, anyway. Fancy doing *that* for a living! Or was he just taking her along? Trying to get fresh with her?

'What you do when you climb the pole?' she said.

'Oh, things. Fix the lines. Put in new ones. Tend them in general.'

That made sense at least. The lines *would* need fixing. Somehow she had never thought of it before. What a lot of queer occupations there must be in the world. So many queer jobs to be done. Somebody had to do them. It was the same all over the world. Her job for instance. Taking care of her sister-in-law, her brother's children. That was one of them. Somebody had to do it. That was why her brother didn't want her to have any friends. Because he wanted her to do that job. He had a long head to his body; her brother.

It was dangerous work too. He might easily get killed fooling with them wires. They were charged with electricity. She knew that. She could see him, without thinking about it, atop one of them poles, caught somehow in amongst the wires, burning up.

'Isn't it dangerous?' she said.

'Not worth speaking of,' he said. 'That is, if you know what you're doing. Them wires carry a powerful lot of volts. If I was to tell you how much you wouldn't believe me. Some of them. Could kill you quicker than thinking. If you don't mind your step.'

She said: 'I should *think* so!' And he looked at her quickly, and smiled.

So then: 'That don't seem to me much of a way for a man to make his living,' she said.

He laughed at that. Just laughed. As though he was saying to himself, well *she* didn't know anything. A girl like that!

The bus came up to the stop then. Somebody got off. Two people. A girl first, and a man after her. They went on down the road. She saw them without looking at them. The bus went on again.

'Weren't you waiting for the bus?' she said.

'Did I say I was?' he said.

She made no answer.

'Maybe I changed my mind,' he said. Without looking at her.

'You live here,' he said. But he wasn't asking. He had a way of saying things like that. Like he was just thinking out aloud.

She said nothing.

'Maybe you would care to go for a walk,' he said. Looking at her. 'Not tonight,' he said, before she could say anything. 'Some other night.' And left it like that.

'No! No!' she said quickly, shaking her head.

'Why?' he said.

'Don't ask me why. It can't be, that's why.'

He just laughed.

'Maybe you'll change your mind,' he said.

'No! No!' she said.

'All right,' he said. 'I was just saying. Anyone can change their mind.'

A bicycle came round the bend up the road. She knew, without knowing, that it was her brother coming home.

'You must go now,' she said, quickly. 'Please go now.'

He looked at her. His face started to laugh, but dropped it. It was as though he understood everything, without her saying it.

'Your husband, eh?'

'No, my brother. You must go now. Please!'

In those few words he understood everything. More than enough to go on. Things she hadn't meant to let out to him. Had let out without knowing!

You must go now! Please! That made it right with him. That told him something besides. That already there was something between them. Something tacit, and implicit. He wasn't slow in these things.

'Goodnight, then. Be seeing you,' he said, without looking at her.

With his hands in his pockets he sauntered off carelessly. A young man taking the air.

'What you doing here? Who you waiting for?' her brother questioned suspiciously as he came up.

'Nothing. Nobody,' she answered.

'You should be inside,' he said. 'No sense to stand at the gate looking out for nothing.'

The wind died down. Suddenly there was no wind at all. Not so much as would stir a leaf. A great drop of rain fell *plop* against her cheek. She put her hand up to her cheek and took it away wet.

'It's going to rain!' she said, looking at her hand, as though she had made a wonderful discovery.

'Get inside,' he said, harshly. 'Get inside now. You have no business standing out here like that, for nothing.'

She moved slowly to do his bidding. As though it was his will not hers that moved the muscles in her body. That moved her legs along. But her mind. That was not his. She looked up at the face of the moon. Last night it was in eclipse. Tonight it was restless and driven, with great black clouds driving across the face of it.

And suddenly she wanted to cry. But not here, where he could see her. Inside in her own little room. Where no one could see her. She would just put her head down and cry. And not because she was sad. And not because she was happy. She only knew she wanted to put her head down and cry and cry her eyes out. And all for nothing.

SAM SELVON

Song of Sixpence

It had a time when things was really brown in Trinidad, and Razor Blade couldn't make a note nohow, no matter what he do, everywhere he turn, people telling him they ain't have work. It look like if work scarce like gold, and is six months now he ain't working.

Besides that, Razor Blade owe Chin parlour about five dollars, and the last time he went in for a sandwich and a sweet drink, Chin tell him no more trusting until he pay off all he owe. Chin have his name in a copybook under the counter.

'Wait until the calypso season start,' he tell Chin, 'and I go be reaping a harvest. You remember last year how much money I had?'

But though Chin remember last year, that still ain't make him soften up, and it reach a position where he hungry, clothes dirty, and he see nothing at all at all to come, and this time so, the calypso season about three four months off.

On top of all that, rain falling nearly every day, and the shoes he have on have big hole in them, like if they laughing, and the water getting up in the shoes and have his feet wet.

Was the rain what cause him to thief a pair of shoes from by a shoemaker shop in Park Street. Is the first time he ever thief, and it take him a long time to make up his mind. He stand up there on the pavement by this shoemaker shop, and he thinking things like Oh God when I tell you I hungry, and all the shoes around the table, on the ground, some capsize, some old and some new, some getting half-sole and some getting new heel.

It have a pair just like the one he have on.

The table cut up for so, as if the shoemaker blind and cutting the wood instead of the leather, and it have a broken calabash shell with some boil starch in it. The starch look like pap; he so hungry he feel he could eat it.

Well, the shoemaker in the back of the shop, and it only have few people sheltering rain on the pavement. It look so easy for him to put down the old pair and take up another pair – this time so, he done have his eye fix on a pair that look like Technic, and just his size, too, besides.

Razor Blade remember how last year he was sitting pretty – two-tone Technic, gabardine suit, hot tie. Now that he catching his royal, everytime he only making comparison with last year, thinking in his mind how them was the good old days, and wondering if they go ever come back again.

And it look to him as if thiefing could be easy, because plenty time people does leave things alone and go away, like how now the shoemaker in the back of the shop, and all he have to do is take up a pair of shoes and walk off in cool blood.

Well, it don't take plenty to make a thief. All you have to do is have a fellar catching his royal, and can't get a work noway, and bam! by the time he make two three rounds he bounce something somewhere, an orange from a tray, or he snatch a bread in a parlour, or something.

Like how he bounce the shoes.

So though he frighten like hell and part of him going like a pliers, Razor Blade playing victor brave boy and whistling as he go down the road.

The only thing now is that he hungry.

Right there by Queen Street, in front a Chinese restaurant, he get an idea. Not an idea in truth; all he did think was: In for a shilling in for a pound. But when he think that, is as if he begin to realize that if he going to get stick for the shoes, he might as well start thiefing black is white.

So he open now to anything; all you need is a start, all you need is a crank up, and it come easy after that.

What you think he planning to do? He planning to walk in the Chinee restaurant and sit down and eat a major meal, and then out off without paying. It look so easy, he wonder why he never think of it before.

The waitress come up while he looking at the menu. She stand up there, with a pencil stick up on she ears like a real test, and when he take a pin-t at she he realize that this restaurant work only part-time as far as she concern, because she look as if she sleepy, she body bend up like a piece of copper wire.

What you go do? She must be only getting a few dollars from the Chinee man, and she can't live on that.

He realize suddenly that he bothering about the woman when he himself catching his tail, so he shake his head and watch down at the menu.

He mad to order a portion of everything: fry rice, chicken chop-suey, roast pork, chicken chow-min, birdnest soup, chicken broth, and one of them big salad with big slice of tomato and onion.

He begin to think again about the last calypso season, when he was holding big, and uses to go up by the high-class Chinee restaurant in St Vincent Street. He think how is a funny thing how sometimes you does have so much food that you eat till you sick, and another time you can't even see you way to hustle a rock and mauby.

It should have some way that when you have the chance you could eat enough to last you for a week or a month, and he make a plan right there, that the next time he have money (oh God) he go make a big deposit in a restaurant, so that all he have to do is walk in and eat like stupidness.

But the woman getting impatient. She say: 'You taking a long time to make up you mind, like you never eat in restaurant before.'

And he think about the time when he had money, how no frowsy woman could have talk to him so. He remember how them waitresses used to hustle to serve him, and one night the talk get around that Razor Blade, the calypsonian, was in the place, and they insist that he give them a number. Which one it was again? The one about Home and the Bachelor.

'Come, come, make up your mind, mister, I have work to do.'

So he order plain boil rice and chicken stew, because the way how he feeling, all them fancy Chinee dish is only joke, he feel as if he want something like roast breadfruit and saltfish, something solid so when it go down in his belly he could feel it there.

An he tell the woman to bring a drink of Barbados rum first thing, because he know how long they does take to bring food in them restaurant, and he could coast with the rum in the meantime.

By the time the food come he feeling so hungry he could hardly wait, he fall down on the plate of rice and chicken as if is the first time he see food, and in three minute everything finish.

And is just as if he seeing the world for the first time, he feel like a million, he feel like a lord; he give a loud belch and bring up some of the chicken and rice to his throat; when he swallow it back down it taste sour.

He thinking how it had a time a American fellar hear a calypso in Trinidad and he went back to the States and he get it set up to music and thing, and he get the Andrew Sisters to sing it, and the song make money like hell, it was on Hit Parade and all; wherever you turn, you could hear people singing that calypso. This time so, the poor calypsonian who really write the song catching hell in Trinidad; it was only when some smart lawyer friend tell him about copyright and that sort of business that he wake up. He went to America; and how you don't know he get a lot of money after the case did fix up in New York?

Razor Blade know the story good; whenever he write a calypso, he always praying that some big-shot from America would hear it and like it, and want to set it up good. The Blade uses to go in Frederick Street and Marine Square by the one-two music shops, and look at all the popular songs, set up in notes and words, with the name of the fellar who write it big on the front, and sometimes his photograph too. And Razor Blade uses to think: But why I can't write song like that too, and have my name all over the place?

And when things was good with him, he went inside now and then, and tell the clerks and them that he does write calypsos. But they only laugh at him, because they does think that calypso is no song at all, that what is song is numbers like 'I've Got You Under My Skin' and 'Sentimental Journey', what American composers write.

And the Blade uses to argue that every dog has his day, and that a time would come when people singing calypso all over the world like stupidness.

He thinking about all that as he lean back there in the Chinee man restaurant.

Is to peel off now without paying!

The best way is to play brassface, do as if you own the damn restaurant, and walk out cool.

So he get up and he notice the waitress not around (she must be serving somebody else) and he take time and walk out, passing by the cashier who writing something in a book.

But all this time, no matter how boldface you try to be, you can't stop part of you from going like a pliers, clip clip, and he feel as if he want to draw his legs together and walk with two feet as one.

When the waitress find out Razor Blade gone without paying, she start to make one set of noise, and a Chinee man from the kitchen dash outside to see if he could see him, but this time so Razor Blade making races down Frederick Street.

The owner of the restaurant tell the woman she have to pay for the food that Razor Blade eat, that was she fault, and she begin to cry big water, because is a lot of food that Razor Blade put away, and she know that that mean two three dollars from she salary.

This time so, Razor Blade laughing like hell; he quite down by the railway station, and he know nobody could catch him now.

One set of rain start to fall suddenly; Razor Blade walking like a king in his new shoes, and no water getting up his foot this time, so he ain't even bothering to shelter.

And he don't know why, but same time he get a sharp idea for a calypso. About how a man does catch his royal when he can't get a work noway. The calypso would say about how he see some real hard days; he start to think up words right away as he walking in the rain:

> It had a time in this colony
> When everybody have money excepting me
> I can't get a work no matter how I try
> It look as if good times pass me by

He start to hum it to the tune of a old calypso (Man Centipede Bad Too Bad) just to see how it shaping up.

And he think about One Foot Harper, the one man who could help him out with a tune.

It had a big joke with One Foot one time. Somebody thief One Foot crutch one day when he was catching a sleep under a weeping willow tree in Woodford Square, and One Foot had was to stay in the square for a whole day and night. You could imagine how he curse stink; everybody only standing up and laughing like hell; nobody won't lend a hand, and if wasn't for Razor Blade, now so One Foot might still be waiting under the weeping willow tree for somebody to get a crutch for him.

But the old Blade help out the situation, and since that time, the both of them good friends.

So Razor Blade start making a tack for the tailor shop which part One Foot does always be hanging out, because One Foot ain't working noway, and every day he there by the tailor shop, sitting down on a soapbox and talking balls whole day.

But don't fret you head. One Foot ain't no fool; it had a time in the old days when they uses to call him King of Calypso, and he was really good. If he did have money, or education business, is a sure thing he would have been up the ladder, because he was the first man who ever had the idea that calypsonians should go away and sing in America and England. But people only laugh at One Foot when he say that.

Razor Blade meet One Foot in a big old talk about the time when the town hall burn down (One Foot saying he know the fellar who start the fire). When One Foot see him, he stop arguing right away and he say:

'What happening paleets, long time no see.'

Razor Blade say: 'Look man, I have a sharp idea for a calypso. Let we go in the back of the shop and work it out.'

But One Foot feeling comfortable on the soapbox. He say: 'Take ease, don't rush me. What about the shilling you have for me, that you borrow last week.'

The Blade turn his pockets inside out, and a pair of dice roll out, and a penknife fall on the ground.

'Boy, I ain't have a cent. I broken. I bawling. If you stick me with a pin you won't draw blood.'

'Don't worry with that kind of talk, is so with all-you fellars, you does borrow a man money and then forget his address.'

'I telling you man,' Razor Blade talk as if he in a hurry, but is only to get away from the topic, 'you don't believe me?'

But the Foot cagey. He say, 'All right, all right, but I telling you in front that if you want money borrow again, you come to the wrong man. I ain't lending you a nail till you pay me back that shilling that you have for me.' The Foot move off the soapbox, and stand up balancing on the crutch.

'Come man, do quick,' Razor Blade make as if to go behind the shop in the backroom. Same time he see Rahamut, the Indian tailor.

'What happening, Indian, things looking good with you?'

Rahamut stop stitching a khaki pants and look at the Blade.

'You and One Foot always writing calypso in this shop, all-you will have to give me a commission.'

'Well you know how it is, sometimes you up, sometimes you down. Right now I so down that bottom and I same thing.'

'Well old man is a funny thing but I never see you when you up.'

'Ah, but wait till the calypso season start.'

'Then you won't come round here at all. Then you is bigshot, you forget small fry like Rahamut.'

Well, Razor Blade don't know what again to tell Rahamut, because is really true all what the Indian saying about he and One Foot hanging out behind the shop. And he think about these days when anybody tell him anything, all he could say is: 'Wait till the calypso season start up,' as if when the calypso season start up God go come to earth, and make everybody happy.

So what he do is laugh kiff-kiff and give Rahamut a pat on the back, like they is good friends.

Same time One Foot come up, so they went and sit down by a break-up table.

Razor Blade say: 'Listen to these words old man, you never hear calypso like this in you born days,' and he start to give the Foot the words.

But from the time he start, One Foot chook his fingers in his ears and bawl out: 'Oh God old man, you can't think up something new, is the same old words every year.'

'But how you mean man,' the Blade say, 'this is calypso father. Wait until you hear the whole thing.'

They begin to work on the song, and One Foot so good that in two twos he fix up a tune. So Razor Blade pick up a empty bottle and a piece of stick, and One Foot start beating the table, and is so they getting on, singing this new calypso that they invent.

Well, Rahamut and another Indian fellar who does help him out with the sewing come up and listen.

'What you think of this new number, papa?' the Blade ask Rahamut.

Rahamut scratch his head and say: 'Let me get that tune again.'

So they begin again, beating on the table and the bottle and Razor Blade imagine that he singing to a big audience in the Calypso Tent, so he putting all he have in it.

When they finish the fellar who does help Rahamut say: 'That is hearts.'

But Rahamut say: 'Why you don't shut you mouth? What all-you Indian know about calypso?'

And that cause a big laugh, everybody begin to laugh kya-kya, because Rahamut himself is a Indian.

One Foot turn to Razor Blade and say: 'Listen to them two Indian how they arguing about we creole calypso. I never see that in my born days!'

Rahamut say: 'Man, I is a creolize Trinidadian, *oui*.'

Razor Blade say: 'All right, joke is joke, but all-you think it good? It really good?'

Rahamut want to say yes, it good, but he beating about the bush, he hemming and hawing, he saying: 'Well, it so-so', and 'it not so bad', and 'I hear a lot of worse ones'.

But the fellar who does help Rahamut, he getting on as if he mad, he only hitting Razor Blade and One Foot on the shoulder and saying how he never hear a calypso like that, how it sure to be the Road March for next year Carnival. He swinging his hands all about in the air while he talking, and his hand hit Rahamut hand and Rahamut get a chook in his finger with a needle he was holding.

Well, Rahamut put the finger in his mouth and start to suck it, and he turn round and start to abuse the other tailor fellar, saying why you don't keep you tail quiet, look you make me chook my hand with the blasted needle?

'Well what happen for that? You go dead because a needle chook you?' the fellar say.

Big argument start up; they forget all about Razor Blade calypso and start to talk about how people does get blood poison from pin and needle chook.

Well, it don't have anything to write down as far as the calypso concern. Razor Blade memorize the words and tune, and that is the case. Is so a calypso born, cool cool, without any fuss. Is so all them big number like 'Yes, I Catch Him Last Night', and 'That is a Thing I Can Do Anytime Anywhere', and 'Old Lady Your Bloomers Falling Down', born right there behind Rahamut tailor shop.

After the big talk about pin and needle Rahamut and the fellar who does assist him went back to finish off a zootsuit that a fellar was going to call for in the evening.

Now Razor Blade want to ask One Foot to borrow him a shilling, but he don't know how to start, especially as he owe him already. So he begin to talk sweet, praising up the tune that One Foot invent for the calypso, saying he never hear a tune so sweet, that the melody smooth like sweetoil.

But as soon as he start to come like that, the old Foot begin to get cagey, and say, 'Oh God old man, don't mamaguile me.'

The Blade not so very fussy, because a solid meal in his belly. But same time he trying to guile One Foot into lending him a little thing, he get an idea.

He begin to tell One Foot how he spend the morning, how he ups the shoes from the shoemaker shop in Park Street, and how he eat big for nothing.

One Foot say: 'I bet you get in trouble, all-you fellars does take some brave risk, *oui*.'

Razor say: 'Man, it easy as kissing hand, is only because you have one foot and can't run fast, that's why you talking so.'

Foot say: 'No jokes about my one foot.'

Razor say: 'But listen man, you too stupid again! You and me could work up a good scheme to get some money. If you thiefing, you might as well thief big.'

'Is you is the thief, not me.'

'But listen man Foot,' the Blade gone down in low voice, 'I go do everything, all I want you to do is to keep watchman for me, to see if anybody coming.'

'What is the scheme you have?'

To tell truth, Blade ain't have nothing cut and dry in the old brain; all he thinking is that he go make a big thief somewhere where have money. He scratch his head and pull his ears like he did see Spencer Tracy do in a picture, and he say: 'What about the Roxy Theatre down St James?'

Same time he talking, he feeling excitement in his body, like if waves going up and coming down and he hold on to One Foot hand.

The Foot say: 'Well yes, the day reach when you really catching you royal. I never thought I would see the time when my good friend Razor Blade turn thief. Man, you sure to get catch. Why you don't try for a work somewhere until the calypso season start up?'

'I tired try to get work. It ain't have work noway.'

'Well, you ain't no thief. You sure to get catch, I tell you.'

'But man look how I get away with the shoes and the meal! I tell you all you have to do is play boldface, and you could commit murder and get away free.'

The Foot start to hum a old calypso:

> 'If a man have money today . . .
> He could commit murder and get away free
> And live in the Governor's company . . .'

The Blade began to get vex. 'So you don't like the idea? You think I can't get away with it?'

'You ain't have no practice. You is a novice. Crime does not pay.'

'You is a damn coward!'

'Us calypsonians have to keep we dignity.'

'You go to hell! If you won't help me I go do it by myself, you go see! And I not thiefing small, I thiefing big! If I going down the river, I making sure is for plenty money, and not for no small-time job.'

'Well, papa, don't say I ain't tell you you looking for trouble.'

'Man Foot, the trouble with you is you only have one foot so you can't think like me.'

The Foot get hot. He say: 'Listen, I tell you already no jokes about my one foot, you hear? I ain't taking no jokes about that. Curse my mother, curse my father, but don't tell me nothing about my foot.'

The Blade relent. 'I sorry, Foot, I know you don't like nobody to give you jokes.'

Same time Rahamut call out and ask why they keeping so much noise, if they think they in the fishmarket.

So they finish the talk. Razor Blade tell One Foot he would see him later, and One Foot say: 'Righto, boy, don't forget the words for the song. And I warning you for the last time to keep out of trouble.'

But the minute he leave the tailor shop Razor Blade thinking how easy it go be to pull off this big deal. He alone would do it, without any gun, too besides.

Imagine the Foot saying he is a novice! All you need is brassface; play brazen; do as if you is a saint, as if you still have your mother innocent features, and if anybody ask you anything, lift up your eyebrows and throw your hands up in the air and say: 'Oh Lord, who, *me?*'

He find himself quite round by the Queen's Park Savannah, walking and thinking. And he see a old woman selling orange. The woman as if she sleeping in the heat, she propping up she chin with one hand, and she head bend down. Few people passing: Razor Blade size up the situation in one glance.

He mad to bounce a orange from the tray, just to show that he could do it and get away. Just pass up near – don't even look down at the tray – and just lift one up easy as you walking, and put it in you pocket.

He wish One Foot was there to see how easy it was to do.

But he hardly put the orange in his pocket when the old woman jump up and start to make one set of noise, bawling out: 'Thief, Thief! Look a man thief a orange from me! Help! Hold him! Don't let 'im get away!'

And is as if that bawling start the pliers working on him right away; he forget everything he was thinking, and he start to make races across the savannah.

He look back and see three fellas chasing him. And is just as if he can't feel nothing at all, as if he not running, as if he standing up in one spot. The only thing is the pliers going clip clip, and he gasping: Oh God! Oh God!

SAM SELVON

My Girl and the City

All these words that I hope to write, I have written them already many times in my mind. I have had many beginnings, each as good or as bad as the other. Hurtling in the underground from station to station, mind the doors, missed it!, there is no substitute for wool: waiting for a bus in Piccadilly Circus: walking across Waterloo bridge: watching the bed of the Thames when the tide is out – choose one, choose a time, a place, any time or any place, and take off, as if this were interrupted conversation, as if you and I were earnest friends and there is no need for preliminary remark.

One day of any day it is like this. I wait for my girl on Waterloo bridge, and when she comes there is a mighty wind blowing across the river, and we lean against it and laugh, her skirt skylarking, her hair whipping across her face.

I wooed my girl, mostly on her way home from work, and I talked a great deal. Often, it was as if I had never spoken, I heard my words echo in deep caverns of thought, as if they hung about like cigarette smoke in a still room, missionless; or else they were lost for ever in the sounds of the city.

We used to wait for a 196 under the railway bridge across the Waterloo Road. There were always long queues and it looked like we would never get a bus. Fidgeting in that line of impatient humanity I got in precious words edgeways, and a train would rumble and drown my words in thundering steel. Still, it was important to talk. In the crowded bus, as if I wooed three or four instead of one. I shot words over my shoulder, across seats; once past a bespectacled man reading the *Evening News*, who lowered his paper and eyed me that I was mad. My words bumped against people's faces, on the glass window of the bus; they found passage between 'fares please' and once I got to writing things on a piece of paper and pushing my hand over two seats.

The journey ended, there was urgent need to communicate before we parted.

All these things I say, I said, waving my hand in the air as if to catch the words floating about me and give them mission. I say them because I want you to know, I don't ever want to regret afterwards that I didn't say enough, I would rather say too much.

Take that Saturday evening, I am waiting for her in Victoria station. When she comes we take the Northern Line to Belsize Park (I know a way to the heath from there, I said). When we get out of the lift and step outside there is a sudden downpour and everyone scampers back into the station. We wait a while, then go out in it. We get lost. I say, Let us ask that fellow the way. But she says No, fancy asking someone the way to the heath on this rainy night, just find out how to get back to the tube station.

We go back, I get my bearings afresh, and we set off. She is hungry. Wait here, I say, under a tree at the side of the road, and I go to a pub for some sandwiches. Water slips off me and makes puddles on the counter as I place my order. The man is taking a long time and I go to the door and wave to her across the street signifying I shan't be too long.

When I go out she has crossed the road and is sheltering in a doorway pouting. You leave me standing in the rain and stay such a long time, she says. I had to wait for the sandwiches, I say, what do you think, I was having a quick one? Yes, she says.

We walk on through the rain and we get to the heath and the rain is falling slantways and carefree and miserable. For a minute we move around in an indecisive way as if we're looking for some particular spot. Then we see a tree which might offer some shelter and we go there and sit on a bench wet and bedraggled.

I am sorry for all this rain, I say, as if I were responsible. I take off her raincoat and make her put on my quilted jacket. She takes off her soaking shoes and tucks her feet under her skirt on the bench. She tries to dry her hair with a handkerchief. I offer her the sandwiches and light a cigarette for myself. Go on, have one, she says. I take a half and munch it, and smoke.

It is cold there. The wind is raging in the leaves of the trees, and the rain is pelting. But abruptly it ceases, the clouds break up in the sky, and the moon shines. When the moon shines, it shines on her face, and I look at her, the beauty of her washed by rain, and I think many things.

Suddenly we are kissing and I wish I could die there and then and there's an end to everything, to all the Jesus-Christ thoughts that make up every moment of my existence.

Writing all this now – and some weeks have gone by since I started – it is lifeless and insipid and useless. Only at the time, there was something, a thought that propelled me. Always, in looking back, there was something, and at the time I am aware of it, and the creation goes on and on in my mind while I look at all the faces around me in the tube, the restless rustle of newspapers, the hiss of air as the doors close, the enaction of life in a variety of form.

Once I told her and she said, as she was a stenographer, that she would come with me and we would ride the Inner Circle and I would just voice my thoughts and she would write them down, and that way we could make something of it. Once the train was crowded and she sat opposite to me and after a while I looked at her and she smiled and turned away. What is all this, what is the meaning of all these things that happen to people, the movement from one place to another, lighting a cigarette, slipping a coin into a slot and pulling a drawer for chocolate, buying a return ticket, waiting for a bus, working the crossword puzzle in the *Evening Standard*?

Sometimes you are in the underground and you have no idea what the weather is like, and the train shoots out of a tunnel and sunlight floods you, falls across your newspaper, makes the passengers squint and look up.

There is a face you have for sitting at home and talking, there is a face you have for working in the office, there is a face, a bearing, a demeanour for each time and place. There is above all a face for travelling, and when you have seen one you have seen all. In a rush hour, when we are breathing down each other's neck, we look at each other and glance quickly away. There is not a great deal to look at in the narrow confines of a carriage except people, and the faces of people, but no one deserves a glass of Hall's wine more than you do. We justle in the subway from train to lift, we wait, shifting our feet. When we are all herded inside we hear the footsteps of a straggler for whom the operator waits, and we try to figure out what sort of a footstep it is, if he feels the lift will wait for him; we are glad if he is left waiting while we shoot upward. Out of the lift, down the street, up the road: in ten seconds flat it is over, and we have to begin again.

One morning I am coming into the city by the night bus 287 from Streatham. It is after one o'clock; I have been stranded again after seeing my girl home. When we get to Westminster bridge the sky is marvellously clear with a few stray patches of beautiful cloud among which stars sparkle. The moon stands over Waterloo bridge, above the Houses of Parliament sharply outlined, and it throws gold on the waters of the Thames. The Embankment is quiet, only a few people loiter around the public convenience near to the Charing Cross underground which is open all night. A man sleeps on a bench. His head is resting under headlines: Suez Deadlock.

Going back to that same spot about five o'clock in the evening, there was absolutely nothing to recall the atmosphere of the early morning hours. Life had taken over completely, and there was nothing but people. People waiting for buses, people hustling for trains.

I go to Waterloo bridge and they come pouring out of the offices and they bob up and down as they walk across the bridge. From the station green trains come and go relentlessly. Motion mesmerizes me into immobility. There are lines of motion across the river, on the river.

Sometimes we sat on a bench near the river, and if the tide was out you could see the muddy bed of the river and the swans grubbing. Such spots, when found, are pleasant to loiter in. Sitting in one of those places – choose one, and choose a time – where it is possible to escape for a brief spell from Christ and the cup of tea, I have known a great frustration and weariness. All these things, said, have been said before, the river seen, the skirt pressed against the swelling thigh noted, the lunch hour eating apples in the sphinx's lap under Cleopatra's Needle observed and duly registered: even to talk of the frustration is a repetition. What am I to do, am I to take each circumstance, each thing seen, noted, and mill them in my mind and spit out something entirely different from the reality?

My girl is very real. She hated the city, I don't know why. It's like that sometimes, a person doesn't have to have a reason. A lot of people don't like London that way, you ask them why and they shrug, and a shrug is sometimes a powerful reply to a question.

She shrugged when I asked her why, and when she asked me why I loved London I too shrugged. But after a minute I thought I would try to explain, because too a shrug is an easy way out of a lot of things.

Falteringly I told her how one night it was late and I found a fish and chip shop open in the East End and I bought and ate in the dark street walking; and of the cup of tea in an all-night café in Kensington one grim winter morning; and of the first time I ever queued in this country in '50 to see the Swan Lake ballet, and the friend who was with me gave a busker two and six because he was playing Sentimental Journey on a mouth-organ.

But why do you love London, she said.

You can't talk about a thing like that, not really. Maybe I could have told her because one evening in the summer I was waiting for her, only it wasn't like summer at all. Rain had been falling all day, and a haze hung about the bridges across the river, and the water was muddy and brown, and there was a kind of wistfulness and sadness about the evening. The way St Paul's was, half-hidden in the rain, the motionless trees along the Embankment. But you say a thing like that and people don't understand at all. How sometimes a surge of greatness could sweep over you when you see something.

But even if I had said all that and much more, it would not have been what I meant. You could be lonely as hell in the city, then one day you look around you and you realize everybody else is lonely too, withdrawn, locked, rushing home out of the chaos: blank faces, unseeing eyes, millions and millions of them, up the Strand, down the Strand, jostling in Charing Cross for the 5.20: in Victoria station, a pretty continental girl wearing a light, becoming shade of lipstick stands away from the board on which the departures of trains appear and cocks her head sideways, hands thrust into pockets of a fawn raincoat.

I catch the eyes of this girl with my own: we each register sight, appreciation: we look away, our eyes pick up casual station activities:

she turns to an automatic refreshment machine, hesitant, not sure if she would be able to operate it.

Things happen, and are finished with for ever: I did not talk to her, I did not look her way again, or even think of her.

I look on the wall of the station at the clock, it is after half-past eight, and my girl was to have met me since six o'clock. I feel in my pockets for pennies to telephone. I only have two. I ask change of a stander with the usual embarrassment: when I telephone, the line is engaged. I alternate between standing in the spot we have arranged to meet and telephoning, but each time the line is engaged. I call the exchange: they ascertain that something is wrong with the line.

At ten minutes to nine I am eating a corned-beef sandwich when she comes. Suddenly now nothing matters except that she is here. She never expected that I would still be waiting, but she came on the offchance. I never expected that she would come, but I waited on the offchance.

Now I have a different word for this thing that happened – an offchance, but that does not explain why it happens, and what it is that really happens. We go to St James's Park, we sit under a tree, we kiss, the moon can be seen between leaves.

Wooing my way towards, sometimes in our casual conversation we came near to great, fundamental truths, and it was a little frightening. It wasn't like wooing at all, it was more discussion of when will it end, and must it ever end, and how did it begin, and how go on from here? We scattered words on the green summer grass, under trees, on dry leaves in a wood of quivering aspens, and sometimes it was as if I was struck speechless with too much to say, and held my tongue between thoughts frightened of utterance.

Once again I am on a green train returning to the heart from the suburbs, and I look out of window into windows of private lives flashed on my brain. Bread being sliced, a man taking off a jacket, an old woman knitting. And all these things I see – the curve of a woman's arm, undressing, the blankets being tucked, and once a solitary figure staring at trains as I stared at windows. All the way into London Bridge – is falling down, is falling down, the wheels say: one must have a thought – where buildings and the shadows of them encroach on the railway tracks. Now the train crawls across the bridges, dark steel in the darkness:

the thoughtful gloom of Waterloo: Charing Cross bridge, Thames reflecting lights, and the silhouettes of city buildings against the sky of the night.

When I was in New York, many times I went into that city late at night after a sally to the outskirts, it lighted up with a million lights, but never a feeling as on entering London. Each return to the city is loaded with thought, so that by the time I take the Inner Circle I am as light as air.

At last I think I know what it is all about. I move around in a world of words. Everything that happens is words. But pure expression is nothing. One must build on the things that happen: it is insufficient to say I sat in the underground and the train hurtled through the darkness and someone isn't using Amplex. So what? So now I weave, I say there was an old man on whose face wrinkles rivered, whose hands were shapeful with arthritis but when he spoke, oddly enough, his voice was young and gay.

But there was no old man, there was nothing, and there is never ever anything.

My girl, she is beautiful to look at. I have seen her in sunlight and in moonlight, and her face carves an exquisite shape in darkness.

These things we talk, I burst out, why mustn't I say them? If I love you, why shouldn't I tell you so?

I love London, she said.

GARTH ST OMER

The Departure

They were sitting at one end of the low counter in the Customs House and it was hot because of the people and of the presence of the strong light in the centre of the ceiling. There was much talking and it was not very intelligent because of the numbers of people who were talking at the same time and because of the noises which the porters made as they carried the things from the boat. It was very bright inside the Customs House and, sitting near to his mother, he was afraid of the noises and the brightness and of the strangeness of everything. The sounds of the voices filled the room and in the light he saw the dirty marks on the white-painted walls of the building and the Customs guards standing, in their khaki uniforms and their caps, at the doors. Then he saw his uncle come in past one of the guards and stand for a little while in the centre of the room looking for them. He touched his mother and pointed to where his uncle was standing. His uncle was small and short and he wore a crumpled coat and a black crumpled tie. His pants were baggy and lay in thick folds over his shoes and there were abrasions in the cloth where it dragged over the ground. As the boy and his mother looked they saw him brush his clothes where a porter had touched him and look at the man and say something to him. The porter moved away, and he saw his uncle make as if to follow him and then his mother had run over and called his uncle and they were coming now after they had talked there in the centre of the room for a short while.

'I only wanted to make him say that he was sorry,' his uncle was saying. 'That was all.'

'You always get yourself in trouble,' his mother said.

'Which trouble,' his uncle said, 'do I always get myself in? The man touched me so that I nearly fell and when I prepare to speak to him about it you talk of trouble. There is no trouble.'

'The man hardly touched you,' she said.

'He dirtied my clothes and he would not apologize when I asked him to.'

'All right, well forget it,' his mother said.

'These fellows on the wharf are too rude,' his uncle said. 'Somebody will have to teach them manners.'

'Does it have to be you?'

'Me or anybody else. But they have to be taught manners. And if I have to do it I will do it.'

'You know these fellows. You will ask him to say he is sorry and he will curse you.'

'Let him curse; his cursing does nothing to me.'

'If it was only curse he would curse. But he would want to fight and you know you can't fight with anybody.'

'I would not fight him. What do you take me for? And I know my rights. You think anybody can just decide that he will beat me up?'

'What will you do, Albert? You're so small.'

'Ah. That's what you always say: I am so small. But a man does not have to be big to know how to get along. He knows what will happen to him if he touches me.'

'What's the use? You will get a beating, perhaps a very bad one. He will either go to gaol or pay some money in court. In the end it is you who has got the worst of it. Gaol means nothing to these men. You know that.'

'But he will know that he has not got to touch me again,' his uncle said. He removed his hat from his head and scratched his scalp with the fingers of the same hand.

'Albert, you must behave yourself,' the boy's mother said.

'How do you mean behave myself? Now you are starting this same foolishness again. "Albert behave yourself." What have I done?' He stopped scratching and put on his hat again.

'You are so stubborn,' she said.

'How am I stubborn? So I must let everybody do with me as they like?'

'No, Albert, but you could try to be more understanding, you must learn to give and take.'

'Nonsense.'

'Always that's the same answer. Always nonsense, stupidness. And in the end it is you who get the worst of it. It's you who got the brick on the head and had to spend a month in hospital and up to now they do not know who did it. And you say you do not care. You're so troublesome.'

'Yes, go on. I am your little child. I am troublesome, I need someone to watch over me, I can't take care of myself, I talk too much . . .'

'You know you say a lot of things you shouldn't say.'

'I said them, on the contrary, because they had to be said.'

'Why did you not let someone else say them?'

'Because I saw that they were to be said and that there was no reason why I could not say them.'

'But why *you?*'

'Why not?'

'Why not let someone else do it who might be able to stand the trouble.'

'I am afraid of nobody, Agnes, nobody at all.'

'That's what I know, that's what I know only too well. And that's why you always come out worse in the end.'

'What do you want me to do, stifle my conscience?'

'All right, Albert, you are raising your voice. Let's stop this thing now.'

'What do you want me to do? Stand there and do everything you say, and accept everything that people do to me, and not expose some of the things that people say to fool us poor people with? Every crap that Mr So and So say I must believe? I'll talk whenever I think I ought to talk and I don't care what happens afterwards.'

'Yes, you don't care. You can come here in the Customs where there are so many people and shout at me and make me ashamed. You don't care. And you have a wife and seven small children at home.'

'The Lord will provide for them.'

'It's easy to say that. But it's time that you changed. It's time you decided that it's you who must strive and then only will the Lord provide.'

'The Lord has provided,' Albert said. 'What do you think I am, a child? I'll be thirty-five next month and you tell me it's time I changed. I am not your child, I am a big man.'

'Albert you are shouting at me in the Customs House.'

'So what?'

'Please, let's stop it.'

'Who started it?'

'All right I did. Now let's stop this talk, please. You came to see me off. Not quarrel with me.'

'I am not quarrelling.'

He stood in front of the low counter upon which the boy and his mother were sitting. He was remembering the men he had left at the back room of the rum shop and he was sorry that he had come so early. He had left them and come here and now it was this quarrelling instead. That was what was wrong with him. He felt too much of a sense of obligation to his sister. There was no need for him to have come here to say goodbye to her. He had told her goodbye at home, hadn't he? He need not have come here at all. And then as soon as he was here she was quarrelling with him. He sucked his teeth softly to himself. She was too squeamish, that was what. Afraid of her own shadow. Always, 'Albert be careful; Albert don't say anything at the meeting that you should not say. Albert you should not stay out so late after what happened the other night.' Always warnings, warnings. And he had left his pals and the good time in the rum shop for this.

He could see the four of them at the table now, Joe, Calderon, Harry and Slim. Having fun and perhaps laughing at him that he had gone and had left it all there.

'Bustamante, you leaving already?' Joe had said.

'I am coming back,' he had said, 'soon. Don't drink all of it.'

'No, Sir Sec.,' Calderon said. Calderon was his assistant. He, Albert, was secretary of the Seamen and Waterfront Union. Although he was not a seaman yet he was one of them. He had drunk with them and he had said some things in the local papers on their behalf. And he was intelligent and could read and write much better than they could.

'I better have one for the road,' he had said, 'just in case.' And he had nearly filled his glass.

'Whopes,' Harry said, 'there's four of us still to drink, yes.'

'Take it easy,' Joe said, 'easy, Bustamante.'

'Don't go, chaps,' he had said, 'I'm only going to see my sister off. I'll be back in a minute.'

'It's too early.'

'No it isn't. She said that the boat was supposed to leave at ten. It's already half-past nine.'

'The boat is late. It's only just come in.'

'You are not renowned for your veracity, Slim.'

'What the hell does that mean,' Slim asked. He was foreman of the stevedores and he was very fond of Albert.

'That you are a blasted liar,' Albert said.

'Two of us both,' Slim said. 'But what I say is true.'

'Is that so?' Albert asked Joe.

'Dunno,' Joe said.

'I had better go and see anyhow,' Albert said. 'One for the road.'

'Well then one for the road.'

'Two you mean,' Harry said.

'Jesus Christ,' Slim said.

'Don't swear, Slim,' Albert said. 'Against the laws of God.'

'Sorry, Parson,' Slim said. 'I had forgot.'

'Your sins are forgiven you,' Albert said.

'Amen,' Slim said.

'Anyhow, don't forget I said one for the road.'

'And I corrected you,' Harry said.

'It's twenty to ten now,' Joe said.

Albert filled the glass and drank. Then he took some water from the iced enamel jug and drank it. He put some more water into the glass, swirled the water in it, and then drank that too.

'You're missing a piece of bread,' Joe said.

'Bread,' Slim asked, 'what for?'

'Bustamante knows,' Joe said.

'Blasphemy, Joe,' Albert said, 'blasphemy. You should go to Confession some time.'

'That's nonsense,' Harry said.

'Unbelief, a sin against Faith,' Albert said. 'I am in bad company.'

'What time did you say it was?' Calderon asked Joe with a wink and a smile.

'I said it was twenty to ten. Now it is a quarter to.'

'Anybody can confess his sins at home,' Harry said.

'Still early,' Albert said, 'I hate to leave this.'

'Gluttony,' Calderon said, 'what's that a sin against?'

'You will miss the boat,' Slim said.

'I am not the one going, remember,' Albert said. 'Only my sister.'

'Well, you have to see her off, don't you?'

'I don't have to, but I will. I'll see you all when I come back.'

'How about one for the road?' Joe said.

'Three for the road, Joe,' Albert said. He drank this one alone and said, 'I want to have a head start on you boys so that you can catch up with me while I am on the wharf.'

'Five to ten,' Joe said. Albert put down the glass and went out.

Now he was thinking, and I had to leave all that and only to find that the boat had just arrived and a quarrel ready for me. It is a wonder she has not told me that I have been drinking, though by now there must be enough smell to push a horse over. And look at the way the little brat looks at me. I bet he would beat me if he had the chance to do so.

'What are you looking at, David?' he asked his nephew.

'Nothing, uncle.'

'How do you feel going away tonight?'

'Well, uncle.'

'You are not afraid?'

'No, uncle.'

'I would be afraid,' he said, 'especially if I had to travel with your mother. She can't swim you know.'

'Yes, uncle.'

'Yes what, David?'

'I don't know, uncle.'

'I am sure,' he said.

'Leave the boy alone,' his sister said.

'Your mother can't swim,' he said to the boy.

'Yes, uncle.'

'And if the boat sinks you will drown. You know that?'

The boy was afraid now and he began to sniffle. If this thing continued he would cry. Albert wanted the boy to cry. His sister said, 'Don't frighten the child, Albert.'

'David is not a child,' Albert said, 'are you, David?'

'Yes, uncle.'

'No. You are not a child. You are a man. Aren't you?'

'Yes, uncle.'

'So you are both man and child, eh, David?'

'Yes, uncle.'

'That's true. The father is child of the man.'

'The child is father of the man,' his sister said.

'Bravo,' he said.

'The boat will sink and you will drown,' he told his nephew. The boy began to cry.

'Albert,' his sister said, 'you have been drinking again.'

'Yes.'

'And you have not gone for supper yet I am sure.'

'No, I have not been home, if you want to know, since I left it at twelve. And it is now after ten o'clock p.m. Don't you think it is a shame?'

'I don't know how your wife can stand it,' his sister said.

'She isn't doing too badly,' he said.

'And she's expecting another baby.'

'That is the chief function of married women.'

He was a little sorry immediately he said so. David was his sister's child out of marriage. He tried to change the conversation quickly.

'What time does the boat expect to leave?'

'I don't know,' she said.

'Next two hours or thereabouts. They are still unloading her.'

'I hope nothing is wrong,' she said, 'with the engine.'

'I doubt it,' he said. 'The only thing is that it must have been delayed taking cargo at the last port. Oh I remember there was a strike at Barbados and the police had to unload her. It must have taken them some time.'

She said nothing. Then he said, 'It is about time we have a strike here. It would teach the government something.'

'Albert, you don't have to talk so loud.'

'We need to have one here to show them that we mean business.'

'All right Albert, but please don't say it. They will think you are one of the ringleaders.'

'They will be afraid of me.'

'They will dislike you.'

'And be afraid of me.'

'Perhaps, Albert, but they could hurt you.'

'They will pay for it.'

The crowd in the Customs House was beginning to thin now and the men had stopped unloading the ship. The incoming passengers had gone and there were only a few people inside of the building. He was thinking: I could go back and spend another hour with the boys, you know. I should not have left in the first place. Slim would know what he was talking about. I was a fool to disbelieve him. And now there is nothing to do but stand here and talk nonsense. If I tell her I am going she will become suspicious and start to preach to me. I know what I will do. I'll make it so sudden she will not have time to think much less to say anything. He said, 'Excuse me, I'll be back.' He was going even before he had completed the sentence. 'Where are you going to?' she asked. But he was disappearing around the doorway. He said, 'I am going back just now.'

2

In the Customs House the few passengers who were waiting to embark sat down on the low counter, their baggage checked, and waited for the time when they could get aboard ship. There were eight of them and of these, four sat in a group on the centre of the counter. The other two, a man and his wife, had got up and were walking slowly up and down the floor of the building and the woman was telling her husband something to which he was interestedly listening. At the end of the counter, David was asleep against his mother who herself dozed. It was not as hot as it had been before in the crowded room, but there was still some heat coming from the powerful bulb in the ceiling. It was almost eleven o'clock. The baggage lay on the low counter and there were the initials of the Customs' clerk written in coloured chalk on each piece. The boy's mother was thinking about her brother and where he was drinking his rum. She was sure that he was drinking rum. And if only she knew where he was and did not believe that she should stay here to wait for the ship, she would have gone after him. But he drank in so many places that if you were not lucky you could go into all the rum shops and meet him only in the last one. To catch him in one of them, unless you knew that he was in there certainly, was a stroke of luck. So she decided she would wait for him to return. Nearly an hour after his departure he had not done so. And now she was afraid that he would not come and that she would have to leave without having seen him this last time. For him she was sorry that she was going away. She could not influence him, it was true, but she believed that her presence had, more than once, softened his attitude a little when it should have been softened much. And even though he never showed it, because it was not in his nature to show that he accepted correction, she was sure that some of what she had told him had had some effect. Now with her gone there would be nobody to try to influence him. There was his wife, of course. But she was useless. She was afraid to tell him anything. There were two things she was not afraid to do for him, bear his children and tell other people of the hardships that his rum drinking and his political statements placed upon her home. Since their marriage, her friends, and some of his too, had known more about her husband than Agnes herself knew. Relations between the man and his wife were very bad, she believed, and one of the reasons for his not going home when he should, though it was not the main reason, was that his wife did nothing to encourage him to stop his drinking and to come home and find there a comfortable place to spend his leisure hours in. If I were married, Agnes thought, I would do my best to have him come back. I would not let him do that to himself to me and to the children. I would speak to him about it instead of going about and telling other people things about him. Especially when, in this small town, he would get to hear most of it, anyway, from those to whom I had told it. I would make his home some place he would feel like coming to after work on afternoons instead of going about becoming drunk and coming home at twelve each night. And now, after he has promised, he is not even here to see me off.

Now a porter came and put all the baggage on to a truck and took it to the ship. The passengers went outside to the wharf. There was one light from the lamp-post in front of the Customs House and the rest of the wharf was lighted only by the reflection of the lights from the ship. There were a few people standing on the wharf and there was a policeman to keep them away from the ship. The ship was lighted in parts only and it was high above the level of the wharf and the noise of its engines came through its sides resting against the wharf. The passengers were beginning to embark.

So, the boy's mother was thinking, he will not come now. He probably is so drunk now that he does not even remember that I am sailing tonight and that he promised to see me off. I am sure he has not gone home yet even though it is after eleven and the rum shops are nearly all closed. He must be lying across some table, drunk, his feet spread out beneath it, his hat on the floor, his jacket ends hanging below the level of his stretched-out thighs, his head lolling. Gone, dead to the world.

The man and his wife were going up the gangway now and the other passengers were clustered at the foot of the gangway under the light from the ship. The ship smelt of dirty oil and of greased cable. From one of the portholes near the stern of the ship dirty water was falling into the sea. The man and his wife had almost reached the top of the swaying gangway. Three policemen stood together a little way from the group of passengers, dressed all in black except for the silver in their buttons and at the top of their cork hats. They stood easily with their hands held behind their backs and they were laughing at something that one of them had said. The man and his wife, the wife in front, came to the end of the gangway and climbed on to the deck. The mother of the little boy, holding her son's hand, began to go up the gangway. Then she heard 'Agnes, Agnes,' and looking around she saw Albert running across from the Customs House, his coat-tails flapping behind him, and his hat held in place on his head by his left hand placed on the crown. She came down from the gangway and allowed the other passengers to climb. Albert came to where the passengers had been standing near to the bottom of the gangway. He seemed about to choke from the tightness of the knotted long black tie that he wore.

'Goodbye, Agnes,' he said.

'Albert, where have you been?'

'I was with the boys. Let me kiss you goodbye.'

He kissed her. 'Goodbye, David.' The boy was half asleep against his mother. He mumbled, 'Bye, uncle.'

'I have to go now,' his sister said.

One of the policemen came now to where they were standing and said 'Only passengers allowed here, mister.'

'I will come up with you.'

'It's all right,' Albert said, 'it's my sister. She is going away and I am seeing her off.'

'Passengers only allowed here,' the policeman repeated.

'It's all right, I tell you.'

'Goodbye, Albert,' Agnes said, 'now please go.'

'I am seeing you to the top of the gangway,' he said. 'It's dangerous for you to climb it alone with the boy.'

'I'll manage, Albert. Now go. You can't stay here.'

'Come on,' the policeman said.

'I'm seeing my sister to the deck of this ship.'

'No sir, not this ship. You're going back right now.' He held Albert firmly by the arm and began to walk with him away from the ship.

'Let me go,' Albert said, and wrenched his arm away. His sister was already going up the gangway. She was afraid that, standing there, alone of all the passengers, she would be keeping back the boat. And she did not want to miss it either. But she feared for her brother. She knew how stubborn he could be. Besides, he was drunk. She said, 'Albert, behave yourself, please. Don't make any trouble.'

From the top of the gangway one of the sailors was saying, 'Come on, Lady, we've got to get 'er up.'

She walked slowly up watching the policeman and her brother. Her brother said, 'Let me go. I'll walk off. You don't have to put your dirty hands on me.'

'Dirty hands, eh,' the policeman said. He placed his hands on Albert's chest and pushed him so violently that he fell over backwards, his feet in the air.

'No,' Agnes shouted from the gangway and made as if to go back. But she was already more than halfway up and now the gangway was going up very slowly. She saw him get up from the ground and rush towards the policeman, and then the three of them were on him and she could only see the lifting and dropping of their arms holding their truncheons and hear the sound of the wood on her brother's body. Her brother was shouting, 'You have no right to do this to me, you can't treat me this way,' and he was hitting back, but she could see that he was not hurting them in any way whatever and that there was blood now on his face.

She was forced by the angle of the rising gangway to get to the deck, and from the deck she could see them hammer him with their sticks and then he was not retaliating and they were hitting him again and again, and, seeing that, she felt the suddenly heavy throb in the ship as it began to move, and saw them carrying him, holding him under the armpits and with his feet dragging a path in the ground over which they passed, out from the wharf, through the gate, and out of sight. She was crying softly now as the ship moved away from the wharf and went far out into the middle of the harbour to turn, and then it had turned and she was seeing the lights of the town recede as the ship headed for the entrance of the bay, and as she looked at the wharf speeding by she saw his hat where it had fallen on the concrete wide edge of the wharf and then the single light before the Customs House was put out and there was darkness except beyond the wharf where the street lights showed.

V. S. NAIPAUL

The Baker's Story

Look at me. Black as the Ace of Spades, and ugly to match. Nobody looking at me would believe they looking at one of the richest men in this city of Port of Spain. Sometimes I find it hard to believe it myself, you know, especially when I go out on some of the holidays that I start taking the wife and children to these days, and I catch sight of the obzocky black face in one of those fancy mirrors that expensive hotels have all over the place, as if to spite people like me.

Now everybody – particularly black people – forever asking me how this thing start, and I does always tell them I make my dough from dough. Ha! You like that one? But how it start? Well, you hearing me talk, and I don't have to tell you I didn't have no education. In Grenada, where I come from – and that is one thing these Trinidad black people don't forgive a man for being: a black Grenadian – in Grenada I was one of ten children, I believe – everything kind of mix up out there – and I don't even know who was the feller who hit my mother. I believe he hit a lot of women in all the other parishes of that island, too, because whenever I go back to Grenada for one of those holidays I tell you about, people always telling me that I remind them of this one and that one, and they always mistaking me for a shop assistant whenever I in a shop. (If this thing go on, one day I going to sell somebody something, just for spite.) And even in Trinidad, whenever I run into another Grenadian, the same thing does happen.

Well, I don't know what happen in Grenada, but mammy bring me alone over to Trinidad when she was still young. I don't know what she do with the others, but perhaps they wasn't even she own. Anyway, she get a work with some white people in St Ann's. They give she a uniform; they give she three meals a day; and they give she a few dollars a month besides. Somehow she get another man, a real Trinidad 'rangoutang, and somehow, I don't know how, she get somebody else to look after me while she was living with this man, for the money and the food she was getting was scarcely enough to support this low-minded Trinidad rango she take up with.

It used to have a Chinee shop not far from this new aunty I was living with, and one day, when the old girl couldn't find the cash no how to buy a bread – is a hell of a thing, come to think of it now, that it have people in this island who can't lay their hands on enough of the ready to buy a bread – well, when she couldn't buy this bread she send me over to this Chinee shop to ask for trust. The Chinee woman – eh, but how these Chinee people does make children! – was big like anything, and I believe I catch she at a good moment, because she say nothing doing, no trust, but if I want a little work that was different, because she want somebody to take some bread she bake for some Indian people. But how she could trust me with the bread? This was a question. And then I pull out my crucifix from under my dirty merino that was more holes than cloth and I tell she to keep it until I come back with the money for the bake bread. I don't know what sort of religion these Chinee people have, but that woman looked impressed like anything. But she was smart, though. She keep the crucifix and she send me off with the bread, which was wrap up in a big old *châle-au-pain*,* just two or three floursack sew together. I collect the money, bring it back, and she give me back the crucifix with a few cents and a bread.

And that was how this thing really begin. I always tell black people that was God give me my start in life, and don't mind these Trinidadians who does always tell you that Grenadians always praying. Is a true thing, though, because whenever I in any little business difficulty even these days I get down bam! straight on my two knees and I start praying like hell, boy.

Well, so this thing went on, until it was a regular afternoon work for me to deliver people bread. The bakery uses to bake ordinary bread – hops and pan and machine – which they uses to sell to the poorer classes. And how those Chinee people uses to work! This woman, with

* *châle-au-pain*: bread-sack.

she big-big belly, clothes all dirty, sweating in front of the oven, making all this bread and making all this money, and I don't know what they doing with it, because all the time they living poor-poor in the back room, with only a bed, some hammocks for the young ones, and a few boxes. I couldn't talk to the husband at all. He didn't know a word of English and all the writing he uses to write uses to be Chinee. He was a thin nashy feller, with those funny flapping khaki short pants and white merino that Chinee people always wear. He uses to work like a bitch too. We Grenadians understand hard work, so that is why I suppose I uses to get on so well with these Chinee people, and that is why these lazy black Trinidadians is jealous of we. But was a funny thing. They uses to live so dirty. But the children, man, uses to leave that ramshackle old back room as clean as new bread, and they always had this neatness, always with their little pencil-case and their little rubbers and rulers and blotters, and they never losing anything. They leaving in the morning in one nice little line and in the afternoon they coming back in this same little line, still cool and clean, as though nothing at all touch them all day. Is something they could teach black people children.

But as I was saying, this bakery uses to bake ordinary bread for the poorer classes. For the richer classes they uses to bake, too. But what they would do would be to collect the dough from those people house, bake it, and send it back as bread, hot and sweet. I uses to fetch and deliver for this class of customer. They never let me serve in the shop; it was as though they couldn't trust me selling across the counter and collecting money in that rush. Always it had this rush. You know black people: even if it only have one man in the shop he always getting on as if it have one hell of a crowd.

Well, one day when I deliver some bread in this *châle-au-pain* to a family, there was a woman, a neighbour, who start saying how nice it is to get bread which you knead with your own hands and not mix up with all sort of people sweat. And this give me the idea. A oven is a oven. It have to go on, whether it baking one bread or two. So I tell this woman, was a Potogee woman, that I would take she dough and bring it back bake for she, and that it would cost she next to nothing. I say this in a sort of way that she wouldn't know whether I was going to give the money to the Chinee people, or whether it was going to cost she next to nothing because it would be I who was going to take the money. But she give me a look which tell me right away that she wanted me to take the money. So matter fix. So. Back in the *châle-au-pain* the next few days I take some dough, hanging it in the carrier of the bakery bicycle. I take it inside, as though I just didn't bother to wrap up the *châle-au-pain*, and the next thing is that this dough mix up with the other dough, and see me kneading and baking, as though all is one. The thing is, when you go in for a thing like that, to go in brave-brave. It have some who make so much fuss when they doing one little thing that they bound to get catch. So, and I was surprise like hell, mind you. I get this stuff push in the oven, and is this said Chinee man, always with this sad and sorrowful Chinee face, who pulling it out of the oven with the long-handle shovel, looking at it, and pushing it back in.

And when I take the bread back, with some other bread, I collect the money cool-cool. The thing with a thing like this is that once you start is damn hard to stop. You start calculating this way and that way. And I have a calculating mind. I forever sitting down and working out how much say .50 a day every day for seven days, and every week for a year, coming to. And so this thing get to be a big thing with me. I wouldn't recommend this to any and everybody who want to go into business. But is what I mean when I tell people that I make my dough by dough.

The Chinee woman wasn't too well now. And the old man was getting on a little funny in a Chinee way. You know how those Chinee fellers does gamble. You drive past Marine Square in the early hours of the Sabbath and is two to one if you don't see some of those Chinee fellers sitting down outside the Treasury, as though they want to be near money, and gambling like hell. Well, the old man was gambling and the old girl was sick, and I was pretty well the only person looking after the bakery. I work damn hard for them, I could tell you. I even pick up two or three words of Chinee, and some of those rude black people start calling me Black Chinee, because at this time I was beginning to dress in short khaki pants and merino like a Chinee and I was drinking that tea Chinee people drinking all day long and I was walking and not saying much like a Chinee. And, now, don't believe what these black people say about Chinee and prejudice, eh. They have nothing at all against black people, provided they is hard-working and grateful.

But life is a funny thing. Now when it look that I all set, that everything going fine and dandy, a whole set of things happen that start me bawling. First, the Chinee lady catch a pleurisy and dead. Was a hell of a thing, but what else you expect when she was always bending down in front of that fire and then getting wet and going out in the dew and everything, and then always making these children too besides. I was sorry like hell, and a little frighten. Because I wasn't too sure how I was going to manage alone with the old man. All the time I work with him he never speak one word straight to me, but he always talking to me through his wife.

And now, look at my crosses. As soon as the woman dead, the Chinee man like he get mad. He didn't cry or anything like that, but he start gambling like a bitch, and the upshot was that one day, perhaps about a month after the old lady dead, the man tell his children to pack up and start leaving, because he gamble and lose the shop to another Chinee feller. I didn't know where I was standing, and nobody telling me nothing. They only packing. I don't know, I suppose they begin to feel that I was just part of the shop, and the old man not even saying that he sorry he lose me. And, you know, as soon as I drop to my knees and start praying, I see it was really God who right from the start put that idea of the dough into my head, because without that I would have been nowhere at all. Because the new feller who take over the shop say he don't want me. He was going to close the bakery and set up a regular grocery, and he didn't want me serving there because the grocery customers wouldn't like black people serving them. So look at me. Twenty-three years old and no work. No nothing. Only I have this Chinee-ness and I know how to bake bread and I have this extra bit of cash I save up over the years.

I slip out of the old khaki short pants and merino and I cruise around the town a little, looking for work. But nobody want bakers. I had about $700.00, and I see that this cruising around would do but it wouldn't pay, because the money was going fast. Now look at this. You know, it never cross my mind in those days that I could open a shop of my own. Is how it is with black people. They get so use to working for other people that they get to believe that because they black they can't do nothing else but work for other people. And I must tell you that when

I start praying and God tell me to go out and open a shop for myself I feel that perhaps God did mistake or that I hadn't hear him good. Because God only saying to me, 'Youngman, take your money and open a bakery. You could bake good bread.' He didn't say to open a parlour, which a few black fellers do, selling rock cakes and mauby and other soft drinks. No, he say open a bakery. Look at my crosses.

I had a lot of trouble borrowing the extra few hundred dollars, but I eventually get a Indian feller to lend me. And this is what I always tell young fellers. That getting credit ain't no trouble at all if you know exactly what you want to do. I didn't go round telling people to lend me money because I want to build house or buy lorry. I just did want to bake bread. Well, to cut a long story short, I buy a break-down old place near Arouca, and I spend most of what I had trying to fix the place up. Nothing extravagant, you understand, because Arouca is Arouca and you don't want to frighten off the country-bookies with anything too sharp. Too besides, I didn't have the cash. I just put in a few second-hand glass cases and things like that. I write up my name on a board, and look, I in business.

Now the funny thing happen. In Laventille the people couldn't have enough of the bread I was baking – and in the last few months was me was doing the baking. But now trouble. I baking better bread than the people of Arouca ever see, and I can't get one single feller to come in like man through my rickety old front door and buy a penny hops bread. You hear all this talk about quality being its own advertisement? Don't believe it, boy. Is quality plus something else. And I didn't have this something else. I begin to wonder what the hell it could be. I say is because I new in Arouca that this thing happening. But no, I new, I get stale, and the people not flocking in their hundreds to the old shop. Day after day I baking two or three quarts good and all this just remaining and going dry and stale, and the only bread I selling is to the man from the government farm, buying stale cakes and bread for the cows or pigs or whatever they have up there. And was good bread. So I get down on the old knees and I pray as though I want to wear them out. And still I getting the same answer: 'Youngman' – was always the way I uses to get call in these prayers – 'Youngman, you just bake bread.'

Pappa! This was a thing. Interest on the loan piling up every month.

Some months I borrow from aunty and anybody else who kind enough to listen just to pay off the interest. And things get so low that I uses to have to go out and pretend to people that I was working for another man bakery and that I was going to bake their dough cheap-cheap. And in Arouca cheap mean cheap. And the little cash I picking up in this disgraceful way just about enough to keep the wolf from the door, I tell you.

Jeezan. Look at confusion. The old place in Arouca so damn out of the way – was why I did buy it, too, thinking that they didn't have no bakery there and that they would be glad of the good Grenadian-baked – the place so out of the way nobody would want to buy it. It ain't even insure or anything, so it can't get in a little fire accident or anything – not that I went in for that sort of thing. And every time I go down on my knees, the answer coming straight back at me: 'Youngman, you just bake bread.'

Well, for the sake of the Lord I baking one or two quarts regular every day, though I begin to feel that the Lord want to break me, and I begin to feel too that it was his punishment for what I uses to do to the Chinee people in their bakery. I was beginning to feel bad and real ignorant. I uses to stay away from the bakery after baking those quarts for the Lord – nothing to lock up, nothing to thief – and, when any of the Laventille boys drop in on the way to Manzanilla and Balandra and those other beaches on the Sabbath, I uses to tell them, making a joke out of it, that I was 'loafing'. They uses to laugh like hell, too. It have nothing in the whole world so funny as to see a man you know flat out on his arse and catching good hell.

The Indian feller was getting anxious about his cash, and you couldn't blame him, either, because some months now he not even seeing his interest. And this begin to get me down, too. I remember how all the man did ask me when I went to him for money was: 'You sure you want to bake bread? You feel you have a hand for baking bread?' And yes-yes, I tell him, and just like that he shell out the cash. And now he was getting anxious. So one day, after baking those loaves for the Lord, I take a Arima Bus Service bus to Port of Spain to see this feller. I was feeling brave enough on the way. But as soon as I see the old sea and get a whiff of South Quay and the bus touch the railway station terminus, my belly start going pweh-pweh. I decide to roam about the city for a little.

Was a hot morning, *petit-carême** weather, and in those days a coconut uses still to cost .04. Well, it had this coconut cart in the old square and I stop by it. It was a damn funny thing to see. The seller was a black feller. And you wouldn't know how funny this was, unless you know that every coconut seller in the island is Indian. They have this way of handling a cutlass that black people don't have. Coconut in left hand; with right hand bam, bam, bam with cutlass, and coconut cut open, ready to drink. I ain't never see a coconut seller chop his hand. And here was this black feller doing this bam-bam business on a coconut with a cutlass. It was as funny as seeing a black man wearing dhoti and turban. The sweetest part of the whole business was that this black feller was, forgetting looks, just like an Indian. He was talking Hindustani to a lot of Indian fellers, who was giving him jokes like hell, but he wasn't minding. It does happen like that sometimes with black fellers who live a lot with Indians in the country. They putting away curry, talking Indian, and behaving just like Indians. Well, I take a coconut from this black man and then went on to see the feller about the money.

He was more sad than vex when I tell him, and if I was in his shoes I woulda be sad, too. Is a hell of a thing when you see your money gone and you ain't getting the sweet little kisses from the interest every month. Anyway, he say he would give me three more months' grace, but that if I didn't start shelling out at the agreed rate he would have to foreclose. 'You put me in a hell of a position,' he say. 'Look at me. You think I want a shop in Arouca?'

I was feeling a little better when I leave the feller, and who I should see when I leave but Percy. Percy was an old rango who uses to go to the Laventille elementary school with me. I never know a boy get so much cut-arse as Percy. But he grow up real hard and ignorant with it, and now he wearing fancy clothes like a saga boy, and talking about various business offers. I believe he was selling insurance – is a thing that nearly every idler doing in Trinidad, and, mark my words, the day coming when you going to see those fellers trying to sell insurance to one another. Anyway, Percy getting on real flash, and he say he want to

---

* *petit-carême*: the kind of weather just before Easter time.

stand me a lunch for old times' sake. He makes a few of the usual ignorant Trinidadian jokes about Grenadians, and we went up to the Angostura Bar. I did never go there before, and wasn't the sort of place you would expect a rango like Percy to be welcome. But we went up there and Percy start throwing his weight around with the waiters, and mind you, they wasn't even a quarter as black as Percy. Is a wonder they didn't abuse him, especially with all those fair people around. After the drinks Percy say, 'Where you want to have this lunch?'

Me, I don't know a thing about the city restaurants, and when Percy talk about food all I was expecting was rice and peas or a roti off a Indian stall or a mauby and rock cake in some parlour. And is a damn hard thing to have people, even people as ignorant as Percy, showing off on you, especially when you carrying two nails in your pocket to make the jingling noise. So I tell Percy we could go to a parlour or a bar. But he say, 'No, no. When I treat my friends, I don't like black people meddling with my food.'

And was only then that the thing hit me. I suppose that what Trinidadians say about the stupidness of Grenadians have a little truth, though you have to live in a place for a long time before you get to know it really well. Then the thing hit me, man.

When black people in Trinidad go to a restaurant they don't like to see black people meddling with their food. And then I see that though Trinidad have every race and every colour, every race have to do special things. But look, man. If you want to buy a snowball, who you buying it from? You wouldn't buy it from a Indian or a Chinee or a Potogee. You would buy it from a black man. And I myself, when I was getting my place in Arouca fix up, I didn't employ Indian carpenters or masons. If a Indian in Trinidad decide to go into the carpentering business the man would starve. Who ever see a Indian carpenter? I suppose the only place in the world where they have Indian carpenters and Indian masons is India. Is a damn funny thing. One of these days I must make a trip to that country, to just see this thing. And as we walking I see the names of bakers: Coelho, Pantin, Stauble. Potogee or Swiss, or something, and then all those other Chinee places. And, look at the laundries. If a black man open a laundry, you would take your clothes to it? *I* wouldn't take my clothes there. Well, I walking to this restaurant, but I jumping for joy. And then all sorts of things fit into place. You remember that the Chinee people didn't let me serve bread across the counter? I uses to think it was because they didn't trust me with the rush. But it wasn't that. It was that, if they did let me serve, they would have had no rush at all. You ever see anybody buying their bread off a black man?

I ask Percy why he didn't like black people meddling with his food in public places. The question throw him a little. He stop and think and say, 'It don't *look* nice.'

Well, you could guess the rest of the story. Before I went back to Arouca that day I made contact with a yellow boy call Macnab. This boy was half black and half Chinee, and, though he had a little brown colour and the hair a little curly, he could pass for one of those Cantonese. They a little darker than the other Chinee people, I believe. Macnab I find beating a steel pan in somebody yard – they was practising for Carnival – and I suppose the only reason that Macnab was willing to come all the way to Arouca was because he was short of the cash to buy his costume for the Carnival island.

But he went up with me. I put him in front of the shop, give him a merino and a pair of khaki short pants, and tell him to talk as Chinee as he could, if he wanted to get that Carnival bonus. I stay in the back room, and I start baking bread. I even give Macnab a old Chinee paper, not to read, because Macnab could scarcely read English, but just to leave lying around, to make it look good. And I get hold of one of those big Chinee calendars with Chinee women and flowers and waterfalls and hang it up on the wall. And when this was all ready, I went down on my knees and thank God. And still the old message coming, but friendly and happy now: 'Youngman, you just bake bread.'

And, you know, that solve another problem. I was worrying to hell about the name I should give the place. New Shanghai, Canton, Hong-kong, Nanking, Yangtse-Kiang. But when the old message came over I know right away what the name should be. I scrub off the old name – no need to tell you what that was – and I get a proper sign painter to copy a few letters from the Chinee newspaper. Below that, in big letters, I make him write:

YUNG MAN BAKER

I never show my face in the front of the shop again. And I tell you, without boasting, that I bake damn good bread. And the people of Arouca ain't that foolish. They know a good thing. And soon I was making so much money that I was able to open a branch in Arima and then another in Port of Spain self. Was hard in the beginning to get real Chinee people to work for a black man. But money have it own way of talking, and when today you pass any of the Yung Man establishments all you seeing behind the counter is Chinee. Some of them ain't even know they working for a black man. My wife handling that side of the business, and the wife is Chinee. She come from down Cedros way. So look at me now, in Port of Spain, giving Stauble and Pantin and Coelho a run for their money. As I say, I only going in the shops from the back. But every Monday morning I walking brave brave to Marine Square and going in the bank, from the front.

PAULE MARSHALL

Barbados

Dawn, like night which had preceded it, came from the sea. In a white mist tumbling like spume over the fishing boats leaving the island and the hunched, ghost shapes of the fishermen. In a white, wet wind breathing over the villages scattered amid the tall canes. The cabbage palms roused, their high headdresses solemnly saluting the wind, and along the white beach which ringed the island the casuarina trees began their moaning – a sound of women lamenting their dead within a cave.

The wind, smarting of the sea, threaded a wet skein through Mr Watford's five hundred dwarf coconut trees and around his house at the edge of the grove. The house, Colonial American in design, seemed created by the mist – as if out of the dawn's formlessness had come, magically, the solid stone walls, the blind, broad windows and the portico of fat columns which embraced the main story. When the mist cleared, the house remained – pure, proud, a pristine white – disdaining the crude wooden houses in the village outside its high gate.

It was not the dawn settling around his house which awakened Mr Watford, but the call of his Barbary doves from their hutch in the yard. And it was more the feel of that sound than the sound itself. His hands had retained, from the many times a day he held the doves, the feel of their throats swelling with that murmurous, mournful note. He lay abed now, his hands – as cracked and callused as a cane cutter's – filled with the sound and against the white sheet which flowed out to the white walls he appeared profoundly alone, yet secure in loneliness, contained. His face was fleshless and severe, his black skin sucked deep into the hollow of his jaw, while under a high brow, which was like a bastion raised against the world, his eyes were indrawn and pure. It was as if during all his seventy years, Mr Watford had permitted nothing to sight which could have affected him.

He stood up, and his body, muscular but stripped of flesh, appeared to be absolved from time, still young. Yet each clenched gesture of his arms, of his lean shank as he dressed in a faded shirt and work pants, each vigilant, snapping motion of his head betrayed tension. Ruthlessly he spurred his body to perform like a younger man's. Savagely he denied the accumulated fatigue of the years. Only sometimes when he paused in his grove of coconut trees during the day, his eyes tearing and the breath torn from his lungs, did it seem that if he could find a place hidden from the world and himself he would give way to exhaustion and weep from weariness.

Dressed, he strode through the house, his step tense, his rough hand touching the furniture from Grand Rapids which crowded each room. For some reason, Mr Watford had never completed the house. Everywhere the walls were raw and unpainted, the furniture unarranged. In the drawing-room with its coffered ceiling, he stood before his favorite piece, an old mantel clock which eked out time. Reluctantly it whirred five and Mr Watford nodded. His day had begun.

It was no different from all the days which made up the five years since his return to Barbados. Downstairs in the unfinished kitchen, he prepared his morning tea – tea with canned milk and fried bakes – and ate standing at the stove while lizards skittered over the unplastered walls. Then, belching and snuffling the way a child would, he put on a pith helmet, secured his pants legs with bicycle clasps and stepped into the yard. There he fed the doves, holding them so that their sound poured into his hands and laughing gently – but the laugh gave way to an irritable grunt as he saw the mongoose tracks under the hutch. He set the trap again.

The first heat had swept the island like a huge tidal wave when Mr Watford, with that tense, headlong stride, entered the grove. He had planted the dwarf coconut trees because of their quick yield and because, with their stunted trunks, they always appeared young. Now as he worked, rearranging the complex of pipes which irrigated the land, stripping off the dead leaves, the trees were like cool, moving presences; the stiletto fronds wove a protective dome above him and slowly, as the day soared toward noon, his mind filled with the slivers of sunlight through the trees and the feel of earth in his hands, as it might have been filled with thoughts.

Except for a meal at noon, he remained in the grove until dusk surged up from the sea; then returning to the house, he bathed and dressed in a medical doctor's white uniform, turned on the lights in the parlor and opened the tall doors to the portico. Then the old women of the village on their way to church, the last hawkers caroling, 'Fish, flying fish, a penny, my lady,' the roistering saga-boys lugging their heavy steel drums to the crossroad where they would rehearse under the street lamp – all passing could glimpse Mr Watford, stiff in his white uniform and with his head bent heavily over a Boston newspaper. The papers reached him weeks late but he read them anyway, giving a little savage chuckle at the thought that beyond his world that other world went its senseless way. As he read, the night sounds of the village welled into a joyous chorale against the sea's muffled cadence and the hollow, haunting music of the steel band. Soon the moths, lured in by the light, fought to die on the lamp, the beetles crashed drunkenly against the walls and the night – like a woman offering herself to him – became fragrant with the night-blooming cactus.

Even in America Mr Watford had spent his evenings this way. Coming home from the hospital, where he worked in the boiler-room, he would dress in his white uniform and read in the basement of the large rooming-house he owned. He had lived closeted like this, detached, because America – despite the money and property he had slowly accumulated – had meant nothing to him. Each morning, walking to the hospital along the rutted Boston streets, through the smoky dawn light, he had known – although it had never been a thought – that his allegiance, his place, lay elsewhere. Neither had the few acquaintances he had made mattered. Nor the women he had occasionally kept as a younger man. After the first months their bodies would grow coarse to his hand and he would begin edging away ... So that he had felt no regret when, the year before his retirement, he resigned his job, liquidated his properties and, his fifty-year exile over, returned home.

The clock doled out eight and Mr Watford folded the newspaper and brushed the burnt moths from the lamp base. His lips still shaped the last words he had read as he moved through the rooms, fastening the windows against the night air, which he had dreaded even as a boy. Something palpable but unseen was always, he believed, crouched in the night's dim recess, waiting to snare him ... Once in bed in his sealed room, Mr Watford fell asleep quickly.

The next day was no different except that Mr Goodman, the local shopkeeper, sent the boy for coconuts to sell at the racetrack and then came that evening to pay for them and to herald – although Mr Watford did not know this – the coming of the girl.

That morning, taking his tea, Mr Watford heard the careful tap of the mule's hoofs and looking out saw the wagon jolting through the dawn and the boy, still lax with sleep, swaying on the seat. He was perhaps eighteen and the muscles packed tightly beneath his lustrous black skin gave him a brooding strength. He came and stood outside the back door, his hands and lowered head performing the small, subtle rites of deference.

Mr Watford's pleasure was full, for the gestures were those given only to a white man in his time. Yet the boy always nettled him. He sensed a natural arrogance like a pinpoint of light within his dark stare. The boy's stance exhumed a memory buried under the years. He remembered, staring at him, the time when he had worked as a yard boy for a white family, and had had to assume the same respectful pose while their flat, raw, Barbadian voices assailed him with orders. He remembered the muscles in his neck straining as he nodded deeply and a taste like alum on his tongue as he repeated the 'Yes, please,' as in a litany. But because of their whiteness and wealth, he had never dared hate them. Instead his rancor, like a boomerang, had rebounded, glancing past him to strike all the dark ones like himself, even his mother with her spindled arms and her stomach sagging with a child who was, invariably, dead at birth. He had been the only one of ten to live, the only one to escape. But he had never lost the sense of being pursued by the same dread presence which had claimed them. He had never lost the fear that if he lived too fully he would tire and death would quickly close the gap. His only defense had been a cautious life and work. He had been almost broken by work at the age of twenty when his parents died, leaving him enough money for the passage to America. Gladly had he fled the island. But nothing had mattered after his flight.

The boy's foot stirred the dust. He murmured, 'Please, sir, Mr Watford, Mr Goodman at the shop send me to pick the coconuts.'

Mr Watford's head snapped up. A caustic word flared, but died as he noticed a political button pinned to the boy's patched shirt with 'Vote for the Barbados People's Party' printed boldly on it, and below that the motto of the party: 'The Old Shall Pass'. At this ludicrous touch (for what could this boy, with his splayed and shigoed feet and blunted mind, understand about politics?) he became suddenly nervous, angry. The button and its motto seemed, somehow, directed at him. He said roughly, 'Well, come then. You can't pick any coconuts standing there looking foolish!' – and he led the way to the grove.

The coconuts, he knew, would sell well at the booths in the center of the track, where the poor were penned in like cattle. As the heat thickened and the betting grew desperate, they would clamor: 'Man, how you selling the water coconuts?' and hacking off the tops they would pour rum into the water within the hollow centers, then tilt the coconuts to their heads so that the rum-sweetened water skimmed their tongues and trickled bright down their dark chins. Mr Watford had stood among them at the track as a young man, as poor as they were, but proud. And he had always found something unutterably graceful and free in their gestures, something which had roused contradictory feelings in him: admiration, but just as strong, impatience at their easy ways, and shame . . .

That night, as he sat in his white uniform reading, he heard Mr Goodman's heavy step and went out and stood at the head of the stairs in a formal, proprietary pose. Mr Goodman's face floated up into the light – the loose folds of flesh, the skin slick with sweat as if oiled, the eyes scribbled with veins and mottled, bold – as if each blemish there was a sin he proudly displayed or a scar which proved he had met life head-on. His body, unlike Mr Watford's, was corpulent and, with the trousers caught up around his full crotch, openly concupiscent. He owned the one shop in the village which gave credit and a booth which sold coconuts at the racetrack, kept a wife and two outside women, drank a rum with each customer at his bar, regularly caned his fourteen children, who still followed him everywhere (even now they were waiting for him in the darkness beyond Mr Watford's gate) and bet heavily at the races, and when he lost gave a loud hacking laugh which squeezed his body like a pain and left him gasping.

The laugh clutched him now as he flung his pendulous flesh into a chair and wheezed, 'Watford, how? Man, I near lose house, shop, shirt and all at races today. I tell you, they got some horses from Trinidad in this meet that's making ours look like they running backwards. Be Jese, I wouldn't bet on a Bajan horse tomorrow if Christ heself was to give me the tip. Those bitches might look good but they's nothing 'pon a track.'

Mr Watford, his back straight as the pillar he leaned against, his eyes unstained, his gaunt face planed by contempt, gave Mr Goodman his cold, measured smile, thinking that the man would be dead soon, bloated with rice and rum – and somehow this made his own life more certain.

Sputtering with his amiable laughter, Mr Goodman paid for the coconuts, but instead of leaving then as he usually did, he lingered, his eyes probing for a glimpse inside the house. Mr Watford waited, his head snapping warily; then, impatient, he started toward the door and Mr Goodman said, 'I tell you, your coconut trees bearing fast enough even for dwarfs. You's lucky, man.'

Ordinarily Mr Watford would have waved both the man and his remark aside, but repelled more than usual tonight by Mr Goodman's gross form and immodest laugh, he said – glad of the cold edge his slight American accent gave the words – 'What luck got to do with it? I does care the trees properly and they bear, that's all. Luck! People, especially this bunch around here, is always looking to luck when the only answer is a little brains and plenty of hard work . . .' Suddenly remembering the boy that morning and the political button, he added in loud disgust, 'Look that half-foolish boy you does send here to pick the coconuts. Instead of him learning a trade and going to England where he might find work he's walking about with a political button. He and all in politics now! But that's the way with these down here. They'll do some of everything but work. They don't want work!' He gestured violently, almost dancing in anger. 'They too busy spreeing.'

The chair creaked as Mr Goodman sketched a pained and gentle denial. 'No, man,' he said, 'you wrong. Things is different to before. I mean to say, the young people nowadays is different to how we was.

They not just sitting back and taking things no more. They not so frighten for the white people as we was. No, man. Now take that said same boy, for an example. I don't say he don't like a spree, but he's serious, you see him there. He's a member of this new Barbados People's Party. He wants to see his own color running the government. He wants to be able to make a living right here in Barbados instead of going to any cold England. And he's right!' Mr Goodman paused at a vehement pitch, then shrugged heavily. 'What the young people must do, nuh? They got to look to something . . .'

'Look to work!' and Mr Watford thrust out a hand so that the horned knuckles caught the light.

'Yes, that's true – and it's up to we that got little something to give them work,' Mr Goodman said, and a sadness filtered among the dissipations in his eyes. 'I mean to say we that got little something got to help out. In a manner of speaking, we's responsible . . .'

'Responsible!' The word circled Mr Watford's head like a gnat and he wanted to reach up and haul it down, to squash it underfoot.

Mr Goodman spread his hands; his breathing rumbled with a sigh. 'Yes, in a manner of speaking. That's why, Watford man, you got to provide little work for some poor person down in here. Hire a servant at least! 'Cause I gon tell you something . . .' And he hitched forward his chair, his voice dropped to a wheeze. 'People talking. Here you come back rich from big America and build a swell house and plant 'nough coconut trees and you still cleaning and cooking and thing like some woman. Man, it don't look good!' His face screwed in emphasis and he sat back. 'Now, there's this girl, the daughter of a friend that just dead, and she need work bad enough. But I wouldn't like to see she working for these white people 'cause you know how those men will take advantage of she. And she'd make a good servant, man. Quiet and quick so, and nothing a-tall to feed and she can sleep anywhere about the place. And she don't have no boys always around her either . . .' Still talking, Mr Goodman eased from his chair and reached the stairs with surprising agility. 'You need a servant,' he whispered, leaning close to Mr Watford as he passed. 'It don't look good, man, people talking. I gon send she.'

Mr Watford was overcome by nausea. Not only from Mr Goodman's smell – a stench of salt fish, rum and sweat – but from an outrage which was like a sediment in his stomach. For a long time he stood there almost kecking from disgust, until his clock struck eight, reminding him of the sanctuary within – and suddenly his cold laugh dismissed Mr Goodman and his proposal. Hurrying in, he locked the doors and windows against the night air and, still laughing, he slept.

The next day, coming from the grove to prepare his noon meal, he saw her. She was standing in his driveway, her bare feet like strong dark roots amid the jagged stones, her face tilted toward the sun – and she might have been standing there always waiting for him. She seemed of the sun, of the earth. The folk-tale of creation might have been true with her: that along a riverbank a god had scooped up the earth – rich and black and warmed by the sun – and molded her poised head with its tufted braids and then with a whimsical touch crowned it with a sober brown felt hat which should have been worn by some stout English matron in a London suburb, had sculptured the passionless face and drawn a screen of gossamer across her eyes to hide the void behind. Beneath her bodice her small breasts were smooth at the crest. Below her waist, her hips branched wide, the place prepared for its load of life. But it was the bold and sensual strength of her legs which completely unstrung Mr Watford. He wanted to grab a hoe and drive her off.

'What it 'tis you want?' he called sharply.

'Mr Goodman send me.'

'Send you for what?' His voice was shrill in the glare.

She moved. Holding a caved-in valise and a pair of white sandals, her head weaving slightly as though she bore a pail of water there or a tray of mangoes, she glided over the stones as if they were smooth ground. Her bland expression did not change, but her eyes, meeting his, held a vague trust. Pausing a few feet away, she curtsied deeply. 'I's the new servant.'

Only Mr Watford's cold laugh saved him from anger. As always it raised him to a height where everything below appeared senseless and insignificant – especially his people, whom the girl embodied. From this height, he could even be charitable. And thinking suddenly of how she had waited in the brutal sun since morning without taking shelter under the nearby tamarind tree, he said, not unkindly, 'Well, girl, go back and tell Mr Goodman for me that I don't need no servant.'

'I can't go back.'

'How you mean can't?' His head gave its angry snap.

'I'll get lashes,' she said simply. 'My mother say I must work the day and then if you don't wish me, I can come back. But I's not to leave till night falling, if not I get lashes.'

He was shaken by her dispassion. So much so that his head dropped from its disdaining angle and his hands twitched with helplessness. Despite anything he might say or do, her fear of the whipping would keep her there until nightfall, the valise and shoes in hand. He felt his day with its order and quiet rhythms threatened by her intrusion – and suddenly waving her off as if she were an evil visitation, he hurried into the kitchen to prepare his meal.

But he paused, confused, in front of the stove, knowing that he could not cook and leave her hungry at the door, nor could he cook and serve her as though he were the servant.

'Yes, please.'

They said nothing more. She entered the room with a firm step and an air of almost familiarity, placed her valise and shoes in a corner and went directly to the larder. For a time Mr Watford stood by, his muscles flexing with anger and his eyes bounding ahead of her every move, until feeling foolish and frighteningly useless, he went out to feed his doves.

The meal was quickly done and as he ate he heard the dry slap of her feet behind him – a pleasant sound – and then silence. When he glanced back she was squatting in the doorway, the sunlight aslant the absurd hat and her face bent to a bowl she held in one palm. She ate slowly, thoughtfully, as if fixing the taste of each spoonful in her mind.

It was then that he decided to let her work the day and at nightfall to pay her a dollar and dismiss her. His decision held when he returned later from the grove and found tea awaiting him, and then through the supper she prepared. Afterward, dressed in his white uniform, he patiently waited out the day's end on the portico, his face setting into a grim mold. Then just as dusk etched the first dark line between the sea and sky, he took out a dollar and went downstairs.

She was not in the kitchen, but the table was set for his morning tea. Muttering at her persistence, he charged down the corridor, which ran the length of the basement, flinging open the doors to the damp, empty rooms on either side, and sending the lizards and the shadows long entrenched there scuttling to safety.

He found her in the small slanted room under the stoop, asleep on an old cot he kept there, her suitcase turned down beside the bed, and the shoes, dress and the ridiculous hat piled on top. A loose nightshift muted the outline of her body and hid her legs, so that she appeared suddenly defenseless, innocent, with a child's trust in her curled hand and in her deep breathing. Standing in the doorway, with his own breathing snarled and his eyes averted, Mr Watford felt like an intruder. She had claimed the room. Quivering with frustration, he slowly turned away, vowing that in the morning he would shove the dollar at her and lead her like a cow out of his house . . .

Dawn brought rain and a hot wind which set the leaves rattling and swiping at the air like distraught arms. Dressing in the dawn darkness, Mr Watford again armed himself with the dollar and, with his shoulders at an uncompromising set, plunged downstairs. He descended into the warm smell of bakes and this smell, along with the thought that she had been up before him, made his hand knot with exasperation on the banister. The knot tightened as he saw her, dust swirling at her feet as she swept the corridor, her face bent solemn to the task. Shutting her out with a lifted hand, he shouted, 'Don't bother sweeping. Here's a dollar. G'long back.'

The broom paused and although she did not raise her head, he sensed her groping through the shadowy maze of her mind toward his voice. Behind the dollar which he waved in her face, her eyes slowly cleared. And, surprisingly, they held no fear. Only anticipation and a tenuous trust. It was as if she expected him to say something kind.

'G'long back!' His angry cry was a plea.

Like a small, starved flame, her trust and expectancy died and she said, almost with reproof, 'The rain falling.'

To confirm this, the wind set the rain stinging across the windows and he could say nothing, even though the words sputtered at his lips. It was useless. There was nothing inside her to comprehend that she was not wanted. His shoulders sagged under the weight of her ignorance, and with a futile gesture he swung away, the dollar hanging from his hand like a small sword gone limp.

She became as fixed and familiar a part of the house as the stones –
and as silent. He paid her five dollars a week, gave her Mondays off and
in the evenings, after a time, even allowed her to sit in the alcove off
the parlor, while he read with his back to her, taking no more notice of
her than he did the moths on the lamp.

But once, after many silent evenings together, he detected a sound
apart from the night murmurs of the sea and village and the metallic
tuning of the steel band, a low, almost inhuman cry of loneliness which
chilled him. Frightened, he turned to find her leaning hesitantly toward
him, her eyes dark with urgency, and her face tight with bewilderment
and a growing anger. He started, not understanding, and her arm lifted
to stay him. Eagerly she bent closer. But as she uttered the low cry again,
as her fingers described her wish to talk, he jerked around, afraid that
she would be foolish enough to speak and that once she did they would
be brought close. He would be forced then to acknowledge something
about her which he refused to grant; above all, he would be called upon
to share a little of himself. Quickly he returned to his newspaper, rustling
it to settle the air, and after a time he felt her slowly, bitterly, return to
her silence . . .

Like sand poured in a careful measure from the hand, the weeks
flowed down to August and on the first Monday, August bank holiday,
Mr Watford awoke to the sound of the excursion buses leaving the
village for the annual outing, their backfire pelleting the dawn calm and
the ancient motors protesting the overcrowding. Lying there, listening,
he saw with disturbing clarity his mother dressed for an excursion – the
white headtie wound above her dark face and her head poised like a
dancer's under the heavy outing basket of food. That set of her head
had haunted his years, reappearing in the girl as she walked toward him
the first day. Aching with the memory, yet annoyed with himself for
remembering, he went downstairs.

The girl had already left for the excursion, and although it was her
day off, he felt vaguely betrayed by her eagerness to leave him. Somehow
it suggested ingratitude. It was as if his doves were suddenly to refuse
him their song or his trees their fruit, despite the care he gave them.
Some vital past which shaped the simple mosaic of his life seemed
suddenly missing. An alien silence curled like coal gas throughout the

house. To escape it he remained in the grove all day and, upon his return to the house, dressed with more care than usual, putting on a fresh, starched uniform, and solemnly brushing his hair until it lay in a smooth bush above his brow. Leaning close to the mirror, but avoiding his eyes, he cleaned the white rheum at their corners, and afterward pried loose the dirt under his nails.

Unable to read his papers, he went out on the portico to escape the unnatural silence in the house, and stood with his hands clenched on the balustrade and his taut body straining forward. After a long wait he heard the buses return and voices in gay shreds upon the wind. Slowly his hands relaxed, as did his shoulders under the white uniform; for the first time that day his breathing was regular. She would soon come.

But she did not come and dusk bloomed into night, with a fragrant heat and a full moon which made the leaves glint as though touched with frost. The steel band at the crossroads began the lilting songs of sadness and seduction, and suddenly – like shades roused by the night and the music – images of the girl flitted before Mr Watford's eyes. He saw her lost amid the carousings in the village, despoiled; he imagined someone like Mr Goodman clasping her lewdly or tumbling her in the canebrake. His hand rose, trembling, to rid the air of her; he tried to summon his cold laugh. But, somehow, he could not dismiss her as he had always done with everyone else. Instead, he wanted to punish and protect her, to find and lead her back to the house.

As he leaned there, trying not to give way to the desire to go and find her, his fist striking the balustrade to deny his longing, he saw them. The girl first, with the moonlight like a silver patina on her skin, then the boy whom Mr Goodman sent for the coconuts, whose easy strength and the political button – 'The Old Order Shall Pass' – had always mocked and challenged Mr Watford. They were joined in a tender battle: the boy in a sport shirt riotous with color was reaching for the girl as he leaped and spun, weightless, to the music, while she fended him off with a gesture which was lovely in its promise of surrender. Her protests were little scattered bursts: 'But, man, why don't you stop, nuh . . . ? But, you know, you getting on like a real-real idiot . . .'

Each time she chided him he leaped higher and landed closer, until finally he eluded her arm and caught her by the waist. Boldly he pressed a leg between her tightly closed legs until they opened under his pressure. Their bodies cleaved into one whirling form and while he sang she laughed like a wanton, with her hat cocked over her ear. Dancing, the stones moiling underfoot, they claimed the night. More than the night. The steel band played for them alone. The trees were their frivolous companions, swaying as they swayed. The moon rode the sky because of them.

Mr Watford, hidden by a dense shadow, felt the tendons which strung him together suddenly go limp; above all, an obscure belief which, like rare china, he had stored on a high shelf in his mind began to tilt. He sensed the familiar specter which hovered in the night reaching out to embrace him, just as the two in the yard were embracing. Utterly unstrung, incapable of either speech or action, he stumbled into the house, only to meet there an accusing silence from the clock, which had missed its eight o'clock winding, and his newspapers lying like ruined leaves over the floor.

He lay in bed in the white uniform, waiting for sleep to rescue him, his hands seeking the comforting sound of his doves. But sleep eluded him and instead of the doves, their throats tremulous with sound, his scarred hands filled with the shape of a woman he had once kept: her skin, which had been almost bruising in its softness; the buttocks and breasts spread under his hands to inspire both cruelty and tenderness. His hands closed to softly crush those forms, and the searing thrust of passion, which he had not felt for years, stabbed his dry groin. He imagined the two outside, their passion at a pitch by now, lying together behind the tamarind tree, or perhaps – and he sat up sharply – they had been bold enough to bring their lust into the house. Did he not smell their taint on the air? Restored suddenly, he rushed downstairs. As he reached the corridor, a thread of light beckoned him from her room and he dashed furiously toward it, rehearsing the angry words which would jar their bodies apart. He neared the door, glimpsed her through the small opening, and his step faltered; the words collapsed.

She was seated alone on the cot, tenderly holding the absurd felt hat in her lap, one leg tucked under her while the other trailed down. A white sandal, its strap broken, dangled from the foot and gently knocked the floor as she absently swung her leg. Her dress was twisted around her body – and pinned to the bodice, so that it gathered the cloth between her small breasts, was the political button the boy always wore. She was dreamily fingering it, her mouth shaped by a gentle, ironic smile and her eyes strangely acute and critical. What had transpired on the cot had not only, it seemed, twisted the dress around her, tumbled her hat and broken her sandal, but had also defined her and brought the blurred forms of life into focus for her. There was a woman's force in her aspect now, a tragic knowing and acceptance in her bent head, a hint about her of Cassandra watching the future wheel before her eyes.

Before those eyes which looked to another world, Mr Watford's anger and strength failed him and he held to the wall for support. Unreasonably, he felt that he should assume some hushed and reverent pose, to bow as she had the day she had come. If he had known their names, he would have pleaded forgiveness for the sins he had committed against her and the others all his life, against himself. If he could have borne the thought, he would have confessed that it had been love, terrible in its demand, which he had always fled. And that love had been the reason for his return. If he had been honest, he would have whispered – his head bent and a hand shading his eyes – that unlike Mr Goodman (whom he suddenly envied for his full life) and the boy with his political button (to whom he had lost the girl), he had not been willing to bear the weight of his own responsibility ... But all Mr Watford could admit, clinging there to the wall, was, simply, that he wanted to live – and that the girl held life within her as surely as she held the hat in her hands. If he could prove himself better than the boy, he could win it. Only then, he dimly knew, would he shake off the pursuer which had given him no rest since birth. Hopefully, he staggered forward, his step cautious and contrite, his hands quivering along the wall.

She did not see or hear him as he pushed the door wider. And for some time he stood there, his shoulders hunched in humility, his skin stripped away to reveal each flaw, his whole self offered in one out-stretched hand. Still unaware of him, she swung her leg, and the dangling shoe struck a derisive note. Then, just as he had turned away that evening in the parlor when she had uttered her low call, she turned away now, refusing him.

Mr Watford's body went slack and then stiffened ominously. He knew that he would have to wrest from her the strength needed to sustain him. Slamming the door, he cried, his voice cracked and strangled, 'What you and him was doing in here? Tell me! I'll not have you bringing nastiness round here. Tell me!'

She did not start. Perhaps she had been aware of him all along and had expected his outburst. Or perhaps his demented eye and the desperation rising from him like a musk filled her with pity instead of fear. Whatever, her benign smile held and her eyes remained abstracted until his hand reached out to fling her back on the cot. Then, frowning, she stood up, wobbling a little on the broken shoe and holding the political button as if it was a new power which would steady and protect her. With a cruel flick of her arm she struck aside his hand and, in a voice as cruel, halted him. 'But you best move and don't come holding on to me, you nasty, pissy old man. That's all you is, despite yuh big house and fancy furnitures and yuh newspapers from America. You ain't people, Mr Watford, you ain't people!' And with a look and a lift of her head which made her condemnation final, she placed the hat atop her braids, and turning aside picked up the valise which had always lain, packed, beside the cot – as if even on the first day she had known that this night would come and had been prepared against it . . .

Mr Watford did not see her leave, for a pain squeezed his heart dry and the driven blood was a bright, blinding cataract over his eyes. But his inner eye was suddenly clear. For the first time it gazed mutely upon the waste and pretense which had spanned his years. Flung there against the door by the girl's small blow, his body slowly crumpled under the weariness he had long denied. He sensed that dark but unsubstantial figure which roamed the nights searching for him wind him in its chill embrace. He struggled against it, his hands clutching the air with the spastic eloquence of a drowning man. He moaned – and the anguished sound reached beyond the room to fill the house. It escaped to the yard and his doves swelled their throats, moaning with him.

AUSTIN CLARKE

I Hanging On, Praise God!

'Gawd bless my eyesight! Clemintine!'

'Pinky! The Lord have his mercy, child, I seeing right?'

'Yesss! How long you here in Canada?'

'Child, I here now two years running 'pon three. But I didn't know *you* was up here, too! What the hell bring you in this godforsaken place though?'

'I come up 'pon the Scheme. The Domestic Scheme. First little break in my whole life. And I glad for it. But I hanging on, meanwhile.'

'You damn right to hang on. 'Cause you know as well as I do that there ain' no particular bed o' roses back where we come from. You could live donkey years back in Barbados, and 'cepting you have godfather or iffing you been to Queens College, or maybe you learn little needlework, you ain' getting *nowhere*. But how you making out?'

'Child, now and then. Today, I up, tomorrow, I down.'

'Well, since I meet up with you, you might as well come and see where I lives. You ain' in no hurry, though? 'Cause you don't look like no Canadian what always rushing, running, turning their blood to water, they in so much o' hurry!'

'To tell you the truth, I come downtown to buy two-three item for the Missy, and . . .'

'How you and she gets along?'

'Betwixt me and you, I don't care much for working for these people. They *too* smart! They counting ever' grain o' rice, and watching ever' slice o' bake pork you put 'pon that table. But they want to go to the Islands, and then they would see *how* smart they is!'

'I list'ning.'

'Well, this lady I works for ... up in that place, Forest Hill Village, where all the rich-able Jews does live ... Clemintine, you never see so much o' money in your born days! But they *tight!*'

'You ain' lie, darling.'

'Child, as I standing up here with you in this subway place, I ain' lying. I tell you ... well, since I been working off my tail for her, three years! She ain' give me one blind cent more than the two hundred dollars a month, what I start out with! All kind o' Jamaican gal, who you know can't touch me for the way I does set table with knife and fork ... they getting all up in the three hundreds, and ...'

'You kidding!'

'Child, you gotta open your two eye wide, wide wide, in this country, yuh! If not, these people jook them out! And I complainin' to her 'bout how the hot stove giving me pains right up in my shoulder blade, all 'cross my back, in me stomach-bone, when the nights come. I catching more cold than what John read 'bout. Can't get a decent night's sleep, I so damn stiff all over my body from standing up at the hot stove, the ironing board ... scrubbing the damn floor ... kitchen floor, bedroom floor, living-room, pantry. You see me here? Well, I don't know how I keeping the little fat God give me on these bones! All these years, and only two hundred dollars a month.'

'You look good, though.'

'Nobody mind you. You pulling my legs.'

'We getting off at the next stop.'

'You living 'pon Bloor Street?'

'Three months now. I can't take on the Missy quarters, soul. Nine o'clock I goes up, and I sits down and face them four bare walls. Prison walls I staring at, all the time. It have television, radiogram, record player. You can't ask for more comforts. But it lacking in something basic. It ain' have peace and happiness! You remember back home, when we was working out for them white people in the Garrison Barracks, how when the evenings come, we could stroll round the Garrison Pasture, or the Explanade? Maybe go for a bus drive and let little o' Silver Sands sea breeze blow in we face? Well, that don't happen here! No place to go. Nowhere to enjoy weselves. All we doing is making money. And nothing, nowhere to spend it ...'

'Don't talk so loud, the man in front list'ning ... You been going church lately?'

'Hold over. Lemme tell you something. I get *saved*.'

'No! Clemintine, you lie!'

'Shhh! The whole streetcar ain' talking to you, woman. Only me talking to you. Yesss! I meet my Savior, soul. Is the onliest salvation what going to help soften my burdens, and my troubles. I looks at the situation this way: I here in Canada three years now, going 'pon four. After work, I changes my clothes and sits down in that Baptist church 'pon Soho Street, and praise my Gawd. Is the onliest salvation I sees in this place. I can't say I going looking for friends. Friends does bring yuh grief!'

'You couldn't be serious, though?'

'Don't let we pass the stop. We getting off at the next one. Look, sweetheart, I come in this place with the '57 batch o' girls. And when that big ugly man down at the Negro Citizens Place finish greeting ever'body, and showing we 'bout Toronto, loneliness step' in. Loneliness. I up there in Bayview. Nobody to talk to me. Only work. I ain' see a soul my color, saving the other Bajan girl, Babbsie, what works for that nice doctor family. I spraining my brain. Things ain' working out, at all. 'Cause we is womens together. And as womens, we does feel a certain way lonesome when we lonely.'

'But how you? Engage' yet?'

'Me, darling? Bother out my soul-case with the niggers in this world!'

'You mean you ain' settle down with a man?'

'And what 'bout you?'

'I have God! And my Bible.'

'Uh-huhn? ... I had a man once. I come up in Canada. I work hard as hell. And I saying I sending back money to him in Barbados, to help make up his plane fare. Well, eight months pass', and I still ain' hear one word from that brute. I getting ready all the marrieding things: white dress, veil, even the eats and drinks, 'cause I had a wonderful freeness in mind. I prepared. And you know, as the Regulations say, we could married after one year pass'. Well, I so *good* to that man! And he writing me all these love letters, how: "Darling, you leave me down here, and I lonely for you. Your heart in front o' my eyes all the time." And Clemintine, the sweet words! How he miss' me in a certain way and that he hope the reaches of his letters would find me in a perfect state of good health, praise God! Darling, I don't know what them sweet words do to my heart in this cold place, but I pouring all my money in that man hand when the paydays come. Two days after the month end, brisk! I down in the post office taking out money order. 'Cause, blood more thicker than water. And I know how lonely them winter nights is, up here, child; and iffing I could do little goodness for the man who say he love me, well, you ain' see no crime in that, eh? But, child, when I hear' the *shout!*'

'Wha' happen?'

'Man in the States! He grab-on 'pon my money and run to 'Mer'ca!'

'Another woman, eh, soul?'

'Some slick Yankee rat turn the man head. And that's the last I hear.'

'The dirty, ungrateful rat!'

'Me, soul! I trying to put man outta me mind! . . . and when I gets that certain feeling, I buys a half bottle o' rum and drinks myself in a nice stupor, up in the Missy quarters, where I safe. And when I get enough 'pon that bank account, it is a acre or two o' land up in Highgate Garden that I after. Nice small stone bungalow, and a nice English Austin car . . . I fix up for the rest o' me old days. I out-out man outta my life, honey!'

'You playing the fool, yuh, child. How you mean?'

'Well, I say I not *looking* for *no* man. If when I fix up myself good back home, and some retired old gentleman, with a little cash in his pockets, who ain' have no wife, and who ain' looking for bed companion, want little attention and somebody to take care 'o him well . . . *perhaps* me and him could come to a understanding.'

'Take off yuh coat, lemme make some tea. I have some rum from home. Want little?'

'A drop in the tea, thanks, so the Missy won't smell it on my breath.'

'But I had something to ask you. Who presses your hair? I looking for somebody nice to fix mine. I had such a nice hairdresser back in Barbados! . . . up 'long Jessemy Lane!'

'I does mine myself. But I could do yours too.'

'And bu'n off me two ear hole? I don't know, though, why some o' we girls who pass' the Scheme, don't open up a little nice, hairdressing place?'

'Child . . . heh-heh-heh! . . . they 'fraid.'

'But why we kind always hiding?'

'Ain' no common thing such as hiding, Pinky, darling. I telling you, child, that when you here as long as me or the next one, you going learn that what and what we does with our hair, it ain' no small thing that call for hiding. Them other too malicious. Too fresh! Ever'day, my Missy saying, "Clemmy, dear, who fixes your hair? My! it's always in place. You uses Clairol or Helena Rubinstein shampoo?" I keeps my mout' shut. Let her take *that!* Now, tell me, what I going to go picking my teet' to her, for? I remember one time, I taking my rest period before I go downstairs and put the steak in the oven. I gets so tired in the afternoons! So, I say to myself: "This place so hot and humid, you better lay down here in your slip." Well, I can't tell how long I been laying down. But when I open my eyes! Missy standing over me, look, she there, right over me, examining ever' hair in my head! I carry-on so stink, I make myself shame. She says to me, "But Pinky, I was only trying to wake you. The master coming home early for supper." And Clem, I take such a turn in her arse, she nearly change her color! I says, "Well, niggerwoman, you drunk in Hell? Snooping 'bout the little dirty room you give me, and you think I going to smile up in your face and forgive you, as the rest do? Now lis-ten to me. And listen good good good. Mistress Bergenstein, you make this the last time you come in my room! It may be in your house, but the Regulations says this room is mine. Now, you get to-hell outta here, before I hold on 'pon you, and screel out for blue murder!"'

'Heh-heh-heh-heh-heh!'

'You ain' in 'greement with me?'

'That I is, child. She won't come round again!'

'You damn right she never come round again. You gotta make these whores understan' what the position is.'

'The tea ready, soul. Help yuhself . . . Oh, I forgot to ask you. You ever get black-eye pea, or dry pea, since you here?'

'Mout' ain' touch little home food since I land up here, saying I bettering myself, child.'

'Must get yuh some.'

'Mout' watering for little good bittle!'

'When I say one thing, I got to say the next. You intend to stay in the Domestic Scheme, all the time you in Canada? Or you thinking 'bout taking up something diff'runt? Like nurse aid, or nursing assistant?'

'I don't know yet, child. Sometimes, when I realize that Canada ain' mine, I mad to bound back home where people does smile, and tell me good morning. 'Nother time, I takes a look at the situation, and I have to decide to stick it out. 'Cause where in Barbados people like me and you going get television, telephone, carpet 'pon the floor, inside running water from? Is like that, soul. We here, through the tender mercies o' God. He open this door for us. And we gotta thank him. This Scheme is the best thing ever happen to poor womens like we. Is for that, and *that* alone, we shouldn't complain. Canada ain' no bed o' roses. And since *they* like they ain' want we nowhere in this Christ's world, we have to stick it out wherever the Lord say we going get a little break.'

'Is too nice to have somebody . . . one o' your own . . . to exchange a thought or two with, sometimes. I sits there at that third-floor window up in that Forest Hill Village, and I looks down and see all them people, happy happy, and enjoying themselfs, and I ain' part o' that life, at all. I there looking out like I is some damn monkey. Days come and go, and not a friend to pick my teet' with, or swap two ideas. Only people. All these years, people people people, and more people. Ain' a friend . . . not till I run in you this forenoon down in the subway place.'

'Ain't a pleasant existence, at all . . .'

'More than we mortals can bear! Many's the night when I flood that pillow with tears. Water dropping outta my eyeball like a tap leaking. Cry-water, Clem, tears! 'Cause I don't have a living soul . . . not one living *soul* . . . to say, "white in your eyes!" And yet, I earning more money than I ever had hope to work for in all my lifetime back in that island; and still I spending all my young years in a Missy kitchen. Before the Lord's sun rise up from behind the hills, I down there making breakfast . . . lunch, snacks. Child, you never see a people could eat so much o' snacks in one day! And the suppers at night! They spends all their time eating. Two-pound piece o' steak for a fourteen-year-old kid? Ain' that worthlessness to the height?'

'You is a joker.'

'And I sweating off my behind in front o' the hot stove. But what I going do? Pick up myself and say I looking for another job? It don't have no *other* job, darling!'

'Let we talk 'bout something else, child. Them thoughts does make me too blind drunk with vexatiousness. The more I think 'bout these things, the more I want to puke.'

'This is nice tea. It bringing the air outta my stomach nice.'

'Is the Missy steak you t'ief that giving you gas, soul.'

'How yuh like this fur-imitation coat she give me for my Christmas, last Christmas?'

'Missy give you that? You works for a damn fine lady, then.'

'She have her bad ways. But yuh can't kill her. Live and let them live, too.'

'Can't beat them; have to 'gree with them.'

'I hope you ain' thinking I does work for a slave driver.'

'I know yuh feelings, darling!'

''Cause words does get back to Missy ears.'

'You is a woman and a human being. Ever' human being have feelings. Ever' woman is flesh. That is why it so damn hard 'pon we who come up here adventuring in this rough country, without we mens as companions. And I ain' so drunk saying I tangling up with no white mens. Leave that for the Jamaican girls, love. And Canada ain' no featherbed we laying down 'pon.'

'Is the Gospull!'

'That's why I telling you, child, looka, *hang on*, you hear me? Hang on! Even if it is by the skin o' your teet', hang on! For I hanging on. I take up the Bible. Not causing I is this big-able Christian-minded person. It ain' true. I like my rum, and my dances. But here, if I don't have church to look forward to, well ... Where it have a place for me and you kind to enjoy weselfs? The Granitt Club? The Yacht Club?'

'A shame, a shame! We can't even put on a nice frock and go for even a moonlight walk.'

'Venture outta that place the Missy put you in, and see if man don't snatch you up offa the street! Ravage you! This place bad, it wild, savage. You can't trust *nobody*. We in *barracks*. Permanunt barracks. You see that rubber stamp-thing the Immigration People put on we passport when we land? You know what it say? PERMANUNT! And it mean just that. We permanunt in this hell! . . . but I start out to tell you something else, though . . .'

'Bout the church.'

'Church? What church? I only going there as I tell you, 'cause it don't have no other place for me to go.'

'Hey! I forget . . . what is the hour? It ain' three yet, nuh? Drunk or sober mind yuh damn business. I ha' a work to go to.'

'Three? Today, or tomorrow morning?'

'It pass' three?'

'Five o'clock, honey.'

'Wuh loss! Look my crosses! The lady waiting for the things . . . well, look, Clemintine, child, me and you going have to get together some time soon, and lick we mout' again . . .'

'See yuh Thursdee?'

'God willing . . .'

'Care yuhself. Don't let that Missy put more on you than you able to bear, child.'

'Not me, nuh, soul. Dog my age ain't no pup!'

'Well, you hang on!'

'In the name o' Christ! I hanging on, praise God!'

EARL LOVELACE

A Brief Conversion

I

Every third Sunday just at the hour when the Shouters are holding service in their church up on the hill into which our street disappears, a bicycle bell rings once; and with the bleak brightness of an undertaker, Mr Fitzie, itinerant barber and sweepstake seller, one of his legs shorter than the other, appears out of the clump of trees that rings our house, pushing his bicycle into our yard with his assured hip-shorted walk, a rhythmic drop-rising, up-downing, each step, climbing down from the height it would ascend with the next, prancing with the oiled inhuman smoothness of the pedal of a foot machine, sets down his box on the big stone in the shade of our chenette tree, and calls out to my mother, and she sends us out, my brother and me, with two chairs, one for Mr Fitzie to use and the other for her to sit on to be director and witness of this rite.

Of those mornings, these remain with me: the smell of the blossoms of our cedar tree, the sounds of the Shouters' hypnotic, rhythmic hymns and the clip-clipping of Mr Fitzie's barbering scissors as they helicopter over my head, not yet touching a hair, Mr Fitzie flexing his fingers, flourishing his dexterity and announcing his power over me before he brings the scissors down to engage my hair; the smell of cheap face powder and, on the ground beside my chair, the fluff of my shorn hair. Or was he shearing me of vanity? Do not learn the vanity of a muff. Do not learn the vanity of a covering of hair. There is no mirror to see what is going on. I run my hand over my head. I feel the loss of hair.

I plead, 'Mr Fitzie, it good now? I finish trim now! Enough hair gone now!'

'Hold yer head!' my mother commands.

Mr Fitzie grips my cheekbones with the vice of his fingers and he screws my head in the direction he wants it and bends it at the angle he requires it to stay; and his scissors clip, snip; and I am stifled by his old perspiration smell, and the sickly scent of cedar blossoms hangs in the air; and, from the space below his armpit, behind the flowering bluebells, butterflies fold their wings and settle in the sunshine of the hibiscus hedge, and in the tall elephant grass across the road, Mr Sylvestre's donkey jerks its ears to shake annoying horse-flies from its face.

'Hold your head,' Mr Fitzie grumbles, his fingers tightening on my temples; and the Shouters sing, 'What a friend we have in Jesus', breaking out from words to sounds, sighs, screams, groans, their singing punctuated and harmonized and juxtaposed, each individual rejoicing wail adding its tall sad brightness to the chorused sounds, drawing my mother in, her own humming martyred and remote for most of the hymn, then her voice breaking out in song when they get to the line: 'Pilgrims in this barren land'.

I see me now, riveted to that chair, my eyes bright and round like polished buttons, 'Mr Fitzie, it good now!' as panic grips me.

'Trim him low, Mr Fitzie,' my mother breathes, her voice insistent, in it, more than a declaration of her will, an edge of – but, I must say it – spite.

'But, why, Pearl? Why you have to cut the boy hair like a Nazi for?' Aunt Irene asks as, bristling with a triumphant, buxom, intimidatory and to my way of thinking, unwarranted vexation, my mother marches into the house and I crawl sullen, humbled, to the mirror to check the exact degree of damage done to my appearance. 'Tell me, what reason it have for you to brutalize your boychild head so? I know Indian people does shave their boychild head, but, that is when their father dead. His father dead, Pearl?'

'You all right, yes, Irene,' my mother answers, in a voice of superior wisdom, with its timbre of doom, outraged that she should be required to give any explanation.

And Aunt Irene, lolling in the sunshine of our veranda, a dustercoat on, her hair in curlers and all her jewels on, lifts a luxurious hand, her bangles and bracelets jangling, and with the consciousness of a glamour that everybody associates with her stay in Port of Spain, says, 'Children like to look nice too. You think I could dare trim Ronnie like that?' Ronnie being her son, my cousin, who, when he comes to spend time with us in Cunaripo, wears a wrist-watch, wears a sailor suit. Ronnie has his hair parted and brushed for the waves in it to show. Aunt Irene hugs Ronnie, kisses him: 'Ronnie, darling, what you want to do today?'

Ronnie wants six cents in his pocket to go down the street. He wants a bicycle to ride. 'But, your bicycle is in Port of Spain, darling,' Aunt Irene coos, soothingly, smoothening down his pouting face, her two hands coming together softly at his chin. Sometimes she talks of his deprivation at being in Cunaripo, of the ice-cream cones he misses, the cinema shows, the circus that's visiting. 'Oh, and you know this weekend I was to go horse races in the Savannah with him . . . Anyway, the little outing will do him good. With the sea so near to Cunaripo, at least he'll learn to swim.'

You dream of a place to go to and Ronnie has been there. You doubt him and he turns to his mother, 'Mummie, didn't you take me to the De Luxe cinema to see that Tarzan picture?' in his adult way of talking that makes my mother squirm.

Ronnie is not very athletic. In the races we run, I beat him every time; yet, when we play, he is Tarzan; he is Zorro. He has a little Zorro mask which he never lends me and, like Zorro, he has a whip with which he feels free to lash me, since in all our games Ronnie is the star boy and I am the crook. When we play stick-em-up, my shots are the ones that miss. He never misses. 'I get you!' he cries, celebrating his perfect marksmanship. 'You dead!'

If I argue, he sulks and refuses to play. I try to hold out against his unfairness; but, he knows that I am dying to play, and he waits until I give in and say, OK. I learn to stumble, to hold my shoulder as I fall, pretending to be wounded only in the arm. He stands, at such times, with a cruel and triumphant grin on his face, his gun aimed dead at my head, ready to shoot me down in cold blood, should I seek to escape.

'You all right, yes, Irene,' my mother repeats, hinting not only at Aunt Irene's pampering of Ronnie, but at the pampering of herself, at her dreaming and creamed face and the langour of her stretching; for Aunt Irene has this hoarse seductive voice filled with sighs and secret breaths and dark smoke, and she has a space between her teeth and she stretches and yawns and she puts her feet up on the banister of the veranda and talks of men and she laughs that terrible laughter that makes the dogs bark and the hens scatter and my mother's eyes widen in alarm.

'Pearl, you too old-fashion. You too close to this cocoa estate.' For Aunt Irene's living in Port of Spain has brought her up to date, has given her a knowledge of 'life' and a wisdom about men; and she extends her coquettish charms to anything male, so that even our dog, Hitler, she treats with a warmth she doesn't extend to Flossie.

Dressed in a dustercoat, less frequently in shorts; for, Cunaripo doesn't rate the effort of her dressing up – her creamings and the rest she is here to take are all for Port of Spain – she sits on the rocking chair on our veranda, watching the turkey cocks dance, the yard cocks parade, casting an eye towards the road, where nothing exciting will happen. 'No,' as she puts it, 'nice man appear to make me put on some clothes.'

Seeing her on the veranda, the men who enter our yard, one or two of my father's friends glance up at her with almost sheepish grins, overpowered by her glamorous femaleness, too embarrassed, as they tell her 'good evening', to look at her bare legs or to meet her eyes while she is wearing the dustercoat with its suggestion of undress. From her trips to the market, she returns with sea moss and sour sop and pawpaw and on a Sunday evening she emerges from the kitchen with a mug of creamy thick liquid, these fruit battered and swizzled and sweetened, set on a tray with glasses with ice; and she moves among us, pouring from the mug into the glasses, instructing, 'Drink this. It good for you.'

'You have a girl friend, Travey?' she asks me.

'Irene, what stupidness you putting in the boy head?' my mother inquires.

'Pearl, this is not something I have to put in his head. You think this generation waiting? You know how much girl friends Ronnie have since he going to that school in Belmont? Ronnie!' she calls, 'Ronnie!' And Ronnie who is near by, tying a string on to the abdomen of a dragonfly, lifts his head with his powerful and domineering sullenness.

'Ronnie, how much girl friends you have?'

The severe Ronnie cocks his head and looks at her in silent reprimand; but, he is unable to resist showing off. 'Three,' he says calmly. 'Now, Mummie, don't ask me that stupid question again.'

My mother groans; but, Aunt Irene doesn't even see a problem.

'Look at these lovely boychildren you have, Pearl! Look at them! Is out in the world they have to go. Don't let them go tame. Send them out brave, warriors with tall limbs, their lovely buttocks –'

'Irene!' my mother cautions. 'Irene!'

'. . . their lovely buttocks dancing bold to make the world blink, to make them say,' and this she breathes, 'That is man! That is man! Like Alan Fortune.'

Of course none of us don't know who this Alan Fortune is; but, from the way her eyes close and her mouth curls around his name, he belongs, we're sure to Aunt Irene's Port of Spain, to the Dairies where she buys Ronnie ice-cream cones, to the Savannah and the De Luxe cinema and the Princes Building Ballroom where she dances to Fitz Vaughn Bryan and John Buddy Williams, dressed, of course, in the latest fashion which she feels compelled to model on the stage of our veranda, just to show my mother, 'Just to show you, Pearl, the dress that I kill them with, the outfit that mash up everybody.'

'That is why I give Ronnie the best I can afford, if only for him to look nice. Let them go, Pearl. Let the boys go. Like lions with their manes. Like cocks with their strut and their colours. With the crown of hair on their head. The world belongs to them.'

'To them? The world?' My mother's chuckle is a groan.

'And why not, Pearl? Why not?'

'You all right, yes, Irene,' she begins disdainfully. But, the enormity of Aunt Irene's claim reaches her. She stops. She faces her sister, 'Irene, you think these boys is Ronnie? You think I could let *these lions* loose with their manes?'

It was as if my mother not only had reasons to believe that the world would be gentler with Ronnie, but, was convinced that me and my brother, unknown even to ourselves, carried in our person some more splendid and provoking quality that, without restriction, would be too much for the world to accept; so, she saw her duty as taming the warrior in us, buttoning down the challenge that, with our own innocence and carelessness, she was sure would steal through our ordinary gestures and provoke the trouble she dreaded from the world.

So maybe it was something less simple than her spite. Maybe my mother's rage and pain derived from having to tame in us what she would have loved to see us exalt, at having to send forth camouflaged as clowns the warriors she had birthed. With her voice ranging over the sounds waves make at every tide, their roarings and their sighs, she had her boychildren shorn, zugged and greased down; and she never allowed us to leave the house without the parting command, 'Button up your shirt!' Button up your shirt! As if our beauty was an insolence to be corrected, our spirit a hazard that endangered us.

'Button up your shirt, Travey!' Louder, if my father happened to be present, as if unable to resist deflecting unto him some portion of some blame, of some shame, they both knew of, making him witness to a powerlessness which saw him as the one to correct, daring him, man that he was, if he was man, to come to my assistance so that she would be able to restate what sounded as challenge and accusation, 'You want him to go out there with his shirt open like a bad John for them to knock him down before he even start to live?'

There were times I stood between my parents, my fingers trembling on the topmost button of my shirt, knowing that, with my three-quarter-length pants, my cleaned head, and my socks collapsed around my ankles, to button it would be to complete my costume of clown. I look at my father. There is a distant waiting in his eyes. It is as if at any instant his time can come, but that right then is not his time. His ambition is to open a radio repairs shop. That will come when he has completed the radio repairs course he has been taking off and on for as long as I can remember. His real work is a woodcutter. He is an axe man. They have given him the name Bull. He is a strong man, with strong arms and neck and a face unto which in times like these he is always trying to force a smile. He has learnt that the smile is a superior weapon, that it can create ease, give a sense of control; but, it is not a weapon that he has mastered; it is one that masters him; so that far from giving the effect he desires, it twists his face into another truth, the truth. It makes him look weak, appealing, sly, as someone who is telling a lie.

Life has embarrassed him. It is always proving him wrong. 'It is my fault,' he says, triumphantly. He has chosen to be loyal to unprofitable enterprises and to have as friends people who cannot help him, and has allowed currents that he could have floated on to pass him by. All sorts of opportunities have passed him in this way. Sometimes he talks in a wistful voice of the Water Scheme days when so much timber was there to be reaped. And where was he? He was bound on another man's estate, planting orange trees and a mango orchard. The same thing happened when the Americans opened their base. The radio repairs course, that is what he looks forward to completing now.

'Button up your shirt,' he says, after a long enough pause, finally, as if each time, this time too, he had thought it through and, sadly, saw no alternative but to bend to the weight and sway of the world. 'Button it up!' his voice trying to be firm, in it the mild, the tentative promise of a future time when by some power yet unknown – win a sweepstake maybe, complete the radio repairs course – he will provide us with the freedom to be free.

And my mother, hearing this dream and treason in his voice, but, happy that she had got him to acknowledge the predominance of a power greater than all our efforts, says, almost with sorrow, 'Yes, let him button it up. When he get big, he could be a stickfighter like you and your brother, Bango.'

I look at my father. It occurs to me that he is in some kind of a jam, some trap, some hole, something that has to do with money and stickfighting and jail: that has to do with setting a proper example for his children, with his inviting his friends home to eat, my mother would say, 'as if we own a grocery', and when the drums beat at Carnival time, the disappearing, with the stickmen led by his brother Bango, to Sangre Grande and Moruga and Mayaro. My mother say to him, 'Follow Bango, Bango aint have a child to his name. Follow Bango. Bango have three woman to mind him.'

On the day of Christmas Eve my father usually went and helped Mr Sylvestre butcher a pig, and in the evening he would come home with a few drinks of rum in his head and in his hands a choice piece of pork and a coiled length of black pudding, and after he put down the meat and had a bath and something to eat, he would take up his *cuatro* and his two *shac shacs* and go into the kitchen where my mother would have started seasoning the meat, 'I going down the road to see what the boys doing.' And he would be gone until maybe, sometime, Christmas Day when he would come up the front steps with the rest of the *parang* band and stand on the veranda, with his head bent sideways and his eyes closed, singing in his rasping bass voice the plaintive serenades, his fingers flying over the strings of the *cuatro* cradled in his arms, and my mother would throw open the door for him, for them, and, with the rest of the band, he would enter, like a stranger, the drawing-room, with its curtains and its polish and its paint, with everything already on the table, the rum and the wine and the ham and the sweetbread and the ginger beer and the sorrel and the cake, the magnificent testament of her servitude, the yearly affirmation of her martyrdom and reproach. He would enter, saying to the men accompanying him, 'Wipe your foot. Wipe your foot! Don't dirty the lady floor.' And he would play music and sing and drink and eat and leave with them, returning home maybe a day or two later, not content simply with making the rounds of the village, but, finding it necessary to go by his sister in Valencia, by his brother-in-law in Sangre Grande or by one of his cousins in Biche. And he would stand before my mother with his cap twisted on his head, his face wrinkled and his eyes twinkling with a guilty and refreshed look, for my mother to say, 'Be glad that you have a woman like me,' turning away from his attempt to embrace her and so make what might have passed for forgiveness its own punishment.

At such times, the lie of his smile would weaken his face, and with his fumbly muscular awkwardness, he would look from my mother to Michael and me; and again I would get this sense of a man mired in some swamp, stuck in some muddy hole in a world that was not the world, this sense of a strength that could not find a way to break through to that world, to that freedom that I was learning we did not yet possess.

'Somebody have to keep it up, Pearl. Somebody have to play the music and go round by people for Christmas and bring some merriment,' he would say.

'And you always have to be the one,' my mother says.

'Somebody have to keep up these things. Somebody,' astonished at her show of indifference.

'You want me to stop?' he asked one day.

'I don't want you to dead,' my mother said.

And he limped away with his wound and his strength, with his *cuatro* like a toy in his fist, to bleed slowly from the wounds of his loyalties and his guilt, to grow quiet with the routine of his woodcutting and the slow magical fiddling with the derelict radios which people had abandoned and brought for him to resurrect, until Carnival came and, as my mother would say, 'the blood fly up in his head', and he leave again, leave radio and axe and forest and take up his stick and go down to the junction to the stickfights by Loy shop and meet Bango and Mano and John and Ragoo and William and go until Ash Wednesday when he would return home, burdened with repentance.

'Leave him alone, Pearl,' Aunt Irene advises. 'He don't gamble. He don't drink too much rum. And, as far as I know, he not friending with no other woman.'

'You see me interfering with him? You see me holding his foot? He is a man do exactly what he want. I don't ask him no question. He go, he come . . .' she said, with a kind of righteous exasperation.

One day we were all in the kitchen, my mother, Aunt Irene, Michael and Ronnie and me. My father wasn't there.

'Me and your father getting married,' my mother said. 'Not anything big. Just a few of us. Just family.' As if she felt that she had been too casual, she added, 'I telling you all this so you will know, not for you to broadcast anything. Is between us, you understand. We not having anything big. Just a few of us in the church. We'll have to get new shoes for the two of you.'

'Kiss your mother,' Aunt Irene said to us. 'Say congratulations.'

Michael kissed her first. Then I went and threw my arms around her neck.

'If is anybody to kiss is their father,' Ma said. 'Is his idea. He's the one who decide after thirteen years living together to do this thing. He believe it will bring him luck, will change him, make him stop galavanting.'

'You can't believe that that is all, Pearl. Love. The man love you. He don't want you to leave him.'

'Leave? Where I leaving to go at this hour of my life?' my mother asks. She turns to us: 'Is for you all,' she said, 'to give you a name now that you getting big in the world. So don't let him down. He have his ways, but, he try. He trying.'

'You not frighten, Pearl?' Aunt Irene asks.

'Sure I frighten,' Ma said, jokingly. 'You know they say when the living good without wedding, the ring does spoil the thing.'

'Let it spoil, Pearl. You is Mistress Jordan now. Mistress Jordan! Let them take that!' Aunt Irene's full-throated, victorious laughter suggesting that the impending marriage was my mother's personal triumph accomplished against the wishes and will of the world.

Ma smiled charitably, 'Darling, I don't worry with people. People could say what they want.'

I was surprised. Seeing me looking at her, she signalled away Michael and me, 'Big people talking now.'

With the wedding coming, a quietness settled upon our household. In it, relatives descended. It was the women who came, the big, majestic women of our family, with their colourful headties and their scents of herbs and incense, with the mysterious air of priestesses who had come to initiate my mother into new rites connected with marriage. Suddenly, they were everywhere, cooking and baking and cleaning. My mother worked among them, allowing herself to be directed by this strong female force, and, for once, she was the woman, bride, fussed over and waited upon.

With relatives among us, and about to enter her new status, she grew calm, gentle. Now she was less strict, her voice was softer and had in it lots of patient laughter. It was a period of grace for Michael and me, and we took advantage of it, figuring that she wouldn't bawl us out in front of these strangers. And she tried to keep up the fiction of softness and gentle persuasion; but, on occasions, she would pull us aside, 'What the hell wrong with you? You don't know how to behave.' But, in front of her sisters or cousins, she would say sweetly, 'Michael and Travey, boys, you not tired of hearing me talk?' as if she had all the patience in the world.

My father had brought in a few of his friends from the village to help him build a tent in the yard. The quality of his silence was different too. The house, always a place where my mother reigned, had never been his domain; now, with all these women about, he seemed an intruder.

In a way, the presence of outsiders brought him closer to my mother. Suddenly I realized that they had secret signs between them, glances, gestures, lifting of eyebrows, at which signals they would move towards each other to discuss what they felt needed to be discussed. My father had a sense of satisfaction about him. It was as if he accepted to himself that he was doing something noble, something that would make my mother happy. He was overjoyed. It was almost embarrassing seeing him so pleased with himself. When he spoke to her out in the yard, he would linger, holding her hands in his own, or place a hand on her shoulders, making a public declaration of the nobility of his resolve. He expressed this warmth to my brother and me as well, involving us in the work around the house, directing us to sweep the yard or to do any other chore which our skill and size permitted.

Holding the two of us around our shoulders, he would say, 'You, bring the water; you, go and get the coconut branches.' It felt good.

Seeing him in this mood, Uncle Bango, who was helping with the building of the tent, said, 'You shoulda do this thing thirteen years ago.'

'Yes,' Pa said, 'I really waste time. But now all that change. I am a family man now.'

Sometimes, though, listening to him talk about stickfighting and the musicians and the rum drinking, I got to glimpse a new side of him, that side that had always been outside of home, outside with the men. It was this he was trying to give up, this part of his life that had to do with the men, the stickfighting and *parang*. After such bouts of reminiscence, he would say, almost as a joke, 'Well, all that done now. I hope everybody hearing me. After this wedding, don't look for me in the stickfight and *parang*. I is a family man now. Is me and my wife and my children.'

'Pearl, you must help him,' Aunt Irene said. 'These things is his life.'

'And I and his children not his life?' Ma asked.

'You is his life in a different way.'

'Bertie is not a young man again, you know. Bertie is not twenty. Today everybody looking to progress. These things must stop. These friends can't put him nowhere.'

'You know him better than me,' Aunt Irene said. 'Is your husband.'

For the wedding day, Aunt Irene left with my mother to go by another aunt where she would dress to go to the church. We were left with my father and another aunt, my father's sister.

'How I look?' Pa asked, when he was ready to leave for the church. 'Too dress up, eh?'

He had bought a new pair of trousers and new shoes, but he had on the same jacket that he used for funerals. He stood with his broad shoulders, big, new-looking, with a rosebud in the lapel of his jacket, and a small handkerchief in his breast pocket.

'Just good,' Aunt Hilda said. 'Today is a day to dress up.'

'I feel too dress up, though. This dressing up business is not for me.' I could see that he was pleased with how he was looking.

We went with them to the church, Michael and me. I saw my mother standing in her white dress, with her bouquet, not looking like my mother at all, but strangely glamorous and bewildered. She had gloves on.

Michael and me were dressed alike, shirt, short pants and a tie; Ronnie wore long pants and a scissors-tail jacket, and he wore gloves.

Aunt Irene wore gloves too, pink, like the rest of her outfit. The only other colour was the black lace over her hat.

After the ceremony in the church, we all went home, and it was fête, with a small band of musicians, Ambrose and the Boys. It was supposed to be a small thing; but, in Cunaripo, you didn't have a small fête. People didn't have to be invited. They just came. All about, men were in jackets and ties in the hot afternoon and food was sharing and people were eating. We were just churning the second batch of ice cream when Uncle Bango came outside and said, 'Everybody, inside!' The music had stopped and there was to be speech-making. They had invited the Forest Ranger of the district to say a few words as well as Uncle Pascal, who was a guard on the railways. Uncle Bango said that he couldn't let the occasion pass without saying something, got up and made a speech. The Forest Ranger talked. Uncle Pascal talked.

Then it was my father's turn. I watched him standing huge and awkward in his shirt and tie (he had taken off his jacket). 'You know I is no speech-maker,' he said. 'Just that I glad that you all come, and everybody having a good time. Only one thing I want everybody to know is that now I married and I intend to live like a married man. Now, let's take a drink to the bride, Mistress Jordan.'

Everybody applauded and then they had the cake sticking, with Aunt Irene singing the song, and then it was back to dancing and I to eating cake and drinking ice cream.

After the wedding, Pa was in the radio repairs room often, and sometimes in the night, doing my home lessons, I would hear the scratching and screeching of the radio and sometimes snatches of Spanish from the radio he was repairing. We had a lot of cake left over from the wedding, after giving to all our relatives. A month after the wedding, we were still eating cake.

Then Christmas was coming, and the *parang* band was beginning to go about the village, serenading people. Pa's *cuatro* remained hanging from a string in the living-room near the hat rack. It was strange to hear the music and to know that he wasn't there with them. Nobody didn't talk about it. Then, with a week to go before Christmas Day, he left one evening, saying to my mother, 'I just going down the road to carry this *cuatro* for Felix.' It was a Friday evening. Monday morning they brought him home. It was Christmas Eve too.

It was the day after that same Christmas. We were going to church. He wasn't going. He had long since given up going to church; but, he had come out on the veranda to watch us go. Aunt Irene and my mother were still inside finishing dressing, and down in the yard, Ronnie, dressed already in his cowboy suit and with a toy pistol in a holster, one of the gifts from his mother, was drawing his gun and firing at Michael who, more indifferent to Ronnie than I could ever be, stood at the edge of the flower garden oblivious to the shots that were speeding through his body.

I come out of the house and am going to meet Michael and Ronnie. I pause. 'I going, Pa.'

He looks at me. I suppose that he sees that I am growing. I am eleven. Next September I will be twelve.

'You going,' he says, and pushes a hand into a side pocket and brings out a coin, the royal sum of six cents. 'Change it,' he says, handing it to me. 'Don't put all in the collection plate.'

'Thanks,' I am watching him. He is beginning to grey. It is really strange to see him at home on Boxing Day. He grins uncomfortably.

'Your mother tell me you doing well at school. That is good. That is very good, eh?'

I nod, yes. In fact, I had passed to go to the exhibition class, and Ma had made a great fuss over me.

'And in the new year coming here you going to be in Teacher George class. They say he is a serious teacher, eh?'

'Yes, Pa.'

'Good. It good to have a serious teacher. You can't skylark when you have a serious teacher. You can't skylark at all . . . Eh?'

I smiled.

'You not going to be like me, you know. No. You not going to be like your father. Last year . . . When it was that William son make a place in the exhibition and went to the college?'

'It wasn't last year.'

'No,' he said, correcting himself. 'Wasn't last year. Was two, three . . . Yes, three years. Time. Look at time, eh? But William son wasn't just bright. William son use to study. Sometimes your mother is right,' he said, pushing his hand into his pocket. 'You have to learn to leave people behind you if you want to move on. You have to learn to be alone. You can't carry friends with you. You can't carry people with you. William son study alone.'

While we were talking, we had walked away from the door to the other end of the veranda.

Then they appeared, my mother first, her handbag over one arm, in the same hand, her fan, in the other, her prayerbook. Her hat tilted saucily at an angle, Aunt Irene's doing I was sure, stout, her dress fluffy, fanning herself already; and behind her, Aunt Irene, poised, serene, with the spectacles she sometimes wore as part of her fashion, her slim, thick body rustling, on her face a flustered assurance in anticipation of the stir she would create, Pa saying, 'Nice! Nice!' bowing his head and smiling. Aunt Irene singing out, 'How you like how your girls looking?'

'Champion,' Pa saying, a bit too gaily, trying to get the attention of my mother who, self-conscious and with her own rustling, descended the steps with an air of grandeur, acting out a rebuke that we did not believe she felt.

I turn to follow them. I look at my father, 'I going, Pa.'

He looks at me. 'Wait.' He makes a step towards me, on his face is a humbled softness now that he no longer sought to struggle with the imitation of a smile. 'Button up your shirt, Travey.' And as I looked at him, 'Yes. Don't frighten, button it up,' nodding encouragement as if, yes, it was all right. It was the thing to be done.

I felt a strange relief and a flow of sadness. It was as if we had come to an end, the two of us. The hoping was done. It was as if he had come finally to acknowledge that he could no longer ask me to wait upon his dreams, that my freedom was to be severed from his own, that I was to go on alone. 'Button up your shirt, man,' gently, firmly, with comradeship and compassion and love, laying a hand on my shoulder, his eyes lighting up with a new wisdom, as if he had just glimpsed the possibility that this burden that he had come to acknowledge that I must bear might be the armour to protect me against that power that he had himself not triumphed over, but had not surrendered to.

2

Let me not make a martyr of myself. I begin to button up my shirt. It is an act that becomes for me quite grave, almost holy. I feel myself the bearer of a redemptive penance that shall lead me to glory, that shall remove the strange burden from my father and make my mother proud of me. I am our hope. I shall become a scholar, a saint.

Now, without complaint, I suffer myself to endure Mr Fitzie's shearing, so much that my mother, who had come to expect the ritual of my protest, becomes puzzled; then she gets worried.

There is a sense of largeness about my mother. Not only is she physically large, she moves large, she talks loud, she fusses, she bustles, she flies up. She prowls our world like a setting hen, with its eyes suspicious and its wings fluffed, as if to present a greater mass against the catastrophes she predicts and expects. She is suspicious of too much tenderness. It is a luxury she is not sure we can afford. It is to be disguised, dispensed discreetly. One time I saw her come from cooking to the kitchen window to look at a scene of my father coming in from the garden to the back of the house.

My father is carrying a bundle of grass on his head. He is also bringing in our two goats. With one hand he holds the two ropes binding the goats, the other he uses to steady the grass on his head. The goats tug, each in a different direction. My father strains to hold them, using the one hand. My mother is looking at him. On her face is the woman she had succeeded so well in hiding, caring, wonder, fascination, humour. That woman has been superseded by The Mother, the great pillar and presence anchored in enduring. She turns and sees that I am looking at her. 'Boy!' she cries, suddenly flustered, as if she had been caught in an act of subversion, as if she had revealed to me too much of that other person that is also herself, 'What you stand up there looking up in my face for? Go and help him!'

Oh, Mother! I want to cry out. I want to run and hug her. She allows herself a smile, shooing me away.

When she worries, it is with the hen's boisterous camouflage, as if fussiness and bustle will turn back the problem. I read of mothers who pick up their children and kiss their hurt. Aunt Irene acts like that with Ronnie: 'Come, sweetheart. What wrong with my baby?' My mother looks on in amusement, believing that Aunt Irene is performing something she has seen acted on the screen of, maybe, the De Luxe cinema.

My mother says, 'Come on. Get up,' as if tenderness, when we fall, must not be allowed to get in the way of our rising again.

After she had puzzled and wondered about me long enough, she confronts me, large, Amazonian, 'What happen to you?'

And already I am trembling, for in our household illness is also an extravagance. 'What you mean, Ma?'

'You very well know what I mean. You about the house poorly poorly; you sitting down quiet and getting your hair trim; you buttoning up your shirt without nobody telling you nothing. You very well know what I mean. You sick? Somebody cuff you in your belly? You get a fall? You was in a fight?' All while she is firing her questions, she is pressing the back of her hand against my cheek, on the skin of my neck, checking my temperature. She peers into my eyes. Her frown deepens. 'Take off your shirt!'

'Ma?'

'Take off your shirt!'

I take off my shirt. She thumps my chest with the back of a crooked index finger, sounding me.

'Ma, nothing aint happen to me.'

She questions my brother in the same aggressive style, 'Michael, what it is happen to Travey? He was in a fight? He get a fall?'

Michael is a born suspect. He stammers, he fumbles, he looks around furtively. It appears to her that he is hiding something. Michael, however, doesn't know yet of my conversion, my sainthood.

'He get a fall? Michael, did your brother get a fall?'

Baffled, she circles. Later she returns to me, 'You have worms!' she announces, with an incontestable certainty, a little bit amazed that the diagnosis could have escaped her. 'Purge!' with a kind of glee, the one prescriptive word, remedy and punishment.

'But, Pearl?' And now it is Aunt Irene's turn to be amused. 'Pearl, what it is you want this boy to do? You cut his hair like a Nazi and you get vex when he complain; he stop complaining, and now you find he acting strange. What you really want him to do?'

Quickly, before she can hide it, a smile flashes across my mother's face, and, for a moment she seems constrained to give an explanation, but, she doesn't. 'Purge!' she repeats, insistently, hurrying away, trying to contain the smile and return the severity to her look.

But, I had seen her smile. It puzzles me. This same mother, who forces me to have my head trimmed clean and my shirt buttoned up, is the mother who wants me to struggle against having these things done to me. Oh, mother!

Purged, buttoned up, greased down and tame, I go to school with the quiet pathos of a clown, in the masquerade that undermines my natural male aura. I am bullied by the boys, dismissed by the girls. They sense my meekness. They give me the nickname, 'Mice', in reference to my fine, protruding teeth. On those days when my haircut is fresh, the boys surround me, pull my cap down over my eyes and rain clouts on my head. I am confused. I wonder if I should fight back. Do saints fight back?

To my brother Michael, my distress is all a joke. He laughs when the boys clout me. Sometimes at home he teases me and, in a mood of mischief, he tells Ronnie what the boys at school do to me. Now Ronnie begins to call me 'Mice'. Now Ronnie wants to clout me.

'Ronnie!' I warn. 'Ronnie!' But, Ronnie is not easily put off. He persists. He believes that among us, he has a special licence. 'Ronnie!'

Even my mother grows impatient with me, 'Sit down there and bawl, "Ronnie! Ronnie!"' she shouts, tired of my whining.

Michael, the traitor, laughs; and Ronnie makes a funny face at me. It is Michael's behaviour that most pains me.

Michael is fourteen. He has already lost his chance at a college exhibition. Now he must study to get his School Leaving Certificate. In another year he will leave school, 'To dig dirt,' my mother says, 'Or to pick coconut on the white people estate ... You will be an A-one coconut picker,' she tells him. 'Don't learn your lessons. Follow Alexis' son and the other nowherian one they calling Scull. Follow them. You will have good dirt-digging companions.'

Michael is unworried. He protests nothing. He sits down in perfect peace while Mr Fitzie trims him. The cleaner the trim, the more is Michael delighted. If there are zugs on his head, he wears them as medals. Nobody needs to tell Michael to button up his shirt. Michael buttons every button right up to his neck.

'You look like you from the orphanage,' my mother tells him, trying to shame him. 'Like you have no owner.' Michael grins. He doesn't have in his possession a school shirt which is not stained with cashew juice or mango sap, nor one with a complete set of buttons. Michael buttons up his shirt with pins. With his impassive face and occasional wry grin, he goes to school with the solemn air of a triumphant clown, in a parody of the neatness which my mother and the school seek to impose upon him. At school, 'Priest' is the nickname they have given him. He spends his time with a gang of boys even more worthless than himself. Their nicknames are self-explanatory: Scull, Belly, Police. They steal children's lunches; they raid mangoes from the estate; they leave school to go fishing and smoke cigarettes; and once the principal promised to expel them when he caught them underneath the school house peering into a mirror they had placed underneath a hole in the flooring, above which one of the Standard Five girls was sitting. They were tough.

As Michael's brother, I had been somewhat exempted from the terrors of their attention; but, now, with my sainthood, they feel no restraint. I had changed. As a candidate for the college exhibition, I suspect that I had begun to draw myself away from them. I was becoming the scholar, the hope. I was becoming tame. Now, on the playing-field and at the pipe where we drink water, they jostle me. They are out for me, I think.

Earlier the clouts I received from them when I went to school with a freshly trimmed head were simply ritual, something that made me feel part of the school, part of the boys, part of a brotherhood. There was never anything vicious about them. Now, thanks to Scull and company, these clouts begin to sting. I began to feel humiliated, abused. At first I accepted them as part of the price I had to pay for my escape, my sainthood. They wouldn't go on for ever. Soon, I would pass my examination and leave them and the school. I tried to buoy myself up with thoughts of my ascension, my coming glory; but, having to face these fellows every third Monday morning, in meekness, I felt something surrendering in myself, a pride, a spirit, a self. I began to feel myself getting away from me. I realized that I had to pay attention to the presentness of my world or for ever surrender. I thought of my father and the promise that I had made that morning. I went to Michael.

'Michael, tell Scull and them that I don't want them to clout me.'

To Michael, that is not possible. As far as he is concerned, it is a rule. 'They clout everybody,' he says. 'They clout me too. They can't change the rules for you.'

'Is not the same, Michael. You is their friend. They want to hurt me.'

Michael cannot understand what I am saying. He doesn't want to. We quarrel.

'Just tell them I don't want any one of them touching my head. Rule or no rule. I not playing. I don't clout nobody and I don't want nobody to clout me.'

I do not know if Michael told them how I felt. For my part, I tried to keep out of their way. I cannot escape them; they are everywhere. In all of it, Michael is an onlooker. I am alone. One Monday morning I go to school with a freshly trimmed head, courtesy of Mr Fitzie. The band of fellows is in the schoolyard waiting for me. In front is Scull, next to him stand Police and Belly. Michael is with them. I am wearing a cap.

'You have a nice trim,' Scull says, grinning.

Scull is long, bony and tough. He is, what is called, double-jointed, a condition which denotes abnormal strength. He is the wicketkeeper for the school's cricket team. At football, he is the goalkeeper. He makes flips and walks on his hands. His bleary eyes and frightening grin have earned him his nickname.

I say nothing.

'We mustn't touch his head. His head is too precious,' Belly says, mocking me, at the same time edging closer.

'No, we mustn't touch his head,' Scull says; and with one deft movement of his long bony hand, makes a snatch at my cap. Only after I had ducked, did I realize that he hadn't meant seriously to remove the cap. For the moment, he was just playing with me.

'A very nice trim,' said Belly, also making a snatch at my cap.

The boys had closed in. I was surrounded.

Making fun of me, Police clapped his hands and at the same instant reached out to touch my head. Seeing him in the motion, I started to swing, and, to his surprise and mine, my fist sank into the firm flesh of his belly. As he stepped back to move in more seriously, the school bell rang.

'Friday,' gasped Police, as we made for the lines.

Friday is the day for fighting. Being the last day of school for the week, it is the safest day to get your clothes dirty; and, being two days before the start of the new week, it allows the possibility that the news would not get to the schoolmaster, and if it did there would be two days for him either to forget or for it to seem distant on the following Monday.

'You crazy or what?' Michael said to me, when we were home that evening. 'You going to fight Police? Police will kill you. Don't expect me to come in, you know.'

Of the gang, Police is the most dangerous because he is the one with the least sense of humour. He will be the most unforgiving. Scull is their leader, Belly is a comic. He is nothing himself, but gets his status from being with the others. He is their caddy boy. Police doesn't laugh. He is fourteen, like Michael. He has an inner vexation and viciousness. He is a bully. He wears his stepfather's cut-down blue serge trousers which still carry the wide loops made especially for the thick police belt. On his arms are outlined belt marks, stripes, where the lashes from his stepfather's floggings have left their mark.

'Say sorry. Go and tell him you sorry,' Michael says.

'Say sorry? I can't go and tell the man I sorry.'

'Give him something, then. You have a pan of marbles. Give them to him.'

'You feel he will take it?'

'I will talk to him,' Michael said.

Next day Michael came to tell me that it was OK. I could give Police the pan of marbles and all would be forgiven. The pan of marbles was a Christmas present from Aunt Irene. I had kept them safely because I hardly used them. I didn't like to play marbles. The fact is, I wasn't too good at it. Sometimes I played with Ronnie, who was the only one around who was a worse player than me; but, we always ended up quarrelling. I didn't need the marbles.

I put the marbles in my book bag next day and went to school. I saw Police, but I didn't give them to him.

'Why you didn't give him the marbles?' Michael asked.

I didn't even know why. Really, I didn't know. I had intended to give them to him. 'Tomorrow,' I said. 'I will give them tomorrow.'

Michael is dissatisfied. He had already told the fellows of my forth-coming peace offering. Now I was making him look like a fool. 'What you waiting for?' he asks. 'You want to fight him? I not going to come in, you know.'

'You want to give them to him for me?'

'No,' says Michael. 'He want them from you.'

For three days of that week I took the marbles to school with me. Thursday evening I still had them. Somehow I had not been able to bring myself to give them over.

'Tomorrow is Friday,' Michael said. 'That is all I have to say.'

On a Thursday evening in Cunaripo, the stores are closed and the rum shops shut. This evening Main Street is quiet and looks wide and the sun is bright. Charcoal burners, on their way to the forest and their charcoal pits, sit on a bench in front of Kee's rum shop, drinking and making merry, singing old love songs and ancient calypsos. Mano, my uncle, is playing his *cuatro*, accompanying them. With them is Priscilla, the only woman there, dancing by herself, her shoulders bent in a tender crouch, her arms wrapped around her body and her eyes closed with the sweetness of memories.

'Good evening, Miss Priscilla,' I say.

'Good evening, lover,' she answers, opening reddened eyes that sparkle with sorrow, winking at me, closing them again.

When Priscilla was young, my mother says, it didn't have anybody in Cunaripo who could dress like her, and nobody so good looking. When it had a dance fellars used to line up just to dance with her, she was so popular. People see a drunkard now, my mother says. But, in those days, Priscilla was a star. Then she went to the city. She went to Venezuela. Her pictures used to be in the papers. She was a model. She used to give away dresses to her relatives. Good good dresses, she used to give away; pretty pretty dresses. A big-shot man was engaged to marry her. She had a good job in the civil service. She was up in society. But, poor Priscilla see what she shouldn't see; she hear what she shouldn't hear. Her boss was a big racketeer, defrauding the country of thousands and thousands of dollars. He bribe everybody, but not Priscilla. She give evidence against him in the inquiry. That was the end of her. She lose her job. The man that she was to marry leave her. Her family who she used to give those pretty dresses to disown her. They try to poison her. She come back to Cunaripo to try to catch herself. They drag her down. They drag her down. She start to drink rum. She lose her looks, her reputation. People forget her, my mother says; but, not my mother. Aunt Irene remembers her too. They talk of her. They remember when she was a star. She, my mother, demands that, no matter what, we be respectful to Priscilla. Whenever I see her, I say 'Good evening, Priscilla'; and she says, 'Good evening, lover'. I am a little scared of her.

In front of the rum shop now, the scene, that a while ago was so merry, turns ugly. Priscilla's performance had taken her to where the men have their bottle of rum. She attempts to take a drink. One of the men protests.

'Get away from here, you dirty woman. Go and bathe before you touch that rum.'

'You talking to me?' Priscilla puts on a baby voice and rolls her eyes flirtatiously. She thinks she knows how to break their hearts.

'You, yes,' the man shouts. 'Go and bathe before you touch this rum.'

'You talking to me? He talking to me?' Priscilla, looking around, now the centre of attention. With the coquetry of a striptease, she lifts her dress and shows her petticoat. Swinging her hips, fluttering her eyelids, she cries, 'Who is dirty? Look! Look!' lifting her dress higher.

Provoked further, for there are those who egg her on, 'Show more! Show more! Show everything!' she lifts her petticoat and reveals her undergarment and her scrawny legs. 'You see it? You see how clean?' She advance upon the man who had made the remark, gyrating her hips, 'Come on, show your drawers. Show them. I show you mine, now, show yours. See who is dirty.'

'Show it, Johnny!' the other men chant. 'Don't make her make you shame.'

Johnny begins to laugh, an embarrassed laughter. His laughter is his surrender, 'Come, Priscilla, come,' he invites her. 'Come and take a drink. Go on children, go on.'

I walk away, leaving behind me their laughter. There at the roundabout is Corporal, barebacked, wearing his own home-made baton at his waist, standing in the middle of the road, directing traffic. On his head is a chamber pot, his helmet; his leggings are a tangle of dried banana leaves wrapped around his feet, from ankles to his knees. He is barefooted.

Earlier, I had passed Mussolini on a bench. He is an old stickfighter who keeps vigil at that corner, with a stick in his hand. He wears a battered black jacket, its pockets stuffed with stones, for he is at war with the schoolchildren who tease him about a sore that is rotting away one of his feet. Some of us run when we see him, others stand a safe distance away and taunt him, and run when he gets up to give chase.

When I get to Federation Café, I will see Science Man, who my father says, 'book send mad', who, during the war, they say, was sentenced to a term in prison for making a radio. Now Science Man prowls the street with a grimace on his face and now and again butts his head forcefully against the wood of the telephone post. Britain, in her unchanged dress of red, white and blue; Graham, with his hernia; Pretty Foot, our transvestite; Fowl, who still crows like the cock he stole from Mother Alice; the Shango priestess. These are our celebrities. Their escapades, their fights, their moments of madness, their sayings, these are the subjects of our conversations. And about each of them is a story: pride that has fallen; ambition that overleaped itself. Each story ends victoriously in defeat, penance, apology. This was our folklore. Until that Thursday evening, I had not put them all together in that way. It was then that I felt the weight of their apology and defeat for the first time; and, for the first time, I looked at our town.

The architects of Cunaripo have placed the police station on a hill commanding the main street. On another hill, the steeple of the Roman Catholic church rises against the sky like a shaft of white light; seeing it, men make the sign of the cross, women genuflect. Men, coming out of Kee's rum shop, stumble upon the serene and anchored power of the police station, with its thick masonry and its Union Jack and its walk of whitewashed flagstones, about it a distant and secret air, like that of a monastery; and they make a bow, not a bow of bending the back, but one of straightening the knees, recognizing before them a power that can render them as sober as the surrounding estate's cocoa trees, standing in their green and lavish silence, offering pods that are crimson breasts, golden eyes; while behind these, below the bulging muscles of the mountain's back, the suspenseful forest watches through the window panes of white eyes. Overpowered by the sense of penance and apology, I head for home.

I must escape. Tomorrow, for sure, I will make Police a gift of my marbles and I would be done with them, with this. I was thinking how wonderful it would be to win a college exhibition and leave and go to college and get away from this place.

I must have bent my head just then to blink away the water that filled my eyes. When I lifted it again, there, through the glaze of tears, I see coming towards me this giant, dancing in a tall loose-jointed ease, his shirt collar turned up, his chest unbuttoned, his hat at a tilt and the sunshine glinting off his face. It was my uncle, Bango. He was whistling. I felt a sudden thrill. I stopped and gazed at him. He waved a hand and winked in salute in recognition, 'Bull!' he exclaimed, calling me by my father's nickname; and, still in his beat, in tune with his rhythm, he went on. Bull, he had called me. In that call was comradeship, acknowledgement, was a pride in me, in himself, in all our family. I felt a sense of thankfulness, I felt saved. Out of this landscape, I had plucked a hero.

I would like to embellish Uncle Bango with power and purpose and a war, give him two pistols and a rifle and a double bandolier; and, with a sombrero tied around his neck and falling on his shoulders, put him on a white horse and make him a bandit chieftain at the head of forty, fifty, a hundred lean desperadoes who appear out of nowhere to battle for the poor. I would like to tell of his being pursued by the cavalry, riding through a hail of bullets to meet the woman that is waiting for him, and his name will be Pancho or Fidel or Che. But that would obscure the truth of this story. I am not blinded by Uncle Bango.

I know he was a hero of a world shrunken to the size of a village street or gambling club or stickfight ring, that his name was linked with streetfighting and gambling, that beyond the limits of Cunaripo hardly anyone would know him. We talked about him at home. He worked irregularly. My mother says he had three women minding him. Pa knows him as a woodworker. He could dance bongo, fight stick and he sculptured heads from dried coconuts. But, he was all I had to pit against the desolate humbling of our landscape. What did he bring?

I suppose I must call it style. It was not style as adornment, but style as substance. His style was not something that he had acquired to enhance an ability; rather, it existed prior to any ability or accomplishment – it was affirmation and self looking for a skill to wed it to, to save it and maintain it, to express it; it was self searching for substance, for meaning. He sometimes wore white, buff shoes. They were always spotless. One night at a fête, Cut Cake, a petty thief, stepped on his shoes and refused to say sorry. When he admonished him, Cut Cake drew a knife. The story, which circulated through the village afterwards, and which came to us at school, was that Uncle Bango paused. And before he butt Cut Cake, he said, 'Don't do that stuff, kid.' No doubt it was something that he had heard in a movie; but, the spirit, the desire for meaning, the style, that was Uncle Bango's.

That evening, though, his one word, salutation, greeting, 'Bull!' conveyed that he was proud of me, that I was part of the struggle, that he was depending on me to achieve with my education the substance that he had been seeking all his life. In a way, I was a hero to him too, to his whole generation. For them, heroism had never meant the surrender of the self.

Next day, as soon as I step out of range of our house, I turn up my shirt collar, undo the topmost button of my shirt, give my khaki pants an added fold, my costume of clown had been transformed to that of warrior, I became, 'Young Bull', nephew of Bango the stickfighter.

'What you doing?' Michael asked in consternation when he saw me making these adjustments to my person. 'Where the marbles?'

'I don't have them. They home.'

'You don't have them? I serious, you know. If you fighting Police, I not putting a hand.'

'Suit yourself,' I said. At last I was feeling that my life was my own, that somehow I had found a way to confront the penance and apology of our town. I had had a brief conversion; I knew I was saying goodbye to my ambition to be other than my father's son.

That Friday evening as school was out for the day, for the week, two heroes, borne along by the press of their supporters, head for the little clearing behind the playing field on the edge of the forest. I am one of them. Michael is nowhere in sight. I have no idea of tactics, all I know is that I am going to fight Police.

Somebody held my book bag, someone holds my cap. The noise dies down and I square off before Police. Out of the corner of my eyes, I get a look of Michael's face, with a grin on it. What am I really doing here, I am asking myself when I feel myself pushed forward and I find that I am surprised when Police hits me, but I feel a sense of relief at being able to withstand his blow. I strike out. The fight is on. All that I am trying to do is to control my trembling. I am glad when we clinch. Then we are on the ground and I am squirming and squirming to get out of his grasp; and then, by some miracle, I find that I have his neck in the crook of my arm. I press and I squeeze and I hold on for dear life, not because I want to hurt him, but, because I know that if I let go, I am dead. After an eternity, I hear myself scream. Police had clamped his teeth on to my arm. Police had bitten me. The bigger boys part us and we get up. Confusion. Some are inspecting my bitten arm, some are restraining Police roughly. In keeping with my role as a combatant, I rush to the attack once more, but they hold me back. The fight is over. All around there are outraged voices, 'You bite him! You bite him!' It is a transgression of the rules.

'But, he was choking me,' Police shouts. They don't want to hear him. His supporters feel let down.

'A big man like you,' Scull was saying disdainfully. 'You is a girl or what?'

'I tell you he was choking me,' Police appealed.

I had won the fight on the technicality of the bite.

Suddenly, Michael materializes, 'Look at your clothes!' In rolling on the ground my clothes had become all dirty, my elbows were bruised as were my knees, and Police's teeth marks were printed on my forearm.

'It bad?' I asked Michael, thinking about my clothes.

'Ma going to soak your tail,' he said.

I dusted myself as best I could, retrieved my belongings and in the middle of a press of supporters, I made for home.

Ma is at the gate waiting for me. My supporters melt. The crook, Michael, had reached home ahead of me and has, no doubt, given her the story.

'Pass in,' she instructs. I go into the house and she follows me. I put down my bag, take off my cap. Arms akimbo, she surveys me. 'Travey, I send you to school to do what?'

I do not answer.

'You don't know what I send you to school for?'

If to such an absurd question I give no answer, it is insolence; if I do answer, I lead myself into the trap she is setting, 'Ma, he hit me first,' I say.

'I am not talking about hitting. I talking about school. I send you to school to do what?'

'But, if he hit me first? Ma, if somebody hit you? If somebody want to clout you?'

'What I send you to school for?'

'To learn, Ma.'

'Yes, to learn. Not to be a fighter; not to be Joe Louis. If somebody hit you, you know what to do. You don't know what to do?'

'Ma, I was outside. I couldn't tell the teacher.'

'Ah, so you know you must tell the teacher if somebody hit you?'

'Yes, Ma.'

'And where Michael was?'

'Michael was there.'

'Michael!' she calls. 'Michael!' My brother appears in his doleful costume of priest. 'Michael, where you was? You mean you stand up there and let them beat your brother?'

Michael starts to give his version of the story. It is jerky and meandering. He tells of his suggestion that I make peace. He tells of his attempts at reconciliation between Police and me.

'So you decide to fight?' Ma asks.

'Ma, I couldn't give him the marbles.'

'And you couldn't tell the teacher either.'

'I beg him to give the marbles to Police. If he did give him the marbles nothing would of happen,' Michael says.

'And because he didn't give the marbles, you stand up and watch them beat him. What kind of brother you is? What happen to the two of you?'

'Nobody aint beat him, Ma. He was winning. He had Police neck locked, and to get away Police had to bite him.'

'Bite? Let me see the bite.'

I show her the teeth marks on my arm. She orders Michael to get the iodine.

'So you is a fighter now,' she says, not without tenderness, holding my arm while I close my eyes and brace myself for the sting of the iodine. 'As for you, Michael, I will speak to your father about you.'

I closed my eyes tightly as the iodine stung. I thought of my father, I felt that I had let him down. The burden that I had agreed to carry, I had rather hurriedly put down. It had seemed so simple then.

'Keep this hand out of water,' she said, daubing the iodine on my elbows now.

'Yes, Ma.'

'It's these games you boys play. This haircut is the whole cause.'

I was glad that I had escaped a flogging. I was ready to rush off.

'And those clothes,' she said sternly. 'You will please wash them yourself.'

'Yes, Ma,' happy that this was to be the price of my reprieve.

'And that head. You better get one of your friends to cut your hair. Fitzie does trim too clean.'

'Yes, Ma. Thank you, Ma.' I wanted to hug her. It was in my eyes.

'Boy,' she said looking down at me. 'What wrong with you now?'

I wanted to hug her, to say, 'I love you.'

'Nothing,' I smiled. With us love had always been expressed in language more tender and tough than words.

E. A. MARKHAM

Miss Joyce and Bobcat

I

Miss Joyce came out on the veranda and sniffed the air and wrinkled up her nose.

'Lord, Lord, have mercy,' she said. 'Why things always work out so? You work, you plan, you prepare; you pay for it with you own money – hard, hard-earned money. But is grudge they grudge. You work and pay, and everything turn out so. I'm too damned soft, that's my trouble. But what's a poor woman to do, a single woman at that? The men have it all their way, the brutes, as always. Bobcat! . . .' Here she shouted at the man in the garden, trying to make herself heard above the sound of the machine. 'Bobcat, you brute. Who paying you to desecrate me so?'

Bobcat, the brute, unaware of Miss Joyce, continued his desecration of Miss Joyce's lawn, digging a hole with an impressive-looking machine.

'We going to have to use the back terrace now,' Miss Joyce sighed. Then she called to someone out of sight: 'Prudence, we'll have to use the back terrace. I'm sure the grass dying already. Prudence!'

Miss Joyce turned to go back into the house but stopped. Bobcat had seen her but pretended not to. The sound of the machine was not so much deafening as conquering; he was hiding behind that. Now that he was performing for her she didn't know whether to suppress or to encourage thoughts about the nature of the man's machine, the maleness of the thing, the authority of that tool smacking into her lawn, gorging great chunks of soil which left the place so wounded and vulnerable –

and the beast, sitting up there on that high seat, like some sort of religion, directing it.

Then Bobcat decided to acknowledge Miss Joyce; he looked up from the still-shuddering machine, the tool suspended in mid-air, and tipped an imaginary hat to her. Miss Joyce refused to be impressed. She wanted the man to know that she was angry, damned angry. She refused to notice the filth that was on the end of the tool.

Bobcat had tipped his hat; who did that sort of thing nowadays? In the old days, when she was a young girl, that sort of thing meant that a man had good manners; then after all the politics and overcoming; after all the raising up of consciousness and women wanting to respect themselves – all that seemed to stop, and only the old-timers were left tipping; clergymen of the old school; the odd businessman from the country who was thinking perhaps of going into politics. Or the odder arse returning damaged from England. Even the grammar-school boys didn't tip hat anymore. Anyway now was no time, a big woman with so much to do, to be encouraging thoughts about grammar-school boys. And tipping hat was like everything else, just what men did to preen themselves and confuse women.

Miss Joyce started as Prudence silently appeared from the house and stood beside her; she had come with a glass of wine on a tray.

'Don't creep up on me so, you want to kill me? Who ask you to bring out the wine?'

'The cakes ready, Miss Joyce.'

'Prudence, you is a human being.'

'Miss Joyce.'

'Then act like a human being. What you doing with wine in the middle of the day; you want to turn me into a drunkard? Look at the state I'm in already; look at that wild man digging up my front lawn as if it belong to him? Shaking up the house and thing. I getting hot and sweaty again. Do I look ready for a garden party, Prudence?'

'Miss Joyce.'

'I going cancel the whole damn thing.'

'The wine for the gentleman; is he ask for it.'

'Well, that's really good to know. You better go and turn down the oven and don't let the cakes and them burn, eh. So he asking for wine now!' They both stood looking at Bobcat who was enjoying this without appearing to.

'So you all think we running a hotel here? A wine shop? I tell you to offer him a cold drink, and you go and open up the wine put aside for my guests; you know what wine cost in this place?'

'You want me to take it back again?'

'Like the man already move into my home. Ordering this and that. Making demands. Is not just the wine I'm talking about, you know.' And here she shouted at Bobcat: 'So you think this is wine shop? Rum shop?'

Bobcat signalled that he would soon be over, and Miss Joyce said to nobody in particular: 'He can hear. He only playing tricks.' Then she turned again to Prudence. 'Woman, you going let the cakes burn to ashes?'

As Prudence turned to go into the house, Miss Joyce had another thought: 'And you better water the grass, eh?'

'The grass not supposed to water. In the hot sun.'

'Since when you're an expert on grass?'

'Is what they say.'

'Who say? So now you're a doctor of grass? They give you degree in grass when you was down in the Virgin Islands? That grass come all the way from the nursery. I shame to tell you what it cost.'

'Well, if it dead, don't blame me.' And Prudence went off, unruffled, into the house.

'Is me you all going to kill. I'm only in this world to take a beating.' This time when she called to the man on the lawn, it was with new resolution, and a new name. 'Leslie!' She signalled and he looked up. 'Stop the damn machine.'

The sudden silence made her a little conscious of her agitation. God, why was it a woman always felt herself in the wrong? The more they abuse you the more you feel guilty. Life unfair, eh?

'Leslie, you nearly finish?'

'Close to.'

'"Close to" not good enough. You promise to come last week.'

'I already explain, Miss Joyce.'

'What good is explanation when I have people coming here in . . .'

she looked at her watch '. . . practically anytime now. I'm not a laughing-stock, you know.'

'The smell completely gone now.'

'Maybe the smell nearly gone, but it look bad. In this day and age no one putting in pit latrine in front of they house. I should have build from scratch like everybody else instead of buying from these foreign people.'

'It's the modern thing, you know.'

'They must be addle your brains in London. Since when pit latrine come modern thing?'

'Is septic tank they call it. All the Americans and Canadians put them in.'

'Thanks for the history lesson. Do I look like I in school? I'm not no American and Canadian. I don't have to follow their nastiness.'

'Anyway, you taking out, not putting in.'

'A half-empty bottle look the same like a half-full bottle to them that don't know.'

'You have a way with words, you know? But as I was saying, some-times, these people, they put them right next to the swimming-pool.'

The man was becoming familiar; she would make him keep his dis-tance, put an end to the conversation. 'This is my front lawn,' she told him. 'No man have the right to pollute it with coarseness, and rudeness and what I call this kind of scatological talk.' Before she disappeared into the house she informed him, in a rather grand manner, that the woman had brought the wine he had ordered.

Bobcat soon collected himself and blew a long whistle in appreciation and tipped his imaginary hat. Not long afterwards, the shudder of his machine could be felt throughout the house.

2

Halfway through the party Miss Joyce, looking cool and unflustered, drifted back to the front terrace to observe the newly laid turf being watered by a sprinkler. She delayed her re-entry as another guest, an elegantly dressed young woman, approached the house.

'Celestine, you look nice,' she said. 'Your better half's here ahead of you.'

'Hello, Miss Joyce. You look nice too.'

'Call me Joyce, man.'

'The weather too hot for clothes. I thought you were putting in a pool here.'

'What do I want with pool? I'm not so desperate to let people see me naked. I have two bathrooms in my house, that's enough for me. So child, I'm glad you come. The Very Reverend missing you inside.'

'I doubt that. Papa doesn't believe the cloth should interfere with having a good time.'

'Is Papa you call the Reverend?'

'Got to call him something, Miss Joyce.'

'People might get the wrong idea when you call him Papa.'

'Well, they say he's old enough to be my daddy.'

'People in this place too wicked. Wicked and bad minded.'

'Well, as Papa says: we have to show we're not as small as the island. We have to go against the trend.'

'You get punished for that too, child. But what we doing out here talking? Come and join the party. You look nice in truth. The Reverend Doctor must be very good to you.'

A short time later, Celestine was back on the front veranda sobbing in Miss Joyce's arms.

'Brutes, that's what they are. Men are brutes,' Miss Joyce consolidated. 'Don't cry, child; they not worth it, none of them. Priest and beggar, all the same. Black and white, no difference.'

Prudence approached from the house with a glass of water on a tray.

'He still playing the fool in there?' Miss Joyce wanted to know. But Prudence remained silent.

'Prudence, you don't hear me talking to you?'

'Is not me invite him here.'

'What's that supposed to mean? Is your family. You all country people together. But it serve me right, I should mix with my own kind.'

'Everybody is family. Me not responsible for that. Reverend Doctor don't change people. Is not me invite him here.'

'I'm sorry I upset your Ladyship.'

'I know him since he small, know how he is. When he use to come up to the big house, Mrs Parkinson old house where I used to work, and that man didn't have nothing, not even a little cardboard suitcase to he name, nothing. And these kind people take he in, buy him clothes. Is me who used to wash them. And he look nice, you know? He always look nice. The boy poor but he could preach even in them days. And they help him along, and they help him along till he marry into the family. And as they help him along he let them down, and as he let them down they forgive he. Every time. And though he married he go and make baby with all kind of dirty, stinking woman. And still they forgive he. And even in the very kitchen, you know where you peeling breadfruit and green banana, he coming in to feel-up you breast.'

Celestine, who had been sobbing all the while, was virtually howling now. So Miss Joyce spoke to Prudence in some anger.

'Woman, you not shame to be talking like that in front of this poor child? Don't no one have any little sensitivity or delicacy in this place?'

But Prudence was unrelenting. 'Excuse my manners. I know what I know. He borrow money and they have to pay it back. He bad, bad, bad. Is preaching save he. Every Sunday when he call the Lord down on we, we frighten, frighten.'

'Jesus God.'

'. . . And when he get into more trouble, they send he away to come Preacher. I tell you when Miss Polly marry he I did cry. I cry bitter tears because I know how it go turn out. And they say even to this day he would have other wife and family in foreign country . . .'

Prudence stopped as the Reverend Doctor appeared in the doorway. 'Ladies, ladies . . .' he hesitated, not sure which one to approach. 'Ladies, excuse my . . . tardiness.' Then he took the glass of water from Prudence. But before taking it to Celestine, he lingered to rebuke Prudence, hardly bothering to lower his voice: 'You never did have any breasts worth talking about.'

3

That evening, after the party, Miss Joyce was sitting on the front terrace, from time to time sipping her drink. She was bothered by a mosquito or a fly and clumsily tried to deal with it, but her mind was elsewhere.

She was wondering why she was making a fool of herself. The effort of the party had left her, not drained but agitated. Not even that. Deflated. Why didn't anything ever turn out as planned? When she had lived abroad and couldn't live as she wanted, she had always promised herself that one day it would be different. And she had saved her money. It wasn't easy lifting up racists off their hospital beds to clean them, but she had gritted her teeth and held her breath and done it in the hope that one day she would be able to live again like a human being.

She was aware that there was someone on the lawn, but she was in no hurry. She thought a bit more of what she would or would not suffer in this place. Finally, in her own time, she addressed the shadow on the lawn:

'Bobcat, what are you doing on my lawn this time of night?'

'I come to apologize, Miss Joyce.'

'What for?'

'For missing the party.'

'Too late as usual. Apologies not accepted. Too bad there's no wine in the house. Rum shop close.'

'What can I do, Miss Joyce?'

'I'm not your father and your mother. You can leave my lawn and take your apology with you.'

'Let me explain.'

'I've heard the explanations. Story of my life.'

'May I have a little drink?'

'Never say the bitch so stingy she wouldn't even let them come and drink her out of house and home.' She got up to go into the house. 'Maybe I'll be a bartender in the next life.'

Bobcat came out of the shadows and up to the edge of the veranda, but didn't mount the steps. And it was here that Miss Joyce passed over his drink.

She was very calm when she spoke. 'If you want to cross this threshold, Leslie, you have to make me feel like a human being.'

'You're something special, you know, Miss Joyce.'

'Everything on this earth is special. God see to that. Even the crappo you hear waking up the dead is in some way special.'

'No, no. But I mean, really special.'

'You not giving me anything, Bobcat, to call me special.'

'God, you going to be hard to please.'

'You find the foreign ladies easy?'

'I made a mistake, man.'

'You're damn right I'm hard to please. If you have an interest in me you have to find out where I am and meet me there. Is the only thing will compensate for the beating and the punishment.'

'Miss Joyce, you have the wrong man.'

'Every woman in this world have the wrong man. We all have the scars to prove it. But I'm not a child, Leslie, I'm not looking for Mr Right. Over the years, I've learnt the value of compromise. Let's drink to that.'

'Let me come up and sit down, eh. Because I have to talk to you real serious.'

Miss Joyce didn't object. But Bobcat found it hard to start.

'I don't know what you think about anything,' Miss Joyce encouraged.

'Like what?'

'I don't know you, man. You must have views. Views on . . . on the President of France, the cutting down of Brazilian rain forests . . .'

'I'm in business, you know, not politics.'

'Oh Leslie, are you a man of imagination or a miser?' She stopped him trying to answer and rushed on: 'Your vocabulary, Leslie: where are the gentle words to cancel out the rest? I expect finesse from a man. I expect something uplifting, not talk about pit latrine and nastiness. I expect reassurance from a man. I want him to tell me that in spite of everything, we're not turning into brutes.'

'Everything like what?'

'Oh God. Everything, man. Everything in the world. Violence. Brutishness: do I have to spell it out? You have to talk to me.'

'Miss Joyce, you're a Philosopher, in truth.'

'When you're up there, high up on your machine, I want to know what you thinking.'

'I like you, you know. That's what I'm thinking. You hear me?'

'That's a cool way to say something, in such a hot climate. You like me like you like rum and cricket?'

'I love you, man.'

'It hurt to say it?'

'Joyce, I love you.'

'That's nice.' Then a little shift of tone. 'You can't imagine that's all a woman want to hear.'

'You going to make me make a fool of meself.'

'That's bad? You don't like me enough to risk making fool of yourself? Maybe you should send me a letter in a brown envelope. In some other language. In French. *M. Bobcat, 48 Terresseur. Bel homme, très sympathique* (you have to lie, they all lie), *entreprenant, d'un naturel réserve, très sympathique des affaires, etc.*'

Bobcat blew another long whistle of appreciation.

'Then maybe I could accept that as a starter,' Miss Joyce said flatly.

'You can toy with a man just so much,' Bobcat threatened, advancing on Miss Joyce. 'I running out of patience, rapidly.'

'So run.'

'I ain't running, Joyce.' His hands were on her.

'So you like me?'

'I love you, man.'

'You like me?'

'Oh God.'

'*C'est vrai?*'

'Oh God. Oh God.'

N. D. WILLIAMS

Cats in the Eyes of the Pig

(Once the waiter had padded off with our order I lit a cigarette and relaxed. I hadn't really expected her to show up, yet here she was sitting beside me. You were telling me about this fellow you once met, I said.)

It happened last summer. My friends had all gone off to England. I never much cared for summer travels. I'd always find some reason to stay home. Couldn't afford it, I told Frieda, my best friend. I couldn't see myself gallivanting through cities and villages, a huddle of girls in jeans, poking about here and there.

The truth is I'm a grounded bird. My wings were trimmed in early childhood. At home my parents allowed me as much freedom as I wished, but travelling beyond the borders of Germany was expressly forbidden. They were afraid something terrible would happen; I'd come back a pot smoker; I'd be killed in a highway accident; or worse, I wouldn't come back at all. When you're an adopted child you have to live with a surfeit of love and concern.

Even after I'd moved into my own apartment, found a job, learnt to manage a separate life, the impulse to fly, to test my wings in open sky, never quickened inside me. So this gentle timid bird was quite content to stay in her gilded cage. Until the day I met Cats.

I'd just finished lunch and was strolling back to the office. I'd stopped at the pedestrian crossing, bunched with everyone. Cats was waiting for the lights on the other side. I remember how he stood out in the crowd: a tall thin frame, the sunglasses, his hair in weird pigtails. He was carrying a musical instrument case and he just couldn't keep still.

Accidentally the case touched an elderly woman. He looked down at her, flashed a gleaming smile and patted her with affection on the shoulder.

There was novelty in that gesture, magic in his courtesy. I couldn't take my eyes off him. He wasn't looking at the lights like everyone else but at the traffic churning by, as if weighing his chances of making a sudden streak through a gap between cars. So desperate, so bent on going somewhere!

He caught me staring at him. At least I felt *caught*, in the act of stealing whatever it was his restlessness concealed. And we might have passed each other, might never have seen each other again, were it not for this incident: right at the moment our bodies near-touched, in the middle of the road, the case flew open and a saxophone, a splash of gold in the afternoon light, fell out. Our four hands dived and saved it from the hurrying crush.

Right there, in my eyes, Cats was an awkward boy on his way to music lessons, fumbling in the middle of the zebra crossing, his mission exposed. The attention of the whole shuffling world had been arrested, if only for seconds, and made to focus on his clumsy soul.

And though I had no real reason to, I felt responsible. *I should not have stared.* I didn't have to stop and help either. Now I had seen inside the closet where every heart hangs its ache, its deep wish.

Cats wanted to be a musician, the finest saxophonist in Europe.

We scrambled to safety on his side of the road. Seconds after he had thanked me in terrible German, and I had smiled, and we both hesitated, knowing our separate lives seemed signposted in opposite directions. In the twilight of that moment Cats tucked his arm in mine and said, 'I've been wandering all these years, searching for the way, I know it must be wherever you're going. Shall we?'

Magical grace, swift courtesy!

What glued me to him as we marched off was his laughter. A startlingly fresh beautiful sound, filling the afternoon air, subsuming the dull grind of traffic. Cats's spirit came through in that sound. His eyes, his cheeks, his skin were aflame with that sound. He seemed so happy to be alive.

Which is why I didn't mind him moving in with me.

He turned up at my door laden with suitcase, travelling bag, the saxophone, a pile of records. My apartment was transformed into a junk shop; Cats dumped things everywhere.

I suddenly realized how constricted my life was, how shaped for comfort and dull ease by all the objects I'd taken so much trouble to purchase, to place here, not there. Imagine the marvellous freedom I felt inside the new disorder.

The only room Cats insisted on maintaining some appearance of order was the kitchen. That was because he liked cooking. He kept it clean, furiously washing and wiping. Force of habit, he explained. As a boy he'd helped his mother in her kitchen. At weekends it became my province, but most evenings I'd come home from work, open the door and be swept inside by the aroma of dinner in preparation. After the meal, the dishes put away, we'd listen to his records.

Cats believed in *pure communication* through sound. He would come in and find me reading a book; he'd frown and say, 'Why must you keep throwing parties in your head?' Then he'd put on some reggae, or Miles Davis who was his hero: 'A black aristocrat if ever there was one. Just listen to the refinement in that horn.'

I couldn't explain to Frieda and the others the night they came clattering up the stairs and hammered on my door, 'Come on, open up', bursting with travel anecdotes. It was their habit to convene in my apartment and relive the pleasures and horrors of that summer. Later they'd show slides.

Imagine their open-mouthed shock when they discovered Cats lounging in his pigtail plaits, ash dangling from the cigarette in his mouth. He waved a languid hand of greeting then resumed his intake of the Modern Jazz Quartet on the stereo. We had to shout to be heard above the music, until Cats swung his long legs off the couch, turned the volume down, then stood his full height to be introduced.

By then Frieda had seen enough and was making excuses for interrupting, and the others were suddenly very tired and had just dropped by to say hello.

Later they phoned. I tried to tell them about Cats, how like a tempest he had swept into my life, bringing fresh rains to my dry routines. I don't think they fully understood.

I couldn't satisfy their curiosity about him because Cats was evasive about his past. He resisted my attempts to pry it out of him. He'd drop bits and pieces of revelation like so much disposable tissue after he'd blown his nose.

'What was it like growing up on an island?' I once asked.

He'd just finished blowing apart 'Round Midnight'. His lips relinquished the mouthpiece, his head turned slowly; he looked at me over his shoulder. He'd tried once to get a job as a film actor in London. This movement of the head might have been something he'd chosen to do for a screen test, something he'd now perfected just in case he was asked again.

'Well, what was it like?' I persisted.

He unhooked the saxophone and sighed.

'It was like if a whole world of ... possibilities was racing through your blood, and with each year passing some of them die like blood cells giving out on you and your vision slowly darkens, and one day you realize ... if you don't do something, something will do you!'

He collapsed in a chair with an actor's exhaustion after that great effort, spilling his drink on the carpet. I fed him questions even as I fetched him a fresh one.

I sat cross-legged that evening, looking suitably captive, telling myself it was all coming out at last.

'I left home because I was young and I'd had enough of being enslaved by older generations. The only future for young men like me, a dropout from the island's high school, was playing cricket. I didn't have much talent for that game.'

He took off for England full of confidence he would *make it*. Make *what* was never too clear in his mind. Within forty-eight hours his dreams got lost in the wet streets and biting cold. He'd spent most of his time after that *staying out of trouble*.

Always when I was supremely receptive to what he was saying Cats would cut it short. How it burned me! I pained at these amputations. But that's the way he was. Some demon in his soul had him zigging and zagging, sliding this way and that, evading completion. I'd bite my lips and wait.

I told myself it was all *here* in my apartment – his dreams, his cooking, his tireless lovemaking, the way he unhooked the instrument after he'd blown out everything I wanted him to talk to me about, the way his limbs elongated on the divan listening to Miles Davis. It was all here with me, this journeyman's life. One day it would be mine to possess. I didn't have to hurry.

(You have to be careful with a girl like this. You should never let your attention stray. Creep up on her, as it were, with your silence, the sword of your love.)

One evening I came home thinking how lucky I was to have someone like Cats to come home to, and thinking of the conversation I'd had with Frieda that afternoon during which she kept asking, 'Are you sure you know what you're doing?' as if someone who didn't go off on summer jaunts wasn't supposed to know what she was doing.

I opened the door and walked right into the stereo at full blast. He didn't answer me when I said 'Hello'. I knew something was wrong. He snapped when I turned the volume down. He was lying on his back, his hands behind his head, staring at the ceiling. I went inside the bedroom, undressed and discovered I wanted to cry.

For an hour I lay on the bed listening to the stereo firing away at Cats outside. It was almost an endurance test. The darkness in my room was as solid as ice. I held my breath and waited. I wondered: was this not my act of sacrificial readiness?

The stereo eventually stopped. The door opened quietly. Cats not wanting to disturb me, knowing very well I was awake; Cats taking off his clothes, standing above me, Cats contemplating my body, then sitting on the bed, shaking my shoulders, finishing his cigarette, saying he was sorry. That was *his* ritual of readiness.

How did we come by *his* arrangement of our pleasure: the distancing then the intimacy, Cats driving into me on and on until I screamed like his saxophone going berserk in those wild passages, until I was babbling my astonishment that such joy was possible between us, until my confused words told him my pleasure was complete?

He curled up like a child at my breasts afterwards. He would offer a little more about the island. I said nothing. I listened. He kept talking until he fell asleep.

One persistent theme: Cats had this overwhelming sense of being entirely on his own. One man and his canoe. It caught him like a heart attack in the oddest place, at the most unlikely moment.

Once, for instance, in a phone booth, while he was calling up *a bird* in London, and she was taking a long time to pick up the phone. He'd hung up and had wandered through the streets of the city for hours, asking himself, 'What am I doing here?' Another occasion was in an airport lounge as he waited for a flight call. One man and his canoe.

One man and his saxophone!

That was the only thing he really loved, he confessed one night. He couldn't get attached to a woman or *a bird* the way he felt for that instrument. He used to play gigs in London. He loved the moment when he was blowing off the end of his solo, and the other fellow was taking over, continuing that long quest of the spirit. He felt, then, tremendously a part of *something moving*. Nothing else, not politics, not *the race thing* gave him that feeling.

Though he never openly admitted it, Cats was soon feeling guilty about the way we lived. He wasn't working; he felt like a leech; it was eating away at his pride.

I tried to reassure him. I talked about how important it was for one of us to live creatively, rather than work in that dull routine way I went off to the job each day. But Cats was too wrapped up in brooding to understand.

'I've got this great idea,' he shouted, as I came in one evening. 'I've been waiting to tell you about it all afternoon.'

I barely had time to catch my breath. 'What's happened?' I asked.

'Sit down here and listen to this.'

His great idea was to open a discothèque. He had gone into this bar some blocks away from the apartment. Business, it seemed, was slow. Cats talked to the owner about music, and sold him the idea of turning the bar into a place for young people, a discothèque with a difference – the music would be louder: reggae, calypso, American soul. People would be eaten alive by rhythm. Imagine, he said, the steel drums ravaging their bodies, the bass guitar making craters of their minds: a deafening immersion into sound never before heard this side of Africa. The owner of the bar was thinking it over.

The idea caught afire. Several nights I sat and watched the dancers being mauled by the lights and the sounds, pleasure cells running riot in their bodies. Cats was master at the controls, keeping up a stream of talk in between records.

'They're like robots,' he declared one night, laughing. 'They're twitch-ing and jerking, but they're not *dancing* yet.'

He decided he'd have to teach them how to dance. This was how Paulette turned up.

She was one of his London *birds*, a pretty long-limbed West Indian. Cats had her up on a raised platform (sometimes he joined her) doing demonstration acts.

And all went well. Too well, in fact.

Cats and Paulette came out one evening to find me settled in for the night with a book.

'Aren't you coming with us?' Paulette asked, a hint of resentment in her voice (something I'd noticed the first time Cats introduced us).

'I think I'll stay home tonight. Catch up on my reading,' I said. Cats made a brief show of disappointment.

After they'd left I tried to silence my suspicious heart, tried not to imagine what they did in the apartment after I'd set off to work, which was sometimes mere hours after they'd come in from night life. I told myself it really didn't matter. Cats wasn't my property after all.

He must have divined my thoughts, for once he came close to me, pinched my cheeks and said, 'Come on, there's nothing to worry about. I'm packing her off in another week. Just as soon as she's shown these zombies how to *dance*.'

By then something else made me anxious – the saxophone! Cats hadn't picked it up since the discothèque idea came to him. He hadn't even blown a celebratory note. After the way he'd spoken about the instrument, success for him would mean nothing unless the saxophone was part of it. I began to feel its neglect, its enormous patience. I watched it leaning against the wall in a corner waiting to absorb fresh pain and joy.

The night Cats vanished, I came home, glanced at the saxophone and told myself that once it was there Cats couldn't be far away. I didn't see him that night, nor the following morning.

It didn't occur to me that something was wrong until the next evening I entered the apartment. I had the funny feeling nothing had been disturbed during my absence. The saxophone was still there. Cats wasn't.

I phoned the discothèque. No one could tell me where he might be. I looked around the apartment. His suitcase, his clothes were gone. So were Paulette's bags. Everything else was much the same. He'd left his record collection.

In the weeks that followed I went through the house chores, my job, the business of living in a state of suspended animation. Frieda showed up barely days after Cats had disappeared, speaking softly, and wearing the half-frown, half-smile of someone anxious to be my confidante if only I'd open up and let her in. I felt no need to explain anything to Frieda.

She wandered around, making desultory remarks, probing with a question or two. Suddenly she declared, 'This place is such a mess!' No doubt that was meant to jolt me into putting things in order, the way they were before.

She picked up the saxophone case. 'Don't touch that,' I screamed.

That must have hurt her. If she expected me to soften next, burst into tears and tell everything, she was disappointed. She called the next day, struggling to be casual and disinterested. I knew what she had imagined: my attempt at suicide, or some bizarre crime: my body discovered one morning in a blood-spattered room bearing multiple stab wounds, the obvious clues suggesting that the wild man I'd been living with had returned, had done his brutal business, had vanished to wherever he'd come from.

I cherished one bright hope: I would return one day to find that wild man waiting for me in the apartment. I'd come in and act surprised to see him. It would be the end of our beginning.

And then Christmas came. It seemed the right time for Cats to turn up, to discover how lost, how deprived he really was without his saxophone. On New Year's Eve I opened the case, took out the instrument and blew a single strangled note. Through the window I watched as the sound took off like a bird into the cold night sky, winging across land and sea to wherever Cats was – playing a gig, waiting for a flight call, turning over a cold memory on its stomach as he waited.

(I glanced at my watch and signalled the waiter. It's getting late, I said, stroking my good luck. Would you like to take a walk?)

CLYDE HOSEIN

Crow

Crow sat in the tall savannah grass and sang to himself, more softly than in the church, when, wearing his pinstriped Indian whipcord suit, he let his voice warble from the choir loft until the altar hummed with the 'Ave Maria', 'Salve Regina' or 'Veni Creator'.

He sang in all seven churches in Esperance; his clear baritone was in constant demand. But he preferred the more flexible program of the Protestant churches, where often the songs to mark the ring and register ceremonies were the same as those on the hit parade. When a Presbyterian or Methodist bride requested a song he would happily croon 'I believe, be my love' or 'Where have all the flowers gone', not only for the two or three dollars the best man pressed into his palm, but also in the hope that he might be launched on his career; for who knew in which congregation lurked the impresario, radio producer or record manufacturer from Port of Spain.

From where he sat Crow saw his father's house crowded with idlers and customers waiting for haircuts and shaves. In the front gallery his brothers and his father, old Kernahan, worked with scissors and razor. Crow could catch on the warm wind the chatter about crab catches, the sugar factory and recent events in Esperance.

Occasionally one of the idlers would go from his seat on one of the long benches in the front, along the side or through the house, to the back gallery where more young men were playing cards and draughts and members of Dynamos Sports Club were meeting.

Crow watched the bus slow at the STOP sign nailed to the almond tree and heard the men in the front gallery laugh, as they always did, at some strained face at a bus window.

A longing possessed him to escape Esperance, the heat, the cinema, the cricket, the farting contests, the endless punning.

He rose from the grass, adjusted his athletic wrist brace and began to walk towards the house.

'The old Crow,' cried the man in the back gallery.

'You cutting hair today, Indian?' asked Dingo.

With a feeling of resignation Crow went to his bedroom and brought out his box of barbering tools. He set it upon the brick balustrade. 'Sit down,' he told Dingo. He sent the card players with their bench into the yard. He sharpened the razor on the strop that hung from the kitchen wall. From up front, barely audible between joke and exploding laughter, four pairs of scissors clipped in unison.

Lying on his bed he watched the lights of a passing vehicle travel the ceiling. Again he had worked far into the night, writing jingles for products he thought needed such an impetus. He was experimenting with a blend of calypso melody and American rock rhythm.

He had plunged with all his energy into that activity and felt grateful for the advice of the bus driver from Arouca who had been in the chorus for a washing-powder radio commercial and soon was leaving for New York.

Crow had spent many months studying the structure of popular jingles like 'Brush your teeth with Colgate', 'Tide's in; dirt's out', and 'You can trust your car to the man who wears the star'. He was sure he had discovered the laws that governed their success.

His thoughts wandered to his earliest attempts at songwriting. He was nearing sixteen and had hoped to sell song poems to Five Star Music Masters, New York or Los Angeles – he still was not sure which.

But he was then too inexperienced to write of love. And despite the localization of the lyrics – keskidee for sparrow, governor-plum for elm, Esperance for San Francisco – every song he produced sounded like one he knew.

When he blew out the lamp the first bus to Port of Spain was straining along the road in the muddy dawn light.

Across the savannah the grandstand stood dark. Seed-hunting tanagers broke the silence. He felt pride and pity as he watched his brothers' faces. Late the previous evening they had played ninety minutes of football for Dynamos and sent a visiting squad back home with a seven to one licking.

He emptied the bucket of its red almond leaves, filled it at the standpipe, jumped the drain and went along the side of the house to the roofless bathroom. He took off his T-shirt, picked up the tin cup from the stone floor and poured water on his head.

The dawning sun had begun to filigree the wet savannah grass when, in his whipcord suit, Crow stepped aboard the second bus and sat at the rear.

Two hours later, after they had rattled through canefields and hamlets, he alighted on South Quay and walked along Frederick Street. Only once before, when he had gone to the Red House for his birth certificate, had he been so far into the core of the city. He came to the same intersection twice, and then he found the building on Gordon Street.

Crow approached the bronze directory on the white wall. HUMPHREY, LEWIS & GRAHAM. He checked the name against the card the Arouca bus driver had given him. At the bottom of the card he read: F. A. Alcazar, Account Executive.

Crow looked up at the sunburnt hills. He felt disoriented but had memorized landmarks along the way; he could retrace his steps to the bus stand. He walked along the wall and peered through the pikes that rose through periwinkle and ixora. In the lower Palladian window a young woman was busy at a typewriter.

He walked back to the gate. PUSH said the sign. His heart beat faster and faster. Except for Father Kennedy at Esperance RC, he had never spoken to a white person.

At noon, when the street overflowed with blue-uniformed schoolgirls and office workers had got into the parked cars and driven away, Crow still stood near the gate with the lyrics of a Malta Stout jingle in the envelope in his hand.

He walked down the street, coming to a café on a corner. Behind the counter an old Chinese man was serving black children sandwiches and peanut punch. Crow went in and bought a hops bread and ham.

Not until 2.30 did he summon up the courage to push open the gate.

He was halfway up one of the flanking granite stairways when a khaki-clad man challenged him from a dark cubicle under the building.

'Who you come to see here, man?'

Crow mumbled something about a wrong address and escaped to the safety of the sidewalk. The sun had stewed the asphalt. He gazed at the bubbles of tar on the pavement as he sat on the kerb with his jacket off.

He went back to the ixora and saw an Indian in a blue uniform standing at the secretary's desk. When the messenger looked out Crow gestured with an upraised hand, which the man correctly assessed as a sign for help, for he came out and Crow gave him the card.

'Why don't you go in and see Mr Alcazar?' the man rebuked. 'Don't you have an appointment?'

When Crow did not reply the man added, 'Alright, wait here. I'll find out if he can see you.'

Soon the messenger re-emerged with a fistful of letters. 'Go up the stairs,' he said.

The secretary had come to the door. Crow held out the card and tiptoed behind her. The messenger and the man in the khaki suit stood side by side below, scowling at him.

He sat in the chair at the side of the desk and when Alcazar swung around from the credenza Crow stared into his blue eyes and could not utter a word. He thrust the sheet of paper at Alcazar.

'From Esperance, eh.' Alcazar read the top of the sheet where Crow had written his name and address below *Respectfully Submitted*. 'My uncle was an overseer on the sugar estate there,' Alcazar said.

'Radio commercials. I want to make radio commercials, sir,' Crow blurted. The argument he had practised eluded him, and the more he tried to coordinate his thoughts the more frantic he became. He held his wrist in his hand, covering up his identification bracelet.

Alcazar studied the Malta Stout lyrics. 'Do you have anything on the air?' he asked.

'No sir, but I sing at weddings.' Crow avoided Alcazar's eyes.

'Ah, you sing too. What songs besides those at weddings?'

'The classics sir,' Crow answered. 'My favourite is "Old Cape Cod".'

Alcazar smiled. He was much younger than Crow had imagined, with a boyish voice that softened further when he spoke into the telephone, 'Is the Turner Tissue recording still on?' Then, addressing Crow, he went on, 'Let me put you in the picture, Mr Kernahan. We employ professional people: copywriters, calypsonians, all kinds of musicians. It's a pity . . .' He handed Crow the lyrics.

'. . . because you've sold me on Malta Stout. This is good clean hard-selling copy, but, unfortunately, our staff handles all the writing. However, we are always looking for good singers. Are you interested in a tissue ad?'

'Oh yes,' Crow, at the edge of his seat, replied.

'It'll be an audition, you understand.' Alcazar wrote in his desk diary.

'I'll be pleased sir,' Crow said.

The first bus took him to the city with hours to spare. He walked the almost deserted streets, found Tragarete Road and headed north.

Above a grocery he saw the sign, CALDERON STUDIOS. He sat under an old samaan tree in the square opposite and watched the street come to life.

The technician arrived and let in the men who had been waiting at the door. Crow crossed the street and followed them up the stairs. He sat, as directed, in the studio and studied the typewritten lyrics.

The band began to play and Alcazar arrived. The band-leader hummed a few bars for the benefit of the singers.

The technician said, 'Singer one, take one,' and the band-leader called the first man to the microphone.

Crow listened to performer after performer. He found it difficult to swallow. And then his turn came.

He sang erratically, forcing the musicians to change pace to keep in time. Alcazar, sitting with the technician behind the glass panel in the control room, added to his unease.

'I'll phone you,' Alcazar said through the partly opened door. The eighth singer was getting ready.

'I don't have a phone.'

'I'll write you then.'

Down the stairs, on the long walk to the stand, and sitting in the bus watching the ajoupas and cane patches fly by, Crow's dislocated brain replayed the lines he had fluffed:

> 'We have the tissue for every issue
> Cold, fever, cough and ague
> Turner's Tissue for you.'

The rainy season came. The drain below the front gallery gurgled all day. Sometimes a truck or a taxi sped through the puddles and a fine mist blew into the gallery where Crow and his father and brothers worked, surrounded by chatter and horseplay. Crow wanted to run into the rain, far from the overrun house.

He said, 'I cut my last head for the day.' He took his toolbox in. He emptied his pockets on his bed and counted the money. Three dollars; twelve customers.

He walked across the savannah through the midget football game, listening to the squelch of his shoes.

The sun came out suddenly, and before he reached the grandstand the water on the asphalt walkways began to evaporate in curling wisps. He sat in the top tier and watched the boys kick the football to the canefield. He went from thought to thought and dark came down.

It gave him a thrill to sit in one place and watch the earth change. Across the fields, in the canecutters' mud hutments orange flambeaux flared. Stars began to show in the powder-blue sky. A bullfinch flew down to the lowest tier.

A great sadness overcame him; yet, he began to sing: 'And the little señorita'.

He sang for the croaking frogs, for the cane, the savannah, the poor people huddled before their rag-and-bottle lamps, for his dead mother, the boredom and materialism of Esperance: 'You're breaking my heart', 'Unforgettable', 'Some enchanted evening'.

When the moon rose over the guava trees he thought of other lands where the same light spread its ghostly sheet, of breakers foaming on white beaches and people going home from work. He thought of different ways of life, of women, of love. He cried as he sang 'Green eyes', 'Lady of Spain', 'No other love'.

The last bus had gone and the road was deserted. He got up and stood for a long time before he walked across the moonlit grass towards the shadowed house.

In the morning the letter came. As soon as the postman put it in his hand Crow ran far into the savannah, tearing at the envelope. In it was a cheque for $15; and the letter:

Dear Mr Kernahan,
Thank you for your audition tape for our client's product, Turner's Tissue.
We enclose the standard fee of fifteen dollars.

> Best wishes,
> F. A. Alcazar

Sunday. The gathering had begun. The young men, bleary-eyed from graveyard shifts at the sugar factory, crammed the galleries. Some sat with their buttocks overhanging the balustrade. If one lost his balance he would plunge to the concrete drain with its ribbon of water.

Old Kernahan leaned across the drain near the almond tree. He had his scissors and comb in hand and talked to the policeman who sat on his bicycle with one foot resting on the kerb. Kernahan cackled with glee when the corporal told him how difficult it was for couples to find a singer for their weddings.

Dingo drove up in his fish van. He rolled down the window and shouted, 'Mr K., what's the latest from the old Crow?'

'I was telling the corporal,' Kernahan said, 'Crow's doing really well. He got another promotion. Assistant Night-shift Supervisor. Get that, *Supervisor!* The man's top brass in that factory in Leeds.'

I-Calypso

There was a lot of laughter that April Fools' Day when the Sunday papers were read. All caused by a three-column by two-inch advertisement in very bold type.

PERSONAL
TO ERMA
PLEASE CONFESS

This is to advise Erma to confess her indiscretions to her husband. He will forgive her if she tells all, but he is getting suspicious and if he finds out for himself, trouble!

The young clerk who took the ad for the paper was new. It didn't even occur to him that there was anything wrong with it. In any case he was alone on the night shift and he didn't want to look foolish by consulting about every little thing. He processed the ad and sent it to the composing room, where it relieved the tedium of the night's work by providing a few laughs as to who Erma might be and why somebody had 'put her in the paper'. Some thought it might be the husband himself, but the clerk reported that it was a woman who brought it in. Perhaps it was Erma's friend? Or her rival? Whoever had done it, it was a good All Fools' Day joke and everybody laughed.

Erma One

'But Erma! Who could be calling the house so early on a Sunday morning! Answer the phone, no!'

'Hello! 80900. Good morning.'

'Erma girl. Is that you! Chile, you read the paper since morning?'

'Eh, eh! Myrtle. You know what time it is? Six o'clock big, big Sunday morning. I just waking up. What happen so?'

'Girl, you name in the paper.'

'What you saying?'

'Look it here. Big advertisement. You can't miss it. Erma please confess.'

'What you talking 'bout?'

'Yes, chile. It right here. What you been up to? It also say you gwine get licks if you don't confess to you husband.'

'Listen, Myrtle, if you drink mad puss piss, keep it to youself and don't provoke me peace this Lord's day morning, hear! Why you don't keep your nastiness to youself? Is me one in the world name Erma? If somebody put somebody name Erma in the paper, it have to be me? Well Miss Gossip, I sorry to disappoint you, but is not me, you hear!'

'Girl, I don't know. But you never see smoke without fire and the pig squealing loudest is the one the stone ketch!'

'Myrtle, I warning you. It's a good thing you on the telephone else I'd be tempted to clap you face for you. Leave me alone and go make you husband breakfast. God knows he look like he need looking after.'

'Erma, who that calling so early?'

'That Myrtle. She make me so angry. Always putting she nasty mouth on people.'

'Who she macoing now?'

'Somebody name Erma.'

'You?'

'Not me at all, boy. Not me.'

Chorus

Erma, honey! Is what you do?
Mek the whole town laughing at you.
Erma what you doing wrong?
Calypsonian soon put you in song.
Everybody teasing, jeering, sorrying for your man.
Chile, mend your ways
Crime never pays.

Erma Two

'John boy. How you going?'

'Fine, partner. Jus tekkin the morning constitutional, as usual.'

'Boy, I admire the way you tek the exercise thing serious.'

'Yes, you know. Have to keep the body fit or the women will leave you out.'

'How Erma?'

'She OK. Can't get she to join me for the morning walk. She say is only fowl cock must wake up so early.'

'You see the Sunday paper yet?'

'No. I usually get it at the corner.'

'A big ad in there bout somebody named Erma. I never know you was having trouble with she, boy.'

'What you talking bout?'

'See it here. Will Erma confess! Is you put she in?'

'What?'

'But careful, John boy. Mind you get a heart attack this big Lord's day morning.'

'I gwine buss she ass, you hear. Give me that.'

'Erma! Erma!'

'Hmm? What you makin up so much noise for so early in the morning?'

'Makin up noise? You don't hear noise yet. What this mean?'

'What, John, man?'

'Read this. Is who put you in the paper? What going on behind me back?'

'Pass me glasses. But, John! How you could think this could be me!'

'Me trust no woman, you hear. How much woman you know name Erma? Somebody talk you business. Tell me what going on before I loss me temper.'

'But John!'

'Don't, "But John" me. Jesus! Look how scandal ketch me this big Sunday morning. I feel I could buss you ass for true!'

'John! What you doing with that belt? Is who you planning to pelt? You mad? But look trouble this morning! Look me crosses this morning. Look how I lying down peaceful in me bed this Lord's day morning and the man come threatening to sweeten me tea with salt, for no reason at all.'

'No reason at all? Erma, you better tell me what going on!'

Chorus

> Erma girl! Is it really true
> That you sins at last ketch up with you?
> Erma, how you could carry on so?
> You had the man like sof sof dough.
> Now somebody squeal an you sins reveal.
> Chile, mend you ways
> Crime never pays.

Erma Three

'Hello.'

'It's only me, darling. So! Somebody put your wife in the papers!'

'I told you not to call me on a Sunday. What're you talking about?'

'You haven't read the papers yet? There's a big ad. Can't miss it. Erma, please confess. It goes on to say that her husband is getting suspicious and that if she doesn't confess she is going to get her tail cut. Why, darling! I didn't know you were violent.'

'What the hell are you talking about? Is this more of your nastiness?'

'But sweetheart! Why are you abusing me? Why would I want to be nasty? Erma is doing it herself. You think she's so pure and righteous. Not like me, a loose woman, eh? But nobody has my name in the papers.'

'Listen, woman! You taking a joke too far. You taking this jealous thing too far. I finish with you if I find out you have anything to do with this. You hear me!'

'Jerry! Oh sorry. I didn't know you were on the phone. Here're the papers. What's the matter, love? You look upset.'

'Some people only like to make life miserable for others. Some foolish person phone telling me about some ad in the paper about an Erma. They want to find out if it's you.'

'What!'

'Wait. Let me see the papers. Oh yes. Here it is: Erma please confess. But anybody ever see anything like this. Some idle person with money to waste. Imagine anybody thinking it could be you, love.'

'Oh, Jerry. How people so wicked. I suppose a whole lot of people will be calling with their bad jokes.'

'Hello, Sheila? Erma here ... No. I'm all right. I don't want Jerry to hear me. You read the papers yet? ... What happen? Girl, I nearly drop dead with fright. Somebody put me in the paper ... Yes. An ad saying Erma must confess her indiscretions. Somebody call Jerry first thing this morning and point it out to him. But he so sweet and trusting. He was laughing with me about it ...

'Girl! I don't know who could be so wicked to do such a thing, but Sheila, I fraid. Suppose he find out in truth? Suppose he get suspicious? ... Yes, I know you was warning me, but you know how it go? I never dream somebody could do such a thing ...

'How you mean stay calm. I biting me nails. You know how them quiet man stay. If he find out, crapaud go smoke me pipe!'

Chorus

Erma! Erma! What you going to do?
Jus yesterday I was warning you.
Is play you say you playing
Jus tekkin a lil chance.
Now the whole world know about you and your romance.
Chile, mend you ways
Crime never pays.

Finale

So all you Erma that doing wrong
All you who going around fooling with man
You might think you get away
But crime will never pay
Man mek to do what he want to do.
Woman mek to do what man tell she to do.
So woman, mend you ways
And forever win his praise.
And if you think is a lie
Check out me and me sweetie-pie.

WAYNE BROWN

Waiting for Jumbies to Cross

Vision is singular: in a crowd, the eye picks out a face, holds it, passes on, picks out another, flickers away. The Red Indian whom Wanda's gaze fell on, in the teeming western approach to the Savannah stage, was huge, swarthy and malevolent-looking. Long-striding, impervious to the opposing tide of spectators (which parted like the biblical sea to let him through) he was making straight for her, towering and unsmiling. There must be some mistake, Wanda thought.

Startled, she glanced for reassurance at the girl from the Tourist Board, but Marilyn Niles, inclining her head to hear something Wanda's husband was shouting into her ear, a small smile on her lips, did not see her. The Red Indian was almost upon her before she realized that his glowering gaze was fixed, not on her, but on the setting sun beyond her shoulder. She had a confused glimpse of a chest black-gleaming with grease, of something metal shining at his throat, of the diagonal of a strap – and then she was twisting sideways to him – too late. The Red Indian strode brutally between her and her husband. His arm struck wrenchingly across her breast, his swinging flask banged her hip bone and he was gone. She reeled away; saw, through the pain, her husband holding his own shoulder and looking almost thoughtfully after the departing, swinging head-dress, and she cried in exasperation, 'Jer-ree!' Then they were with her, Jerry's handsome, still-boyish, crewcut face peering with concern into hers, him saying, 'Hey, Wanda, you OK?' and the pain beginning to subside, resolving into separate tendernesses, into a stinging flaring ache below, and the deep hurt over her heart.

'Of course I'm not OK!' she cried irritably, 'That – brute!'

'You got a good bounce,' the girl from the Tourist Board said sympathetically. 'Look' – she wiped her fingers on the upper sleeve of the blond woman's blouse and held them up – 'Grease paint.'

'She'll be OK,' Jerry told the girl; and they both looked encouragingly at Wanda. ('He's *apologizing*,' Wanda thought. She cupped the wrenched breast and leaned forward slightly, taking its weight in her hand, feeling for the depth of the hurt.)

'He didn't mean anything, Mrs Schulman,' Marilyn Niles said consolingly. 'He was just passin'.' Taking the older woman's silence for assent, she went on brightly: 'You know, we have a saying in this country: "You can't play mas' and be afraid of the powder."'

'But I wasn't playing mas'!' said Wanda irritably. It sounded petulant and childish as she said it, and she straightened up and looked around her, gingerly rubbing her hip bone where it protruded from the waistband of her hipster denims. 'I'm OK,' she said to her husband, and he smiled, relieved.

'She's better now,' he told the girl.

Marilyn Niles, looking at him, smiled. To the woman, she said, 'That's good. I knew it would pass.' Then she glanced away, amused. This was the third year she had hired on for Carnival as an escort with the Tourist Board; in three years, not one of the couples she'd escorted had had, as far as she could tell, anything like the absolutely fantastic time they tirelessly professed to be having; and yet, she supposed, they had all returned to their home towns in the States or Canada or West Germany, and been the envy of their friends with their terrific tans, their treasure troves of photographs, and their tales of an orgiastic tropical paradise; as this couple, no doubt, would, too. Well, that was OK by her. Everything was what you made of it, thought Marilyn Niles sagely.

And that was OK too. Her job was to show these people a good time, and if a good time was what they were determined at all cost to have, who was she to nitpick? Her only problem right now was keeping this one's interest in her short of the point where his wife would notice, take offence, perhaps even lodge a complaint about her to her employers; and she didn't think it would be a big problem.

At their first meeting, she had been routinely aware of her effect upon Jerry Schulman. Lightly and cheerfully in the days that followed, she had let him come on, since that was part of the game, up to a point, since she had to admit that he wasn't exactly hard on the eyes, especially not by comparison with the odious, fat man from Arkansas she'd had the previous year, and since, most of all, to tell the truth, she had been first intrigued, and then animated, by the measured, cautious, slow concentration of the forces of his attention upon her, until now, five o'clock on Carnival Tuesday afternoon, she felt for the first time an instinct to draw back from him, not only for tactical reasons but out of self-protection.

Still – it wasn't a big problem. In fact, it wouldn't have been a problem at all, she thought, if he hadn't started drinking; but he had. Not a lot, not so that it showed; but slowly, steadily, like the way he'd been closing in on her, once he'd started, Jerry Schulman had gone on drinking. He'd been drinking now for three days, and was flushed beneath his tan, and there was a certain heavy watchfulness behind his boyish smile when he turned to her, and his shirt was unbuttoned all the way down the front. Still (and here Marilyn Niles's heart skipped lightly, as though at a pleasurable thought she had tossed her head) nothing untoward was going to come of it.

They were basically OK, these Schulmans, so far as she could judge, and basically OK with each other as well. In their early thirties, married for six years – she'd made a point of finding that out – that was no more nor less than you'd expect, she concluded.

Marilyn Niles had an ingenuously simple idea of marriage. She thought of marriage as a chalice from which the liquid of intimacy slowly evaporated, so that, full to the brim on the wedding day, its level sank imperceptibly but inexorably thereafter, until one day, fifteen or twenty-five years later, the chalice was empty, and husband and wife, looking up from the dinner table, each looked into a perfect stranger's eyes.

It was an image Marilyn Niles countenanced with fatalistic resignation, as though it represented a law of Nature. Her own four-year-old marriage to Charlie, she fancied, confirmed it (for wasn't his ardour that much less than it had been?) and while, fearing at first to hasten that slow slide, she had postponed having a baby, of late she had begun to feel the future coming upon her from another direction, and she felt that if she didn't have a baby soon, 'the time would pass'.

All these were vague premonitions. If anyone had asked her, she would have replied, truthfully enough, that she was still in love with Charlie and he with her, and that their marriage was still good, better than good. But no one could deny, it was not as it had been; and as for these two here, surmised Marilyn Niles, although their marriage looked to be basically OK, despite a li'l 'Carnival madness' on his part, one thing was as certain as the stars above, and that was that it was two years less OK than her own.

She glanced at them, and met Jerry's intent look. Subconsciously she'd been prepared for it, but now it occurred to her, 'He was waiting', and the thought made her blush. To cover her confusion, she said: 'I think we better get closer. To the stage. I mean' – one of Edmond Hart's trucks came abreast of them and she had to cup her mouth and shout into his ear – '*I don't want to miss Charlie!*'

Yelled like that it sounded wrong, and she flushed again.

'We're looking forward to seeing your husband again,' Jerry bawled back obligingly, but the look with which he concluded the words complicated their meaning. She was glad when Sophie Johnson, a Bee-Wee counter clerk, came dancing towards her out of the last Hart section, to stand before her in a limbo crouch (feet spread, knees flexed, hands palm upward at her sides) crying jubilantly, 'Marilyn! O Gawd, chile, whuh yuh doin'?' Girl grabbed girl; hugged; pranced in a tight circle; and then Sophie Johnson let go and was gone, pausing once to clasp her hands between her thighs and shake her bottom at them (grinning back over her shoulder mischievously) before prancing off down the grass corridor, arms pedalling. To the Schulmans, Marilyn Niles said, with the bright inanity of a guide: 'Well! That's Carnival!'

Wanda gave her a neutral smile. To her husband, she said: 'So, what's the plan?'

'The plan,' Jerry told her, 'is to try and get closer to the stage and wait for Jumbies, and after they come offstage we're all going to jump up with the band: you, me, Marilyn, and Charlie.'

'Who's Charlie?' Wanda asked.

Jerry looked at her oddly. 'Who's Charlie? Charlie's Marilyn's husband, for Chrissakes; don't you remember we met . . .'

'Oh. That Charlie.' She glanced around Jerry to see if an apology were required, but the girl from the Tourist Board had evidently not heard.

'OK,' she said, 'I'm game. Let's go.' She smiled what she hoped was a brave smile, but he hardly noticed, and as the three of them began moving east again, making their way against the stragglers coming off stage from the Edmond Hart band, she slipped back into the private misery of her thoughts, and the strange torpor of bewildered helplessness they evoked in her . . .

Thought is active and purposeful, so it would be inaccurate to say, as they wended their way towards the exit ramp of the Savannah stage, with Jerry in the middle, holding each woman now by the hand, that Wanda was 'thinking'. Outwardly she seemed only subdued – a natural response, thought Jerry, glancing at her, to being struck like that by the monomaniac Red Indian – but inwardly, secretly, she was entirely passive. Wanda felt herself strangely at the mercy of all manner of inchoate and fragmentary sensations, emotions and images; and it was this novel sensation of helplessness, of being pinned to a wall and assailed by a world she could not begin to comprehend, that constituted the real misery she dared not let her husband see.

She had known of course, from the moment they met her, that Jerry was attracted to this child (for that was how Wanda thought of Marilyn Niles, a mere five years her junior, and married as well, but, unlike herself, still childless, and therefore still, in some obscure way, unpossessed) and at that first meeting – while she, Wanda, still felt like herself, and like Jerry's wife – she had appraised her, covertly and swiftly, as she had appraised more than one potential rival in the past. She had registered the wide mouth, gleaming cheek bones and tight black curls, the snub nose and elongated eyes, and she had glanced with envy at the younger woman's lithe brown legs in which, as yet, no varicose vein showed, not even behind the knees (the latter were the reason why she, Wanda, oftener than not these days, opted to wear slacks).

Yet at the first meeting, nothing about the girl had particularly fazed her. Wanda had known for many years that the world considered her a beauty, if in a slightly old-fashioned way, with her perfect mouth, squarish jaw, and wide-set almond eyes, blond hair and fine throat (by contrast, this girl's neck was piggishly short and plump) and at thirty-two she had kept her figure. The varicose veins were her only blemish – that, and the slight, very slight, slackening of skin on her abdomen and breasts, something no woman, having given birth, could avoid. No – what fazed her was not the girl but Jerry's reaction to her. He was seeing something in the child she had not seen.

The thought frightened her. In this hot little country, so far away from Springfield, Illinois, from their house with the newly painted wicker-work on the veranda, the musty attic Jerry kept putting off cleaning, the drained swimming-pool out back – in this unfamiliar, bacchanalian place, bereft of all the habitual references of his life and hers (she even had trouble imagining clearly what Randy and Joanne, left behind with his grandparents, might be doing at any particular moment) she felt uncharacteristically unsure of herself. She watched with strange passivity, and growing dread, Jerry's deepening response to this girl, whose name she'd been told but had forgotten, and now had the utmost difficulty in recalling, no matter how often she heard the name from Jerry's lips.

And as the days passed, and Jerry began drinking and went on drinking, slowly, remorselessly, it seemed, she had felt the texture of their lives together thinning out, had felt him withdrawing more and more of the deep roots of his nature from her and directing them, progressively, towards this negligible girl – and she had felt strangely powerless to act. Beset by incomprehension, bereft of support, she had become a spectator at a scene of untellable misery: the slow extraction of his life from their life, and the unexpected emptiness where once she had unthinkingly leaned for support.

Heat, noise. Her days lost sequence. Always the girl wore those fashionable, flared shorts with the cuffs. Lights, noise: each excursion into the evening darkness seemed the same. Always, it seemed, they ended up in this dusty arena; or if not, she couldn't tell where. The girl changed her shoes but not her lipstick, to match her shorts. Always her lipstick was the same dark red. Traffic, dust, lights, noise. People! Pulling the drapes in the hotel at night tight, tight! Speech between them becoming perfunctory, incomprehensible. 'I'm fine ... wasn't that ... didn't you ... it certainly was ... yeah ... fine.' She lay in the dark, a crystal vase, waiting to shatter. 'Jerry? ... Yeah ... Fine.' In the mirror, she probed her face experimentally with fine fingers. Her nights were limbos of suspension, presided over by the intermittent shudder of the air-conditioning. She slept badly, drifting in and out of sleep. Glare. Noise. Dust.

'Pardon?'

They were in the grassy walkway between the North Stand and the stage, and a band on a truck was approaching, and there was an inexplicable deep ache over her heart, and someone, Jerry, was holding her hand, and the brown girl in the shorts was looking at her expectantly. She saw they had stopped walking, and she looked around.

To her husband, she said, smiling: 'Here?'

He nodded. 'Marilyn says this is close enough,' he told her.

Like a ponderous boat pushing a bow wave of revellers before it, a McWilliams truck came towards them down the grass corridor between the North Stand and the stage. Wanda stood at a loss, watching it come, until the girl from the Tourist Board, taking her hand, led her over to a low concrete bunker-like shed roofed in corrugated zinc, on which a couple of young black men were already sitting. To Wanda's husband, Marilyn Niles said: 'Hoist me up.' Turning full-face to him, placing her hands on his shoulders like a child.

Wanda watched as Jerry, stooping slightly, took hold of the brown girl's waist and swung her up ('My, he's strong!' thought Marilyn Niles). Before she could protest he had done the same with her, though his hand on her bare waist pulled the skin tight over her bruised hip and sent a flash of pain through her so that she hissed: 'Owww!' Then he hoisted himself up into the narrow space between them. Wanda, flinching away from the sudden weight of his hip against the tender bone of her own, shoved against the young man in the fishnet vest sitting on the other side of her. She turned to him, smiling confusedly, saying, 'I'm sorry'; but the young man only looked intently into her face and she flushed and looked away, toward the empty stage (at the eastern end of which a band was massing) waiting for her husband's voice to rescue her, to rescue them both; looking meanwhile straight ahead, at nothing.

The bow wave of revellers passed below them. The truck, a slow boat inhabited by black-silhouetted, bellowing demons, passed, inches from their knees. A little boy, leaning outboard, banged a bottle with a spoon intently in their faces, looking back at them for some moments after he'd passed. The band burst on to the stage. Jerry shouted into Wanda's ear, 'Isn't it something?' and she turned to him with a sweet, drowned smile, which irritated him. In the corner of his eye he saw the unknowable brown girl lean forward, bending almost double to shout a greeting at a noble-looking middle-aged black man with a beard whitened with powder. Jerry saw the man, beaming, reach up and take her face in both hands and kiss it hard on the mouth, before moving on with a departing wave, not looking back; and he turned and stared at her face in profile, at the broad cheekbone, the snub nose, the full lips with their blood-dark lipstick slightly smudged, and at the little beads of sweat on her neck and on her forehead just below the hairline. He stared, and knew she was aware of him staring; but she refused to meet his gaze, and went on looking straight ahead of her with a vague smile; and, baffled, not knowing how to proceed, he drew back in uncertainty into himself, saying as an afterthought to Wanda: 'How's the hip?'

The bruise was already purpling. The childish gesture with which she showed it, tugging the waist-band away from her flesh for his inspection, touched him with something like sorrow, and he mussed her hair briefly, saying, 'You're a brave girl.' Then Marilyn Niles leaned across him to say, 'You sure you OK, Mrs Schulman?' and he smelt her perfume and sweat, and her breast was hard against his arm.

On stage the figures in coruscating gold and blue chipped and pranced, or jumped, or merely walked, or, singly or in twosomes or threesomes, planted themselves and wined. In the flesh they looked less exuberant, more exhausted, than they had on television earlier that afternoon. Except for the walking ones, there was a curious air of determination about their movements, and on their faces Jerry saw a slack-mouthed, lidded look, a suffused daze, and here and there a secret, silly smile. 'They've forgotten their faces,' Jerry thought; and here a young Indian girl, scantily clad but for her cape, came and stood at the edge of the stage directly opposite to him, shouting and gesturing at him, 'Leave those two and come with me!' For answer he pulled his shirt-tails wide with both hands, baring his belly at her in a gesture simultaneously of challenge and helplessness, and she threw herself down on the stage floor and writhed in a paroxysm of feigned passion before getting to her feet and walking away from him with a scornful look. At his side Marilyn Niles laughed and laughed. 'You see everything at Carnival,' she told him. 'Any an' everything you ever wanted to see is right here.' This time she held his gaze for a reckless moment, before looking away with a little private laugh. Then she looked around her, businesslike. 'I think Jumbies might be next,' she told him.

The day was fading; the stage lights came on; a light drizzle began. The young men sitting next to Wanda fished behind them and came up with a loose sheet of galvanize which they held over their heads like an awning. The one in the fishnet vest offered to hold an end over Wanda – offering this wordlessly, with an inquiring, unsmiling look – but she shook her head, smiling wanly: 'It's OK,' She caught his glance down at her breasts before he looked away. It gave her a dull feeling, and she started to wonder whether she shouldn't untie the shirt-tail knot under her ribs and button up her blouse instead. But vaguely she couldn't think why, and the ache over her heart intervened, and the thought never completed itself. She sat slumped forward, hands clasped loosely between her thighs, and tried to imagine what her children might be doing at that moment. 'What's the time back home?' she asked Jerry suddenly.

Jerry looked annoyed. 'Well, what's the time here?' he demanded.

She started to answer – then stopped and stared in dismay at the band and disk of untanned white flesh where her wristwatch had been.

'My watch is gone!'

The loss startled her momentarily out of her torpor. The Rolex had been a gift from Jerry four years ago. It had been intended to commemorate a double celebration: his promotion to branch manager of the insurance company in Springfield, and the birth of Joanne, their first child. She had worn it unfailingly ever since; had even told the child it would be hers one day. Now her wrist felt orphaned. She looked at the disk of white flesh, pale in the deepening gloom, and for the first time that day – for the first time since they had arrived in this hot and festive country – felt herself close to tears.

'Well, that's that, then,' Jerry said coldly. 'I told you you should have changed the band before we came.' And he turned away to explain, in answer to the inquiring, light hand on his knee, that his wife had lost her perfectly good Rolex watch.

'It's twenty to seven,' the man in the fishnet vest said to Wanda.

She turned to him in sudden gratitude, trying to make out his face. But it was shrouded by the galvanize, and in the deepening dark and the drizzle all she could see clearly were his eyes. She murmured 'Thank you,' and looked away in confusion. The thought occurred to her that she had made a mistake in thus acknowledging him, but she couldn't think why this should be so. It occurred to her once more to button her blouse, but in a dullness of lethargy she let the thought go. The man said something to his companion, and they both looked at her. She felt them looking at her, and the dullness grew heavier. In a half-stupor, she gazed through the drizzle at the brightly lit stage, from which the last of the coruscating figures were now draining, and thought: 'Now I've lost his watch.' When the man in the fishnet vest abruptly moved the galvanized sheet over her head, bringing her into the rainless dark of him and his companion, she didn't react.

Her hair was wet. With both hands she slicked it back on either side of her neck. The water trickled down on to her chest, cold, then warm.

Jerry was talking to Randy in his mind. 'Randy,' he said silently, seeing clearly before him the bright inquisitive face of the three-year-old, 'when you grow up you'll understand a lot of things. You'll understand how full of shit the world is. You'll understand how hard it is to be a man. Who made it so, I don't know. I came and found it so, is all I can say. But it isn't a small thing – not this and that. You can't say, I'll keep this and change that. It's a whole great thing wrapped up together. You have to take it all, or reject it all. I love you so much, little fella, you'll never know. But I've taken it for nine years now, all of it. I guess you could say I've given you a good start. I guess you'll have to admit that yourself, one day. Randy, I have to tell you about the world . . .'

He stopped. The child was vivid before him, with his tousled brown curls and broad and shining forehead, and his mother's wide-set almond eyes, staring and waiting for him to go on; but for a moment he could not go on. He didn't know what he was telling the child, or why. He didn't know how Randy had suddenly appeared to him, more real than his surroundings, brighter than the stage, more intensely apprehended, even, than this woman-presence sitting next to him, its shoulder pressed against his shoulder, its thigh against his thigh. He only knew that the pain in his chest, which had begun, quietly, from the moment he first set eyes on her three days ago, had gone on, growing stronger and sinking ever deeper into him, until now it was like a bloodbeat of anguish in the deepest part of his being, and he felt himself flushed and slowed with it, and strong with the power of anguish. Invisibly his skin crawled, the words were deep in his throat, the metal band around his chest tightened and tightened; and the woman-presence was there, pressed against his side.

Out of all that, and Wanda's loss of her watch, the kid had suddenly appeared before him. As though, with her betrayal of the Rolex, the last present he had given her out of sheer happiness, out of the exultation of his young manhood and the promise of a still-shining world, the skein of irritation through which he had come to see her abruptly burst, and beyond it was the kid, sitting splay-legged on the apron of the swimming-pool with a plastic battleship between his knees, twisting around to look up, grinning at his approach, and he had known there were things he must say to him.

He said: 'Randy, you see, the world . . .'

The band around his chest tightened again. The kid was watching him, clear-eyed, waiting. In his anguish he felt portentous, huge. He said: 'Not the world, but society. Society is something different from a man. We live in society; but life is so short! Men understand things we cannot say. One day you'll be a man; you'll understand. I wish I could change the world they made for you, but I can't. You'll understand then. You'll understand your father. Nine years is a long time; I'm thirty-three, Randy. I'm not a kid, anymore. And I love you so much . . .'

He stopped, startled, feeling the woman-presence thrust against him hard. He was instantly, overwhelmingly aware of her – yet, turning to her, he was also aware, separately and distinctly, as in a drug trance, that a din of anticipation had risen in the dark stand behind him, and that a band had surged on to the entry ramp of the stage.

'Jumbies!' cried Marilyn Niles, thrusting her arms into the air, ten fingers spread. Twisting around like that, so that her arm was momentarily against his face, she cried heraldically again to the cavernous North Stand: 'Jumbies!'

Her wet cheekbone was six inches from his eye. He saw with startling clarity the mascara smudge, the tilt of her snub nose, the fine hairs above her lip – and below that, at the edge of his vision, the wide and blood-dark mouth, with its perfect teeth.

The band surged on to the entry ramp – and stopped. Out of the milling mass, indistinct in the gloom, stick-figures, two, then three, then four, advanced teeteringly on to the stage. The first two, eight feet tall, came long-striding down the northern edge of the stage, androgynously slender and sinuous in polka-dotted body stockings, black-on-white, white-on-black.

To Jerry, watching them approach in the strengthening light, they seemed heralds of a kind: twins, as the lit and dark sides of the moon are twins; and their meaning felt portentous and indecipherable. 'What are they supposed to represent?' he asked the girl beside him, raising his voice above the din: 'The age of unisex?'

'I suppose you could say so,' she shouted back gaily.

He saw that she didn't know and didn't care. He looked at her and felt for the first time a welling-up of enormous uncertainty; but it subsided, giving way almost at once to the tightening of the metal band around his chest. He tried once more to conjure up Randy, obscurely aware of something unfinished between them, but the image of the child, when it returned this time, was disaffected, blurred and far, and the feeling of urgency faded. Now a female figure on stilts came staggering towards him: a lurid, blue and yellow stick-female, its breasts and pubic triangle outlined in red, with a featureless, eggshell face, black holes for eyes. He smiled, uncomprehending, and, turning to Wanda, saw her sitting away from him, one of a trio (the other two were young black men whose features he couldn't discern) sheltering from the drizzle in the gloaming under a sheet of corrugated zinc. He nudged her, meaning to ask, 'Hey, you OK?' – and recoiled from the blank gaze she turned to him. 'Hey, you OK?' he asked her.

Wanda nodded, but coldly; as if – Jerry thought – he were a stranger who had presumed to intrude upon her solitude. Directing her gaze with a slight gesture at the female stick-figure still teetering towards them on the stage, he said conversationally: 'That's a terrific costume. Looks like a colour photo printed in negative; but see? There's no face.'

Wanda looked, not really seeing. Then Jerry saw her look. Placing the heels of her palms on the zinc roof behind her, Wanda leaned back, inclining her head to one side, and looked at the Queen of the Jumbies. Then she jerked forward, pulled her knees up to her chest, applied her cheek to her shoulder; and sitting so, hugging her knees and rocking slightly, she considered the lurid stick-female (now rising above them) with a wincing smile.

His wife was being difficult again. Jerry looked away. There was a truck approaching along the grass swathe, the din of its music rising, and Marilyn Niles's fists and shoulders were rolling to the beat, and she was shifting her weight from buttock to buttock, against him, away from him, against, away. 'Jumbies!' she barked. 'Jumbies!' Naughtily she dug Jerry in the ribs. 'Leh we get high wid de Jumbies,' she sang with the singer, laughing into his face. Jerry lunged for her mouth; as quickly she pulled her face away. 'Jumbies,' she sang softly, not missing a beat – not glancing at him anymore, still smiling, but with a sideways wariness of him now in her face; 'Jumbies,' she sang, fists, shoulders and buttocks rolling, against, away, against, away. 'You little bitch,' Jerry told her, and Marilyn Niles threw back her head and laughed at his adoration, and dug him remonstratively in the ribs again, just in case, looking away from him. 'Jumbies,' she crooned, everything rolling. 'Dese jumbies is it!'

The truck came abreast of them and slowly passed, and in the reverberation of its crescendo they saw that the band was now on stage: a bobbing mêlée of black and white whose individual forms the stage lights weren't quite strong enough to render. They looked like a tossing sea under the moon, with the infernal stick-figures, waist-deep, rising from it; and towering above them all, Jerry now saw, was a near-naked, gleaming, brown-skinned figure with a winged Darth Vader mask for a face.

The Darth Vader figure advanced emphatically, stagger-striding, swinging its arms across its torso like a race-walker. Jerry was about to laugh with pleasure at the invention when the face drew nearer and he saw it was not what he had imagined. Not malevolence but anguish was what shone in the black eggshell face with its gaping eyesockets, its grid for a mouth, its diamond noseplate and barred forehead – not fury, but loneliness and torture. Hoisted aloft, the imprisoning mask came on, arms pumping, but with the head strangely lolling; and in it Jerry saw the crucifixion of his age, the merciless imprisonment of a man in his own life, and in the life around him, and in the inexpressive metal of the world he had himself made. He said in desperation, 'Randy, this is *it* –.' And stopped.

He had spoken aloud. Marilyn Niles, all motion, stopped dead, and gave him a hard look. 'What you said?'

'Nothing,' Jerry said.

She looked at him a moment longer, her fists and shoulders still frozen in mid-roll. Then: 'Oh-ho,' she said, mock-threateningly, as if he had nearly been a bad boy and aroused her ire; and she resumed her sedentary dancing, rolling her shoulders and shifting her weight from buttock to buttock, against him, away from him, humming, under her breath now, the Tambu song.

Now, though he didn't know it, Jerry had misconstrued Marilyn Niles's animation. It wasn't that she was any especial fan of the Jumbies' band-leader (she herself had played regularly with Garib before her marriage to Charlie) nor was it due to loyalty to her husband's band. What mattered to Marilyn Niles was that whenever Charlie caught sight of her – which would probably be before she saw *him* – he should see her having a good time.

A better than good time, in fact – for Marilyn Niles had obscurely sensed that her marriage had reached the stage where it would do her no harm at all to be seen by her husband, in the first flash of recognition, not as 'his wife', but as a woman animated and desirable in her own right, and not necessarily dependent on him for her happiness. If this was teasing, thought Marilyn Niles, it was teasing in a good cause; and so, the moment the band came on stage, the moment it was even theoretically possible that her husband's eyes might pick her out, perched on the little galvanized roof with her two charges, she had set herself in motion, fists, shoulders and buttocks all rolling – and her animation had instantly been increased to the level of something like exaltation by the effect it had had on this Mr Jerry Schulman of Illinois here. His hapless lunge for her mouth minutes ago had been like homage; and now, in the secondary realization that with her husband near she could freely play with him and have nothing to fear, she revelled in the delight of her power.

Besides, there was something vaguely humiliating, Marilyn Niles thought, about being a tourist guide and having always to explain things that in your own life you took for granted. Now, in the moment of their release, she discovered a muted irritation and resentment at the role she had played for the past three Carnivals; and a little impulse of vengeance further heightened her exaltation; as though, sitting, dancing there for Charlie's eyes, and dancing up against this one here, the baffled force of him at her side like a homage or like a goad, she was also reclaiming her life: reaffirming her oneness with her people and their Carnival, which was her Carnival too, and putting a decisive distance between herself and her two charges, the insurance man from Illinois and his unhappy blond wife.

Add to these that a young body in motion, as Marilyn Niles's was, insensibly increases its elation, and it will be appreciated that by the time that Charlie, from behind his mask, did in fact pick her out, Marilyn Niles seemed transported. So radiant, so more-than-herself she seemed, that Charlie's gaze went reflexively to the crew-cut white man sitting pressed up against her, his face flushed, his shirt unbuttoned all the way, and – forgetting for a moment the unexpected good time which the young thing from the typing pool had shown him on the road, all the way from the cemetery to Memorial Park, and what vistas might thus open up to him, come Ash Wednesday morning at the office – he stopped chipping and said to himself, a trifle grimly, 'Well-well. We shall see what we shall see.'

The Jumbies were beginning to leave the stage. A slight strain had entered Marilyn Niles's sedentary dancing, and her humming had grown abstracted, almost inaudible. She had been scanning the stage without seeming to and not catching sight of Charlie; and the ghost of a question had begun intruding upon her exaltation with a wife's subconscious alarm. Where was Charlie? And what explanation could there be for his absence from the stage, other than some bacchanalian subterfuge?

She had faced the worst, and was preparing some gay dismissive explanation of his non-appearance for the benefit of her charges here, when a large, black and white, wedge-shaped mask thrust itself between her knees, and a deep voice said: 'Boo.'

Marilyn Niles gave a little shriek. Then: 'Charlie!' she cried. 'You beast!'

Charlie tugged off the mask as she leaned forward to take his head in both hands and shake it briefly in remonstration and relief. He was a young man of average good looks, lighter-skinned than she, with a neat Mugabe beard. In his face, the played-out, slack grin of the masquerader, come Tuesday night, was leavened by a certain alertness. Marilyn Niles saw it, and, throwing her arms around his neck, she laughed and nibbled his ear. 'We thought you were never comin'!' she cried. 'We thought some jumbie had got you, taken you off!'

Charlie grinned at her. 'How yuh doing there, Mr Schulman?' he said drawlingly.

Marilyn Niles laughed. With inexplicable gaiety, she cried: 'Jerry! You remember my husband!'

'Good to see you, Charlie,' Jerry Schulman said levelly.

'And Mrs Schulman?' cried Marilyn Niles to her husband. 'Say hi to Mrs Schulman, Charlie, she got a good bounce!'

Then they were down from the wall and, forming a wavering, unsteady line, pressed upon by bodies in front of them and by more bodies behind them, had joined the river of masqueraders winding westward across the Savannah in the thickening night. Jerry, with Marilyn Niles on one side of him – on her near-side shoulder her husband's wrist rested limply, in casual possession – was surprised to find on his other side, not Wanda, but a man in a fishnet vest, looking straight ahead, his hand around Jerry's neck. He leaned back and saw his wife beyond Fishnet, with another man on the other side of her; and for a brief moment he tried to catch her gaze and reassure himself that she was OK. But Wanda, looking down at her feet – she was dully trying to match her chip-step to those of the experienced feet on either side of her – did not see him.

Jerry looked straight ahead. Beneath his hand was the damp khaki of Marilyn Niles's blouse, and beneath that the thickness of her waist, and her own hand was light on his flank. In the dark he surged against her slightly, and felt her hand reflexively tightening on his waist, and the hand of Fishnet slipped from his neck; but it returned. He was about to shout something into Marilyn Niles's ear when the next thing happened. It happened quickly and all but invisibly, and it was over at once.

The line of six, with Jerry near the centre of it, began once more to sway to the left. Then it began to sway back to the right – except that Jerry, from a sudden lack of resistance on his left, discovered that Fishnet and by extension Wanda and her other companion were no longer there. Instinctively he lunged leftward in search of them – and in the same moment Marilyn Niles tightened her hand on his waist, spreading her fingers so that the tips slipped into the waistband of his trousers. Jerry surged back against her, so hard that she tumbled against Charlie and grabbed him for support – and it was over. In her ear, Jerry bawled, 'Wanda's gone,' and Marilyn Niles, ascertaining with a quick glance across his chest that this was so, yet postponed her reaction to this news to deal first with Charlie, whom she felt glancing at her on her other side. 'I stumbled!' she cried to her husband in explanation, but making it sound like a child's complaint. 'I nearly fell!'

Hardly were the words out than she believed them utterly herself. That was what had happened. She had stumbled and grabbed both men for support; that was all. Charlie mussed her hair, and she squeezed his waist. To Jerry she shouted, 'Not to worry, we'll catch up with her later!'

She knew this to be untrue as she said it, and the thought occurred to her that what was going to happen to Mrs Schulman before the night was over would indubitably get her, Marilyn Niles, in some serious trouble with her employers at the Tourist Board. And it was her lack of concern over this prospect that made her realize that her days as a Carnival escort were over. She was going, Marilyn Niles knew now, to start a baby with Charlie soon. Yes, definitely. Not later than Easter.

And so they surged on in the bellowing dark towards the neon lights of the road, lurching, and stopping, and pulling from side to side as before, only they were three now where they had been six. Over their heads, intermittently silhouetted against the nightsky, the gesticulating, hoarse figure of David Rudder shifted from foot to foot. 'We are children of Africa!' bellowed the truck into the surging dark. 'Children of Africa! Yay-hay! Yay-hay!'

OLIVE SENIOR

Country of the One Eye God

She heard the news on the little transistor radio her granddaughter had
sent her from the States. She who had lived so long she felt drained of
all emotion, now experienced nothing but a confirmation of the news
which had come floating down in scraps and whispers last year: her
grandson was a thief, a murderer, a hired gunman, a rapist, a jailbird, a
jail breaker, and now, at nineteen, a man with a price on his head.

From the time the first scraps of news had made their way from town,
even as she expressed disbelief to keep up appearances, she knew that
everything they said about him was the truth. She firmly believed that
every evil deed, evil thought, of all the generations had finally been
distilled into this one boy. Ever since the beginning when he had left
home, she had coldly cast her mind back to every thing she knew about
every single member of the family to discern if there was something
hidden in her tribe that betokened this ending, and she could find nothing
that warranted such a hard and final cruelty. They had faced deaths
starvation hurricane earthquake cholera typhoid malaria tuberculosis fire
diphtheria and travel to dangerous and distant places in search of work.
But beyond everything that they did, Ma Bell saw them as nothing more
than victims struggling against the forces of a God who was sometimes
deaf and blind.

Still, Ma Bell found the Lord a comforting presence. Since the last
grandchild had left – the rapist, the thief, the hired gun, the murderer
– Ma Bell had got into the habit of talking directly to the Lord. He was
everywhere. She spent so much of her life in the consolation of his
company that she could easily conduct dialogue with him for she knew
his answers so well. And without having to let him know her whereabouts, she could continue her conversation with him anywhere in the

house, in the yard, walking slowly and painfully down the lane to the Pentecostal Church of Christ the Redeemer. All her life, since she had first given birth at sixteen, sixty years ago, Ma Bell had spent her time addressing children and she saw nothing incongruous about addressing the Lord in the same manner for he failed her and tested her as surely as they did. Now she addressed him on the subject uppermost in her mind:

'Is wanting to better yuself a sin? Then if is sin, we have sinned. But nothing more than that. I know yu going pick on me first. But dont bother. If I did give short in my higglering days it was because I needed it, Lord. Pickney a yard needing shoes and books and clothes so they could learn to hold their head up high. And dont you see that it was right after all? Look how they turn out. Dont you please? Granted them forget me. You even. They dont write. Sometime I would starve if it was for them. Once in a blue moon a get a letter with a two, three dollar. But Lord, I ever get news yet that any of them in prison? That any of them thief? That any of them is murderer? Eh? You answer me that for you know even more than I hear. Never mind that I take their children and raise them till their mumma and puppa get establish in foreign and sometime when they done get establish they forget all we poor one still a scuffle down here. But dont you think a little cutting corner here and there is worth it? Talk truth now.'

'Ma B, Ma B,' a hurried and anxious voice called from the doorway. 'You hear the news?'

'Come in, Jacob. Dont excite up yuself so. Yu know is not good for the pressure.'

'Ma B you did have yu radio on? Yu hear the news bout Jacko? Ma B, two thousand dollar reward.'

Jacob was Ma Bell's seventy-year-old nephew but since he had never acquired her calm, she treated him just like a boy.

She now said patiently, 'Yes Jacob. Jacko is now big wanted man. So what yu expect me to do?'

'But Ma B yu dont see what going to happen?'

'What, Jacob Sawyers?'

'If him on the run where the first place yu think him come?'

'Well if you think is here yu is a bigger fool than I think.'

'How yu mean, dont is you grow him?'

'Jacob Sawyers, yu know that I never hear one living word from Jacko from December eighteen gone two year now him tief mi little coffee money and tek off. That is how him treat him gran that raise him from him born. But that blood in him was bad from the start. A beat and a beat and it never come out. A never see a child come tough so. Yu could beat Jacko from morning till night and not a drop of eye water ever come. Is the times breeding them tough pickney. But he dont get no bad blood from my family I dont have to tell you. And he would have nerves coming here. Nobody in this family was ever a criminal. Nobody ever a thief. And I can go back five generation to my mother Iris Jestina Howell born in 1884 the same year as Bustamante and to her mother Myrtelle Dawkin Nathan born in 1863 and fe her mother Lucilda who was born a slave and get her emancipate from Queen Victoria with the rest of the slave them 1838. And on your side of the family my lawful husband Nathaniel Jacob Sawyers and his father Isiah Sawyers and his father father Lemonius Sawyers that go to Colón in 1849. All their generation. Not one is robber. Not one is thief. Not one raise gun or other implement against other human being to earn money. No. Mark you I never encourage my son when he start courting that Carter gal for everybody round here know that them not a family that can hold up their head for reason I dont have to go into. But it not nice. But Jacob, never on this earth there is a generation like thisa one. They is truly a generation of vipers. But God see and know everything and one day one day, Jacob. But how they come so eh? How we that dont do nobody nothing bring children into world and before them old enough to spit, is animal them turn?'

'Oh Ma B evil evil evil in this land.'

'A-men.'

'But it predick you know Ma B. As the Good Book say Job Thirtieth Verse Twelve upon my right hand rise the youth they push away my feet and raise up against me the ways of their destruction.'

'Ah Jacob, true word.'

'But Ma B, if him come here. What yu going to do?'

'Jacob Sawyers, dont vex mi spirit ya. The boy have him combolo all over the place. No dem he did run way with. Mek him go to them.'

But even as Ma Bell spoke she could feel the thread that bound her grandson to her rewinding, tightening around her heart. With every tremor of a sunset cloud which came together, melted and dissolved, with the chirping of a tree frog, the flicker of a pennie-wallie, she felt her heart leap, had a premonition of the world all cata-corner and moving off course.

The boy came near dawn when she had almost given up expecting him. She knew that now with a price on his head if he did not come tonight he probably would never come again. When she heard the scratching at her door, Ma Bell was pleased that after all the call of blood remained so strong, even as she feared to open her door to this stranger. For stranger he was. In the pale moon glow, for she was afraid to bring the lamp to the door lest it attract her neighbours, she saw a bearded and hairy stranger with a countenance that would frighten children. She could discern nothing of family in this person and for a moment feared that it was in fact a stranger come to do her harm. But from the familiar way he came into the house she knew that it was he.

'So yu came?'

'What yu expect?'

'Dont yu have friend?'

'Fren a dawg.'

'Is friend yu run away with from here.'

'Ol lady, that time so long ago it long like from here to moon.'

Even his voice had changed and it was not only that it had deepened with age but it held an edge of bitterness even as it suggested the weariness of an old man.

She didn't know what to expect and wasn't sure about why she wanted the boy here. But she thought that even though he was now a man with a price on his head beyond any sum she had ever conceived of owning in her life, she was still his gran and had a right to expect a show of respect, even warmth, from him. But not this cold detachment.

He followed her into the kitchen attached to the house at the back and carefully put the latch on the door. From beneath the ashes of the fireplace she unearthed the roast yam and from a pan on the fireside took a piece of fried saltfish which she put on top of the yam as the 'rider'. Ma Bell had known that at whatever hour he came he would be hungry. He wolfed down the food like a starving man while from the battered Thermos she poured him a mug of sweetened bissy.

'Nuh have no rum?'

'Rum? Listen no bwoy. Just because yu is bull buck and duppy conqueror everywhere else yu is still bwoy in this yard. So just know yu place. Rum in this house is big man sinting.'

Without answering or looking at her he coolly stretched across to the tiny kitchen cupboard and took out a flask of white rum which he knew she always kept there as a medicine against cold, fevers and a wetting in the rain. He put the flask to his head and drank, then set it down on the table in front of him while he finished eating.

Ma Bell shrank away. Never before in her house had anyone shown such a lack of manners, for if the children she raised acquired nothing else, it was manners that she hammered into their heads from birth.

'A need some money.'

O God O God she asked herself. Is family this? This is what it come to Lord? O rid me and deliver me from the hands of strange children whose mouth speaketh vanity and their right hand is the right hand of falsehood.

'What yu want money for? Nobody can help you now. Only Jesus can help you.'

He sucked his teeth.

'A haffe leave.'

'Leave? Go where?'

'Where yu think? Yu think is holiday I come spend?'

'How far yu think yu can get?'

'You dont worry. I have mi passport.'

'What? Yu plan to go to foreign?'

'What else? Dont I have mother, dont I have father in foreign?'

'Jesus no. You wouldnt go over there and bring no shame on them Jacko. No. They been fighting all their life over there to lift their head up. Even if I had it I would never give you money to see yu shame them and them family.'

'Oh. So me not family? Them never shame me? Them never shame me when they walk way leave me? Look how long I wait for them to send for me and all I ever hear is next year next year. Next year never did come for me for every year them breed up a new pickney. They could never afford to send me. Well, long time now I decide to start take my next year this year. I couldnt wait no more.'

'Jacko. No. How yu so bold. Keep yu badness to yuself. Turn yourself in and take your punishment. Dont inflict it on anybody else.'

'Is bury you want bury me alive. Me hear enough talk and get enough battering from you when I small. Me no need no more talk any more. Just give me the money – thats all I come for.'

'Where yu expect an old woman like me to get money?'

'A who yu a talk to? Dont your whole generation dem in foreign. Yu was always proud of that. Not like we poor one that turn down back here.'

She was suddenly afraid, hardly listening to what he was saying, wondering if Jacko when he lived with her had somehow discovered the secret that nobody knew – where she kept her money. For Ma Bell did have a cache of money which she hoarded for a purpose. Every extra cent she could squeeze from her frugal living she kept in this special fund. She kept this money for one reason only. When Ma Bell died, she wanted the most beautiful coffin that the undertaker could provide – the real undertaker from town and not Brother Bertie who sent off everyone around in plain cedar coffins. The coffin was something that Ma Bell had to provide for herself; she did not believe that anyone in her family would go to that sort of expense when she was not around to see. Ma Bell had arrived at the decision about the coffin late in life when she saw that none of her other secret longings would ever be fulfilled. Ma Bell used to say to the Lord:

'Poor people just come into world so and is just so they must leave? Well I ent leaving that way and I dont care if you dont like it.'

She wanted to leave this world and enter the next cocooned in the luxury she never had in life and she sometimes grew impatient at the slowness with which the fund had accumulated for she was anxious to lie in the splendour of white satin surrounded by polished wood and silver fittings, in a coffin so heavy it would take twelve men to lift it. Ma B hoped that the undertaker would make her face beautiful at last so that everyone for miles around would come to ooh and aah as they

walked past the open coffin where she lay in state. That is why she
became fearful at the boy's mention of money for she would rather die
than part with it.

Ma Bell kept this money in a long piece of cloth which she rolled
and tied round her waist. Also in the cloth in her spidery handwriting
on thin paper were her most careful instructions for her burial. Like all
old women, Ma Bell had such a collection of baggy old clothes and bits
of string and cloth tied around her that no one ever suspected that her
garments held a secret.

The boy had finished the food and was leaning back in her one good
chair. Ma Bell searched his face to see in it the signs that would tell her
that this was one of the most wanted criminals in the country but could
discern nothing that set him apart from the boys his age around except
for an assurance of manner and a hardness in his eyes. He had a presence
that forced even his grandmother to look away. She shivered, and knew
that someone had walked over her grave. In the pale light, Ma Bell
suddenly wondered how such a little boy could suddenly grow so huge
as to fill all the spaces in the room. She felt shrivelled and light, com-
pressed into the interstices of space by his nearness.

'Money,' he said again.

Ma Bell said nothing but abruptly rose and squeezed past him into
the room where she slept and came back with a cocoa tin stuffed full
of papers which she emptied on the table. Coins rolled on to the floor
and the papers turned out to be old envelopes and scraps wrapped
around the small sums she apportioned for her various needs.

'Seetya, you can have all of it. Three dollar that I was saving to pay
doctor on the bill I owe him. Two dollar buy a little soup bone from
Ba Daniel Saturday. One dollar eighteen cent for my tithe O God you
wouldnt take this is the Lord's money. This is five dollar I just get from
the fowl I sell Jestina Dawson.'

She was muttering to herself as she slowly unrolled each bit of money
but the boy said nothing, looking only with anxious eyes to see if there
was more. His grandmother, sensing this anxiety for a moment felt a
surge of power over him. He searched beneath the table for the coins
which had fallen and including the tithe money over her protests, counted
all there was.

'Twenty-eight dollar two cents. Cho. How far yu expect me to get with that? I cant reach anybody else with money now Babylon a watch them. Just bring out the real dunza ya.'

'Jacko. Dont try mi patience. Blood or no blood bother me long enough and a bawl out fe murder so loud that every single soul for ten mile bout hear me.'

'Yeah. A would like to see you bawl for once for all the bawling you mek me do in my life. That is all your generation ever know to do. How to drop lick and chastisement.'

'Jacko, you have walked far from the ways of the Lord. My heart bleed to see what you turn into. But it is not too late to repent and give yourself up. Judgement Day must begin at the house of the Lord.'

The boy laughed a sneering laugh.

'Nutten change, eh? Same ol foolishness bout God and judgement. That is the trouble with the whole lot a unno. All unno think bout is judgement and future life. But from morning me study seh in this country fe yu God is a one eye God. Him only open him good eye to people who have everything already so him can pile up more thing on top of that. Him no business with rag tag and bobtail like unno. God up a top a laugh keh keh keh at the likes of you. Fe see you, so poor and turn down think you can talk to the likes of him so high and mighty. Keh keh keh.'

'Jacko!'

'Fe yu God ever help anybody yu know?'

'Plenty time.'

'Yes? Well yu better start pray to him from now that yu remember where yu put the money. Or yu want me to search for it?'

'Jacko. No. Dont do this to your old gran.'

Ignoring her, he started slowly, methodically, to search the house. There was not much to search, for apart from the kitchen Ma Bell had only two rooms. The boy searched every pot, every vase, every shelf, turned out drawers, battered trunks, cardboard boxes and pressed-paper suitcases sitting in the rafters. He pulled the bed and the mattress apart, lifted all the loose floorboards that he remembered as a child, and turned out the cheese tins in which were growing on the little veranda a few half-dead plants. He took the photographs out of their frames, held Ma

Bell's Bible and shook it, and to her everlasting shame, rummaged among her stiffly starched and pressed undergarments. He conducted the search swiftly and silently, carrying the small kerosene lamp from room to room. Ma Bell followed like a sleepwalker. It never occurred to her to run, to cry out to her neighbours, or to plead with the boy. She suddenly felt very old and with the pounding which had started up in her ears, began to see and hear things as from a great distance. She felt the thread around her heart tightening and tightening so she could hardly breathe. Ma Bell followed her grandson through his path of destruction as if he had already robbed her of her speech, her mind, her bodily strength, her will.

When the boy had finished his search they found themselves back in the kitchen where they started as if there was a certain logic in this night that drew them tightly in this circle.

'OK Ma B. A giving you one more chance. I aint quick to fire blow like yu. A dont even want to hurt yu. But is hard time we living in now and if yu wont give the money to me, a dont care no more. A will find it and take it.'

'I have no money my son,' Ma Bell said in a weak voice.

'Rass. Dont give me that. Me know unno old woman. Yu have the money hide on yu.'

'I have no money, Jacko. Dont shame me so.'

'Ma B, for the last time, give me the money. Yu soon dead and lef it yu know. What you want money for? Let it go nuh. I have the whole of my life still in front of me. Nah give up so.'

Ma B said nothing but closed her eyes.

'Please God O please God dont let what him saying about you be true. That you is a one eye God. I know better than that. Show him what you can do. No matter what he say, dont let him get my burial money. That is my future. O God deliver me from this snare that bind me.'

When she opened her eyes she saw without astonishment that the boy was pointing a gun at her.

'No. If you shoot me Jacko, yu will never leave this place alive. Everybody will hear that gun.'

'Let me worry about that. Me sure no God going to hear yu. This is the country of the one eye God. And he a-see neither you nor me. Ma B, a giving you one more chance. Give me the money. For a not fighting with you. A know you have it, and if a dont get it from you live a wi tek it from you dead.'

'Please God, a know you think is vanity. But I truly dont want to go into the next world as poor and naked as I come into this one. Please God, no matter what happen, dont let him find my burial money. God, he is my very blood. He wouldnt really kill me? Eh God?'

Ma Bell prayed and prayed as the boy carefully lifted the gun.

You Think I Mad, Miss?

1

You think I mad, miss? You see me here with my full head of hair and my notebook and pencil, never go out a street without my stockings straight and shoes shine good for is so my mother did grow me. Beg yu a smalls nuh? Then why your face mek up so? Don't I look like somebody pickney? Don't I look like teacher? Say what? Say why I living on street then? Then is who tell you I living on street? See here, is Sheraton I live. All them box and carochies there on the roadside? Well, I have to whisper and tell you this for I don't want the breeze to catch it. You see the wappen-bappen on the streetside there? Is one old lady ask me to watch it for her till she come back. And cause me heart so good, me say yes. I watching it day and night though is Sheraton I live. For the old lady don't come back yet. Quick before the light change for I don't eat nutten from morning. I don't know is what sweet you so. But thank you all the same. Drive good, yu hear.

2

I hope you don't hear already, sar, what that foolish Doctor Bartholomew saying about me all over town? Is him should lock up in Bellevue and all the people inside there set free, you know. But he couldn't keep me lock up for I smarter than all of them. That's what Teacher used to tell me. I come brighter than all the other pickney around. And tree never grow in my face neither. Beg you a little food money there nuh before the light turn green. A who you calling dutty? A why yu a wind up yu window and mek up yu face? You know say is Isabella Francina Myrtella Jones this yu a talk to? And since when dutty bwoy like you think you can eggs-up so talk to Miss Catherine daughter that studying to turn teacher? Why yu a turn yu head a gwan seh you no see me? I know you see me alright for though I don't behave as if I notice, I know all you young men sitting on the bridge every day there eyeing me as I pass. Would like to drag me down, drag me right down to your level. Have my name outa road like how you all have Canepiece Icilda. And that is why I hold up my head and wear two slip under my skirt. And I don't pay you all no mind. For what I would want with any of you? Then wait, you not even giving me a two cents there and I don't eat from morning? Gwan, you ol red nayga yu. From I see you drive up I shoulda know say is that Bartholomew send you. Send you to torment me. You ugly just like him, to rah. Go weh!

3

Hello my sweet little darling. What you have to give me today? I don't eat a thing from morning, mother. I wouldn't tell you lie in front of your little girl. Is same so my little one did look you know? Seven pound six and a half ounce she did weigh and pretty like a picture. Is bad-minded people make them take her away. Thank you, mother. God bless you and the little darling. Say who take her? Well me have to whisper it for me don't want the breeze to catch it. But is that Elfraida Campbell that's who. The one that did say me did grudge her Jimmy Watson. Then you nuh remember her? Is she and her mother burn bad candle for me mek me buck mi foot and fall. For I never had those intentions. No such intentions. Is two slip I wear under my skirt for I was studying to be teacher. Is Miss Catherine my mother you know. Say the light changing? You gone? God bless you my precious daughter.

4

Young girl, I see you courting. But don't mek that young man behind steering-wheel have business with you before you married, you hear? For once he know you he drag you down, drag you down to nutten. Then is pure ashes you eat. Pure dutty fe yu bed. The two of you a laugh! You better mind is nuh laugh today: cry tomorrow. But what a way you resemble Jimmy Watson, ee. Him was handsome just like you. Thank you mi darling, the two of you drive good, you hear. Say who is Jimmy Watson? Then you never know him? The same Jimmy Watson that did come as the assistant teacher and all the girls did love him off. Well not me. For I didn't have no intention to take on young man before I get certification. Is Shortwood I was going to, you know. Eh-eh, then you just wind up yu window and drive off so? What a bad-mannered set of children, ee.

5

Like I was saying, sar, I was busy with my studying and that is why that Elfraida Campbell did get her hooks into Jimmy Watson. For what Jimmy would really want with girl that can barely sign her name, nuh matter she walk and fling her hips about. So I just study and bide my time. Oh, God bless you sar, I could kiss your hand. Is from morning I don't eat you know. But that Elfraida is such a wicked girl sir, she and her mammy. If you ever see her, please call the constable for me, for is plenty things she have to answer for. Courthouse business sar. If she and her mammy didn't work negromancy on me, Doctor Bartholomew wouldn't be looking for me all now. But he will never never find me. You want to know why? You see that big box there a road side? Is there I hide you know. Once I get inside my box, not a living soul can find me. They could send out one million policeman to search for me. Two million soldier. The whole of Salvation Army. They could look into the box till they turn fool. They could shine they torch, bring searchlight and X-ray and TV and atomic bomb. Not one of them could ever find me. Aright sar. You gone? God bless you.

6

Look at my darling lady in the white car who always give me something. God bless you and keep you my dear. Mine how you travel, you hear. Satan set plenty snares in the world for the innocent. Take me now. Is not me did go after Jimmy Watson. As God is me judge. Him and Elfraida Campbell was getting on good-good there. It was a disgrace that a girl should act so common and make people carry her name all over the district like that. Even the breeze did tek it. And he was man of education too. What about his reputation? So when he first put question to me I didn't business, for I never want people have anything to say about me and I don't get my certificate yet. But it was just as I thought. Jimmy Watson wanted a woman that wouldn't shame him, a decent woman with broughtupcy and plenty book learning. That is how he put it to me. And I resist and I resist but after a while, that Jimmy Watson so handsome and have sweet-mout so, him confabulation just wear down mi resistance. Never mind bout certification and teacher college – Eh-eh, you gone already. God bless you, sweetheart.

7

Sir, you see that police fellow there from morning? The constable that is like a thorn in my side? Can't get a good night rest from him beating on my bedroom with him stick. Is what do him ee? Is Satan send him to torment me you know. You know who Satan is? Beg you a dollar nuh? A hungry, yu see. A don't eat a thing from morning. Satan and Bartholomew is one and the same. Then you never know? And you look so bright? Look as if is university you come from. Don't is so? Well thank you sar. The good Lord will bless you. And if you see Bartholomew there up at U C, tell him is lie. Is lie he telling about the baby. Say it was all in my mind. You ever hear a piece of madness like that? Is Bartholomew they suppose to lock up and the child weight eight and three-quarter pound? A spaking baby boy. Is that cause Elfraida Campbell to burn bad candle for me. Jealousy just drive her crazy. Eh-he. Drive good ya. And beg you tell government what Bartholomew going on with, you hear?

8

From I born and grow I never know man could be like that Jimmy Thomas. Is only Bartholomew like good like him, you know, my lady and gentleman. Thank you for a smalls, sir, for a cup of tea. Nothing pass my lips from morning. Thank you sar. God bless, you did know Jimmy Thomas swear to my mother he never touch me? Never have a thing to do with me? Fancy that! So is who was lying with me every night there? Who was plunging into me like St George with his sword? He cry the living eye water the day my mother ask if he business with me for that time the baby already on the way. I could feel it kicking inside me. And that lying Jimmy Thomas say he never lay hands on me. Same thing the lying Bartholomew did tell my mother. That no man ever touch me. How man can lie so, ee? So is how the baby did come then, answer me that? How baby can born so, without father? Ten and a half pound it weigh. Say what, sar? Say why if I have children I living on street? Then is why unno red nayga so fas' and facety ee? Answer me that? You see me asking you question bout fe you pickney? Unno gwan! Think because you see me look so I don't come from nowhere? Ever see me without my paper and pencil yet? Ever see me without my shoes and stocking and two slip under my dress? Think I wear them little clingy-clingy frock without slip like that Elfraida Campbell so every man could see my backside swing when I walk? Unno gwan!

9

So is what sweet yu so, yu little facety bwoy? Yu never see stone fling after car yet? Yu want me bus' one in yu head? Say somebody shoulda call police? So why you don't do it, since yu so shurance and force-ripe. Mek that constable bwoy come near me today. Mek them send that Bartholomew. Send for them. Do. I want them to arrest me at Lady

Musgrave Road traffic-light here today. I want them to take me down to courthouse. I want to have my day in court. I want to stand up in front of judge and jury. I want to say 'Justice' and beg him to ask them certain question. He-hey. Don't mek I laugh here today. You want to know something, sweet boy. Them not going to do a thing about me, you know. Say wha mek? Well, me have to whisper it, for me nuh want no breeze catch hold of it. But the reason is because they fraid. Fraid to give me my day in court. Fraid to have me ask my question there. All of them fraid. Even the judge. Even Massa God himself. For nobody want to take responsibility to answer me. Gwan, yu little dutty bwoy. Yu face favour!

10

Good day, missis. You say you want to hear my question? Well, beg you a money there nuh please. I don't get a thing to eat from morning. Thank you, miss. You want to hear my question please? So why yu winding up yu glass? Why yu unmannersable so? Well, whether you want to hear or not you stupid bitch, I Isabella Francine Myrtella Jones am going to tell you. So you can ease down all you want. I going to shout it from Lady Musgrave Road traffic-light. I going to make the breeze take it to the four corners of everywhere. First: Is who take away my child? Second: Why Jimmy Thomas lie so and say he never lie with me? Third: Why they let that Elfraida Campbell and her mother tie Jimmy Thomas so I never even have a chance with him? Fourth: Why my mother Miss Catherine never believe anything I say again. Why she let me down so? Is obeah them obeah her too why she hand me over to that Bartholomew? Fifth: Why that Bartholomew madder than mad and he walking about free as a bird? Who give him the right to lock up people in Bellevue and burn bright light all night and ask them all sort of foolish question? Sixth: What is the government going to do about these things? Seventh: If there is still Massa God up above, is what I do why him have to tek everybody side against me?

WILLI CHEN

Moro

Moro arrived in Esperanza late one afternoon in an antiquated Chevrolet loaded with bamboo cages filled with game cocks. Like other cock breeders who moved from district to district in Trinidad, he was carefree and enjoyed a cavalier bachelorhood. Moro's leatherlike, spice-coloured cheeks jutted beneath eyes that shone with the mirth of songs. A single plait of rich, dark hair was held at the back of his head by a twist of crimson ribbon.

Moro sat as if welded to the seat, his short frame in stark contrast to the long arms that gripped the wheel.

'Hi-yahh!' he called pleasantly as the clanking car rolled to a halt.

Moro's Doms and Clarets had conquered the fiercest Reds and Greys from St Raphael, Valencia and Malgrétoute. His birds were victorious in Rancho Quemado and even in La Brea, where the cocks were almost night-black, like the pitch that oozed from the great lake around them.

Moro was serious in his training. He would stoop for hours with his legs parted, keeping his forearms laced up, protected from the spurs. He pushed the game cocks between and around his legs in a figure eight, taunting them until their heads reddened with rage and their beaks snapped open for battle. Again and again he tossed their lithe bodies aloft, their long clean necks toughened by continuous massage with bay rum and clove. With his hands beneath the long tails, he pushed them up and away, their wings flapping in the air, their beaks and spurs arched forward and moving at a devastating speed. Then he would put them on a rope stretched tautly between the paling and a tree in the yard. There they would rock back and forth until their leg muscles finally hardened under the strain and their talons tightened.

Moro followed the same routine each day, beginning before dawn with a quick shower and black coffee, his life as disciplined as that of the birds. Then he would gently bring out the game cocks, speaking quietly to them, blowing his warm breath on their heads, caressing the combs so their backs arched in response. They tipped their heads to listen to his whispers and the mellow monotone of his deep, soothing voice. Then, suddenly, the peaceful scene would be changed by the early morning breeze which scattered the dead leaves in the yard and ruffled the down on the birds. As their feathers lifted, the thick muscular thighs would be exposed and a fierceness would come into their eyes. It was the same sharp ferocity that appeared in the gayelle at the moment of battle.

Moro was working with his birds one morning when a long, blue Buick pulled into the yard. Through the bougainvillea Moro was able to see the white sidewall tyres and a glint of chrome, but he did not recognize the man who stepped from behind the wheel. He was black, middle-aged, and his face was crumpled and tired-looking. He wore a faded khaki shirt which was wet at the armpits.

'Morning.'

Moro nodded, but did not move. The man moved towards him, with a limp in his heavy stride.

'You is Moro, the cockfighter?'

Moro turned towards the visitor, putting down a cock on a bamboo pole.

'What is it?'

'Boss send me. Want to see you . . . is about game cocks. What to tell him? He say you must come up.'

Moro frowned. 'Wey he living?'

'Never hear about Mr Holman? He is the overseer in Caroni. House by de side road after Milton Number Two. One ah dem backra quarters, white and green windows. Big yard.'

'You mean the boss in the game? How much cocks he have?' Moro asked.

The black man shrugged. 'Is plenty and all kind. You coming?'

Moro nodded.

The next day he stood before the white mansion, enthralled by its green tarpaulin awnings and fine mosquito netting in a paler shade. The estate was magnificent, the house stood on whitewashed concrete pillars surrounded by potted palms.

Moro heard the sudden crow of a cock. Then the chicken run came into view, running through the pillars at the back of the building.

'Mr Holman!' he called, trying to make himself heard over the crowing cocks penned in the coops. 'Mr Holman! Mr Holman!' he yelled louder, his growing anxiety obvious in his voice.

A tall man, clad all in white, came down the back steps. He shook hands with Moro.

Moro felt the power of the big man.

'Hear about you, man,' Mr Holman spoke in a surprisingly soft voice. 'Think you could fly my birds for me? Look after them? Will pay you well, man.'

Holman did not wait for a reply, but turned to lead the way into the great house, passing the Buick with its cloth hood down, its fancy metallic buttons on the dashboard standing out in contrast to the soft leather upholstery. There were clothes hanging on a line strung between the huge pillars at the back of the house.

They descended the concrete aisle, the coops arranged wall to wall high off the ground so that the droppings would fall and be washed away by the continuous rush of water below. The cells were constructed of expanded wire mesh, each separated by solid polished pitch-pine walls to prevent the birds from seeing one another. Inside, the cocks stood on two-inch diameter perches, swaying and crowing in a continuous staccato of piercing cries.

'That is Satan,' Holman pointed. 'Black Devil never lost a battle yet. Watch that beak and how he shakes his head from the right to the left . . . so fast. That is the sign of a good fighter. This one is Banana Bottom, champion of champions, a legend for destroying over twenty-five cocks and,' Holman smiled, 'bringing in $22,000 for me.'

'Nice cocks, Mr Holman,' Moro complimented. 'They looking good, man.'

'Not good enough, Moro.'

'What you mean?'

'Ever heard of De Pas and Vasquez?'

Moro nodded.

'The greatest cocks are from Cuba ... Vasquez. He is a fanatic,' Holman explained. 'You heard of him. Well, whenever there is a fight and he attends, the gayelle is closed until he is through.'

'Why is that?'

'Man, he is crazy about fighting cocks. Have you heard of St Eves and Guichard from Martinique, Malaban from Guadeloupe? Well, Little Guadeloupe is getting strong breeds from France and Puerto Rico, Hernandez and dos Pasos from Santo Domingo and de Jesus from Haiti. They are the giants in cock fighting ... they are the giants from Guadeloupe and Martinique. These are crazy men, wild about cocks. They would leave their wives for their battlers, starve for them. They give them only the very best. Their coops are under mosquito netting to avoid sandflies. It is honey in the morning and boiled eggs and greens in the evening,' Holman shook his head. 'I tell you, Moro, they count every grain of cracked corn, every capsule of vitamins. They record their rest periods, hours of sleep ... they even count the drops of water the birds drink. They know when their birds will sneeze, when they will cough, and in the ring they know exactly at what time the opponent's cock will strangle on its own blood and when it will be torn to shreds. They never lose, Moro. Never. They live cocks. They breed and breathe cocks. They are the champions, Moro ... for now they are the champions. But you know something?'

Moro nodded. He did know.

'I have to beat them,' Holman said, his eyes piercing Moro's with an intense stare. 'I must win. Otherwise all my efforts will have been in vain. I have everything, Moro ... feed, medicines, nice pens, the best birds. Five of the cocks are from Cuba out of Vasquez's own broods. Only the trainer is missing, and I think that is you.'

'Why me?'

'Because I have a challenge. Ever heard of El Diablo?'

Moro turned excitedly. 'Yes, dat's the greatest cock in the Caribbean, man. Dat from Santo Domingo.'

Holman rubbed his hands together anxiously. 'Well, they have challenged us, but Motilal and Rienzi ... you know Rienzi, the big man from the north ... they both refused.'

'They have a right to refuse. Boss, everybody know about dat game cock. It is the baddest thing with spurs,' Moro said. 'It kill Corriea bird and Clarke, two champions, one after the other. Man cry too bad when dey see dat bird. Money lost, lots a money lost, and Corriea hold he head and bawl because his cock was the greatest thing to pass through Valencia . . . bad as Banana Boat, he was.'

The men stepped from the runs into the sunshine and walked to the low shed.

'So, what you think?' Holman asked.

'Don't know.'

'Pay will be good. You will have meals and Boyo will be your assistant. He is a good boy. You will be in charge of feeding, training and preparing them for fights. You will have freedom to do anything you want in handling the birds . . . you can organize a new schedule if you wish.'

They stood in the middle of the shed underneath a bank of fluorescent lights. Around them were sacks of corn, oats, bags of grits and specially mixed grain packed off the floor on ramps. In the open cupboards stood rows and rows of phials, large bottles, small demijohns, packages of tablets, boxes of disposable gloves and cartons of syringes, each item serving a special purpose in training and maintaining the health of Holman's fighting cocks. It was an impressive place.

'So, what you say?' Holman asked again.

'Deal,' Moro agreed.

The rigid programme of training began and continued over the next twelve months. Moro would arrive long before dawn, a new twist in the bundle of hair at the back of his head and the faint smile of a man never in a hurry turning up the corners of his mouth. One after the other, the twelve cocks took turns alighting on to his leather-wrapped forearm to take their dose of medicine before beginning the exercises. Each bird was allotted a specific amount of time for its feed and exercise on the pole, then Moro would hold each one on his lap to rub down its head and neck, massaging the strong thighs and chest with brandy and ginger. Gently, sweetly, he caressed them and spoke to them as they bent their necks to take the grains he offered in his palm.

Then, after months of training, it was time. Holman stepped into the yard and hollered, 'Moro, next Saturday, man. Hear them Cubans and Spaniards coming . . . and you can guess who . . .'

'El Diablo, boss?'

'Right. Think we have a chance, Moro? Think Trinidad might finally be in the picture?'

'Time'll tell, boss,' Moro answered.

'Well, you are the trainer. You should know.'

'Boss, dem oversea cocks is world-class, but dat doh mean a thing. A good fighter cock could come from de bush. Get what ah say?'

'Well, De Pas and Vasquez will be there.'

'Let them come, boss. We go be there too!'

Early the next Saturday, they followed the winding road that took them through overgrown weeds into a mushy path of ruts and hoofprints. The black sticky mud made the journey perilous for the station wagon filled with stacked cages of fighting cocks.

They arrived long before daybreak, but they were not the first. There were others, consumed by anxiety and overwhelmed by their passion for action, who had long been camped beneath the forest shade. Green tents were pegged to the ground scout-style, and their own cages of birds were under careful watch as they awaited the beginning of the first contest.

The gayelle shimmered in the slow-rising sun, its small enclosure of sand encircled by the seats made of rough-hewn planks. At the side was the cubicle for the trainers, who held their birds in small cages, the officials and the bettors. On the far side, the foreigners, mostly Spanish-speaking people, clenched foul-smelling cigars between chubby fingers ringed with gold.

Holman leaned close to Moro to whisper in his ear, 'That's Malaban over there in the panama hat. See his big moustache? More hair in it than feathers on the birds he breeds. That man has killers.'

'El Diablo is the one we have to watch, boss,' Moro said.

'Think Satan will make it?'

'He have a chance. He jumping good these days.'

In minutes the gayelle blossomed into a riotous blaze of hot-pink shirts, fancy hats and black spectacles worn on sweaty foreheads, as if to compete with the colourful plumage of the game cocks. The contest began quickly. The barricade bent forward under the strain of the pressing crowd which craned over in an effort to see the fighting cocks in action.

The first fight was brief. There was a flurry of feathers, sharp beaks and bloody spurs punctuated by the loud voices of those who bet and lost. Someone swore in Spanish, a bottle of mountain dew changed hands, and more notes were peeled off thick wads from waistcoat pockets. Five local birds, two of the best from Malgrétoute, succumbed to the spurs of the foreign champions and were soaked in their own blood. They were destroyed by sheer speed and power, the like of which had never been seen from the local fighters. Then, the long-awaited moment arrived. The battler with an unbeaten record, the king of cocks, the terrible killer came into the ring. El Diablo.

By this time the crowd had swelled and the trainers had taken their cocks into the gayelle. Moro stood with Satan, the bird black and gleaming in the sunlight, a wild look in its eyes as it scratched the sand with its feet. El Diablo stood its ground fearlessly, the long tail curving in an arch of brilliant red, touching the sand far behind. Its head was almost flat at the top; its strong, pointed beaks were nearly as sharp as its pair of deadly spurs which had been chiselled to a fine point.

The cocks flew and clawed at each other in the ring. As Satan jumped into the air, both feet pumped with mechanical efficiency. Landing on its feet, it soared again, driving its spurs ahead.

Ready for battle, the great Spanish bird retaliated. True to its name it recoiled instantly and dived under its opponent, keeping low to the ground as the clatter of spurs echoed overhead and the flapping of wings churned the sand around.

'Caramaba,' a Spaniard muttered as the others puffed on their cigars and laughed.

El Diablo rushed forward in a red rage, attacking in strong thrusts with its beak, but Satan had long moved its head in fast feinting movements until they flew up together in a clash of feathers. Again the pumping legs, the curved half-open deadly beaks – and this time blood spattered on the sand.

They rose and clashed again and again, beaks digging into reddened flesh, bloody spurs stabbing in a flurry of attack. Feathers were scattered over the ground and tossed about by the breeze. El Diablo wheeled around, its head so low it nearly touched the ground. Satan fired its spurs once, but the Spanish bird was too fast. It soared in the air in one jump as if prodded by some mysterious force, and its feet tore into the neck and head of the black opponent. Satan crumpled, drenched in blood, as the mutterings of the crowd rose. El Diablo rushed in for the kill, a twisted mass of beak and spurs, pouncing on to the writhing form of Satan stretched out in the dust.

Holman jumped into the arena to gather up his bird. A Spaniard leaned forward and caught El Diablo, to pat its head. He kissed El Diablo's red comb, smoothed its feathers and lifted the wings to examine the bird for wounds. The cries of the foreigners rose above the crowd.

With just three victories to the Trinidadians, they acknowledged defeat. There was an aggressiveness in the foreign birds which could never be found in their own cocks. Holman recognized the superiority and fighting instincts in the five cocks from Haiti and Martinique, and knew there was a strong need for more training and breeding to develop a better fighting strain.

He turned away from the gayelle, Satan in his arms. The bird was bloodied and dying from deep lacerations over its head, neck and breast. He jostled out of the trainers' cubicle, into the open, and looked about.

'Where is Moro?' he asked under his breath.

The deafening voices of the Cubans and Spaniards rose afresh as they began their celebration. It was then that Moro appeared, slowly walking into the arena, the plait of hair at the back of his neck and the slight smile on his spice-coloured cheeks. Perched on his forearm, its feet clasping on to leather, was a red and black Dom. It stood tall, its head almost round, but it had no tail.

'Thought you left us, Moro.'

'No, boss. I know that El Diablo was too good for us.'

'Where you got that bird?'

'This is one ah mine own. I bring two cocks just in case. This one good boss.'

'You entering that?'

'Yes, only way to know. Nothing to lose.'

Holman smiled as he scrutinized the cock on Moro's arm. It was odd-looking with its large, round head and the stump of short feathers behind. Once in the arena, the tailless bird evoked laughter from the crowd. It was weighed, and someone remarked about going back home for its clothes, but Moro stood his ground proudly. He patted the bird's back, speaking encouraging words as if the cock could understand what he was saying.

In the gayelle, El Diablo stood like a pillar of fire, red down to its toes. Groomed afresh, its eyes burned for more blood, the loud cackle from its throat rattling like a chac-chac shaken after a victory. The Spaniards threw their hats into the sand, and clouds of cigar smoke drifted across the gayelle.

Again there was laughter at the tailless Trinidad bird, though it stood taller than the red Spanish terror. It even drew a smile from the Trinidad crowd, though they had suffered their fifth straight defeat at the hands of the foreigners.

Sand and loose feathers torn from the underside of El Diablo flew when the fighting cocks began their battle. The betting resumed, though many were hesitant to place their money on the Trinidad fighter. El Diablo was the red menace, conqueror from overseas, the one always victorious.

In a flash, El Diablo whirled around thrusting its spurs with deadly accuracy, but Tailless counter-attacked, springing higher as they clashed in the air. When they landed, Tailless had already planted four strokes on El Diablo's head, and a hush fell over the Spaniards, who looked amazed. Again, the barricades bent forward under the pressing weight of the crowd. Holman edged closer to Moro. Moro remained cool, pensive, watchful.

Driven into a greater frenzy, El Diablo charged again. At first it kept its head very low, crawling along the ground like a snake, dodging from side to side, holding the crowd spellbound with its crafty wile. A murmur of surprise rose from the foreigners upon seeing the true mettle of their great fighter. They whispered to one another, as El Diablo renewed its terrifying assaults. Tailless retreated from the stabbing spurs that had already ripped across an unguarded chest, blood spewing off its flanks on to the sand.

El Diablo flapped its wings and bounded into the air. With a drop of its mighty head, its beak found the target in the underside of its adversary.

Then it happened. El Diablo retreated; low on the ground, thrusting its head forward, wings unfolded, as it prepared to leap again. Tailless waited, and when they rose, El Diablo had already torn into the exposed thighs of the Trinidad bird. Feathers blew across the arena, and the Spaniards chuckled around their fat cigars.

It was only when the flapping wings were folded and the cocks landed from their short flight that they saw the pointed spur sticking through the neck of El Diablo.

'Look!' someone shouted.

'*Mammá miá*,' a Spaniard gasped.

Holman looked closely, as the sand around the cocks reddened. El Diablo fluttered, then stretched out in the throes of defeat. It attempted to flap its once-proud plumage, tarnished by its own sticky gore. The crowd jumped to its feet, and someone rushed into the ring. Another dived in to pull Tailless away as it pounced on the fallen cock to pick at its victim's eyes.

Moro gently lifted Tailless into his arms, caressing his bird. As he lifted its wings, a gasp escaped his throat when he felt his hands moistened. Furtively, he turned away clutching his bird deep into his chest.

It was sudden pandemonium as everyone pushed into the arena. In the uproar, someone picked up El Diablo, its mouth wide open, the head and neck wet with blood that oozed from its wounds.

Holman smiled. His own people hugged him in congratulation. They jumped the barricades into the arena to slap him on the back for winning the most important fight of the season. At last they had produced a great champion, gaining the prestigious Caribbean title for the first time in the history of the games. To Holman and his fellow trainers, it meant that they had arrived at a milestone in the sport, and that with dedication and continuous training and breeding, they would be able to produce their own successful strain. Moro had proved that by entering his tailless battler, which he had raised in his own yard. With his expertise and Holman's excellent facilities, they knew they would make a great team.

'No more Venezuelan cocks,' Moro heard someone say. 'Just now we goh do we own exporting.'

'Never see a cock fight so yet,' another remarked. 'Imagine if he had a tail!'

Alcohol flowed in celebration. Then Holman moved out of the enclosure and turned toward the trainers. He looked over their heads, into the faces of the foreigners, once again searching for Moro. He had disappeared, as before, into the crowd.

Holman elbowed and pushed, trying to edge his way out of the crowd that held him back to shake his hand and congratulate him. He asked everyone he met on his way out if they had seen Moro. Finally, he shook the hand of a man who said he had seen someone leave the gayelle alone, his hair plaited at the back of his head, walking in a peculiar shuffle.

'He was walking straight ahead without looking back. About five minutes now. Look, he gone up de road,' the little man explained. 'He have a dead fowl cock in he hand that ent have no tail.'

PAULINE MELVILLE

You Left the Door Open

Some events defy scrutiny. Like electrons in a bubble-chamber, the act of looking at them disturbs them. All that can be seen are traces of recent passage, tracks left behind. The electron itself remains unseen, its form only to be guessed at, a ghost in the atom.

The attack – and it was a violent one, a murderous one, at night, as I lay sleeping – was just such an event. Under close examination, the meaning of it began to dance. There were traces, both before and after, that served as clues; synchronicities, unaccountable coincidences, signs even, as well as solid facts and evidence. But, at the heart of the matter lay impenetrable ambiguity, like the infuriating Necker cube – a cube drawn in such a way that one minute it appears solid and facing in one direction and then, through an involuntary shift in the mechanism of the eye, it appears to be hollow and facing the other way.

The paradigm, the lens through which something is viewed, determines what is seen. Psychologists, with their particular conceptual spectacles, saw the attack as the work of a paranoid schizophrenic. Sociologists would doubtless have some other explanation for the epidemic of stranglings and rapes that plagued London throughout the long, hot summer of that year. Theories that include the idea of a demon are, of course, out of the question in this day and age. Demons have lost their footing on the hierarchy of scientific disciplines. The police lay yet another template on events. Their gaze rests only on the physical, forensic evidence and facts.

'Did you notice anyone suspicious hanging around the area before you were attacked?' A buxom policewoman in a spotlessly white blouse and neat skirt was taking down my statement.

'Yes, I did. A few days earlier I saw a man sitting on the low wall outside one of the houses a few doors down the street.'

'What did this man look like?' she asked.

'He looked as though he had the soul of a wolf,' I replied.

The policewoman did not write this down. Her pen remained poised over the sheaf of statement papers. It was not the sort of fact the police wish to accumulate:

'Did you notice what he was wearing?' she asked.

I tried to remember the physical details. It had been a warm day, yet he had been wearing a jacket, blue or grey, I think. I passed him, sitting on the wall, as I returned home from the shops; a man in his late thirties, with a broad forehead and fairish hair receding at the temples, lean in build. As I approached him, the hairs on the back of my hands prickled and rose. There seemed to be some sort of aura around him like an electromagnetic force field. He stared at me and through me and past me. What struck me was that he looked more utterly alone than anyone I have ever seen. Schoolchildren were tumbling out of the gates of the school across the road. For a moment I felt a brief, inexplicable concern for their safety, but I gave him no more than a glance as I returned home. A couple of hours later, I went out again. The man was still sitting there.

I am a cabaret artist. I specialize in impersonations. Not for me the grand, plush venues of London, I work in the tiny clubs, the underground cellars hung with black drapes where the audiences are impecunious and raucous. On this circuit, there is usually one cramped room put aside as a dressing-room. Jugglers, comics, fire-eaters and musicians vie for space amid dirty tables, empty beer cans and plastic cups sprouting cigarette ends hastily doused as some performer hears his name being announced by the compère on stage. A few months before the main events of this story took place – the attack occurred in the summer and I suppose the idea first came to me in February – I was becoming bored with my act and I conceived the idea of doing some male impersonation. One night, alone at home, I found myself in the bathroom looking in the cabinet mirror. I took a black eyebrow pencil from my make-up bag and drew a moustache on my upper lip. It was too thick. I made it thinner. Then I took some hair gel from the shelf and smarmed my hair back off my face. I spent an inordinate amount of time combing my hair. I thickened my eyebrows and looked at the face in the mirror. It grinned. It was the face of a small-time crook, a petty thief. I settled on a name for him – Charlie. The next day, I went to the market to find Charlie some clothes. A cold drizzle fell on the stalls of second-hand clothes and cheap jewellery. I selected the following items for him:

> A black nylon roll-neck sweater, the type worn by spivs
> A calf-length camel-hair coat
> Some flashy, fake gold rings and a neck-chain
> A pork-pie hat, brown with a feather in it
> Hush Puppy shoes, soft and noiseless
> Second-hand grey trousers with a sharp crease.

That evening, Charlie regarded me confidently from the full-length mirror in my bedroom. I decided to take him out in the street. The night was damp and freezing cold. I hate the cold. Charlie seemed to love it. He had not spoken much but when he had it was with a northern accent. One odd thing I noticed. Normally, I am short-sighted, but that evening I could see far, way down the street. Outside, standing on the pavement, I knew immediately that Charlie was vicious and predatory. All he wanted to do was to wait in shop doorways and pounce on passers-by. I didn't let him, of course. But before I could stop him, he had taken my car keys and let himself into my car. He drove too fast, cursing and swearing at any delay, pushing the nose of the car right up against the bumpers of other, slower cars in front. He wanted to hurt people. There was a certain thrill to his viciousness. I took him home. I was exhausted. He wasn't. I undressed and went to bed.

A short while later, I took him on stage for the first time. It was a mistake. He had not the least intention of amusing the audience. He wanted to frighten them. He said horrible things. Quickly, I took Charlie home and put him away in the cupboard.

'What happened to that character you were creating?' a friend inquired of me, a week or so after his début.

'Oh, he was too violent and dangerous,' I giggled. 'He had to be locked up in a mental hospital.'

Around the time I discovered Charlie, a man was, in fact, released from one of the big hospitals for the criminally insane in the north of England. Later, he was to weep, his head on the table in the police interview room, saying that the hospital was the only place where he had ever been happy. Outside, apparently, a voice kept getting into his head telling him to do certain things. He consistently denied the attack. 'It wasn't me,' he repeated again and again. 'It wasn't me.' In some ways, he may have been right.

In May, I read in the local newspaper that a woman who lived near by had been savagely attacked and raped by a man who was skilful and cunning enough to leave not a fingerprint or trace of himself behind. I soon forgot about it.

A sizzling summer arrived. A Jamaican friend of mine came to stay while she finalized the last details of the publication of her book. On the day she was to leave, we were sitting with friends who had come to say goodbye. The flat was a welter of half-packed suitcases, pages of manuscript, scattered books and possible designs for her book cover.

'I don't like any of these designs for the book jacket,' she grumbled. 'I won't have them on the front of my book.' She shoved some clothes into a bag and turned to one of the other girls:

'Mary, your designs are better than these. Go and do some sketches for me, quick. Take them down to the publishers on Monday and send me copies to Jamaica. I must have something with more of a Caribbean feel to it.'

Mary was on her knees studying the front covers of several books laid out on the floor. She looked up at the bookshelf and saw, resting there, a painting I had brought back with me from Haiti. Still unframed, it leant against the wall. It is a smallish painting, executed in the most brilliant colours. A leopard, one of the sacred animals of Haiti, sits under a tree in the forest. From the branches of the tree hang large, round fruits, purple, brown and scarlet sliced with yellow. The great cat, black with no markings, gazes out from thick, green foliage. His eyes are bright, lucent and alert. They appear to follow you round the room as you move.

'Let me borrow that painting,' said Mary. 'The colours have the right feel.' I did not want her to borrow the painting. It is my favourite. She will spoil it, I thought, drop coffee on it, sit on it and tear the canvas. I tried to invent an excuse as to why she could not take it:

'Don't take that painting. It protects my house,' I mumbled, feebly. But she took it anyway, promising to bring it back the next day. And that night, without its protection, I was attacked.

In the afternoon, after I had driven my friend to the airport and tidied the flat a little, I sat at the table in the front room trying to complete some work. Once, I looked up and a figure darted behind some bushes that grow by the railings in the front garden. I did not see the face. I thought no more of it. That evening, I visited friends. It must have been about one o'clock in the morning when I returned home. I remember hearing the sound of my heels clicking in the empty street as I ran from my car to the flat. It is always a disturbing sound, running footsteps at night, even if they are your own. The sound of a victim. Inside the flat, I felt safe. It was peaceful and warm. I put my bag and keys on the trunk by the front door and wandered into the large back bedroom. There, I undressed and hung my clothes in the walk-in wardrobe. Naked, I strolled into the bathroom, washed and cleaned my teeth. For some reason, I decided to sleep in the small bedroom that night. It is a tiny room. In the corner opposite the door is a single divan bed. Next to the bed is a small cupboard with a portable television set on it and a radio clock. Apart from that, there is room only for an upright bamboo chair. Two uncurtained windows are set deep in the thick, outside walls of the house. I got into bed and switched on the television. For a while, I read by the light of the television. No other lights in the flat were on. After a bit, I reached over, switched off the television and went to sleep.

What woke me I do not know. I lifted my head from the pillow to see, dimly, a figure in the doorway about four feet away from me. The room was very dark. The figure recoiled for an instant. Then it attacked. I had the impression of something erupting violently from beneath the floorboards at the side of the bed. At the same time, a rough, gloved hand was pushing into and against my mouth, forcing my head down in the pillows. This is real, I thought, this is real. I struggled to breathe and I must have been trying to scream because the voice in my ear was saying:

'Shut up! Shut up! I've got a knife. I've got a knife.'

The voice was coarse and rough as goatskin. Scarcely able to breathe, I turned my head this way and that to get air. The whole weight of his body bore down on me. The rough, woollen-gloved hand clamped like a vice over my mouth was tearing the skin off my face as I twisted my head, trying to get away. I was suffocating. Sound that had its origin in my stomach was issuing out of my mouth, a roaring, black vomit of sound. He was still growling:

'Shut up! Shut up! Don't move! Don't move!'

The fight became a grim battle. Something was being pulled round my neck. Rope. As he tightened it, I put up my right hand and managed to insert my fingers under the rope and pull it away from my windpipe. I pulled and pulled. It came away in my hand and I held on to it tightly. Somehow, I contrived to swing my legs out of the bed. It was too dark to see anything clearly. He was standing over me. I lunged for his balls. We fought violently in the pitch-dark room. The television set crashed to the floor and then the radio clock went as well. The bamboo chair was smashed. I was pinioned back down on the bed, still struggling:

'I want to put a pillowcase over your head,' he grunted.

I bellowed: 'NOOOOOOOOOOOOO!'

The tidal wave of noise that came from me lifted me to my feet and him with me. He darted behind me and locked his left arm tightly round my neck. We were both out of breath. There we stood. I was captured. Naked and cunning as a wild animal, I trembled. I looked about, as far as the dim light would allow, for a weapon. Nothing in sight. I was filled with a sensation of extraordinary physical fitness and well-being. All I knew was that I had no intention of being quenched, snuffed out, extinguished, murdered and silenced. I had no intention of vacating my premises and leaving my empty body in the concrete gully beneath my window. Something diabolical had entered the flat. I would fight. But, he might be too strong in the end. Events seemed to have lifted themselves on to a plane where the struggle which took place felt like the ultimate, gargantuan struggle between good and evil. There was, as yet, no winner.

Suddenly, I punched out hard over my left shoulder. My fist smacked into his eye socket. I lashed out twice more. I tried to look round at his face but he jerked his head back so that I caught the merest glimpse of a high forehead, shining in the meagre light from the window, and a strand or two of fairish hair. I never saw his face. I jabbed my flat, stiffened fingers into his gullet and held them there, pushing hard. He countered by grabbing my hand and bending the fingers back violently. More fighting and we fell to the floor. It ended with my recapture. He sat with his back to the bedside cupboard, his left arm locked once more around my neck. I sat with my legs outstretched, his left leg curled about my waist. My back was to him. I saw the grubby trainer shoe on his foot. I was tired. I wanted to fall into a deep sleep.

'Don't move or I'll hurt you,' he kept saying.

In a mockery of snug intimacy, I sat nestled between the legs of the man whose face I had not seen. We stayed locked together like this for some considerable time, in fact, until the first birdsong at the break of dawn. The battleground changed. It became a battle of wills and of wits. For the first time, we conversed.

'Listen.' The voice was gruff and urgent. 'I want three things. I want money, food and a bath. I've been on the run for three days and I'm filthy. I'm filthy and I'm starving hungry.'

When he said he was filthy, I got the impression he was describing his inner self.

'Look,' he said, 'I've got to put a pillowcase over your head.'

'No,' I replied. 'That's too frightening.'

Now we were to bargain over every move, the advantage slipping from one to the other.

'All right, then. All right. I'm going to tie up your hands and feet. Give me the rope back.'

'No.' I still held tightly on to the thin piece of rope.

'I've got another piece here.' He reached in his pocket with his free hand and dangled a second piece in front of my face.

'I don't want you to tie me up. You might rape me.'

'If I was going to do that, I'd knock you spark out. If I was going to hurt you, I'd have done it by now. Give me my rope back.'

'No. I'm too scared.' My mind raced. I knew I had to keep him talking. 'Where are you on the run from, anyway?' I asked.

'I didn't escape from nick. The police were coming to pick me up and I went on the run from them.'

'My husband's on the run too,' I said, trying to make common ground between us.

'Well, I hope he doesn't end up in the same nick as me after all this.' There was a pause.

'He did diamond robberies,' I said.

'Is that where you got the money for the flat from?' I detected a strong, northern accent.

'Yes,' I said.

'Where is he now?' he asked, suspiciously.

'I dunno.' I tried making a bond between us. 'I'm on your side, you know. Let me go. I won't call the police. Most people I know are on the run, anyway.'

Playing for time, I embarked on a story of how a friend of mine escaped from jail. How she took a chance when one of the screws wasn't looking and ran off from the party working on the outside gardens. How she knocked on the door of a stranger's house and asked to use the telephone to call a taxi. My captor grunted to show that he was listening.

'Naturally, as she'd just done a bunk, she didn't have any money on her. So when the taxi came, she drove to a jeweller's, told the cabbie to stop for a minute, ran into the shop, sold the gold chain from round her neck and that's how she got the money to pay for the taxi.'

'Then what?' he asked.

'Then – and this is brilliant,' I continued, 'she went to a battered wives' hostel, told them she'd run away from a violent husband and they took her in. They hid her, helped her change her name by deed poll and got her re-housed. Now she's living round the corner with her four kids.'

He gave his grunting laugh.

'So why don't you just go away,' I suggested quietly. 'I won't call the police. I don't like them any more than you do. How long do you want me to give you to get away?'

'Three weeks,' he replied. We both laughed.

'Now listen,' he said, 'I want you to put your hands together so I can tie you up.'

'No. That's too scary. You take what you want and I'll just sit here and I won't say anything.'

He became agitated.

'You won't,' he said. 'I don't trust you. I don't trust you. You'll do something. You'll do something.'

'I won't,' I said. But I knew I would, given a chance. And he knew it too.

'Are you a rapist or a burglar?' I asked.

'I'm a professional burglar. I'm a professional burglar.' He spoke with the insistence of a man trying to convince himself.

'Look,' he said. 'I'm not going to hurt you. It's you that's hurt me. I only attacked you once. You've attacked me twice. I'm still seeing stars from where you punched me.'

'Sorry,' I replied with false contrition. 'Anyway, I don't punch hard. I'm no Frank Bruno. I feel more like Barry McGuigan.' I had recently seen Barry McGuigan on television being carried, bloodstained and defeated, from the boxing ring.

The man laughed. I decided to play for sympathy.

'Ooh. I'm feeling sick,' I said. 'I think I'm going to faint.'

'Don't give me that shit,' he hissed and I stopped.

'Don't move,' he said, 'I'm going to roll myself a smoke.' He took his arm from my neck and began to feel for cigarette papers.

'Don't bother to roll one. There's a packet of mine on that little cupboard behind you. I want one too.' He felt around for them in the dark.

'Where?' he asked. 'I can't find them.'

'They must have fallen on the floor in the fight,' I replied.

He found them and lit one for me.

'What's your name?' he asked.

'Carole. What shall I call you?' I phrased the question in that way because I knew he wouldn't give me his real name. He hesitated for a minute and then answered:

'Charlie. Charlie Peace.'

It was not till days later that I discovered the true identity of Charlie Peace. The true historical identity that is – not the identity of the man who held me captive. Charlie Peace was a nineteenth-century murderer. He was born in Sheffield, son of a shoemaker. He was employed as a tinsmith and later as a workman at a rolling mill. Strangely enough, he also worked for a while as a cabaret artist. He appeared on stage in Worksop in 1853, a comic performance in which he impersonated the modern Paganini, playing the violin with one string. His criminal career as a professional burglar began later. He first killed in 1872. Apparently, he eluded capture in a wonderful manner, assuming many disguises and still committing burglaries. He moved to London and lived under the alias of John Ward. He shot a policeman and attempted suicide. He was betrayed in London by a married woman. He confessed to yet another murder before being executed in Manchester in 1876.

I knew none of this as I sat imprisoned by my assailant. In fact, I laughed when he used the name Peace. I thought it ironic that such a violent man should choose to call himself by the name Peace:

'How did you get in, anyway?' I asked.

'You left the door open,' he replied and laughed. 'You left the door open.'

The reply disturbed me. I knew without a doubt that I had locked the front door behind me as I came into the flat. It doesn't shut properly otherwise. It was as though he was referring to some other door, as though I had unwittingly nudged open an invisible door to some infernal region, enabling him to slip through. It occurred to me that I would never know how to shut this intangible door or worse, that I would never know how to avoid accidentally opening it again, this incorporeal door to hell.

'You've got a cut on your back,' he said. 'It looks quite deep.'

'I want an ashtray,' I said. He passed me the empty Silk Cut packet to use as an ashtray. We both stubbed out our cigarettes in it. In the dim light, I caught sight of a large black shape by the wall. I tried to puzzle out what it was. I thought he might have brought a black bag with him, but it turned out to be the overturned television set.

'Put your hands behind your back so I can tie them.'

'No.'

'You're a bloody nuisance, you are.' He sounded exasperated.

'You might want to tie me up because you're a . . .' I could not bring myself to say the word.

'A pervert.' He finished the sentence for me.

'Yes,' I said.

'How do you know I'm not a poof?'

'You can be what you like,' I answered with a liberalism born out of wariness. 'I don't mind.'

'Look. I'm going to get really angry in a minute. If you don't do what I want, I'm going to knock you spark out and then I will rape you. Give me your hands so I can tie them up.'

'Why?' I stalled for time.

'Because I don't want you to see me stark bollock naked in the bath,' he hissed furiously.

'Well, look at me,' I said indignantly. 'How do you think I feel? I haven't got anything on. I feel terrible like this. Let me go and get a dressing-gown.'

'Let me tie your hands and then I'll get you a nightgown.'

'That's no good,' I said. 'If my hands are tied up I won't be able to get them through the sleeves, will I?' My logic made him change tack.

'How old are you?' he asked.

'Twenty-eight,' I lied. I lied for a reason. That summer, in London, a strangler was on the loose. He was called 'The Whispering Strangler' in the press and he only murdered elderly people. It had already occurred to me that this might be the same man, so I knocked a chunk off my age.

'Come off it. How old are you?'

'All right, fifty-eight if that suits you better.'

'Tell me how old you are.'

'No. You might tell the police.' He laughed.

'I'm hungry,' he announced.

'Let me get you something to eat.' I sounded like a new bride.

'No you won't. Don't move. How much money have you got in the flat?'

'Fifteen pounds.'

'Oh, bloody hell.'

'Well, I'm skint. I'll go and get my purse if you like. It's in the hall.' So many small attempts at escape.

'Don't move. Don't move. I'm going to tie your arms and legs.'

'No. You might rape me.'

'How can I rape you if I've tied your legs up?' We seemed equally matched for logic.

Suddenly, his tone changed. He became gentle, almost shy, as if trying to be genuinely helpful:

'Do you want me to fuck you?' he asked.

'No!' I replied. I was exhausted, so much so that I almost yielded. I had sat hugged up in his arms for nearly an hour. My body was telling me what a normal thing it would be to do. But I feared he would kill me afterwards. The first birds of the dawn chorus began to sing. He became fierce:

'Look. It's getting light. It's getting light. I won't have time for a bath.' I could hear the agitation in his voice. There were sound, practical reasons why he should not be abroad in daylight. Someone might see him. He might be recognized. Perhaps there were other reasons too why he had to be gone before the day fully broke.

'Let me tie your hands.'

I was so exhausted that I agreed.

'All right then, you can tie them as long as you tie them up in front of me and you don't tie them too tight.'

'Give me the rope then.' I gave it to him.

'Put your hands over your head.' I put my hands over my head for a minute and then put them down again.

'I don't like doing that. It makes me feel frightened. I'll put them over my shoulder.' I put them over my left shoulder, elbows together, hands opened.

'Put your hands together,' he ordered. I closed my hands and opened my elbows.

'Put your elbows together,' he said. I put my elbows together and my hands flat together and I pulled my wrists as far apart as I could. We used to do this as children, playing games of prisoner and captor, to enable a quick escape. All the frightening games of childhood are a preparation for this sort of experience: skirmishes, hunting, tracking games, tying up to a tree games. It's a shame we stop playing them. We get out of practice. He tied my wrists, knotting the rope carefully between them. From the way I had held my wrists, I knew immediately that there was enough leeway for me to be able to slip the bonds when the opportunity arose. I would wait until it became absolutely necessary.

As soon as my wrists were tied he became more savage. In a sudden outburst of violence, he manhandled me towards the bed. That was to be the pattern. The more concessions I made, the more cruel he became. Any weakness from me generated his power. With hindsight, I under-stand that it is pointless to cooperate with a demon or appeal to his better nature when he has the upper hand.

'Kneel down by the bed. Are you going to do what I say?' He spoke with the same, growling, whispered intensity.

'Yes, sir. No, sir,' I replied, with the cunning obsequiousness of the slave. He held me by the neck while he dragged the woven Mexican blanket off my bed. He draped it over my head and helped me gently to my feet. The blanket hung about two feet over my head. If I held it out in front of me I could see the floor.

'All right. Where's your purse?' he asked.

I walked out into the hallway with him close behind me. I fumbled about on the trunk but couldn't find my purse:

'I can't find it. Let me switch the light on a minute.'

'Don't switch the light on.' The words were spat out. Under the piles of papers and letters on the chest I knew that, somewhere, there was an iron tyre lever. I couldn't risk rummaging around for it. He was too near me. The opportunity slid past like a ship in the night that fails to see the life-raft. I found my purse and opened it. He was still behind me. I felt him come closer. His chin must have been near my shoulder because it was then that I felt his stare. It was a stare of such power and evil that I knew, from that moment, that I must never attempt to look at his face. That was partly prudence. If he knew that I could identify him he would have greater reason to kill. But there was something else. I thought that if I turned, I would see a visage so appalling, so fearful that I would be paralysed with terror. I looked in my purse:

'I'm sorry. There's only ten pounds here.' I handed him the note. I fiddled around in the purse again and found two one-pound coins and a fifty-pence piece. A stubborn meanness came over me that made me want to keep it:

'You don't want all this small change, do you?' I said confidently, as if that was the end of the matter.

'No,' he acquiesced. I seized the advantage.

'You know when your mouth goes all dry because you're frightened,' I said. 'Well, that's how my mouth's gone. I want a glass of water.' Tentatively, I began to call the shots. We walked back along the hall and into the kitchen. The blanket was still over my head. He stayed close behind me. With tied hands I reached for a glass from the shelf over the sink and poured myself a glass of water:

'Do you want some?' I asked.

'No.' I felt him jerk back like a man with hydrophobia. On the draining-board, next to the sink, lay a large Sabatier kitchen knife. My thoughts ran here and there like a rat in a cul-de-sac. I could make a grab for the knife but he might overpower me and use it against me. He was being cooperative at this moment, perhaps it would be better not to antagonize him. But finally, it was the desire to kill that was lacking in me. I let it be, hoping that he had not seen the knife.

Of course, he had seen it.

'What food have you got?' he inquired.

'There's some bread.' I opened the big cupboard and took out a green plastic carrier-bag. Into it I put the remains of a loaf from the bread-bin. On the fridge were three nectarines.

'Why don't you have some of those, they're nice,' I said, sounding like a shop assistant at a greengrocer's.

'What are they? Plums?'

'No. They're nectarines.' I hoped that didn't sound too fancy.

'I'll leave you one for your breakfast,' he said.

'Thanks.' I opened the fridge door, crouched on the floor, the blanket covering my head. The fridge was nearly empty.

'Blimey, there's not much here. There's only a bit of cucumber. Do you want it?'

'No.'

He began to push me towards the bathroom. He picked up a chair from the kitchen:

'I'll take this chair so you've got something to sit on.'

'It's all right. There's one in there,' I said.

In the bathroom he told me to keep the blanket over my head and stand still. He switched on the light. Then he took some books and papers off the chair so that I would be more comfortable. The chair was beside the wash-basin, facing the toilet. I sat down. For the first time, I began to feel sick. Bathrooms are dangerous places to fight in. There are too many hard edges. I thought he was going to run the water in the bath and drown me, or push my head down the toilet bowl and murder me that way. I leaned forward and put the toilet lid down. That would delay him another second or two:

'I'll sit on the toilet seat,' I said.

'No you won't. Don't move.' He didn't want me seated behind him while he was facing the sink in case I saw him in the mirror of the cabinet. I could not see what he was doing. I just heard sounds. I heard the water running in the basin. He seemed to be doing something with his gloves. He asked for soap. I told him where it was. Whatever he was doing, he was doing it carefully and methodically. He asked for a comb. I heard him combing his hair for a long time, slowly, ritualistically. It was then I knew for certain he was no ordinary burglar. I think he used one of my towels. Then he took a damp cloth, lifted the blanket from behind and washed the wound on my back. When he had finished in the bathroom, he announced that we would go and get my dressing-

gown. We walked down the hall and into the big bedroom. I was relieved
to be out of the bathroom.

'Where is it?' he asked.

'Do you see that wardrobe?' From under the blanket I managed to
indicate the walk-in wardrobe. 'Well, it's hanging on the inside of the
door.' He walked round the bed towards the wardrobe.

'Has it got flowers on it?' he asked, sounding innocent.

'Yes.'

He stood behind me and lifted the blanket from my head. Tenderly,
he placed the dressing-gown round my shoulders. I felt the roughness
of his gloves. He draped the blanket back over my head.

'Do you want me to button up the front for you?' he asked.

'No.'

'Now I am going to tie your feet up. Do you want to lie on the bed
or do you want to lie on the floor?'

'I don't want you to tie my feet up. I don't like having my feet tied.
It's horrible.' I shifted the blanket a little.

'Don't move that blanket about.'

'I can't help it. It's hot under here. I can't breathe.'

'They all say that,' he replied, coldly.

We argued for a while. He told me to sit down on the bed. The bed is
just a base with a mattress on it, covered by a red woollen blanket. It
is low on the ground. He told me not to move and he left the room.
The full-length curtains were drawn. There was not much light. He
returned almost immediately and offered me another of my cigarettes.
I held the blanket away from me and he reached down and lit it for me.
I could see the silver-coloured metal lighter. It was the old-fashioned
sort with a flip-top, hinged on the short side. This time he did not
smoke. He knew how to wait.

'I need another ashtray,' I said. He accompanied me back into the
kitchen. I couldn't see an ashtray. I took a small plate and we returned
to the bedroom where I finished my cigarette.

'I'm going to tie your feet.' He became aggressive. I grumbled but
exhaustion had weakened my will. I sat on the end of the bed and he

tied up my feet. He tied them skilfully, kneeling on the floor a little to my left. He tied both feet at the ankles, and knotted the rope in between. I felt miserably powerless. Although I knew I could free my hands when necessary, my feet had been bound too fast for me to loosen the ties.

'You've got hairy legs,' he sneered.

'That's no way to speak to a friend,' I retorted. I used the word 'friend' deliberately, so that he might find it more difficult to kill me. Suddenly, I had a vision of my bloodstained body, lying undiscovered for days. He gave his chuckling grunt:

'Your feet are tiny,' he said, as if to apologize.

He left the room and I heard him go into the kitchen. Moments later, he returned. He stood directly in front of me and thrust a big knife under the blanket. It was the Sabatier kitchen knife. He had taken off his gloves.

'I've got a big knife here. Can you see it? Can you see it?' The voice was fierce and powerful.

'Yes.' His trousers were lowered to just below the top of his thighs. He had an erection.

'You said you wouldn't do this,' I said, sulkily.

'Well, I am,' he replied, spitefully. 'Are you going to do what I say? Yes or no? YES OR NO?'

'I suppose so,' I grumbled.

'Now then, I want you to suck me off.' The blade of the knife was a dull grey under the blanket. A perverse feeling of obstinacy came over me.

'Well, I don't know how to do that,' I said. He seemed bewildered by the reply.

'You just put it in your mouth and suck,' he explained.

'Well, I can't. I don't know how to.' I was careful not to insult him sexually.

'Kneel down by the side of the bed,' he said in a harsh growl. I knelt down facing the bed. 'Lie on your stomach on the bed.' I didn't move. He began to pull at my legs. I was feeling annoyed. I did not cooperate. Eventually he pulled me on to the bed.

'Lie flat and put your arms above your head.'

All my instincts told me not to lie prone. I raised myself on my elbows. If he used the knife I had to be ready.

'Lie flat.'

'No. I'm all right like this.' He was kneeling behind me.

'I'm going to feel you,' he said. He began to fondle my breasts gently and firmly. It was almost pleasurable – if death had not been on my mind. Murder.

'Now I'm going to rub myself against you.' He pushed the blanket and dressing-gown up my back and put his arms underneath my arms. His hands were flat on the bed. For the first time, I was able to see his hands. They were neat, well-proportioned, unremarkable hands, clean with a fine covering of fairish hair. He began to rub his erect penis between the cheeks of my behind. I peeked out from under the blanket to see if I could locate the knife. No sign of it. But I knew that as long as I could see his hands he couldn't use the weapon.

'Sit back on the bed.' I did what he said.

'Right. Now suck me off.'

Thrust under the blanket, his erect penis floated in the air, flanked by two smooth, round balls. I wondered if they were swollen from when I had grabbed them earlier in the fight. I considered biting the penis or freeing my hands and tearing at the genitals, but I did not know where he had put the knife. One thing I did know. I was not going to suck him off.

'I can't. I don't know how to,' I repeated.

'Why won't you suck me off?' he asked, plaintively, a little hurt. I got stubborn. The dynamics of childishness entered into the situation. Cussedness took hold of me.

'Don't want to,' I said.

'Why not?' he complained.

Here was a dilemma. I couldn't say 'Because you're a fucking maniac,' so I bargained.

'I might toss you off,' I said.

'Go on then.'

I rubbed my hands up and down his penis and touched his balls. Then, as women often do, I got bored and stopped.

'I can't do this. It's too difficult with my hands tied.'

'Well squeeze it then.'

I squeezed it unenthusiastically for a second or two and stopped. There was a pause.

'Lie back on the bed. Keep the blanket over your face. I'm going to come over your tits.'

He was forced to do it himself. I lay back and after a while he ejaculated over and between my breasts. It felt warm. He took a cloth which he must have brought with him and wiped me thoroughly. I glimpsed the sleeve of a leather jacket and the slightly worn cuff of a dark nylon sweater. Then he said, quietly:

'It's all over.'

What did he mean? Life?

He left the bedroom and returned quickly. I had sat up on the edge of the bed, the blanket still over my head. He knelt down and cut the rope between my ankles. As he did so, he nicked me with the knife.

'Ouch,' I said.

'Sorry,' he said.

'Thanks,' I said.

'Where's your telephone? Where's your telephone?' He sounded panicky.

'It's in the front room.'

'Where is it exactly?'

'If you go into the front room, it's on the floor over to the left.'

'I'm going to cut the wires.' Suddenly, he began to rummage around among some packages that had been left on the bed from the night before.

'Where's me food bag? Where's me food bag? What's in these bags?' he asked.

'Soap and stuff that someone's taking to my family abroad for me.'

He left the room and I heard his footsteps retreating down the hall. For two seconds I hesitated. Then I quickly freed my hands, keeping them hidden under the blanket lest he returned. I waited for one more second and threw the blanket from my head. I ran across the room to the back window, pushed back the curtain and with one manoeuvre, opened the window. I leapt out into the back garden. The air was chill. I jumped up the four stone steps on to the wet grass. I was exhilarated. Yelling for the people upstairs, I raced across the grass to the fence, scratching myself on the rose bushes. I tried to climb on to the fence but fell back. Then, with one enormous effort, I was on top of the fence with its three-foot-high trellis. I was still naked. Naked and free. It was early dawn. Everywhere was quiet and still. I glanced back at the window to see if a figure was climbing out in pursuit of me and I yelled with the power of an opera singer. I was half-caught in the branches of a pear tree, an early morning goddess, calling and hollering. Slowly, neighbours came to various windows:

'Quick! Get the police.' My voice was huge and clear. Soon the police arrived. There was no sign of the man.

For the first two days afterwards, the police were consideration itself. A plump, brown-haired policewoman was assigned to my case and spent most of the first day taking down my statement. Then she drove me to a friend's house where I was to stay the night while my flat was sealed off for forensic examination. I was, naturally, exhausted. Before I fell asleep, words from the twenty-third psalm floated into my head. I remembered something about lying down in green pastures and walking beside still waters. Suddenly, I experienced the sensation of walking through delightful pastures of long green grass dotted with yellow wild flowers until I came and stood by the stillest of waters. At the same time, my own physical boundaries dissolved and I recognized that those green meadows and rivers were inside me. The experience was so full of wonder that I tried to delay going to sleep in order to prolong it, but soon I fell into the most profound and peaceful of slumbers. I dreamed. I dreamed the dream of the leopard. The leopard was sitting at one end of my hallway. He was half-painting and half-real. At the other end of the passage was a mirror. The leopard was out of alignment with the mirror. He had to be moved so that he could see in the mirror. But I knew that when he was face to face with the mirror, something terrible would happen. Then I woke up.

*   *   *

On the third day the police turned nasty.

'Mrs Atkins, are you sure you didn't know this intruder? We cannot find a point of entry. Are you sure you didn't let him in?'

'I think he must have got in through the front window. I usually keep it locked but I had a friend staying. She might have opened it.'

'And our forensic people have not been able to find a trace of him. There are no fingerprints and we can't even pick up a footprint. Where is the knife he used?'

'He must have taken it with him.'

'And the cloth he used to wipe you down?'

'He must have taken that too.'

'What about the rope he tied you with?'

'It doesn't seem to be here.' (Later, fortunately, I found the rope that had tied my hands, in the garden.)

'Look. We can see that something happened here. We can see there's been a fight of some sort, but it's very unusual for someone to stay this long in a flat and to have been in the bathroom, the kitchen, the hall, both bedrooms and not leave a trace or a clue behind. Where's the comb he used? We might be able to get one of his hairs from that.'

'It's gone.'

'Did he eat anything? Use any cutlery? We might be able to get a saliva trace.'

'What about the cigarette stubs?' I suggested. 'We both smoked a cigarette and stubbed them out in an empty packet. There should be a saliva trace on there.'

'That's already been checked. There was only one stub in the packet and that has your saliva on it.'

'He must be very clever,' I said. 'He's taken all the evidence with him.'

Over the next few days my imagination ran wild over the grid of facts, along the boundaries of reason and unreason that are stalked by the ancient figure of fear. Could it have been part of myself that escaped and attacked me? Had the spirit of a nineteenth-century murderer and cabaret artist entered a contemporary small-time burglar? Did we all overlap? Some months later a young plain-clothes detective appeared at the front door:

'Can I come in?' he said. 'I think we've found your man. Would you mind if I brought a police photographer in with me to take some pictures of the flat?'

He leaned nonchalantly against the kitchen door, drinking a coffee while his colleague took photographs of the other rooms:

'You're a performer, I hear. I used to be an actor myself. I was at Hornchurch Repertory Company for nearly a year. Then I gave it up for this.' His collar-length hair still looked actorish. He continued 'Anyway, we're pretty certain it's him, although it's going to be difficult to prove in court with so little evidence. He may well get off. We think it's him that raped another woman near here. We haven't got a scrap of evidence on that either. He's cunning. Spent two nights at her house with putty softener, then removed a whole pane of glass. He's got a history of this sort of thing. Often attacks on Christmas Day. Clever, you see. He's denying it, mind you. Denying everything. I almost felt sorry for him when I was talking to him. He's in a horrendous mental state. Says someone is trying to get into him and tell him what to do. Someone called John, he says. Maybe, it's this John we should be going after. Don't know him do you?' he asked, jokingly.

Charlie Peace, I thought. Alias John Ward. Betrayed by a married woman in London.

'Don't forget you've got the piece of rope I found in the garden,' I said.

'We're not likely to forget that,' he said. 'It's all we have got.'

In court, the man was not in my direct line of vision and he remained turned slightly away from me. Only once did he look at me, as I was demonstrating to the jury how I had held my wrists apart as he tied them. His head swivelled slowly through an angle of one hundred and eighty degrees like an owl, and he stared with great, blank eyes. It was then that I noticed his camel-hair coat and cheap jewellery and a black nylon roll-neck sweater of the type worn by spivs.

PAULINE MELVILLE

Eat Labba and Drink Creek Water

Lorna fled from Jamaica and came to live in my London flat for a year, recovering from Philip who had gone back to his wife. She arrived with two bulging suitcases and chickenpox:

'I can't bear to live on the island while he's there with her.' The tears were extraordinary. They spouted from the outermost corners of her eyes. When she blinked they squirted out. She consumed quantities of Frascati wine and swallowed all the pills my doctor could provide. Sometimes I heard her shouting in her sleep. Every so often she managed to haul herself by train to the provincial university where she was completing a thesis on the sugar riots of the thirties. I imagined her, this white-looking creole girl, jolting along in a British Rail compartment that smelled of stale smoke, weeping and puffing at cigarettes and staring out at the grey English weather which she hated. In the end:

'I'm going back,' she said.

'I'm going back too, to Guyana.'

'Why?'

'I don't know. I want to see my aunts before they die. They're old. And I want to spend some time in Georgetown, in the house with Evelyn and the others. I miss the landscape. Perhaps I'll buy a piece of land there. I don't know why. I just want to go back.'

'Eat labba and drink creek water and you will always return', so the saying goes.

Once I dreamed I returned by walking in the manner of a high-wire artist, arms outstretched, across a frail spider's thread suspended sixty feet above the Atlantic attached to Big Ben at one end and St George's

Cathedral, Demerara, at the other. It took me twenty-two days to do it and during the whole of that time only the moon shone.

Another time, my dream blew me clean across the ocean like tumble-weed. That took only three days and the sun and the moon shone alternately as per usual.

We do return and leave and return again, criss-crossing the Atlantic, but whichever side of the Atlantic we are on, the dream is always on the other side.

I am splashing in the waters of the lake at Suddie. The waters are a strange reddish colour, the colour of Pepsi-Cola and the lake is fenced in with reeds. The sky is a grey-blue lid with clouds in it – far too big for the lake. Opposite me on the far side, an Amerindian woman sits motionless in the back of a canoe wedged in the reeds. She is clutching a paddle.

They say that the spirit of a pale boy is trapped beneath the waters of one of the creeks near by. You can see him looking up when sunlight penetrates the overhanging branches and green butterfly leaves, caught between the reflections of tree roots that stretch like fins from the banks into the water.

'So you're going back to the West Indies,' says the man at the party, in his blue and white striped shirt. 'I was on holiday in Montego Bay last year. How I envy you. All those white beaches and palm trees.'

But it's not like that, I think to myself. It's not like that at all. I think of Jamaica with its harsh sunlight and stony roads. Everything is more visible there, the gunmen, the politics, the sturdy, outspoken people. And I think of the Guyanese coast, with its crab-infested mud-flats and low trees dipping into the water.

'You've got all that wonderful reggae music too,' the man is saying. But I don't bother to put him right because the buzz of conversation is too loud.

The pale boy's name is Wat. He is standing on the deck of a ship at anchor in the estuary of a great river, screwing up his eyes to scan the coast. The boards of the deck are burning hot underfoot. The sun pulverizes his head. His father, leader of the expedition, comes over to him and puts his hand on the boy's shoulder:

'At last we have found entry into the Guianas,' he says.

Wat's heart beats a little faster. This is it. Somewhere in the interior they will find Manoa which the Spaniards call El Dorado. They will outdo the feats of Cortes and Pizarro. They will discover

The mountain of crystal

The empire where there is more abundance of gold than in Peru

The palaces that contain feathered fish, beasts and birds, all fashioned in gold by men with no iron implements

The pleasure gardens with intricate replicas of trees, herbs and flowers, all wrought in silver and gold.

He gazes eagerly ahead. There is mud, green bush, river and more bush stretching as far as the eye can see. And there are no seagulls. Unlike the coast of England where the birds had shrieked them such a noisy farewell, this coast is utterly silent.

The body of an Amerindian is falling through the mists, a brown leaf curling and twisting downwards until it reaches the earth with a thud like fruit.

A low mournful hoot signals the departure of the SS *Essequibo* as it steams out of the Demerara into the Atlantic.

A young man of twenty-one braces himself against the rail taking deep breaths of the future. There is not much of the African left in his appearance, a hint of it perhaps in the tawny colour of a complexion mixed over generations with Scottish, Amerindian and Portuguese. He lets go of the rail and strolls towards the prow of the ship. His eyes never leave the horizon. Not once does he look back as the land recedes away behind him, because

In England there is a library that contains all the books in the world, a cathedral of knowledge the interior of whose dome shimmers gold from the lettering on spines of ancient volumes.

In England there are theatres and concert halls and galleries hung from ceiling to floor with magnificent gold-framed paintings and all of these are peopled by men in black silk opera hats and women with skins like cream of coconut.

In England there are museums which house the giant skeletons of dinosaurs whose breastbones flute into a ribcage as lofty and vast as the stone ribs inside Westminster Abbey, which he has seen on a postcard.

This is what will happen.

He will disembark in the industrial docks of Liverpool to the delicious shock of seeing, for the first time, white men working with their hands.

For a year he will study law at the Inns of Court in London.

In the Great War of Europe, two of the fingers of his left hand will be torn off by shrapnel. A bluish wound will disfigure the calf of his leg. The thundering of the artillery will render him stone deaf in one ear and after a period of rehabilitation in Shorncliffe, Kent, he will be returned to his native land where his mother, brothers and sisters wait for him on the veranda. He brings with him a letter signed by the King of England which his mother frames and hangs in the living-room. It says:

'A Grateful Mother Country Thanks You For Your Sacrifice.'

They are drenched with spray, Wat, his father and six of the crew, clinging to the rocks at the base of the giant falls of Kaeitur, a waterfall so enormous that it makes the sound of a thousand bells as the column of water falls thousands of feet to the River Potaro below. Each one of them is exhausted, but above all, perplexed. For two weeks they have travelled upriver led by an Arawak guide. Before they set off they explained carefully to him through an interpreter that they were seeking the mountain of crystal. And this is where he has brought them.

'I'm coming on November the sixth,' I yell down the phone to Evelyn. 'I'll go to see my aunts in New Amsterdam for a couple of days then I'll come and stay with you.'

'That is good.' Evelyn's voice is faint and crackly. 'Bring a Gestetner machine with you. They need one at the party headquarters. Really we need a computer but that costs thousands of dollars. We'll pay you for it when you reach.'

'OK Evelyn. I'll see you in two weeks' time. I can't wait. Bye.'

'Bye. Don't forget ink and paper.'

I lie back on the bed wiggling my toes and thinking of Evelyn. She is a stockily built black woman of thirty-six, a financial wizard in the pin-ball economy of the country. She will never leave. Her house is set back a little from the road. On every side of its white-painted exterior, tiers of Demerara shutters open, bottom out, stiff sails designed to catch the last breath of wind. I try to imagine whereabouts she is in the house. She has a cordless telephone now so she could be anywhere – in the kitchen perhaps or wandering about upstairs. When the trade winds blow the upper floors of the house are full of air encrusted with salt and at night the house creaks like a ship resting at anchor in the city of wooden dreams, a city built on stilts, belonging neither to land nor to sea but to land reclaimed from the sea.

Beneath his father's framed certificate from the King of England, a slim youth of nineteen leans his back against the dresser thinking:

'*If I don't get out of this colony I shall suffocate.*'

A problem has arisen over his leaving. His father and Mr Wilkinson, his employer, are discussing it in the stifling inertia of midday. His father is frowning and flexing the stubs of his two fingers, as if they have pins and needles. Mr Wilkinson is one of those gingery, peppery Englishmen whose long stay in the tropics has sucked all the moisture from him, leaving a dry sandy exterior. He too is frowning at the piece of paper in his hand.

'The trouble is with this damn birth certificate. The transfer to London went through all right. The Booker-McConnell people in London agreed to it, then, out of the blue, they ask for his birth certificate. Just a formality I suppose. All the same . . .'

His voice tails off into silence.

On the birth certificate, under the section marked 'Type' are written the words: 'Coloured. Native. Creole.'

The young man's eyes are solemn and watchful as he waits for his elders to find a solution. He has a recurring nightmare which is this: that Crab Island, the chunk of mud and jungle in the estuary of the Berbice River, grows to such enormous proportions that it blocks for ever his escape from New Amsterdam; that he is forced to stay in the stultifyingly dull town with its straggly cabbage palms and telegraph poles whose wires carry singing messages from nowhere to nowhere. He awakes from the dream sweating and in a claustrophobic panic.

In London there is jazz and the Café Royal.

In London you can skate across the Thames when it is frozen and there is snow snow snow in a million crystal flakes.

In London there are debonair, sophisticated, cosmopolitan men. It is impossible to *be* a real man until you have been to London.

He watches them sip their rum punches by the window. In the silence, music drifts up from the phonograph playing in the bottom-house:

> The music goes round and round
> Oh oh oh, Oh oh oh
> And it comes out here.

Gazing at the three of them with blank disdainful eyes is the portrait of an Amerindian.

Mr Wilkinson continues, embarrassed:

'Frankly, I don't expect it will make any difference, but I wouldn't like there to be any foul-up at this late stage. I'll tell you what we'll do. Have you got his baptism certificate? They don't put all this rubbish on the baptism certificate. I'll write a letter to London saying the birth certificate was destroyed by a fire in the records office. I'll enclose the baptism certificate instead. That should fix it. They won't bother once he's there.' He takes another swallow of his drink. 'I suppose they have to be careful. It is the City of London after all, where they set the Gold Standard for the world.' He winks.

The great and golden city is to be discovered in the heart of a large, rich and beautiful empire. The city is well proportioned and has many great towers. Throughout, there are laid out goodly gardens and parks, some of them containing ponds of excellent fish. There are, too, many squares where trading is done and markets are held for the buying and selling of all manner of wares: ornaments of gold, silver, lead, brass and copper; game, birds of every species, rabbits, hares and partridges; vegetables, fish and fruit.

In all the districts of this great city are many temples or houses for their idols.

In one part of the city they have built cages to house large numbers of lions, tigers, wolves, foxes and cats of various kinds.

There are yet other large houses where live many men and women with deformities and various maladies. Likewise there are people to look after them.

In some of these great towers are hollow statues of gold which seem giants and all manner of gold artefacts, even gold that seems like wooden logs to burn. Here dwell men who deal in markets of coffee and sugar and vast numbers of other like commodities. They have eyes in their shoulders, mouths in the middle of their breasts, a long train of hair grows backwards between their shoulders. They sit on finely made leather cushions and there are also men like porters to carry food to them on magnificent plates of gold and silver.

In the uppermost rooms of these towers, which are as we would call palaces, sit stockbrokers, their bodies anointed with white powdered gold blown through hollow canes until they are shining all over. Above their heads hang the skulls of dead company directors, all hung and decked with feathers. Here they sit drinking, hundreds of them together, for as many as six or seven days at a time.

I am squatting on the veranda in the hot yellow afternoon making spills for my grandfather. I tear strips from the *Berbice Advertiser* as he's shown me and fold them carefully into tiny pleats. In the yard is the Po' Boy tree which is supposed to be lucky. Children late for school stop to touch it and recite:

> Pity pity Po' Boy
> Sorry fi me
> If God don' help me
> The devil surely will.

My grandfather rests in his chair, one foot up on the long wooden arm. I want to please him so I place four spills for his pipe on the wicker table at his side but he hardly notices. I try to peek at the hand that has two fingers missing but it is folded in his lap in such a way that I can't see properly.

Aunt Rosa comes out of the living-room to give me a glass of soursop:

'Tomorrow your daddy is coming to take you back to England.'

'England. England. England,' I dance along the veranda.

'Come in out of the sun, chile. You're gettin' all burnt up. I will take you over to the da Silvas to play one last time.'

I stop short, filled with apprehension and start to scuff my shoe on the floor:

'I don' want to go.' I follow her inside where it is darker and cooler: 'What is this foolishness? Why you don' want to go?'

I don't want to tell her. I try to distract her attention from the da Silvas:

'What does my daddy do in London?'

'He works for Booker-McConnell, of course, in a big building called Plantation House in the City of London.' There is a note of pride in her voice which encourages me to lead her further away from the subject of the da Silvas:

'Will you show me the photograph of the men in London again?'

Aunt Rosa goes over to the large, carved oak dresser. She is darker than my father but with the same large creole eyes. Her black hair is in a roll at the front. On top of the dresser are some of my favourite objects: a tumbler full of glass swizzle sticks, a bell jar, glass goblets and, best of all, a garishly painted wooden Chinese god with a face like a gargoyle and a chipped nose. I hang around the edge fingering the carved roses while Aunt Rosa rummages in the drawer:

'Here it is. These men are very important. They are the men who meet every day to fix the price of sugar on the world market.'

She shows a photograph of dull, sombre-suited men with white faces gathered round a table and points to one of them:

'This is the man who owns the company your daddy works for.'

I try to look interested but I can feel the time running out. I am right.

'Now what is all this nonsense about the da Silvas?' she asks.

'I hate the da Silvas. They keep callin' me "ice-cream face".' And I burst into tears.

Later that night I lie in bed under a single sheet. The doors to the adjoining room are fixed back and I can hear Aunt Rosa talking to Mrs Hunter:

'Look how she fair-skinned, Frank's daughter. No one would ever know. An' she complainin' about it.' They laugh and lower their voices, but I can still hear fragments. Mrs Hunter is talking in a troubled voice about her brother:

'. . . the first coloured officer in the British Army . . . imagine how proud . . . other officers would not speak to him . . . the men refused to obey his orders . . . Some incident . . . trumped up, I tell you . . . an excuse . . . cashiered . . . the shock that ran through the family.' I hear the sob in her voice and Aunt Rosa hush-hushing her.

I creep out of bed towards the open doors. Moonlight floods over the leaves of the Molucca pear tree and spills through the jalousies on to the floor, a dark lake of polished wood. Stepping delicately over it is Salamander, the pale, golden gazelle of a cat, thin with pointy ears. He seems to be dancing some sort of minuet, extending each paw, then with a hop tapping the floor. Delighted, I move to take a closer look. And then I see it. Between his paws is a huge cockroach, a great black ugly thing lying on its back, its feelers moving this way and that. I must have squawked because there is a pause in the conversation, then Aunt Rosa says:

'Get back to bed, chile. If you look out of the window on a night like this you will see Moongazer at the cross-roads.'

'Hello, ice-cream face.' It is my father and he is laughing as he lifts me way up into the sky and sing-chants:

> Molasses, molasses
> Sticky sticky goo
> Molasses, molasses
> Will always stick to you.

My aunts, uncles and cousins are standing round by the wooden lattice at the front of the house. Everyone is laughing and I laugh too.

Some time afterwards, in England, I am playing with my doll Lucy in a garden full of browns and greys. Lucy's face is cracked like crazy paving because I left her out in the rain but I love her because her hair is the colour of golden syrup. The cockney boy who lives next door has climbed into the pear tree on his side of the fence and is intoning in a sneery voice:

'Your fahver looks like a monkey. Your fahver looks like a monkey.'

I go inside and tell my mother.

'Mum, Keith says Daddy looks like a monkey. And I think so too.'

My mother stops beating the cake mixture. She looks sad but not the way she looks when she is sad herself. It is the way she looks when she is teaching me what to be sad about:

'Ahh,' she says, as if I have grazed my knee. 'Well don't tell Daddy, you know he would be so hurt.'

They are lost, Wat, his father and the ragged remnants of the crew. They are paddling the small craft which the Arawaks have named 'the eight-legged sea-spider', and they are lost in a labyrinth of rivers, a confluence of streams that branch into rapids and then into more billowing waters all crossing the other, ebbing and flowing. They seem to travel far on the same spot so that it takes an hour to travel a stone's cast. The sun appears in the sky in three places at once and whether they attempt to use the sun as a guide or a compass they are carried in circles amongst a multitude of islands.

I am fourteen and back from England for the summer. My friend Gail Fraser has pestered and pestered her mother to cook labba for me before I return.

Now we sit at the dinner table, Gail's great-aunt Bertha, her mother, her brother Edmund, and me and Gail. Great-aunt Bertha is a yellow-skinned woman whose face is all caught up in leathery pouches under her white wavy hair. Gail's mother is square-jawed with iron-grey crinkly hair and she is too practical for my liking as I judge everybody by how much 'soul' they have. My friend Gail is honey-coloured and round as a butterball. She has brown almond eyes and curly brown hair and scores about eight out of ten for soul. We have spent most of the holiday lying on her bed exchanging passionate secrets and raiding the rumbly old fridge for plum-juice. My deepest secret is that I am so in love with her brother Edmund that I could die. Edmund has what I call a *crème de cacao* complexion, tight black curls, full lips with the first black hairs of a moustache. He is slim and has black eyes that are brimful of soul. I know he would respond to me if he would stop talking about cricket for ONE minute. As it is, I have to be content to breathe the same air as him, which is pretty nice in itself.

Gail and I are trying desperately not to scream out loud with laughter as great-aunt Bertha chides Edmund for not wearing his jacket:

'My father would not see the boys at dinner without their jackets.'

Dreadful snorts are coming out of Gail and Edmund is pulling faces. I can't look up. Gail is heaving and shaking next to me. Great-aunt Bertha turns to me:

'When I was in London I used to look after a sick. She was a real lady. I was her companion. I would have liked to stay in England. I asked to stay but they wouldn't let me.'

Gail explodes and runs out of the room. Her mother looks disapproving. I manage to hang on to myself.

That evening Edmund takes Gail and me in the rowing-boat to the middle of Canje Creek because Gail insists that I drink creek water and I won't drink from the edge because it's too muddy and slimy. We row out on to the midnight black and glittering waters of the creek. It is silent apart from a goat-sucker bird calling 'hoo yoo, hoo yoo' in the distance.

'This time tomorrow I'll be in London.'

'What will you be doing?' asks Gail.

'I don't know. I might be in a coffee bar with my friends playing the juke-box.'

'Play something for me.'

'What?'

'"Blue-suede shoes" by Elvis Presley.'

'Oh phooey that's old. They won't still have it.' I can tell that she is hurt. I am sitting behind Edmund. I kiss him on the back of his shoulder so lightly he doesn't notice. Gail grasses me up:

'She kissin' you, Edmund.' He ignores me.

I lean over the edge of the boat, cup my hands and scoop up some of the water. It is clear and refreshing.

'Now you must come back,' says Gail. 'Now you're bound to come back.' And her voice is full of spite.

Wearied and scorched, they bury Wat as best they can in the muddy bank of the creek. His father's demeanour is grim and he says no prayers. They just sit around for a bit. After they have gone, dead leaves, twigs, bark and moss begin to float and fall on to the burial spot, the first signs of rain. Seed-pods plummet and burst on the water and heavy raindrops start to pock the surface of the creek. Out on the lake torrential rains flatten the reeds at the water's edge. Everything turns grey. Wat's body, loosened from its grave, begins a quest of its own through the network of creeks and streams and rivers.

A month later, Wat's father gives up his search for the tantalizing city of El Dorado and writes in his log:

'It's time to leave Guiana to the sun whom they worship and steer northwards.'

I am back at last. The old metal bucket of a ferry dips in the sweet brown waters of the Berbice River, passes Crab Island and ties up at the stelling.

I walk through the town to the house. The Po' Boy tree is still there but the house looks ramshackle, sagging on its rigid wooden stilts, the wood where the paint has peeled, grey from the sun.

I haven't told my aunts I'm coming. I'm going to surprise them. I go up the steps to the front door and announce myself through the open slats of the jalousies. There is no sign of life.

'It's me. Frank's daughter,' I say, in case in their old age they have forgotten my name.

Through the slatted door I see a shape. It is one of my aunts. She doesn't open the door. I peer through. She is swaying and wringing her hands.

'Avril. It's me. Open the door.'

I can hear her moaning softly:

'Oh this is disastrous. Oh this is disastrous. Deep trouble. We in deep trouble.'

Finally she opens the door. I hear Aunt Rosa's voice on the telephone, shriller than I remembered it:

'I tell you it's a plot, Laura. They're lying to you. They're all on drugs. Don' believe them.' She hangs up and turns around. Both of them are neatly dressed in blouses and slacks. Aunt Rosa's hair is still in the same black roll at the front but her face has shrunk with age and her eyes are blazing:

'So you've come back. I suppose you want our money. Well you're unlucky. We haven't got any.'

We go into the living-room. The place is in dusty disorder. Aunt Rosa stands by the window, angry and troubled:

'I didn't want you to see us like this. Why did you come? We all busted up over here. The family is all busted up. Laura is in the hospital with some kinda sclerosis. She's twisted up in the bed like a hermit crab and all the doctors and nurses are on drugs, I can see it in their eyes.'

Avril is moving about, muttering, picking up things and putting them down again, pulling at the frizzy hair round her dark impassive face:

'STOP STILL FOR ONE MINUTE WILL YOU, AVRIL?' screams Aunt Rosa. 'Your niece is here from England. Don't you remember her? We raised her and then she left.'

'Where's Auntie Florence?' I ask timidly.

'We had to send her up to Canada to your Uncle Bertie's. She livin' in the past. She talkin' to the dead. She thinks they're still alive. She anxious and upset all the time. She thought everything in the house was on fire. Even us, her sisters. She saw us burnin' up burnin' up like paper, black with a red edge. Paper sisters. She's turned into a screwball.'

She moves over to the sofa and sits there gripping her walking-stick and turning it round and round. I try to think of somebody who could help:

'What about the Frasers? Do you still see them?'

'Oh they left a long time ago, Toronto, New Orleans, somewhere. They all left. I didn't think my brothers would leave but they did. They all left and married white, street-walkin' bitches. They left us behind because we were too dark.'

She leans forward and speaks passionately:

'I loved my brothers. My brothers are innocent. It's their wives that keep them from us. Especially that red-headed bitch that stole Bertie.

Mind you, Bertie could charm a cobra. Bertie could charm a camoodie. She drugs Bertie, you know, so that he can't come back.'

She sniffs the air:

'I can smell somethin',' she says suddenly.

'What?'

'Somethin' I shouldn't be smellin',' she snaps. She is glaring at me suspiciously:

'You don' look like you used to.'

'How not?'

'You used to have brown eyes.'

'No I didn't. Look, there's a photo of me on the dresser. I always had blue eyes.' I go and get it. It's dusty like everything else. The sight of it throws her into a venomous rage:

'Just because you've got white skin and blue eyes you think you haven't got coloured blood in you. But you have. Just like me. It's in your veins. You can't escape from it. There's mental illness in the family too.'

I am shocked. She continues in an unstoppable outburst:

'You sent your father's ashes back here because he had mixed blood. You were too ashamed to let him stay in England. And you're black-mailing your cousin over there for the same reason. If anyone finds out he'll lose his job! Why do you do these terrible things? You were a nice chile. Why do you do all these terrible things?'

'Do you have anything to drink in the fridge?' My stomach is churning.

'I don' know. Go and look. Everything's gone middly-muddly over here.'

I open the fridge door and recoil. Inside, the contents are webbed with mould from all the electricity cuts. I go back to the living-room:

'Tomorrow I'll fix for somebody to come in and help you.'

'We don' want strangers pokin' their noses in, seeing what's happened to us.' She lowers her head then jerks it up:

'Your father's skin was whiter than mine. If he'd been my colour your mother never would have married him!'

'Rosa. We're in the nineteen-eighties. Nobody cares about that sort of thing any more.'

'You think I'm crazy?' she sneers. I go over to Avril to give her a hug. She pushes me away:

'I'm not the affectionate type,' she says. 'Oh, this is terrible. This is really awful.'

'AVRIL YOU'RE A DONKEY,' shouts Aunt Rosa. 'She's mentally ill too. She's ashamed of her illness. She hasn't left the house for a year. She too frighten'. I do the shopping. Everything was fine until January the fifth, then it all stopped.' Avril starts to mumble a litany of potential disasters:

'What will happen when she leaves? There will be all those people in the street. What will she do? And it might rain. She might get wet.'

'I hope she melts,' snarls Aunt Rosa.

Suddenly, she puts her head in her hands:

'I don' know what's happened to us,' she says.

That night I try and sleep. The room is musty. The sheet is damp with humidity. The mosquito net has holes all over. Through the night I hear one or other of them pacing the house. I half-sleep and doze because it gets into my head that they might set fire to my room.

It is evening when I reach Georgetown. The great house is just as I remember it.

The sight of Evelyn at the door fills me with relief. I notice the fine net of grey over her coarse tight curls.

'Goodness, Evelyn. My aunts have gone crazy in New Amsterdam.'

'So I hear. Well you know what they say. All the mad people are in Berbice. You should come back here for good. Not just for your aunts. There is so much to do here to turn this country round.'

I follow her up the old circular wooden staircase. Sitting on the steps half-way up is a black woman in a loose skirt. Next to her are two sacks marked: 'US Famine Aid. Destination Ethiopia.' Evelyn sees my curious stare:

'You are shocked? She's a smuggler from the Corentyne. We past shame in this country. There are people for whom crime is still a shock. We way past that stage. Way past. That is wheat flour she tryin' to sell.'

We go into the large kitchen and Evelyn fetches me a glass of freshly squeezed grapefruit juice. It tastes deliciously bitter and cool after the hot journey.

'Have you got a match, Evelyn?' I'm waving a cigarette in the air.

'You din' bring matches?' She laughs. 'You have forgotten what it is like to live in a country that is bankrupt. There is no milk in the country. Dried milk costs twelve US dollars a bag. Money has left the banks. Money is dancin' around in the streets. The black market rules here now. Come and I will show you which room you are staying in. The others are in a political meeting downstairs. They said they will see you in the morning.'

In my room I fix the mosquito net. Evelyn is leaning against the door jamb:

'You have everything you need?'

'Yes. Thanks. I'm going to bed, now. I'm exhausted. We'll talk in the morning.'

'You know,' says Evelyn, 'you should stay. If the party could get hold of two hundred thousand US dollars we could turn this country round. I will get it somehow. I am telling you, this place could be a paradise.'

After she has gone I peer through the jalousies. Outside is a sugar-apple tree and dragon-tongue shrubs by the brick path below. In the yard I can see the rusted shells of two cars.

LAWRENCE SCOTT

The House of Funerals

I

The morning sun blazed down hot on to the small, rusty-roofed houses with filigreed, white, lattice-work verandas, yellowing. Fern baskets, hanging from eaves festooned with cobwebs, dripped.

The tumbledown town tumbled down to the wharf in the bay on the gulf and jangled with Indian music. On the High Street loudspeakers blared from the doorways of Ramnarine's Garment Palace and shattered the glass cases in Patel's Jewel Box.

The sea in the bay on the gulf glinted.

Above the traffic and the commerce of the town, on top of the hill with the fir trees, the jangle achieved a monotony. The heat, like a mirage, floated above the pitch road cut into the ochre earth winding up the hill.

On the gulf the mirage hung above the glinting, clamped downfast, leaden lid of the sea; the grey lid of an ancestral vault.

The jangling tumbled-down town, the sweating morning, the jalousies-shuttered room behind Teresa's Hairdressing Salon to which Gaston, the grandson of Cecile Monagas went 'to play in the dirty water with that coolie girl' as his mother would say, the gravediggers in Paradise Cemetery, the women in the flower shop entwining sweet-lime bushes into wreaths with tuberoses and catalair orchids, the women of the Legion of Mary and Father Sebastian the parish priest, all waited expectantly for the news that Cecile Monagas de los Macajuelos had eventually died.

2

Now on top of the hill in the garden with the fir trees there was the house: a vantage point from which to see the plains seeping from the swamps towards the continental cordillera of mountains in the north; the cocoa hills, ridged and green like the back of an iguana, rising and falling across the centre of the island; the dusty fringes of sugar cane disappearing into the southern forests, black with oil – the blue-stone house in the garden with the fir trees overlooking the gulf; each blue-stone quarried from the cliffs near the sea on the north coast of the island and brought to the top of the hill by African men, women and children: overseered, cajoled and sometimes paid weekly by Carlos Monagas de los Macajuelos; watched by Madoo the nightwatchman, the son of an indentured labourer, so that the people in the shacks below the hill would not steal the bricks and iron rods for the foundations in order to build their own fragile huts in the shadow of the blue-stone house; in the shadow and the shade of its courtyards, terraces, staircases leading to sunken gardens of roses and anthurium lilies growing beneath mango trees – the house with the grotto of the Blessed Virgin Mary at the end of the path near the calabash tree whose interior was cool with ferns potted in damp black earth and palms growing beneath arches and under alcoves in whose recesses there were busts of Venus and other goddesses: floors of polished parquet, mahogany chairs, tables, marble-topped chests of drawers from the sale of Napoleon the Third's palace, crystals and china in cabinets, portraits on the walls. In the bedroom of the house above the orchid house at whose window-sill she used to stand and watch the gulf and pray to the Virgin, Cecile Monagas de los Macajuelos died at dawn. She had been dying for years.

'Poor dear. Mariana my child this is the end of an era.' Marie-Claire, the sister of Cecile, stroked the hair of her niece. They touched their eyes with embroidered, linen handkerchiefs, blotting the first tears.

The purple, pink, white and gold blooms which perched like carnival butterflies upon the rubbery leaves growing out of the dry logs encrusted with dry moss, hung from wires in the orchid house, rotting.

Carlos Monagas, Cecile's husband, had grown them and then died from inhaling nicotine and the fungal dust.

Carlos had died at Pentecost and the church had to be stripped of its festive red and draped in black for the requiem. The vases of red exhoras were banked in the sacristy.

He was buried in the ancestral grave beneath the marble angel with the broken arm. Someone had wanted to steal the bouquet of lilies from the clenched fist of the messenger of heaven.

Cecile then began to die. Carlos her rock of Gibraltar had sunk into the gulf or that is what her sister and family thought. 'This will be the end of Cecile.' What they saw sitting near to the casket like one of Carlos's orchids, white and wearing a purple dress, was a stunned Cecile. Like a butterfly which, buffeted and knocked suddenly to the ground, as suddenly takes to the air for a day, to freedom: Cecile's freedom was like that of the butterfly.

She bought a car and could be seen at all parts of the island recording the changing landscapes of both the dry and wet seasons; holding on for dear life to her easel as she faced the windswept ocean raging in from off the Atlantic, so that she could depict the last detail in the yellowing frond of a coconut tree, bent to the brink of the water with its crown twisted back towards the land by the force of the wind. She became daring and swore at the sky which resisted being captured in a drop of coloured water on her white pad. 'They change so quickly,' she used to say, stamping her feet. She could be found in remote country villages painting the shacks of the poor and village women with baskets on their heads.

Her enthusiasm for life was so intense after the death of Carlos that she would come home quite amazed at the happiness of the world. 'Why was everyone smiling and waving at me today on the way back from mass? The town was so happy as I was going down High Street.'

'But Mummy, you're mad. High Street is a one-way street, an up street.'

'Don't tell me that dear. It could only be Saint Christopher and the hosts of guardian angels who saved me.'

She broke through traffic lights in her eagerness.

But this burst and last claim on life was as short-lived as the life of a butterfly because the pain and endurance of the years had already destroyed her nervous system. Her last paintings became abstract as she could no longer control her fingers. They were splodges, blotches; the bursting of atoms, molecules, elemental. The water and the paints on the window-sill dried up. The last entries in her diary were dots, waiting, trying to steady her fingers.

The tinkle of the viaticum alerted Marie-Claire and Mariana as Father Sebastian entered the house of funerals followed by the acolyte with the bell and the bucket of holy water. Alicia the old nurse followed behind.

The women worked fast fearing putrefaction. They washed the thin, dead limbs of Cecile's body with soap and water. She was dressed in a blue nightgown because blue is the colour of Our Lady. Marie-Claire shook her head remembering, 'Mariana, I can see her now.'

'Aunty don't start remembering. I don't want to know.'

Marie-Claire sprinkled eau-de-Cologne on to a linen handkerchief and dabbed the forehead of Cecile's body. Afterwards she put the handkerchief to her nose and shook her head. 'I can see her now. I can see her as a bride.'

'Mr Samaroo is coming for the body, Aunty, and Father Sebastian is here.'

'Yes, dear. She died before she could receive communion, but now she is in his arms,' she whispered while stroking the limp hair on Cecile's head.

The women knelt and received the viaticum intended for Cecile. Father Sebastian broke the host into four parts with a crumb for the acolyte. 'This will help you on your way,' he chuckled. He anointed the body of Cecile Monagas de los Macajuelos with the extreme unction: her forehead, lips, ears, nose, eyes, and he stroked the fingertips and the extremity of the toes.

'Mr Samaroo, take care,' Mariana helped to lift her mother's corpse. 'Don't let me down.'

'Madam?' Samaroo's had been preparing bodies for burial in San Andres since before the beginning of the century.

'I'm coming for Mummy at two-thirty. The funeral in the church is at four o'clock.'

'Plenty time madam.'

'The funeral in the church is at four o'clock and I don't want anything to interfere with that. You know how many funerals they have in this town.'

'Take care going down the steps,' said Mr Samaroo the professional.

'At twelve o'clock the women of the Legion of Mary will come and say the rosary and keep vigil. Then there is clothes. Aunty what I going to dress Mummy in now?' Mariana's voice cracked.

'We will think of something dear,' Marie-Claire followed behind the little procession down the stairs: Mr Samaroo and his attendant carrying the body helped by Mariana, Father Sebastian, the acolyte and Alicia. From the bay window of the staircase Marie-Claire could see the gulf.

The sea was like a slate in the vanishing dawn. 'So, Mr Samaroo, have your business finish on time.'

'Yes, madam. You want the body to leave the home at three-thirty?'

'She has to leave from here. This is where she lived. This is where her children born and died. She buried them from here, though she believed that they had flown like angels across the gulf.' Mariana's voice trailed off.

'Yes, madam. I see what you mean.'

'Do you? That is more than I can see. But you understand. She is not going to fly out over the gulf; assumed into heaven body and soul this afternoon. So please do your business properly this morning. You see this heat. Take care the body smell.'

'Madam you know how we does do business. Since my great-grandfather doing this thing. OK boy, rest down here, open the hearse door.'

'Take care, she so frail,' Alicia keened.

All the time Marie-Claire muttered, 'May the angels of heaven take her in their arms to Paradise.'

'And the advertisement, madam, since 1888 we working for people in distress and now we have these new methods from America.'

'All the same Mr Samaroo heat is heat.' When she was a little girl her grandmother said that she looked as delicate and pretty as a porcelain figurine on the dressing-table of Marie Antoinette. She had grown old giving birth to sons.

The procession dispersed; Mr Samaroo with the corpse and Father Sebastian's blessing.

'Father Sebastian, the bells, you won't forget to toll the bells?' Mariana cried out to the priest.

'Quite right Mariana. Good of you to remember the bells.' Marie-Claire turned to go into the house.

Alicia, who was reputed to be a hundred years old, returned to the servants' quarters with her ancestry. Her father had been an English overseer and her mother an African slave. She came from Barbados to be nurse to generations of Monagas children. In the courtyard outside her room she looked up to the sky, 'Miss Mariana, Miss Mariana, corbeaux circling in the sky.'

At that moment a fast car with screeching tyres drove up into the yard; skidding on the pods from the flamboyant tree. 'Oh God all yuh, get out me way nuh.' It was Gaston, Mariana's son.

'Where have you been all night? In that dirty water again?' Mariana turned to go into the house.

This was Gaston, grandson of Gaston Monagas de los Macajuelos, great-grandson of Gaston Monagas de los Macajuelos from the matrilineal blood; the descendant of caballeros and conquistadores with fat features and dark shadows over his eyes. His shirt was open and gold chains with medals of Our Lady of the Immaculate Conception and Saint Christopher nestled in the hairs of his chest. He was sweating. 'God all yuh, leave a man alone nuh. Give a man a chance nuh.'

'Your grandmother died in the night and that is where you spend the night, shaming me and your father and the name of your family,' Mariana screamed.

'My father, shame?'

'Madam, son.' Alicia raised her eyes to the sky searching the circling corbeaux.

The bedroom above the orchid house overlooking the gulf was left to air. The bedspreads were pulled off and the mosquito net drawn back. Cecile had died on her marriage bed. It was made of saman wood, cut from a tree in the pasture of her father's and grandfather's estate. The carpenter had built, under the instructions and design of her husband, a canopy giving her the shade which is given beneath those trees. It rose to a crown carved with wild English flowers from which hung the capacious folds of the fine mosquito net, like the train of her daughter-brides, or her own bridal lace, or that of her mother and grandmother before her.

It was a bed of births and deaths into which had soaked the amniotic waters, the blood of the womb and the vaginal tissue. It was the bed into which she had miscarried nine times: baptizing with water from the basin near her bed; with her own hands and prayers; in hope and faith the soul had already filtered like sunlight through muslin or a blue afternoon. She dipped her fingers into the salt of the amniotic water and searched for tongues, ears, noses, fingers, and toes to anoint.

'Do you renounce Satan and all his works?' she asked and immediately whispered back to herself, 'I do.' She whispered again, 'And all his pomp?' Again, 'I do.' She spoke for the formless and speechless lips, wet between her legs, or which she pulled up to her breasts to suckle in hope; umbilically tied so that she was even more entitled to speak for them.

The little white satin-covered coffins which were lined with quilted taffeta were brought to this bedroom nine times for those rescued from limbo by the ministrations of Cecile Monagas de los Macajuelos.

Bells in the parish church of San Andres rang with joy nine times for the little angels assumed into heaven.

Marie-Claire pulled off the linen sheets; damp with the sweat of death. She looked at the bed and shook her head. They had all known and kept silent.

She remembered the convent girl in the dormitory hidden beneath the linen shroud to change her clothes; hiding from her own body, a child of nuns with crisp habits and linen veils.

They had all been so excited. 'We are going to give out Cecile's engagement,' her mother had announced on the veranda. She could see her now in the armchair near the ledge with the angel-hair ferns. She filled the chair with her broad hips sitting with her snow-white hair, the mending basket at her feet and the low mahogany table set with cups and saucers for tea. 'Carlos Monagas has been to see your father.' The old French family to be united with the old Spanish family; there was great excitement.

The grave of his ancestors was in the ancient city of San José de

Orunya, where the river has run dry and the spirits float in the candlelit air on All Souls night.

Mrs de Lapeyrouse had dug deep into her chest for the old, soft lace of her own wedding dress. There was no time to wait for a dress from Paris. Carlos was leaving for South America. The wedding day would be within the month. Cecile wore gold on her wedding day. The lace had turned yellow; penetrated by moths.

Marie-Claire dusted the room. She paused at the window-ledge and stared out over the gulf. The images of her sister's girlhood rose to meet her from the leaden vault.

She had been so frail, so pale; like the white of blanched almonds in her yellowing dress. Carlos had thought of her as an orchid; like the orchid that he had found near the bleached driftwood at Galeota.

Then the morning at the wharf when they all waited to say farewell and to board the old rusting steamer, *La Concepcion*. Marie-Claire remembered turning to her mother, 'Mother, what will she do? What does she know?'

'Carlos Monagas is a gentleman,' her mother smiled, remembering her own wedding night at sixteen.

When Cecile returned from South America it was left to Father Sebastian to guide her soul and to bury the dead angels.

3

The afternoon stretched out into the eternity which Father Sebastian had prayed for. The traffic jam began to build up in the High Street. Gaston, Mariana's son, parked his fast car in the open gutter. He went into the back room at Teresa's Hairdressing Salon. As his mother would say, and Alicia deplore, 'to play in the dirty water', but his father, thumping him on the shoulder, would advise him, 'Take care with them young Indian beti, boy.' The loudspeakers proclaimed their bargains. The Indian music sang high in the telephone and electric wires strung out low over the emblazoned roofs. Zinc creaked and syncopated rhythms throbbed from taxis and transistors.

The verandas dripped.

The sea crinkled like galvanized roofs into the blue afternoon which stretched like membrane over the skeleton of a mountain in Venezuela.

The time of Cecile Monagas lived on. It lived on in the linen sheets; washed in suds and sunned in the courtyard; shaken and ironed by Alicia; folded and brought up on a wooden tray for her madam to count and arrange in the linen press on the landing at the top of the steps in the blue-stone house. Cecile Monagas's time lived on: her fingers lived on in the embroidery on the pillowcases; in the tablecloths bargained for on the front steps of the blue-stone house with the Syrian merchant who brought his suitcases from Lebanon; in the filigreed lace which ran through the brown fingers of Mr Khan from Madras; in the doily mats from Madeira brought by the Portuguese wholesaler who had climbed Mount Mora in the hot sun.

Cecile Monagas had lived her time. It was accounted for in the shopping lists recorded at the back of her diaries, each item costed; in the weekly checks of the linen to see that the servants had not been stealing; in the lists of the babies' layettes; nine layettes kept in tissue-paper and preserved in mothballs, but sweetened with cuscus grass from Dominica. There were christening gowns which had never been worn, lace bonnets and skull caps. Her presence lingered on in the souvenirs of her honeymoon and other paraphernalia of a young bride.

Her time was in the arrangements of flowers which young brides remembered in the sanctuary on their wedding day and which startled first communicants by the perfume of the frangipani bouquets. These were the same first communicants who were instructed in their faith and remembered her like a second mother. She gave them, at seven years old, a profound initiation into the mysteries of the immortality of the soul; why Adam and Eve were banished from the garden of Eden by an angel with a flaming sword and why Eve would bring forth children in sorrow and pain; of mortal sin and how far venial sin stretched; of efficacious grace; the infallibility of the Pope; the transubstantiation of bread into flesh and wine into blood; the ascension of the Lord; his transfiguration and the assumption of his mother, the Virgin, into heaven, complete with body and soul. These truths, like the eternity of the afternoon; these words, possessed the time of Cecile Monagas; so intimately were they part of her that they kept recurring on the lips of the old women of the Legion of Mary that morning in the sacristy while they polished the brass candlesticks which would stand on either side of the black, draped catafalque on which the coffin of Cecile Monagas would rest at the centre of the church.

Ever since early morning, when he had anointed the body of Cecile Monagas, Father Sebastian had been remembering her confessions. He alone possessed a part of her which had now floated above the gulf into the clear dawn of the distant mountains of Venezuela; her invisible soul.

He remembered her, early, before the six o'clock mass, in the line for the confessional.

'Bless me, Father, for I have sinned, Father it is one day since my last confession.'

At first, he used to be surprised when he slid back the varnished, latticed shutters, to hear the small voice of Cecile Monagas yet again, when she had only been there the morning before. But then he became accustomed to her almost daily visits to him, as the representative of her God, the judge and forgiver of her sins.

'My child there is no need for you to come each day.' The priest felt that he had no other alternative but to try and restrain her need to come to him each morning; particularly when Cecile could not formulate precisely the name of her sin and its dimensions, but only that she carried about within her a sense of the enormity of sin and that she was sinful by nature.

'My child, for your penance I want you to say your daily rosary with special devotion for those souls who are trapped in purgatory and for the sins of the world, which weigh down upon the shoulders of our crucified Lord and which pierce the heart of his Virgin Mother.' He knew that these intentions would give her enormous joy and purpose.

It took Cecile years to come to a formulation of her sin. At first she thought that there were so many. Like the story of the gospel: 'My name is Legion for I am many.' She imagined her sin like little devils pricking into her with their tridents, like the *jab molasse* at Carnival or the devils in the murals on the walls of the convent. They were scruples which interrupted her daily activities: that she hadn't kissed her husband's cheek with sufficient fervour before he went to work; she had not completed her mending; or that a crumb had passed her lips inadvertently before going to the six o'clock mass and she had received communion having broken her fast; she had lost her temper with Alicia; she felt too exhausted to play with the children; she had not weeded the rose-bed with Madoo and the bajac ants had invaded on floating leaves upon the water in the anti-formica clay pots and stripped leaves and petals from Our Lady's roses. They arrayed themselves and invaded with such persistence. She had made a noise and disturbed Carlos in the stillness of the orchid house as she crushed the pebbles so they crunched and he was rustled from his velvet scents, nicotine and the fungal dust.

Her visits to Father Sebastian became more frequent. She needed to see him before and after mass. She visited him in his office in the presbytery, because during mass, at the crucial moment of the consecration she was filled with a sense of sin; she remembered seeing her body in the mirror of the bathroom and so she was unworthy to receive the host.

Father Sebastian had to become more than just her parish priest and confessor. He became her spiritual director.

She gave him her soul: the most secret and immortal part of herself; into his hands, soft with blue veins; smelling of hosts, holy oils and incense. His breath always had a stale, sweet smell of the communion wine, the blood of Christ. She gave to him that part of herself she taught the children to take most care of in order to direct it heavenwards away from the pit of hell and its scrupulous devils.

At lunchtime the women of the Legion of Mary went to Samaroo's to keep the afternoon vigil and to say the rosary. They arrived as the attendants wheeled out from the embalming room the prepared body of Cecile in its mahogany casket with simple brass handles and cross upon the lid. She was arranged in quilted satin like an artificial orchid in a plastic box you give loved ones on birthdays and anniversaries. Mariana and Marie-Claire had sent her purple lace dress. Mr Samaroo, with the power of all his art, skills and new methods from America, had arranged what little hair was left into a nimbus of silver curls.

In the presbytery Father Sebastian sat alone at the lunch table gathering the crumbs of bread into little mountains. The fan on top of the corner cupboard whirred and swivelled, giving him an intermittent breeze. The water jug sweated dripping into the tablecloth. He squashed a soft grain of rice between his fingers. That morning he had thought of crushed wheat and stamped grapes at the consecration.

In the orchid house below the bedroom of the blue-stone house the orchids on their logs were still rotting. The birds which were accustomed to sing and flick silver from the bird bath in their flight had vanished into the sizzling stillness. The pipe in the orchid house dripped, filling the barrel so that it eventually overflowed, and the water seeped through the pebbles to the underlying moss, all the time saturating the stone walls, growing with ferns, oozing into the beds with anthurium lilies, like a wet grave.

While the housekeeper did the washing-up Father Sebastian hung up his cassock behind the door of his bedroom and lay down in his vest and underpants beneath the whirr of the ceiling fan. The Indian music from the bargain parade continued to advertise the seventy-five-per-cent discount in honour of the day, the coming weekend, the next weekend, the recession and the inflation. The picture of the Sacred Heart knocked against the wall in the hot air.

Gaston's car was still parked in the gutter with the dirty water running down the drain. He was still in the back room of Teresa's Hairdressing Salon.

The back room of Teresa's Hairdressing Salon kept its shutters closed so that the room sweated and the bedsprings creaked endlessly into the afternoon under the weight of Gaston's oppression. The weight of centuries humped into that ridiculous bottom. He had forgotten that it was the day that his grandmother had died but he kept remembering his father's advice, 'Take care with them beti, boy', and understood that his father's advice had come from experience.

Father Sebastian had a distinct sense of loss. The soul of Cecile Monagas had slipped through his consecrated fingers; young and nervous like a bride on her first night.

He imagined a young bird, fluttering, trapped in a house: the fear of the bird and the fear it engendered in the witness and perpetrator of its entrapment and in him, the person trying to free it, struggling with its rescuer. He was pained by the reverberations of its struggle and its attempt to find an open window.

In the last days it lay still as the body gave up living and the skin seemed to fade over the bones, transparent, so that the soul could slip through. When he anointed her body he did it in the belief that it had been a tabernacle.

The celibate had wooed her soul for Christ. Each morning she brought him her fear.

She had formulated her sin. She could not remember whether she had consummated her marriage.

'Father I can't remember. I am denying my husband his right.'

'My child look at your daughter.'

'But Father I pray to Our Lady of the Immaculate Conception.'

He attempted to remind her of the evidence of her life: her daughter who had lived; the baptisms she had administered; the memory of the nine little angels assumed into heaven. He reminded her of the taffeta-quilted, white satin coffins under the earth in Paradise Cemetery.

But each morning the amnesia returned as she woke with her heart fluttering like the wings of the trapped bird: waking with Carlos near to her before he left to descend to the orchid house for the morning inspection, but not being able to remember. There was a lid over her dreams, memories, as vast as the lid over the gulf; a grey shadow, the Holy Spirit brooding over the waters at the beginning of creation, overshadowing her.

Father Sebastian absolved her so that she could make a new start, each day a new start to try and remember. Then Carlos had died.

Father Sebastian dozed off in his underpants and vest under the whirring fan as he reminded himself that he must tell the sexton to toll the bells.

The mourners began to arrive at the house, standing about the yard in little groups; the relatives and the white friends. In the church the women of the Legion of Mary had begun the fifteen mysteries of the rosary.

The gravediggers endured their vigil with lots of rum, leaning on their forks and spades sunk into the wet earth after they had tidied away the rotting planks of Carlos's coffin and overcome their astonishment at the remnants of the nine white satin coffins.

Alicia could not stay inside her room, battened down in the servants' quarters off the courtyard, outside the kitchen. There was no air. The trees did not stir and there was not a sound of a bird. There was only the monotony of the town and a little nearer the drip of the pipe in the orchid house. She dragged her stool under the arch which opened on to the path to the orchid house and the sunken garden. She liked to sit there because she could see the sea from there.

'So madam gone,' she said to herself with her one hundred years. She stared at the sea and the swoop of the circling corbeaux over the gulf.

The wreaths began to arrive at the house and at the church piled up in the doorways, at the back of cars and on top of the hearse standing in the yard at the front of the blue-stone house; beginning to suffocate the atmosphere with the perfume of their dying blooms.

The women in the flower shops brushed up the wilting sweet-lime leaves and the dust of the asparagus fern.

Father Sebastian had woken and showered and put on a clean white cassock. He sat in his rattan rocker on the veranda of the presbytery behind the ledge with the pots of eucharist lilies, reciting the Magnificat: 'My soul doth magnify the Lord'.

The Indian music, the transistors and the stereo taxis kept up their incessant screech and throb.

These last preparations for the obsequies of Cecile Monagas de los Macajuelos did not penetrate the sunless, shuttered and sweating room at the back of Teresa's Hairdressing Salon. Gaston had forgotten about his car parked in the gutter and that he was to be a pall-bearer. It was creating a traffic jam in the High Street and no one had any idea whose it was, so careful had he been about his incognito. Two policemen kept walking around it, writing down the registration number and the number of the licence and tax disc into little black books and then walking away again. Taxi drivers shouted and gesticulated at it and pedestrians waiting for a taxi leant up on it allowing Coca-Cola and curry juice from *barras* to drip on to it. None of this entered the emptied brain of Gaston. His activity had created a state of amnesia.

Marie-Claire had arrived back at the house in the same sweating afternoon to receive her sister's body from Samaroo's. She had powdered her nose and tidied her grey hair into a bun at the nape of her neck and wore a lilac dress. She had on a white hat with a tulle veil to blur her tears. She stood on the terrace with a cloud of blue plumbago and white

Queen Anne's lace in front of her. She stared out over the gulf towards the mountains; the foothills of the Andes rising to the heights of Venezuela over the archipelago of linking islands, beyond the island of Patos.

'Aunty what you staring at?' Mariana called from the window upstairs. 'Mr Samaroo should be here any minute.'

'Just thinking dear.' She kept on staring, remembering. She remembered her mother and grandmother whose ancestor rode on his horse beside Bolivar.

The leaden lid of the vault would once again open to receive one of her own. She stared at the gulf.

The gulf stared back at her. This was the gulf into which the ships with the slaves of Lopinot and Roume St Laurent had sailed. This was the gulf into which had sunk the burning galleons of Apodoca; the English, French and Spanish ships of plunder. This was the gulf into which had flowed the blood of suicidal Amerindians claiming themselves in death rather than capture. Into this gulf had flowed the disinfectant from off the bodies of indentured Indians whose children and women ate clay in the quarantine camps on the island of Nelson. It was from the waters of this gulf that the baptisms were administered to innocent people. And it was along the shores of this gulf that a young black girl of fourteen had strolled, smoking a cigar, and had later been taken to an upper room in the port and tortured with the chains of the Inquisition.

The gulf stared back, inscrutable and metallic. Marie-Claire arranged a strand of stray grey hair behind her ear and into the folds of her bun. She thought about her own death.

Mr Samaroo delivered the coffin, lifting it carefully, with the help of attendants, into the drawing-room where the murmur of the rosary continued like the tide. Five mysteries of the rosary were recited while the relatives and white friends crushed through the front doors into the hallway, overflowing on to the terraces, until the house was once again a house for a funeral. Women fanned themselves and the men mopped their brows, sweating in their stuffed suits. Eau-de-Cologne and Chanel No. 5 dripped in the perspiration.

'Where is that son of mine?' Mariana came and knelt near to Marie-Claire who was praying into the open coffin.

'Leave it in God's hands, my dear.' Marie-Claire continued with the rosary fingering the crystal beads.

'I wish I could say that he was in God's hands now, instead of you know whose arms.' Mariana stifled her anger out of respect for her mother and because she did not want to cause an embarrassment.

The five mysteries faded into the ejaculations for the dead. The pall-bearers came to lift the coffin. Mr Samaroo, with generations of etiquette and respect, substituted for Gaston.

The doors of the hearse were shut and the last stages of Cecile Monagas de los Macajuelos' funeral procession began to wind its way slowly down from the top of Mount Mora; from the top of the hill with the fir trees in the garden of the blue-stone house overlooking the gulf. It descended, one car behind the other, behind the hearse: brakes creaking, bumpers almost scratching the chrome of the other; each car packed with family, weighted down and suffocating under wreaths stacked behind the back seats and on the bonnets. The procession descended into the jangling, tumbledown town: sweating, throbbing and locked in an inextricable traffic jam, because unknown to them all, family and friends, Gaston's car was holding up the traffic in the High Street, parked in front of Teresa's Hairdressing Salon.

Waiting in the church, the people of the town congregated: the black people who had known Miss Monagas; the women of the Legion of Mary both the Junior and Senior Praesidiums; representatives from the Catholic Youth Organization; the first communion classes and the confirmation classes; the Catholic wing of the Girl Guides and Boy Scouts; nurses from the Red Cross who had laboured over the body of Carlos Monagas; members of the Horticultural Society who had gone to the blue-stone house for orchid exhibitions; the Society of the Sacred Heart; children of Our Lady of Fatima and Our Lady of Lourdes packed the aisles and the porticoes of the side-doors. Black people who usually congregated on the bandstand opposite the Town Hall and Indians who sat on the railings around the statue of Mahatma Gandhi came too, pulled by this throng which had taken centuries to collect. Members of the Protestant community, business associates and the Freemasons took their places.

As four o'clock approached the Mother Superior of the convent of

Cluny proceeded across the promenade with her community of nuns following, heads bowed beneath their fluttering linen veils.

Father Sebastian proceeded down the aisle in his capacious black satin cope, billowing out behind him, preceded by acolytes carrying holy water buckets, thuribles with burning coals for incense and candles. They took up their positions at the entrance of the church to receive the body of Cecile Monagas de los Macajuelos.

Father Sebastian had remembered the bells and he had ordered the sexton to begin tolling them at five minutes to four o'clock.

The clergy from the neighbouring parishes and the abbot of the monastery in the mountains filled the sanctuary. The church was dense with prayer and talcum powder.

The ancestral funeral procession took years to battle through the traffic of the centuries and the streets. The people of the town waited for the cortège and the day to progress to the church and thence to Paradise Cemetery.

The procession was stuck in Cipero Street. The High Street was jammed. The orange-sellers, the peanut and channa-vendors at the library corner did a good trade with passengers hanging out of stationary taxis.

Gaston, the last descendant of the Monagas de los Macajuelos, who in these last days were famed for their still gargantuan stature, the mysterious circulation of their blood and the complexity of their digestive systems, had brought the town to a standstill. The projectors in the Radio City, the Rivoli, the Gaiety and the Globe flickered and went out over the matinee performances because no one could get to see them; Maureen O'Hara dying in the arms of Randolph Scott; the massacre of the North American Indians and the crimes of Chicago gangsters.

The people of the town of San Andres stood on the pavements and looked on at what was taking a long time to pass away. The Bible preachers began their sermons of repentance between hallelujahs and the Baptist women lit their candles and rang their bell calling the people together. People were reminded to look at what was passing away and what was taking its place.

The funeral cortège sat in their misted up Mitsubishis, Toyotas, Mazdas, long American and chunky British limousines, refrigerated by air-conditioning.

At five minutes to four o'clock Father Sebastian sent an acolyte to give the sexton the signal to start with the tolling of the bells.

At each successive boom, the tolling of the funeral bells eventually penetrated the sunless and shuttered room at the back of Teresa's Hairdressing Salon. They eventually bored their way through the amnesiacal barrier into Gaston's memory. He suddenly remembered as he lay there, sweating, that this was the day that his grandmother had died and he was a pall-bearer.

He leapt out of bed and picked up his pants from off the floor. 'Girl, ah go see yuh,' he said as he dashed out into the street pulling up his pants and buttoning his crotch.

The congested town heaved forward with the moving of Gaston's car. It was already growing dark when the funeral procession eventually arrived at the church. Father Sebastian had buried the other dead. The St John Ambulance Brigade had attended to the fainting congregation.

The last obsequies were rushed so that Cecile could be buried before nightfall as the law stipulated.

The last shovel of earth was packed down on to the grave. Gaston's father patted him on the shoulder and said, 'Too much beti, boy.'

Alicia, helped along with her one hundred years by Madoo, shook her head as she left the cemetery, 'So madam gone, eh Madoo, madam gone.'

Moon

'Do you know that there is a connection between lovers and Chinese food?' He looks at her with his 'I can't believe this woman' look. 'What?' 'Yes, it's true. I've never been to a Chinese restaurant where there wasn't at least one pair of lovers somewhere in a corner eating while they ate each other with their eyes. Also, you can tell what is the state of the relationship by how they eat and how much they eat.'

He looks across at her and he can't help himself, but he is slightly annoyed. Her vagueness, her far-out ideas which he finds so endearing sometimes annoy him slightly, now. Sometimes, it's like she goes off on an ethereal journey and he is angry because he cannot go all the way with her. Like this lovers and Chinese food theory, it's interesting but he doesn't enter fully into it right away. Sometimes he misses the sensible down-to-earthness of the familiar woman.

If he were with her, they would probably be talking about ways to make money or they'd be discussing something that they had both read in today's newspaper. Sometimes it became very necessary to be around her, her familiarity was so reassuring; but the flip side of that was dull.

Moon (that was their private name for her), Moon, because she liked silvery things and her face was round and there were strong tides of feelings always flowing through her, Moon was something rare. He balanced both women skilfully, he thought, sometimes he was overawed at the amount of riches he possessed in them collectively.

Moon is smiling now, she bends over and is whispering to him, 'Look over there in that corner, do you see that couple?' He glances over and in the corner there is a man in his early fifties, looking like a business executive. He is with a slender young girl who looks like she could have recently joined his firm as a trainee in the marketing department.

The man is ordering from the menu in a confident and experienced way; the girl looks nervous but she is obviously also quite thrilled. The man is in charge, he says to the girl, 'I'm sure you will like Mushrooms in Oyster Sauce, trust me.' The girl nods and says, 'All right.'

The man is speaking a little too loudly, for his last remark hangs in the air, right up there with the fringed red paper lanterns. In spite of himself, David was drawn into the unfolding of the Lovers and Chinese Food Theory.

'You see,' says Moon, 'that's the early stages. They haven't been to bed together yet, the girl is not sure that she should, but she is responding favourably to his bold, masterful "take charge" attitude, she probably will give him her body, and that's the stage the relationship is at. Now later when they are lovers they won't take so much time ordering, they will have favourites by then.'

Then she said, 'What stage do you think our relationship is at?' (That's another thing about Moon, she resisted all rules, grammatically and otherwise.) David was such an organized businesslike type, he hardly ever used slang. He is unprepared for the question. 'What exactly do you mean by that?' he asks her. 'Think about it before you answer me, please,' says Moon. He finds her very endearing right now, she is very exotic looking, sort of Rasta Chic. Sometimes she was so otherworldly, he wonders if he could live with her every day, it would probably be like drinking champagne in the morning or eating lobster every Monday. Sometimes he saved her up, like he used to relish some particularly nice treat as a child; don't eat it right away, save it for a day or two then go to it with all your strength. She had brought a quality to his life he never expected to find, he had not really looked for it because he didn't know it. Like one midday he had returned to work for a meeting to find a telegram on his desk, it just said, 'Come – Moon.'

He had only just left her a few hours before, so he panicked and called her house. The phone just rang and rang. He was forced to cancel the meeting and dash around to her house ... he arrived to find the front door open, he rushes in to find Moon sitting at the dining-table before a feast of fruit and wine, a fat bird-shaped bread as the centre-piece and flowers and lit candles all around the room ... he is stunned. She says, 'Today is the anniversary of the first time I ever saw you, you were boarding an Air Jamaica plane and I asked somebody what your name was and they said ... forget it, he's not your type ... this feast is to prove that they were wrong.' In spite of himself he is overwhelmed, thrilled, he feels a surge of happiness which almost lifts him off the ground ... he just forgets about his meeting and allows himself to be drawn along by this very strong, powerful and refreshing tide. Sometimes he fears he will drown in one of them, but somehow he always emerges feeling like a new man.

He reaches across the table and holds her face between his hands, 'Why are you asking me this now, Moon?'

'Because you will have to choose, soon.'

'Choose? What do you mean?'

'No, you must not do that ... you and I already know what we mean. I just think now is the time for choosing.'

He says, 'Look, you know I don't take ultimatums from *anybody*,' he stresses the anybody, because this turn in the evening has taken him completely by surprise, and he is angry at being caught off guard.

'Oh yes' she says, 'I know that, but this is not an ultimatum though, it's an invitation to choose. You can't have it all, sweetheart, that's greedy,' she giggles. 'It's like trying to eat too much Chinese food, like that man over there.' She motions to the man in the corner, who in his zeal has ordered enough food for four people. She continues, 'Sometimes too much can make you fat and complacent. Aah, maybe I'm too strange for you anyway.' Her voice has become soft, soft. She is humming, and he looks across the table at her. It is very difficult for him to envisage what his life will be like without her, he thinks back to before her, and quickly comes forward. He says, 'I need time to think about this, you are right.' She stops humming, she says, 'OK, I'm going to be gone until you decide. I'm going away tomorrow afternoon.'

'And you are only just telling me this?'

'I anticipated your response, I'm even more knowing than you think.'

He just looks at her dumbfounded. That was another thing about her: people said she 'knew things', she denied that, but sometimes her 'intuition' was very accurate.

They fall silent now, then she takes out a small notepad and begins to read from a list. It's a list of all the arrangements she has put into place for her journey and for her plans to keep her affairs at home going while she is away. He is amazed at how organized and businesslike she sounds.

JAMAICA KINCAID

Song of Roland

His mouth was like an island in the sea that was his face; I am sure he had ears and nose and eyes and all the rest, but I could see only his mouth, which I knew could do all the things that a mouth usually does, such as eat food, purse in approval or disapproval, smile, twist in thought; inside were his teeth and behind them was his tongue. Why did I see him that way, how did I come to see him that way? It was a mystery to me that he had been alive all along and that I had not known of his existence and I was perfectly fine – I went to sleep at night and I could wake up in the morning and greet the day with indifference if it suited me, I could comb my hair and scratch myself and I was still perfectly fine – and he was alive, sometimes living in a house next to mine, sometimes living in a house far away, and his existence was ordinary and perfect and parallel to mine, but I did not know of it, even though sometimes he was close enough to me for me to notice that he smelt of cargo he had been unloading; he was a stevedore.

His mouth really did look like an island, lying in a twig-brown sea, stretching out from east to west, widest near the centre, with tiny, sharp creases, its colour a shade lighter than that of the twig-brown sea in which it lay, the place where the two lips met disappearing into the pinkest of pinks, and even though I must have held his mouth in mine a thousand times, it was always new to me. He must have smiled at me, though I don't really know, but I don't like to think that I would love someone who hadn't first smiled at me. It had been raining, a heavy downpour, and I took shelter under the gallery of a dry-goods store along with some other people. The rain was an inconvenience, for it was not necessary; there had already been too much of it, and it was no longer only outside, overflowing in the gutters, but inside also, roofs were leaking and then falling in. I was standing under the gallery and had sunk deep within myself, enjoying completely the despair I felt at being myself. I was wearing a dress; I had combed my hair that morning; I had washed myself that morning. I was looking at nothing in particular when I saw his mouth. He was speaking to someone else, but he was looking at me. The someone else he was speaking to was a woman. His mouth then was not like an island at rest in a sea but like a small patch of ground viewed from high above and set in motion by a force not readily seen.

When he saw me looking at him, he opened his mouth wider, and that must have been the smile. I saw then that he had a large gap between his two front teeth, which probably meant that he could not be trusted, but I did not care. My dress was damp, my shoes were wet, my hair was wet, my skin was cold, all around me were people standing in small amounts of water and mud, shivering, but I started to perspire from an effort I wasn't aware I was making; I started to perspire because I felt hot, and I started to perspire because I felt happy. I wore my hair then in two plaits and the ends of them rested just below my collar-bone; all the moisture in my hair collected and ran down my two plaits, as if they were two gutters, and the water seeped through my dress just below the collar-bone and continued to run down my chest, only stopping at the place where the tips of my breasts met the fabric, revealing, plain as a new print, my nipples. He was looking at me and talking to someone else, and his mouth grew wide and narrow, small and large, and I wanted him to notice me, but there was so much noise: all the people standing in the gallery, sheltering themselves from the strong rain, had something they wanted to say, something not about the weather (that was by now beyond comment) but about their lives, their disappointments most likely, for joy is so short-lived there isn't enough time to dwell on its occurrence. The noise, which started as a hum, grew to a loud din, and the loud din had an unpleasant taste of metal and vinegar, but I knew his mouth could take it away if only I could get to it; so I called out my own name, and I knew he heard me immediately, but he wouldn't stop speaking to the woman he was talking to, so I had to call out my name again and again until he stopped, and by that time my name was like a chain around him, as the sight of his mouth was like a chain around me. And when our eyes met, we laughed, because we were happy, but it was frightening, for that gaze asked everything: who would betray whom, who would be captive, who would be captor, who would give and who would take, what would I do. And when our eyes met and we laughed at the same time, I said, 'I love you, I love you,' and he said, 'I know.' He did not say it out of vanity, he did not say it out of conceit, he only said it because it was true.

His name was Roland. He was not a hero, he did not even have a country; he was from an island, a small island that was between a sea and an ocean, and a small island is not a country. And he did not have a history; he was a small event in somebody else's history, but he was a man. I could see him better than he could see himself, and that was because he was who he was and I was myself but also because I was taller than he was. He was unpolished, but he carried himself as if he were precious. His hands were large and thick, and for no reason that I could see he would spread them out in front of him and they looked as if they were the missing parts from a powerful piece of machinery; his legs were straight from hip to knee and then from the knee they bent at an angle as if he had been at sea too long or had never learnt to walk properly to begin with. The hair on his legs was tightly curled as if the hairs were pieces of thread rolled between the thumb and the forefinger in preparation for sewing, and so was the hair on his arms, the hair in his underarms, and the hair on his chest; the hair in those places was black and grew sparsely; the hair on his head and the hair between his legs was black and tightly curled also, but it grew in such abundance that it was impossible for me to move my hands through it. Sitting, standing, walking, or lying down, he carried himself as if he were something precious, but not out of vanity, for it was true, he was something precious; yet when he was lying on top of me he looked down at me as if I were the only woman in the world, the only woman he had ever looked at in that way – but that was not true, a man only does that when it is not true. When he first lay on top of me I was so ashamed of how much pleasure I felt that I bit my bottom lip hard – but I did not bleed, not from biting my lip, not then. His skin was smooth and warm in places I had not kissed him; in the places I had kissed him his skin was cold and coarse, and the pores were open and raised.

Did the world become a beautiful place? The rainy season eventually went away, the sunny season came, and it was too hot; the riverbed grew dry, the mouth of the river became shallow, the heat eventually became as wearying as the rain, and I would have wished it away if I had not become occupied with this other sensation, a sensation I had no single word for. I could feel myself full of happiness, but it was a kind of happiness I had never experienced before, and my happiness would spill out of me and run all the way down a long, long road and then the road would come to an end and I would feel empty and sad, for what could come after this? How would it end?

Not everything has an end, even though the beginning changes. The first time we were in a bed together we were lying on a thin board that was covered with old cloth, and this small detail, evidence of our poverty – people in our position, a stevedore and a doctor's servant, could not afford a proper mattress – was a major contribution to my satisfaction, for it allowed me to brace myself and match him breath for breath. But how can it be that a man who can carry large sacks filled with sugar or bales of cotton on his back from dawn to dusk exhausts himself within five minutes inside a woman? I did not then and I do not now know the answer to that. He kissed me. He fell asleep. I bathed my face then between his legs; he smelt of curry and onions, for those were the things he had been unloading all day; other times when I bathed my face between his legs – for I did it often, I liked doing it – he would smell of sugar, or flour, or the large, cheap bolts of cotton from which he would steal a few yards to give me to make a dress.

What is the everyday? What is the ordinary? One day, as I was walking towards the government dispensary to collect some supplies – one of my duties as a servant to a man who was in love with me beyond anything he could help and so had long since stopped trying, a man I ignored except when I wanted him to please me – I met Roland's wife, face to face, for the first time. She stood in front of me like a sentry – stern, dignified, guarding the noble idea, if not noble ideal, that was her husband. She did not block the sun, it was shining on my right; on my left was a large black cloud; it was raining way in the distance; there was no rainbow on the horizon. We stood on the narrow strip of concrete

that was the sidewalk. One section of a wooden fence that was supposed
to shield a yard from passers-by on the street bulged out and was broken,
and a few tugs from any careless party would end its usefulness; in that
yard a primrose bush bloomed unnaturally, its leaves too large, its flowers
showy, and weeds were everywhere, they had prospered in all the wet.
We were not alone. A man walked past us with a cutlass in his knapsack
and a mistreated dog two steps behind him; a woman walked by with a
large basket of food on her head; some children were walking home
from school, and they were not walking together; a man was leaning out
a window, spitting, he used snuff. I was wearing a pair of modestly high
heels, red, not a colour to wear to work in the middle of the day, but
that was just the way I had been feeling, red with a passion, like that
hibiscus that was growing under the window of the man who kept
spitting from the snuff. And Roland's wife called me a whore, a slut, a
pig, a snake, a viper, a rat, a low-life, a parasite, and an evil woman. I
could see that her mouth formed a familiar hug around these words –
poor thing, she had been used to saying them. I was not surprised. I
could not have loved Roland the way I did if he had not loved other
women. And I was not surprised; I had noticed immediately the space
between his teeth. I was not surprised that she knew about me; a man
cannot keep a secret, a man always wants all the women he knows to
know each other.

I believe I said this: 'I love Roland; when he is with me I want him
to love me; when he is not with me I think of him loving me. I do not
love you. I love Roland.' This is what I wanted to say, and this is what
I believe I said. She slapped me across the face; her hand was wide and
thick like an oar; she, too, was used to doing hard work. Her hand met
the side of my face: my jawbone, the skin below my eye and under my
chin, a small portion of my nose, the lobe of my ear. I was then a young
woman in the early twenties, my skin was supple, smooth, the pores
invisible to the naked eye. It was completely without bitterness that I
thought as I looked at her face, a face I had so little interest in that it
would tire me to describe it, Why is the state of marriage so desirable
that all women are afraid to be caught outside it? And why does this
woman, who has never seen me before, to whom I have never made
any promise, to whom I owe nothing, hate me so much? She expected

me to return her blow but, instead, I said, again completely without bitterness, 'I consider it beneath me to fight over a man.'

I was wearing a dress of light-blue Irish linen. I could not afford to buy such material, because it came from a real country, not a false country like mine; a shipment of this material in blue, in pink, in lime green, and in beige had come from Ireland, I suppose, and Roland had given me yards of each shade from the bolts. I was wearing my blue Irish-linen dress that day, and it was demure enough – a pleated skirt that ended beneath my knees, a belt at my waist, sleeves that buttoned at my wrists, a high neckline that covered my collar-bone – but underneath my dress I wore absolutely nothing, no undergarments of any kind, only my stockings, given to me by Roland and taken from yet another shipment of dry goods, each one held up by two pieces of elastic that I had sewn together to make a garter. My declaration of what I considered beneath me must have enraged Roland's wife, for she grabbed my blue dress at the collar and gave it a huge tug; it rent in two from my neck to my waist. My breasts lay softly on my chest, like two small pieces of unrisen dough, unmoved by the anger of this woman; not so by the touch of her husband's mouth, for he would remove my dress, by first patiently undoing all the buttons and then pulling down the bodice, and then he would take one breast in his mouth, and it would grow to a size much bigger than his mouth could hold, and he would let it go and turn to the other one; the saliva evaporating from the skin on that breast was an altogether different sensation from the sensation of my other breast in his mouth, and I would divide myself in two, for I could not decide which sensation I wanted to take dominance over the other. For an hour he would kiss me in this way and then exhaust himself on top of me in five minutes. I loved him so. In the dark I couldn't see him clearly, only an outline, a solid shadow; when I saw him in the daytime he was fully dressed. His wife, as she rent my dress, a dress made of material she knew very well, for she had a dress made of the same material, told me his history; it was not a long one, it was not a sad one, no one had died in it, no land had been laid waste, no birthright had been stolen; she had a list, and it was full of names, but they were not the names of countries.

What was the colour of her wedding day? When she first saw him was she overwhelmed with desire? The impulse to possess is alive in every heart, and some people choose vast plains, some people choose high mountains, some people choose wide seas, and some people choose husbands; I chose to possess myself. I resembled a tree, a tall tree with long, strong branches; I looked delicate, but any man I held in my arms knew that I was strong; my hair was long and thick and deeply waved naturally, and I wore it braided and pinned up, because when I wore it loosely around my shoulders it caused excitement in other people – some of them men, some of them women, some of them it pleased, some of them it did not. The way I walked depended on who I thought would see me and what effect I wanted my walk to have on them. My face was beautiful, I found it so.

And yet I was standing before a woman who found herself unable to keep her life's booty in its protective sack, a woman whose voice no longer came from her throat but from deep within her stomach, a woman whose hatred was misplaced. I looked down at our feet, hers and mine, and I expected to see my short life flash before me; instead, I saw that her feet were without shoes. She did have a pair of shoes, though, which I had seen: they were white, they were plain, a round toe and flat laces, they took shoe polish well, she wore them only on Sundays and to church. I had many pairs of shoes, in colours meant to attract attention and dazzle the eye; they were uncomfortable, I wore them every day, I never went to church at all.

My strong arms reached around to caress Roland, who was lying on my back naked; I was naked also. I knew his wife's name, but I did not say it; he knew his wife's name, too, but he did not say it. I did not know the long list of names that were not countries that his wife had committed to memory. He himself did not know the long list of names; he had not committed this list to memory. This was not from deceit, and it was not from carelessness. He was someone so used to a large fortune that he took it for granted; he did not have a bank-book, he did not have a ledger, he had a fortune – but still he had not lost interest in acquiring more. Feeling my womb contract, I crossed the room, still naked; small drops of blood spilt from inside me, evidence of my refusal to accept his silent offering. And Roland looked at me, his face expressing confusion. Why did I not bear his children? He could feel the times that I was fertile, and yet each month blood flowed away from me, and each month I expressed confidence at its imminent arrival and departure, and always I was overjoyed at the accuracy of my prediction. When I saw him like that, on his face a look that was a mixture – confusion, dumb-foundedness, defeat – I felt much sorrow for him, for his life was reduced to a list of names that were not countries, and to the number of times he brought the monthly flow of blood to a halt; his life was reduced to women, some of them beautiful, wearing dresses made from yards of cloth he had surreptitiously removed from the bowels of the ships where he worked as a stevedore.

At that time I loved him beyond words; I loved him when he was standing in front of me and I loved him when he was out of my sight. I was still a young woman. No small impressions, the size of a child's forefinger, had yet appeared on the soft parts of my body; my legs were long and hard, as if they had been made to take me a long distance; my arms were long and strong, as if prepared for carrying heavy loads; I was not beautiful, but if I could have been in love with myself I would have been. I was in love with Roland. He was a man. But who was he really? He did not sail the seas, he did not cross the oceans, he only worked in the bottom of vessels that had done so; no mountains were named for him, no valleys, no nothing. But still he was a man, and he wanted something beyond ordinary satisfaction – beyond one wife, one love, and one room with walls made of mud and roof of cane leaves, beyond the small plot of land where the same trees bear the same fruit year following year – for it would all end only in death, for though no history yet written had embraced him, though he could not identify the small uprisings within himself, though he would deny the small uprisings within himself, a strange calm would sometimes come over him, a cold stillness, and since he could find no words for it, he was momentarily blinded with shame.

One night Roland and I were sitting on the steps of the jetty, our backs facing the small world we were from, the world of sharp, dangerous curves in the road, of steep mountains of recent volcanic formations covered in a green so humble no one had ever longed for them, of three hundred and sixty-five small streams that would never meet up to form a majestic roar, of clouds that were nothing but large vessels holding endless days of water, of people who had never been regarded as people at all; we looked into the night, its blackness did not come as a surprise, a moon full of dead white light travelled across the surface of a glittering black sky; I was wearing a dress made from another piece of cloth he had given me, another piece of cloth taken from the bowels of a ship without permission, and there was a false pocket in the skirt, a pocket that did not have a bottom, and Roland placed his hand inside the pocket, reaching all the way down to touch inside of me; I looked at his face, his mouth I could see and it stretched across his face like an island and like an island, too, it held secrets and was dangerous and could swallow things whole that were much larger than itself; I looked out towards the horizon, which I could not see but knew was there all the same, and this was also true of the end of my love for Roland.

MAKEDA SILVERA

Baby

Asha woke up to find Baby close. Her nipple was sore from Baby's hunger of the night before. She was tired, her eyes red from too much crying. She eased Baby away, so as not to wake her. Asha left the bedroom and walked down the hall to the bathroom, avoiding a small stain on the carpet. Shit, one of the cats must have vomited last night.

Downstairs in the kitchen, she made herself a cup of coffee and curled up on the sofa with Mooney, the oldest cat. She had five. Mooney was almost seventeen years old.

She was a sucker for cats. A stray only had to come to the front door or the back yard a few times, with an unkept look, hungry eyes, and she would take it in. Friends teased her often.

'Girl, you should have been a vet, you have no business wasting your time as a schoolteacher, look at all dem hundreds of strays just waiting for a home. If we had money girl, we would done set you up on a farm.' They would laugh, rolling their eyes at each other as if she were the strangest person they had ever met.

She got up from the couch, fed the cats and helped herself to another cup of coffee, this time adding ice. It was daybreak, but she could already feel the approaching heat. The cats circled her, some at her feet, others on the couch. When Asha got up they followed her to the half-open kitchen window.

'Dammit, why am I so absent-minded? I have to remember to close this damn window at nights,' she mumbled to herself as the cats dashed through. Asha paused and whispered a silent prayer: 'Thank God, this isn't back home. They would have climbed in and stolen every goddam thing but the cats.'

She needed to be active, take her mind off last night. Doing housework gave her time to think. She washed towels, sheets and a basket of Baby's clothing. By noon she had changed the cat litter, washed the pots and dishes from the night before, and swept and washed the kitchen floor, working up a bucket of sweat.

Asha felt worn, but still she craved the closeness of Baby. She wanted to lie next to her. To listen to her quiet breath and to feel Baby turn lips to breast.

She went back to bed and stripped to her panties; it was going to be a hot one. Oblivious to the heat and still half asleep, Baby reached for Asha's breast. Despite the soreness and the slight bruise, Asha gave in to her, and feeling a sudden warmth come over her body, she slowly drifted in and out of sleep, barely noticing Baby's pull.

It had been an early night. They'd had supper. Fed the cats. Settled upstairs in bed to watch television. A few sitcoms, a game show, a mystery.

Kneeling in front of Baby, Asha had gently undressed her and stroked her with her tongue.

'I would die for you,' said one. Said the other, 'I would kill for you.'

Passion talk.

Love talk.

Woman talk.

It doesn't matter who said what.

With Baby so close, Asha felt grateful for the privacy Canada had given them. Sleepless, she stood in front of the window, looking out. The moon loomed high. The maple tree outside the window, with its full green protective canopy, made her ache for home. No paradise but full of life. She missed the loud dancehall music pushing itself through closed doors, the boisterous talk in the streets, the boys hanging out on the street corner, the sudden knock on the door from an unexpected friend. No maple trees, but fruit trees of every size and description: mango, coconut, orange, papaya, all luscious. Naseberry, guava, sweetsop, and sugar cane, she could almost taste it, juice so s-sweet. Oh, what joy, what pain, that sugar cane. Turning to molasses, turning to rum, turning to export, sweetening white tongues while black tongues taste ash.

Asha was pulled out of her thoughts by a sudden scream from Baby. Baby sat upright, a sour look on her face.

'What's the matter, Baby?' Asha asked, concerned.

'I had another bad dream. I can't take them anymore. It's the same one. Do you love me, Asha?'

'Baby, you know I do; why are you asking me this?'

'The dream, it comes every now and then, it's always the same. We are in a parade, dressed up in masks, costumes . . . and then you disappear on me. I can't find you anywhere.' Baby sulked.

'Baby, it's only a dream; you know I won't leave you. Not now, not ever.'

Baby jumped up suddenly from the bed, chased the cats out of the room, cursing each one by name, and slammed the bedroom door.

Asha sat quietly, watching Baby.

'We have to talk, Asha. We have to talk about us. I can't go on like this.'

Asha got up quietly and lit two candles to aid the moon's glow as it crept through the windows. In the flicker of the candlelight, Baby's eyes sparked anger and determination.

'We have to talk, I tell you. SOMETHING is wrong with our relationship. That dream is about us.' Baby's voice went higher. 'Talk to me, talk to me!' she demanded. 'We go nowhere together, excepting the Hotspot Restaurant, which don't count. We hardly have any friends. All we do is watch TV. It's like I'm invisible in your life . . .' She was now pacing the floor. She waited for a response, but Asha just sat, staring at no place in particular.

'This goddam TV. Aaah, I wish I were a violent person. You know what I'd do?' Baby paused, and with no reply from Asha, she went on. 'I'd kick the shit out of it and throw it through this goddam window.

'Asha, we can't go on like this. I want out. Do you hear me? O-U-T. Out. Watch my mouth, I want to live like a normal person, not in a closet.'

Asha's face was hidden behind a glass of water. 'What do you mean, Baby?' she asked, just to fill the silence.

What Baby could not express in words she said by raking her hands over Asha's face. 'Stop it,' Asha commanded. 'Let's talk, but don't pounce on me like some animal.' Then, her voice soft, she asked, 'Why are you turning on me, Baby? We were fine a few hours ago. Don't let the dream do this.'

Baby replied in a voice as heavy and dark as the night outside, 'These dreams mean something, Asha. They don't just come from no place. They're in my head and my head don't lie. You know what I mean. You do nothing but watch TV. When was the last time we went to the movies? Or to a woman's bar? Or to a party at one of my friends' house? We've never even gone to a damn gay pride parade. Every time I ask you to go out, it's "Oh Baby, there's a good program on TV tonight." Or "Oh Baby, you know I hate the bars."'

It was Asha's turn to say something. 'Baby, you know I don't like the bars, it's not a lie. I don't like the smoke. Have I ever stopped you from going?'

'Who wants to fucking go out alone? My lover is home watching TV and I'm out all alone. What about bingo? What was your excuse last month? Oh yeah, you didn't like gambling. Then the movie, a clean wholesome environment, with popcorn and a soft drink? "Oh Baby, that will come on TV soon." Christ, Asha. I'm only thirty-five years old. I'm not ready for the cobwebs to start growing on me.'

She stopped there, waiting for Asha to say she'd try to change. Asha said nothing.

'Say something, dammit. Look, you don't even respond. Sometimes I just want to walk out of this house and never look back.'

Asha was sitting up in bed, her eyes filling with tears. She tried to pull Baby close.

'Don't touch me, DON'T. If you can't talk to me, don't touch me. You think you can cry a few tears, and everything will be OK, don't you? I should be the one crying. My name is Baby, isn't it?' she goaded. 'No, Asha, I can't cry, that's reserved for you. My well-cultured, well-classed high-school teacher, and that elegant face all dipped in milk chocolate.' Baby stopped now, her smile sharp.

'Isn't it interesting, every time we have a quarrel, you throw my class, my education and my colour in my face. Why is it only when we disagree that they become a cross?' Asha demanded, her face now bitter chocolate.

A look of satisfaction rushed over Baby's face. She'd cut deep.

'Well, I'm packing.' Baby began pulling sweaters and jeans out of drawers. 'I'm tired of this closet. You enjoy it with the cats.'

'I know what I am,' continued Baby. 'I'm a lesbian. A zami. A sodomite. A black-skinned woman. I got no education or family behind my name. I'm just a woman getting by. Asha, I'm ready for war. And you? You're ready to protect the little you have. Your job. Well, for me it just isn't enough.'

Asha bent over to touch Baby's hands.

'Baby, some of what you say is true, but it's unfair for you to throw class at me every time we fight. And tell me, Baby, do I run back to class for shelter? You are so critical of me. I can't please you, everything I do is wrong. Baby, please try to understand. I love my work. I am a good teacher, and the Black students need that model. They need to see us in positive roles. They need to see more than the pimps—prostitutes—junkies. You know if the school finds out I'm a lesbian, they'll find a reason to get rid of me. And don't even talk about the parents.' She was desperately trying to elicit some response from Baby.

Baby had piled the sweaters and jeans on the floor and was grabbing more clothes out of the closet and throwing them into a suitcase. Asha grabbed her. 'Baby, listen to me. Don't leave. We belong together. We've been together for three years. Why now, why break up now?'

'I can't take it any longer, Asha. I can't. We can't go on gay demos because someone from school might see you on TV. We can't do this, we can't do that. I'm tired. I don't want to live like this. I can't stop my life because some people hate Blacks. And I am bloody well not going to stop living my life because another group hates lesbians. No job will ever keep me in the closet.'

'Baby, are you saying I should just quit my job? Just walk out in the name of being a Black lesbian?'

'For God's sake, Asha, don't be so fucking dramatic. Live your life how you want. Stay in your closet. Me, I need fresh air. And if I have to fight for the right to enjoy it, then I will.'

'I'm not being dramatic, Baby. But what do you want me to do? Just go in tomorrow morning and say "Hey principal, hey fellow teachers, hey students, look at me. I'm a lesbian, have been all my life, just thought I should let you know." Is that what you want?'

'Asha, sometimes I don't know you. Honest to God. Who are you hiding from?' Her voice became softer. 'Asha, I love you. I want you to start living. I want us to start living.'

Baby was the first to hear the sound outside the bedroom door.

'It's only the cats, Baby,' Asha reassured her. 'They want to be in here with us, to feel everything is all right.' In a softer tone she added, 'Baby, they don't like it when we fight, when we get unhappy.' Asha pulled her close to kiss her. Baby didn't pull back. They dropped to the pile of clothes on the floor.

The man standing outside the bedroom door had come into the house through the kitchen window. He was of average height. He had black curly hair, cut close to his scalp. The right side of his mouth pulled up in a nervous twitch. He wore a pair of navy blue cotton shorts and a plain white cotton T-shirt. He wore no mask. He had a white plastic bag in his hand.

He was no stranger, had lived next door in a rooming-house for the past year, but was planning to go out West any day now. The women knew him, too. They didn't know his name, but he was a familiar face in the Hotspot, where they sometimes went to eat or have a beer. The Hotspot served as a hangout for locals. It carried a good Caribbean menu, Caribbean beers and rum. The Hotspot was always jammed – jobless neighbours dropped in on the way back from one more no-go interview. The ones with jobs came to cash a cheque, the hangers-on were there all day, waiting to strike it big in the lottery. The jukebox never stopped playing. The back room housed gamblers and folks with items to sell.

Some of the regular customers paid little notice to the two women who always came together. Others talked about them. The man hung around the Hotspot after work and on weekends, drinking beer and looking for a way to get in on the conversation of the regulars.

'When I win di lottery, I going home to soak up some of dat sun, buy a nice house, car and find myself a good woman.'

'My boss man is like a slave driver. I can't even take a leak without the supervisor coming to look for me.'

'They lay me off after twenty-five years' service and tell me times rough.'

'Bwoy, dem girls different. Dem need a good fuck. Can't understand how nice Black woman like dem get influence in dis lesbian business.'

'Nastiness man, nastiness. Satan work.'

He'd overheard the last comment many times. He'd watched the two women closely each time they came into the Hotspot. They had an independent streak about them. He didn't like it. They come to Canada and they adopt foreign ways, he thought to himself.

He stood silently outside their bedroom door now, fingering the shiny black gun he had removed from its plastic bag. It was a .38 calibre automatic he'd bought from a stranger at the Hotspot Restaurant. The seller was looking for cash, had to leave town in a hurry. The man had the money. 'Why not?' he'd said. Tonight he was going to put a stop to all this nastiness. He'd try to help them, and if they didn't listen, then they'd have to face the consequences. God never intended them to be this way. God wanted man and woman together.

'Oh, Baby, I don't want you to leave me,' whispered Asha. 'Love me for ever, Baby. Don't stop.'

'I won't. But Asha, save some of this for later. Don't let the well run dry,' Baby teased.

He could hear it all through the closed door. The gun was getting warm and sticky in his hand. The front of his shorts jumped like a trapped crab.

'What do you want me to do, Asha?'

'Baby, you know what I like best.' Without another word, she pushed Baby's head down.

The crab jumped higher. He switched the gun from hand to hand. He wanted to fire it through the door. He took the crab out of his pants to give it room. It was hard. He played with it, pulling and squeezing it.

Bitches, sluts, ungodly creatures. He intended to tie them up. Strap their legs against each other. Oh, he was going to teach them a lesson. Let them do those things to each other right before his eyes.

He was excited, the crab more restless, the gun hot in his hand.

Tie up them lezzies. Then fuck them. Let them feel what it's like to get fucked by a real man. He wished he had carried his knife so he could slit their throats, watch the red running down their tits.

The crab throbbed.

Bitches. Let the dirty bitches feel the right thing. He might even let one of them feel it in her mouth.

When he was finished with their bodies, he would rob them, take their money and jewellery. Use the silencer. Do a good clean job, then leave through the kitchen window. He'd already packed his few belongings. Leave early morning on the Greyhound bus. He was tired of his job as a security guard in the stinking rotten high-rise building in downtown Toronto anyway. He'd had enough of Toronto and its dirty filthy morals, its dirty filthy women, dirty filthy life. Things were different in Vancouver, he'd heard. Nice people, nice open land. Mountains and ocean. That's what he needed. A place like back home. A place big enough that he wouldn't have to see women like these, his own people, stooping to this.

Standing at the bedroom door, he was reminded of conversations he'd picked up on at the Hotspot.

'I would like to fuck dem girls. Give it to dem good in di ass.'

'Ass, boy? I want to throw dem legs over di shoulder and pump everything in.'

'Dem gal need to learn lessons. Man fi woman and woman fi man. None of this nastiness, none of this separation.'

The cats had come upstairs. They sat staring at him. He couldn't stand the goddam creatures. Hated their fur and their tongues.

'Can't stand the bitches,' he muttered, wanting to use the gun.

He could hear Asha and Baby clearly. Ignoring the cats as best as he could, he turned his mind to the crab. It couldn't wait. He jerked it back and forth, leaving a small puddle on the red carpet, only partly muffling the grunt that came from his mouth.

'Those damn cats,' Baby muttered.

'Leave them alone, Baby. They're just playing. In fact, they're watching over us. They're our guard cats.'

Asha and Baby had tumbled off the pile of clothes, wrapped around each other.

He stayed outside. The crab had gone to sleep and he was getting tired. They were so loud. Bitches. He'd give them a few more minutes.

Wait for them to start up again, then he would kick down the door and watch them.

'Asha, this doesn't change anything, you know.'

'What do you mean, Baby? What do you want me to do?'

'I love you, Asha, but this isn't the Middle Ages. For God's sake, get involved in a gay group for teachers, or something. I just can't live like this. I won't live like this. I'm tired, Asha.'

He was getting impatient. Too much arguing. He wished he had kicked the door in earlier. He should have done it when the crab was awake. He'd never wake it now.

The gun went back into the plastic bag. He walked down the stairs and climbed out through the kitchen window.

NEIL BISSOONDATH

Security

Alistair Ramgoolam stretched carefully out on the sofa in the living-room, the cushion under his head giving off a newness powerful enough to efface, at least momentarily, the thicker, sweeter scents of the incense sticks he had lit in the corner behind him. He clasped his hands on his paunch – the stomach medicine hadn't yet taken effect on his ulcer – and sighed. The sofa's smell, of factory plastic wrap and newly milled material, distressed him; it conjured up an unfamiliarity and a sense of dislocation he had never expected to experience. His children and his grandchildren, yes, but not he or his wife of so many years. He mumbled, in a voice of grumbling complaint, 'I knew we were insecure on that damned island.'

But only the television responded: 'Althea Wilson, come on down!' And Althea Wilson bounded convulsively from the audience, careered down the stairs, her heavy breasts leaping and swaying as if alive under her blouse, to the podium on the stage.

Mr Ramgoolam thought: Fool, why are you making such a spectacle of yourself? On national television, to boot? But a part of him envied her, coveted this opportunity for wealth that had so easily bartered itself for her dignity.

Althea Wilson squealed and squirmed before the microphone, as if called by nature and not permitted to answer. The television audience applauded, roared its approval of Althea Wilson, of her fellow competitors, of the silver-haired host recoiling with a febrile guardedness. Mr Ramgoolam could not push away the man's silver hair, his wrinkled face, the plasticized smile, and the eyes appalled by, disbelieving of, the thirsts he had unleashed.

Mr Ramgoolam shifted on to his side, away from the bright television, banishing from sight this vision of himself as he might be, as – he was uncomfortably aware – he had partly become. But he could not fully escape Althea Wilson, knew too well the dynamics of the emotion and the manipulated greed, needed too deeply the vicarious thrill of her excitement. His gaze drifted to the balcony doors, rectangles of black aluminum frame and double-glazed panes and wire-mesh screens. He could see the narrow balcony, his backyard now, and the sky grey and unfriendly beyond. These clouds, this deepening greyness: the sky seemed to weigh on him, encasing him like the heavy blankets he'd left behind on the bed not long before.

His wife had removed the drapes before going to work that morning, lifting with them a sense of cloister, baring the living-room to the sky and the clouds and the tops of taller buildings. Earlier that morning, peering through the dusty panes and squared wire-mesh, he had been able to see, as if for the first time because so long unseen, the solid, upward rush of the dense downtown, the trees still stripped to forlorn brown in the fading winter, the distant lake a grey horizontal smudge almost indistinct from the sky. It had been an enervating sight, and he could not prevent a rush of resentment against his wife, against the missing drapes, against the city itself.

Mr Ramgoolam thought with unease of the hours of television that lay ahead, the game shows and the movies and the discussions of beauty and sex. The weekdays were long for him. He had not, even after many months, grown accustomed to the endless stretches of being alone. On the island, someone had always been there: his mother, his wife, a maid. But now – curious thought – his wife went out to work. His eldest son – after years of residence here, Canadian to the point of strangeness – was at his desk in a big, black office tower downtown, a telephone receiver plastered to one ear, a computer terminal sitting luminescent on his desk. Vijay, his second son, having taken to life in the new country more avidly than his father would have guessed after the unhappiness of his university years, was out there somewhere, working on the deals that he mentioned only vaguely, keeping details to himself with a calculated display of irritation. His youngest son was at the university, studying a subject – something to do with electrical impulses in crab legs – that Mr Ramgoolam would have thought foolish were it not for the lucrative job offers his son, not even close to graduation, was already receiving.

Lately Mr Ramgoolam had begun dreaming his own fantasies of easy money, of untold, unearned riches. Every week he threw out handfuls of lottery tickets and horse-race stubs, stepping back from the sense of hope evaporated to the renewed possibilities of fresh numbers and fresh horses. Yet he had earned the right, he thought, had worked hard all his life and did not deserve to find himself returned, in the twilight of his life, to the moneyless uncertainties of his youth.

He closed his eyes, felt consciousness slip. A deep male voice boomed orgasmically over a set of new luggage. His awareness grew listless, and he sensed with nebulous pleasure the tentative encroachment of submerged images.

Images of bustle and fear. Of darkness buzzing with a confusion of rumours. Of shortened breath and the acidic seething of his ulcer.

Vijay, grown mysteriously from a wild-eyed teenager into a gloomy young man, a little extra skin on him now – he looked no longer simply like a rake, but like a rake draped loosely in a flesh-coloured garment – had quietly taken charge. Vijay had surprised his father with his cool efficiency, the effect, Mr Ramgoolam speculated, of the business degree he had paid so dearly for and which had seemed, in the years following Vijay's return to the island from Toronto, to have been utterly useless. But the boy had done well in the multiplying chaos. Had somehow, through whispered telephone calls and furtive car trips into the night, made what he called 'arrangements'.

'Arrangements?' Mr Ramgoolam had said. 'Arrangements for what?'

And he had put it well, the boy, with a subtlety Mr Ramgoolam appreciated even at the time, even as his wife crumpled tearfully into her handkerchief. Vijay had said, 'To go, Pa. To Toronto.' Not, Mr Ramgoolam noted, to *leave* but *go to*: the boy was forward-looking.

'When?'

'In two hours.'

'Two hours!'

'Two hours or nothing.'

'How?'

'By plane.'

'What plane? No planes comin' in these days.'

But Vijay had not replied, had simply gazed back at him with a look that was tired of questions.

Mrs Ramgoolam had said, 'Two hours? But, son, is not enough time to pack, we have too much –'

'Ma.' Vijay's voice was merciless. 'One person, one suitcase.'

Her mouth fell slowly open. 'One person, one suitcase?'

'But you jokin', son.' Mr Ramgoolam reached out a hand to support his wife. 'We live here all our lives, Vijay. How we going to put a lifetime in one suitcase?'

'Pack tight.' Vijay spun on his heel, headed for his bedroom.

Mr Ramgoolam was stunned. But he was, at the same time, pleased to note that his son had made his 'arrangements' as he himself had always conducted his business, deftly, with skill but without fanfare, knowing through experience slyly acquired which string to pull, which button to press. And presenting, then, a *fait accompli*. For the first time, he felt pride in Vijay, felt him to be his son in ways beyond the physical. It made the packing – a discarding of the sentimental in favour of the financial – easier.

Vijay, silent, tension channelled into activity of quiet bustle, loaded family and baggage into his Mercedes convertible. He remained indifferent to his mother's sobbing, seemed himself unmoved by considerations other than those of flight: so what if this was the house he'd grown up in? So what if his parents were leaving behind significant parts of themselves? Vijay's gloominess had nothing nostalgic about it. Mr Ramgoolam knew this about his son, appreciated it, understood that much of his strength – the strength here displayed – came from this bloodless practicality. But it disturbed him, nevertheless. He wished he could have seen in his son the merest hint of regret, the briefest glance backwards. But Vijay would make no concession, concentrated on the task at hand: the easing of the car from the driveway, the chaining of the gate that had to it the feel of ritual, senseless but comforting.

They seemed such a little group, Mr Ramgoolam thought, feeling suddenly vulnerable as they rushed through the quiet night, through its deceptions and its camouflaged perils. He sat in the front seat beside his son while his wife sat sniffling in the back seat beside their hand

–luggage, Vijay driving in his usual anarchic way, the darkness a spur to his recklessness. Mr Ramgoolam shut his eyes, the lids heavy and stinging against the lower rims.

Vijay had not put on the headlights. He didn't want to draw attention, pointed out he would spot the lights of oncoming vehicles before they saw him, would be able to avoid them with ease. Mr Ramgoolam wondered what would happen if the other driver had had the same idea as his son, but he said nothing – Vijay was in charge – and settled for not staring into the nocturnal void ahead. He opened his eyes only occasionally during the drive through the deserted streets, and the sight of blackened vehicles and smouldering ruins, the frantic dishevelment of wilful urban disorder, caused his ulcer to seethe. Only then did he realize that, in the haste of departure, he had neglected to bring along his bottle of stomach medicine.

The airplane flight, offering in its first minutes a distant glimpse of the city below aglow with dim electricity and angry flame, was an agony of pain and uncertainty. Mr Ramgoolam writhed in discomfort and Vijay, function fulfilled, responsibility relieved, lapsed into a reverie of alcohol and pills furtively consumed, while Mrs Ramgoolam seemed suddenly seized by a vein of energy her husband had thought long exhausted. A clearness appeared in her eyes, a sureness in her touch and her words, that made him think of youth. But it took him a while, days, weeks even, to realize that the change in her went much deeper; that she had shucked off a timidity he had always believed innate, as if leaving the island had unclipped her constraints and revealed a self concealed by the demands and expectations of family and of an island small enough to gossip into scandal the slightest deviation from the social code. And it was there, on the airplane, even as she did what little she could to ease his discomfort, that he sensed the shuffling of intangibles that was her taking possession of herself. That was, he saw later, her taking leave of him.

Their two other sons were waiting for them at the airport, smiles creasing through the strain on their faces. The eldest – thoughtful boy! – held a bottle of stomach medicine in his hand. It wasn't Mr Ramgoolam's usual brand, that wasn't available here, but a couple of quick gulps told him it was an effective one none the less. After the embraces and the tears and the murmurs of reassurance, he noticed that his sons had failed to bring coats and, having visited Toronto only in winter, having last seen the city in the aftermath of a blizzard, he began upbraiding them for the oversight: why, they would freeze to death without coats in this devil of a country, they should think of their poor mother, their brother, not to mention their long-suffering father, and – What's this? Laughing? Such insolence! You too, Vijay? You going to freeze, too, you know –

But it was the middle of July and outside, away from the air-conditioned comfort of the terminal, the day was as hot and as humid as the island they'd just left. Even his wife, patting at her forehead and neck with a perfumed handkerchief, twittered at him as they wended their way through the parking garage, the air seeming to suck perspiration from their pores.

When Vijay saw his elder brother's car, he was horrified. A Honda? Didn't he have any shame? Top of the line? So what? It wasn't a Mercedes, was it? He got in the front seat, with an unbecoming delicacy, while his younger brother squeezed into the back between their parents. Mr Ramgoolam, ulcer going dormant, suddenly felt like kicking Vijay. Mercedes? What nonsense was the boy talking? All that was gone now, didn't he realize? But he said nothing. He, too, had his regrets to deal with, his losses to mourn. They all did.

Applause exploded. The blond assistant, smiling through heavy make-up, held a camera up to the contestants. Althea Wilson stared hard. Thirty-five millimetre. Automatic focus. Automatic flash. Black, solid, compact. Great for those vacation shots! How much was it worth? Her brow crinkled into thick parallel cords; perspiration, bright and fresh in the television lights, laminated her skin.

'Two-fifty, you chupid woman,' Mr Ramgoolam muttered. 'Anybody know that.'

Althea Wilson hazarded five hundred.

Mr Ramgoolam sucked his teeth in disgust: Point a television camera at people and they go *bazody*, as if the lens suck out their brains.

A brace of pigeons fluttered on to the balcony railing. Mr Ramgoolam knew he should get up and shoo them away – given half a chance, they would cake the balcony in excrement that dried to the consistency of cement – but he couldn't, just then, be bothered. Pigeons, pigeon feathers, pigeon shit. His eldest son got very exercised over them, running on to the balcony flapping his arms and shouting when they threatened to alight; but Mr Ramgoolam figured that everybody – even birds – needed a safe place to land. Surely their wings would tire, he thought. Surely even pigeons, with their innate sense of direction, occasionally needed a point of reference from which they could reassure themselves of their place in the world.

He watched as the pigeons strutted stiffly on the rail, their round, red-rimmed, manic eyes darting around, oriented themselves, then one after the other plunged off as if diving to the earth. He sighed, noticing only then that he had held his breath throughout their presence, that he had managed in the tension of the long moment – looking for the little shot of excrement that he would have to clean up or risk the wrath of his eldest son – to ignore the abrasive fretting of his ulcer.

The bare windows open to a great barrenness: it was, he knew, his fault in the end. He was the one who had insisted on celebrating Divali in as traditional a manner as possible. He was the one who had ignored the infidel groans of his youngest son, the weary pleas of his wife, the cautions of his eldest son. He was the one who had appealed to an unresponsive Vijay and interpreted his silence as support. He, too, who had gone yesterday to the supermarket to buy the two dozen aluminum muffin cups. (In this pagan society you couldn't find *deeyas*, the little earthenware oil lamps that flickered an air of mystery over the altar.) It was he who had rolled the cottonwool wicks; who had distributed the cups filled with ghee around the living-room, making sure that the wicks were adequately soaked and well placed.

While his wife stirred and fried at various pots in the small kitchen; while his youngest son picked at the plates of sweets and appetizers laid out on the table; while Vijay sat hunched in a corner of the sofa smoking a cigarette of vaguely familiar scent; while his eldest son – deliberately, the father thought – worked late at the office, Mr Ramgoolam girded his loins in a dhoti and meandered around the living-room with a box of matches lighting his modern *deeyas*. The room blazed in the brilliance of the two dozen little flames. Mr Ramgoolam was pleased, was put in mind of his parents' house on Divali evening when much of their meagre

financial solvency was dissolved in hundreds of the little lights, unbroken
lines of them on window-sills, beside pathways, throughout the yard of
hardened clay, even along the branches of the mango tree. Spectacle for
the gods: the way lit, the house exalted.

Mr Ramgoolam stuck twenty incense sticks into a brass cuspidor filled
with potting soil and lit them. 'Ma! Ma!' he called to his wife. 'Come
look.'

Mrs Ramgoolam emerged from the kitchen, perspiring, eyes dull with
fatigue, wringing her hands in a towel. She looked around, smiled thinly,
said, 'It nice, Pa. Very nice. They lookin' like the real thing.' Then she
paused, her eyes blinking. 'But –'

Mr Ramgoolam's glow of achievement converted to irritation. 'But
what?' he demanded.

But she didn't have to tell him: already the living-room was hazy with
the smoke of the burning ghee.

His youngest son suggested opening the balcony door to let out some
of the smoke. Vijay remarked dreamily that it was a cold night. Instead,
Mr Ramgoolam opened the door to the corridor.

His eldest son arrived not two minutes later. He was alarmed. 'What's
going on here? The corridor's thick with smoke –'

'We just airin' out the place, son,' Mr Ramgoolam said. 'Look at the
deeyas, you don't find they pretty –'

'Jesus Christ, Pa, you can hardly breathe in here.'

'Is just temporary, son –'

His son, dropping his briefcase to the floor, swept his hands around
the living-room. 'We've got to put some of these lights out, Pa. Before
someone calls the fire department.'

Mrs Ramgoolam, suppressing a smile of relief, moved to the closest
deeya.

'No, no!' Mr Ramgoolam snatched at his wife's reaching arm. 'Is bad
luck to out a *deeya*, Ma, you don't know that? Don't –'

But he couldn't finish. His words were cut off by the hammering wail
of the fire alarm.

His eldest son covered his face with his hands.

His wife and youngest son whipped around the room extinguishing
the little fires.

Vijay, smiling benignly, remained where he was.

When the *deeyas* were all out, when the alarm had been turned off and the firemen sent away with apologies, when the neighbours had returned to their dinners and their television sets, Mr Ramgoolam stood in the middle of the living-room surveying the damage. The incense sticks continued their slow burn in the cuspidor, but his aluminum *deeyas* had gone cold and dark. The bad luck acquired was incalculable. And in the air cleared of smoke, he saw that the white walls and ceiling now swirled with elegant grey patterns; saw that the white drapes and his shirt and dhoti, and his wife's skirt, had greyed. Tissues were splattered black when he blew his nose, the water in the basin ran grey when he washed his face.

So it had been his fault when, this morning, his wife stood on a chair and unhooked the drapes for washing, when she unwittingly revealed this world to him, and him to this world. But still, he couldn't help feeling that she should have known better, that she should have had a bit more consideration for his bruised feelings and the imminence of their bad luck. He couldn't, despite himself and because of himself, restrain his resentment.

On the television, Althea Wilson pondered a trade: the camera for a hatbox.

'Take the box,' Mr Ramgoolam muttered. 'Take the box, you chupid woman.'

Mr Ramgoolam had wasted no time in attempting to create gainful employment, but he was hindered by the way in which his plans, so well laid, had failed to materialize. It had begun years before, with his eldest son's insistence on spending the Toronto nest-egg on a house. The healthy bank account, to Mr Ramgoolam's distress, had gone suddenly anorexic. He had had to become doubly creative in finding ways of smuggling money out of the island to make the monthly mortgage payments. His son, still at school at the time, had been too busy being independent, going to plays and operas and European films, to find a part-time job.

As the years passed, the value of the house rose almost madly, leaping and jumping for no apparent reason except greed in an overheated market. Mr Ramgoolam's initial anxiety eased, his confidence in his eldest son rising with each new quote received, with each new unsolicited offer to buy the house. Then one day, out of the blue, his son decided to sell the house, informing his father only after the deal had been finalized. Mr Ramgoolam would have preferred to hold on to it – the property not only seemed a phenomenal investment, but also reflected the traditional virtues of independence, stability, and self-reliance that Mr Ramgoolam had learned from his father – but his son had declared it too much trouble; the house was not new, there was always something that needed repairing, it claimed too much of his time. So he'd sold it to a yuppie – he had to explain the word to his father as someone young, rich, and foolish, someone, his father thought, rather like his son himself – and immediately rolled most of the substantial profit into a condominium, less room but less trouble, he'd explained, paying for it in cash.

So when the family arrived unexpectedly, little planning possible in the sudden cartwheeling of politics and fear, there was a place for them to go to, but little money available for them to live on. Mr Ramgoolam had hoped to use the excess from the sale to begin a humble business along the lines he knew best, import-export. But the money, a modest if not insignificant sum, was locked into a term deposit. There was nothing for him to work with.

He turned to the newspapers, discovering there, for the first time in his life, his lack of qualifications and the limitations of a high-school education that had ended almost half a century before. The employment requirements, long lines of incomprehensible terms linked by strings of undefined letters, bewildered him. He gravitated to the simpler jobs, to salaries progressively more modest.

His first job had promised *Progressive Working Conditions. Friendly Supportive Environment. Five Hundred to a Thousand Dollars a Week.* 'Canadians are thirsting for education!' the advertisement had assured him, painting a picture of millions of Canadians, crazed by educational deprivation, scrambling and fighting to place encyclopedia orders. He had trudged from door to unfriendly door for a week, encountering not a single person who lit up with relief and delight at his well-rehearsed opening gambit. Just one woman had invited him in, and only because she had mistaken him for a fellow Jehovah's Witness.

His second job – *Join Our Family! Generous Commissions! Twelve Hundred to Fifteen Hundred Dollars per Week! Free Transportation!* – had lasted for two weeks. Few people, he quickly discovered, were interested in owning an industrial-strength vacuum cleaner, especially once he had washed and groomed their rugs in demonstration. Surprising himself, he actually managed to sell one to a retired janitor, but it quickly became clear to him that most of the people who made demonstration appointments did so because they were old and retired and craved company; they usually could not afford the machine, or had failed to understand that this was a sales demonstration and resented learning the sad truth. And, yes, the company provided free transportation – the machine was heavy, and none of the salespeople he had met earned enough to acquire a car – but there were long waits for pick-up, anywhere from a half-hour to two hours. Sometimes he was served coffee and cookies by sympathetic, always talkative clients; more often than not he was politely but firmly ushered out to wait on the sidewalk. He quit in a huff the day the company van was an hour late, giving enough time for a storm to break, the rain soaking through his suit and through the box of his demonstration machine. The driver, a young man, himself a salesman, a believer in the school of hard sell and irritated by his own recent failures, had greeted Mr Ramgoolam's complaints with a distinct lack of sympathy.

At home later that evening, having changed out of his wet clothes and into his pyjamas, Mr Ramgoolam ran his hands through his damp hair, long silvered and now thinning as his father's had done in his final years, and told himself he was too old for such nonsense. He deserved a position of greater dignity and ease, had earned the right to be treated with respect, especially by pushy, half-educated, foul-mouthed puppies like the van driver.

He was up half the night nursing his burning ulcer, while his wife, solicitous but somehow too methodical, her touch and her words governed by a curious dispatch, ministered to him. When, in the silent hours of the early morning, he bemoaned their losses, when he spoke with pain of their jettisoned houses and cars, she sucked her teeth softly, brushed his hair back from his sweat-slicked forehead with her hand, and said, 'Shh, shh, is not a time to cry, we ain't have time to cry, we have to think 'bout tomorrow.'

And it was the next day, as he remained in bed with a raw throat and soaring temperature, that she went out without saying a word to him and applied for a job as a cook at the Indian restaurant on Bloor Street.

Mr Ramgoolam was infuriated and ashamed at the thought of his wife's working. She had never held a job before, had depended on him for money, she the homemaker, he the provider. And now suddenly, he was the one who remained at home, she the one who dressed and went out. Left to his own devices, he could not deal with the ensuing silence, could not fill the empty spaces by himself. He was grateful for the raucous intervention of the television. It offered company of a sort, helped hold back the deeper silence. And it provided, too, the soothing, if ephemeral and vicarious, fantasies of easy answers.

'A brand-new ... washing machine!'

Althea Wilson was stunned.

Mr Ramgoolam was disappointed. A washing machine: it was like finding jockey shorts under the tree on Christmas morning, or unwrapping a bottle of aftershave lotion on your birthday.

Oh well, he thought, at least she could sell it, pocket the cash. But he found her reaction overdone. It was embarrassing. The sum involved – a few hundred dollars, no more – was barely significant, it hardly justified a further diminution of dignity. He would have shown greater coolness, an I-can-take-it-or-leave-it attitude. But then, he realized, he had never done the wash; that had always been his wife's responsibility. He had no idea of the passion – yes, that was the word, judging by Althea Wilson's reaction – that a washing-machine could arouse in a woman. He was pleased for her when, with a flashing of lights and a clanging of bells, the machine was hers.

Outside, the day remained unfriendly. The thickening clouds had lost luminosity. From time to time, flurries, crazed by unexpected gusts of wind, hurtled down. A clutch of children's balloons lurched drunkenly across the sky.

Mr Ramgoolam thought, with distress, of his wife's going out into this day, into this weather that battered in subtle ways at her body, evoking aches and pains and new abrasions of rheumatism. He thought of her wrapped in a white apron, cutting and chopping and stirring pots not her own. This vision of her, and of the exhaustion she brought home every evening, ripped at him, confronted him with failures and inadequacies he had always attributed only to other people. She had never complained, his wife, had not once accused him of dereliction of husbandly duty. But she didn't have to. His silent self-accusation sufficed.

Althea Wilson stared glassy-eyed at a projected slide of a blue sea and a crescent of white sand dwarfed by a hotel of mammoth proportions. It was a beach such as Mr Ramgoolam had never seen: built up, industrialized. The male voice tripped over exotic foreign names. The audience caught its collective breath on cue.

Mr Ramgoolam thought of the beaches left behind, thought of plunging into warm, salty water, of playing cricket on the sand with his three sons, these boys whose lives he had so carefully nurtured, whose well-being he had so intensely fretted over. He had long known his sons to be distant from him, the major consequence of travel and education and lives led in foreign lands. The discovery years before had been a blow – his ulcer had grated for days, he had sipped at bottles of stomach medicine as at bottles of soft drink – but he had gradually grown to accept the distancing, even in his mellower moments to view it as a sign, distressing though it may have been, of his success as a father.

Now his wife too had grown remote, not through her own fault but through force of circumstance. Yet he could learn to live with even that.

Most frightening of all, though, was the realization that he too had grown away, not just from his sons, not just from his wife, but from himself. He no longer recognized himself, no longer knew who Alistair Ramgoolam was. Was he the independent businessman, proud of his self-sufficiency and success? No, not any more. Was he this man who spent more time than was healthy in front of a television set while his wife and sons went out to earn a living? No, he would not accept that, refused to believe it. But if he was neither of these, then just who was he? More and more, it seemed, he was the Alistair Ramgoolam of the sofa, the Alistair Ramgoolam who found haven in televised thrills of effortless acquisition and in childhood memories, ever sharper, cleansed of ringworm and scorpion stings and vicious parental beatings. It was an Alistair Ramgoolam he did not like. He was becoming the kind of man he had spent much of his life railing against, a man for whom he would have once used the word parasitic. Now, watching Althea Wilson sweat under the television lights, seeing her screw up her face in concentrated thought, acknowledging his own longing to be in her place, he thought it an odious word.

His luck, it had occurred to him, required a measure of divine intervention. He set about erecting, in the tiny den of the condominium apartment, an altar for his morning devotions. He hung various pictures of deities on the wall – the females fair and pink-cheeked, the males black to the point of blueness – constructing below them an altar of stacked milk crates smothered in a length of heavy drapery material.

He located most of the necessary implements in the little Indian-owned stores on Yonge Street, crowded enterprises of glutinous atmosphere and ingratiating service. He had not lingered. The turbaned men and saried women, people so obviously of India in their dress, in their smells, had unsettled him, for while he resembled them, was welcomed as one of them in Hindi, a language familiar to him only in a religious context, he felt himself to be different, found himself distrustful of them and wishing to flee.

But he had acquired enough of the brass vases and plates and idols and muffin cups to suit his needs, to more or less reconstruct the altar he had had at home. The result, a delicate blending of piety and paraphernalia necessary to the full exercise of his devotion, pleased him. There was no longer a dew-smothered garden in which to pick fresh flowers, but a daily trip to the convenience store provided the necessary. There was no longer a large yard in which to plant the *jhandi*, the little flags that fluttered at the top of towering bamboo stalks signalling the completion of devotional duty, but he had found an acceptable compromise in a package of wooden chopsticks and a plant-pot of soil tucked into a corner of the balcony.

Mr Ramgoolam thought of himself as a religious man, but not as a philosophical one. He was punctilious in his performance of ritual, but in obedience only to the talismanic, 'whatif' school of thought: whatif they – and *they* could be anyone with anything to say on religion, even contradictory information finding a home in his fears and uncertainties and still-powerful childhood sense of mystery – whatif they were right?

Whatif opening an umbrella in the house really brought bad luck? Whatif failure to propitiate the gods really attracted their anger? Whatif moving into a house on the astrologically wrong date really led to collapse and personal ruin, even death? Why take the chance? Why not do it all? Why not fulfil all the requirements, only occasionally onerous, and assure a maximum of protection?

He made little adjustments in his life. Beef was banned from the condominium, as was pork. No flesh – no fish, no chicken – was eaten on Fridays. Footwear was left at the door, incense sticks burnt every morning.

His wife paid little attention to his deepening devotions. She was just pleased that he was keeping himself occupied. His sons, less tolerant, protested mildly, but backed down before his adamant rules.

'You always did your pooja, Pa,' his youngest son said to him one evening after being upbraided for wearing his shoes in the living-room, 'but how come you never get into this incense and beef-banning and all this other shit before? How come now, here, of all places?'

But that was the point, Mr Ramgoolam pointed out with glee, wondering in an aside to his wife what all this education was doing to their children's brains. If they were all here now, in this foreign land, with insufficient money, with his mother slaving away in the kitchen of a Bloor Street restaurant, with his father having to put up with indignity after indignity in the little jobs he had tried, it was because they had led improper lives before. They had not prayed enough, they had eaten beef and pork, they had failed to consult the gods adequately. This – and Mr Ramgoolam strode to the window, gestured grandiloquently at the sweep of the city, at the soaring buildings, the dense greenery, the placid blue of the distant lake – this, all this, was their punishment.

His son grinned mischievously. 'If that's so, beat me more,' he said.

Mr Ramgoolam was not amused.

In bed that night, he lamented the inadequate upbringing his sons had received. 'We didn't bring them up as good Hindus, Ma, we didn't give them no culture. And now we payin' for it. Look at them, Ma, look at our sons. Barbarians, every one of them. Stuffin' themselves in restaurants with steak and hotdogs and hamburgers and –' But she was already asleep, head turned away from him, mouth opened in a gentle, riffling snore.

It was once more his youngest son – the scientist, as Mr Ramgoolam began sarcastically calling him – who precipitated a minor theological crisis by pointing out that all of his father's shoes and belts were made of leather: *dead cow skin*. An hour of meditation brought the answer, however: plastic around his waist and running shoes, leatherless, on his feet. His attempt to discard his wife's shoes – she had discovered him in the garbage room attempting to stuff a bag of her footwear into the chute – had met with a hard-eyed rejection.

And she had been less than sympathetic – her response was to twirl her index finger at her temple – when he admitted his growing resentment of the vacuum cleaner and the broom. He objected to the noise of the one, to the stiff man-made fibres of the other. He wished he could lay his hands on a *cocoyea* broom instead, he said, the implement made from the leaves of a dried coconut-tree branch, spines stripped and bound into a crude broom. It made a sweet, soft sound, a soothing swish that evoked in its trail the clucking of chickens and the distant bleat of a grazing goat. And, he claimed, it did a far better job than either vacuum cleaners or these unnatural, new-fangled gizmos. His wife was somewhat less than convinced, reminding him that his mother had used the *cocoyea* broom only to sweep the yard. Inside, she had used a regular, modern broom. Displeased, Mr Ramgoolam resorted in his irritation to sullying his mother's memory by declaring that her house had never really sparkled. 'And the yard was shinin' bright, I suppose?' his wife retorted.

'You coulda eat off it!' he hissed, locking himself away in the bathroom with his sense of his own foolishness.

Mr Ramgoolam began feeling, after a while, that in this unexpected deprivation he was single-handedly fighting a war of domestic skirmishes to uphold traditions which, he acknowledged, had meant little to him before but which suddenly, inexplicably, loomed in importance. Challenged by his sons, he could not explain their new value; could not, when confronted by his wife's weary hesitation, justify his renewed reliance on them; just knew that in this alien land, far from all that had created him, far from all that he had created, they were vital.

On Saturday mornings, Mr Ramgoolam would tune the radio to a program of popular Indian music, turning the volume up until the strains reached into every corner of the apartment. Sunday mornings brought a program of popular music and dance on the television, the saried hostess chattering in Hindi between numbers. Mr Ramgoolam would sit in the living-room, paying full attention to the programs, not understanding a word that was said or sung, not even really wishing to, simply letting the sounds wash over him, honing his sense of self, taking him back decades to the mystery and hubbub of his parents' religious gatherings: to huge cauldrons of food bubbling spicy aromas at blazing fires, to toothless old women singing and chattering as they stirred and sweated in the flickering light, to grizzled men drinking and arguing as they played cards and smoked marijuana cigarettes late into the night. It was always a disappointment when the programs ended and reality came full-force back at him in the form of a jingled advertisement for a hamburger chain or an unfamiliar airline. Then he would feel an ache just under his ribcage, and his ulcer would begin a gentle burn.

And he felt battered the Saturday morning that his eldest son awoke with a hangover to the insistent strains of Bombay film music. Indian female singers, his son had once remarked, all sounded as if they suffered from permanent nasal congestion. He propelled his father out to the balcony, pointed to the slash of blue lake in the distance, and said in a voice rasping with anger, 'You see that, Pa? That is not the Caribbean. You understand? That is *not* the Caribbean you're seeing there.'

It was from this loneliness, this sense of abandonment, that emerged Mr Ramgoolam's deepest worry: would his sons do for him after his death all that he had done for his parents after theirs? Would they – and, beyond this, *could* they, in this country – fulfil their cremation duties, feed his hungry and wandering soul, have themselves ritually shaved beside a river, dispatch his soul to wherever with the final farewell ceremony? He feared they would not, feared they had grown too far from him and from the past that was his. That they knew none of the reasons the ceremonies had to be performed did not disturb him – neither, after all, did he – but their remaining almost wilfully ignorant of even the simplest of the protective and supplicatory gestures conjured up paralysing visions of his soul left to the vagaries of an alien and forbidding void.

Mr Ramgoolam had never credited his imagination with much power; movies, whether in the cinema or on television, had never engaged him, usually lulled him into somnolence after ten or fifteen minutes; books could never hold his attention past the first four or five pages. The images sat dull in his mind, his imagination incapable of sharpening their vagueness into a reality deserving of serious consideration. But now, for the first time in his life, he could imagine only too well the fate that he feared awaited him: could feel himself floating free, out of control in a chilled darkness; could feel his mouth opening and closing in soundless appeals for rescue.

Althea Wilson and a friend would be going to Hawaii. And she was going to have a new camera to take her photographs with. And a set of new luggage to put her new designer wardrobe into. And a thousand dollars spending money. US, Mr Ramgoolam thought, quickly and automatically working out the exchange into Canadian dollars.

His ulcer crabbed at him, its heated pinch spreading and tightening from his belly to under his ribcage and beyond.

Althea Wilson jumped and jumped. She hugged the host, never noticing the momentary look of distaste that crossed his smiling face.

Mr Ramgoolam felt the vice-like grip of Althea Wilson fasten itself around his chest.

The host extricated himself, self-consciously straightening his jacket and tie.

Althea Wilson flung herself into the arms of a beaming relative.

Mr Ramgoolam was puzzled when he felt his breath leave him.

The television screen glowed brightly. The images grew indistinct, edges erasing themselves, light eating rapidly into Althea Wilson, the relatives who had run to join her, the host.

Mr Ramgoolam thought: The tube has blown. Tried to sit up on the sofa. Couldn't. His arms would not rise. Legs would not obey. Lungs would not expand.

Applause filled his head.

Alistair Ramgoolam, come on down!

He thought: But I'm not going down, it's up, I'm going up.

And he was blinded by the lights.

ALECIA McKENZIE

Full Stop

My grandmother writes without commas or full stops She writes My
Dear Carmen Greetings in Jesus Precious name Its so nice hearing from
you The time doesnt matter as long as we are in each others thoughts
Well Im here still holding on praying for a better way of living myself
We just have to keep hoping that our sweet Saviour helps us take each
day one at a time We know not what the future holds but we sure know
who holds the key and its a secret to him only so we just have to keep
praying to him Thanks very much for your letters and money You are
in my thoughts all along the way My knees are very weak now Old age
is on me now I have somebody to take me to church and back Thank
God for that Give regards to your hubby for me until I know him to
do so myself So keep sweet as always Cheerio for now and God Bless
Same old Grand Ma Scottie PS write your mother

   And I write back saying Grandma what do you mean by God bless
And whats this about weak knees You know youre fit as a fiddle Dont
let anybody fool you that 73 is old Normy is fine and he sends you his
love Enclosed is $75 Take care of yourself and I hope to be home one
of these days Love Carmen

   She writes back saying Dear Carmen I got your letter yesterday Why
are you writing me without punctuation Dont you know better Is that
what I worked hard and sent you to school for Dont let me down like
this Thanks for the money It came just in time to buy some paint for
the old shack here But its not enough to pay for a painter so Im going
to do the job myself with Gods help I pray for you every night that you
stay healthy and good I truly hope you make it home for Christmas at
least Love to your hubby God Bless and write your mother Same Grand
Ma Scottie

Dear Grandma,

Please don't go painting at your age. Enclosed is $100 to pay a painter. Remember the last time you painted the house you fell off the ladder? God didn't catch you then, and you spent weeks in the hospital and hated it. Please get someone. Normy sends his love.

Love,
Carmen

Dear Carmen God bless you for the money I put it in the bank You think Im too old to paint my own house The painters on this island are all thieves They charge you a cow and a horse and when theyre done you have to do it over Its better to do the job yourself from the start Child I heard from your mother the other day Shes now in London She wrote that the man shes now living with is working as a hotel doorman and that he really loves his uniform The damn fools She didnt ask a word about how I was doing and she didnt even send a red cent But you cant expect such people to change She said she wrote you many times and you havent replied You should write her She is still your mother Our Saviour says to forgive and forget I must leave you now in the hands of him from whom all blessings flow So keep sweet and take care Yours the same Grand Ma PS Dont make jokes about God not catching me You know better Write your mother and say hello to your hubby

Dear Grandma,

Sorry to take so long to write but I just changed jobs. I'm working at a bigger hospital now, but I'm on the night shift so it's hard to get time to sit down and do anything.

I'm sorry, but every time I try to write my 'mother', no words come. What do you say to somebody you've seen only once? As far as I'm concerned the person who raised me is my mother, and that's you.

I'm glad you managed to paint the house but please don't do it again. Old bones break easily, you know (smile). Enclosed is $75. Normy sends his love.

Love,
Carmen

My Dear Carmen Suppose our Saviour was to say that since Joseph raised him God is not his father Wouldnt God be upset Same for your mother You came from her and nothing can change that Forgive 7 times 7 our Good Lord said Thanks for the money I put half of it in the bank Your brother never writes not a line but Im used to it When last did you hear from him My love things on the island are getting worse but Im too old to move now The thieves are breaking into everybodys house but I suppose its the same in New York The Sweet Lord has spared my old shack But let anyone try to break in and see if I dont chop him up with this machete I keep under my bed Take care of yourself and say hello to hubby Remember to pray Write to your mother She would love to hear from you Same Grand Ma Scottie

Dear Grandma,

Enclosed is $200. Get somebody to put burglar bars over all the windows. Why don't you rent out one of the rooms so that at least you won't be alone in the house at nights?

I got another letter from my 'mother', saying she would love me to come over to England for a holiday. What would I do in England? With the little holidays I get, I'd rather come back home. Besides what would we have to talk about? She's almost a complete stranger to me.

I'm now on the day shift, by the way, which gives me a bit more time to myself in the evenings. Normy is fine. Maybe you'll even have a great-grandchild soon. We're thinking about it.

Love,

Carmen

PS. Richie called me a few days ago. He says he'll write soon.

Dear Carmen You shouldnt talk that way about your mother She was young when she had you and didnt know better I was the one who told her to let me raise you so that she could go to England for a better life for herself When she brought me Richie two years later that was a different story But the good Lord knows best Dont hold it against her Forgive us our sins as we forgive them that sin against us Her problem is that she was born a fool when it comes to men but not everybody can be smart Thank God for your brains my child I always knew you would be a lawyer doctor or Indian Chief ha ha ha I pray for you Thanks for the money you sent I bought a new mattress because the old one was really getting too soft You wouldn't believe the price of mattresses on this island these days I dont know how poor people manage But the Good Lord dont give us more than we can bear Say hello to your hubby and stop thinking about the baby and have it Youll soon be thirty and then youll have a really tough time Same Grand Ma Scottie PS I dont want anybody living with me in the house The people on this island will rob you blind And I dont like burglar bars God will protect me from evil

Dear Grandma,

You shouldn't rely too much on God these days. Please put up some burglar bars. I'm sending the money for it.

The job at the hospital is very stressful, especially when you're on emergency. You wouldn't believe the things people do to one another in New York. Believe me, you're much better off on the island.

By the way, I got a letter from your daughter the same day your letter came. She says she has a cyst in one eye and has to be operated on. She asked me what she should do, as if I'm an eye specialist. She also said she wants to come to New York for the operation. Don't they have plenty doctors in England? I wish she would leave me alone. Let her go to California where Richie is if she wants to do the operation in the States.

By the way, Normy and I have decided we're too busy now for children. So we've put it off for another couple of years. Lots of people have children when they're in their thirties without any problems. Don't be disappointed.

Love,

Carmen

My Dear Carmen Whats wrong with you The Lord said be fruitful and multiply Stop wasting time I would like to see your children before Our Saviour calls me onto him Keep that in mind Your mother wrote me too about the cyst I feel sorry for her but the Lord gives and the Lord takes away Maybe you should let her come and stay with you for just a little while Mr Bax up the road died last week and since I didnt have a thing to wear to the funeral I bought a dress with the money you sent The burglar bars will come another time It was a lovely funeral Everybody turned out We sang Closer My God To Thee Miss Gerdy told me I still have a good voice Did you know that I sang in a choir when I was younger Your mother did too before she met the no good boy your father I forget his name May he rest in peace Its a wonderful thing to give praise onto the Lord I hope you're still saying your prayers Kiss hubby for me and write your mother Same Grand Ma Scottie

Dear Grandma,

Sorry to hear about Mr Bax. He was a nice man. Remember how he always brought me and Richie mangoes from his Bombay tree?

By the way, did you give your daughter my telephone number? She called and said she's definitely coming to New York for the operation. I didn't even recognize her voice until she told me who she was. I'm sure I wouldn't recognize her if I saw her on the street. She says she isn't asking me to put her up, that she'll stay at a hotel. I hope she's already reserved a room because I don't have time for any foolishness.

Did you get a letter from Richie now? He phoned me not too long ago, said he got promoted to assistant manager at his job. He said he sent you some money for your birthday. Did you get my card?

Take care and write soon. Normy sends his love.

Love,

Carmen

My Dear Carmen I didnt get any letter from your brother Ask him if he remembered to post it Thanks for your card and the gift inside I put it in the bank When the Lord calls me this money will all come back to you because he that giveth shall receiveth and you have given me a lot in these years You have given me a lot of joy no matter what your mother may tell you Are you sure she is coming to America Child be careful of her for she is a snake in the grass But still she is your mother and Our Saviour says honour thy father and mother Im feeling very old these days and I would like to see you and get to know my grand son in law before He gathers me onto his bosom Write soon and be nice

to your mother when she comes even though it will be hard Same Grand
Ma Scottie

Dear Grandma,

Well, she showed up. Unfortunately I wasn't at home at the time so
Normy let her in. I almost had a heart attack when I got home and saw
her. She looks much younger than 47 and she was dressed to match.
She brought us lots of presents – bedspreads, tablecloths and all that
old British stuff. She acted as if I was her long lost baby. Do you know
what she said? She said that she and my father made an agreement with
you and that you broke it. She said that because they didn't have any
money when I was born they asked you to keep me for a while. Then
they went to England because there were jobs there. But soon she got
pregnant with Richie and had to bring him to you as well. She said that
when I was six and Richie was four, Daddy was killed on a construction
site. She said that afterwards she came back for us and you refused to
give us up. You hid us with your relatives in St Thomas, she said. She
also said that you hated Daddy from the start because he wouldn't go
to church. I don't believe her but she swears it's true. She cried the
whole night. Please tell me what really happened. I wish she hadn't come.
    Love,
    Carmen

My Dear Carmen Your mother was always a snake in the grass Dont
believe a word she says She and your father were not fit to raise you so
The Good Lord appointed me guardian He did not want you to be
raised in England so he gave you onto my care And look how fine youve
turned out.

Well I finally got a letter from Richard He said he couldnt write before
because he was working overtime he moved into a new apartment and
horse dead and cow fat Excuses and more excuses When are you coming
home I don't have much longer on this earth you know I can hardly
put one foot in front of the other these days Pray for me The thieves
on the island are getting really bold On Tuesday night they broke into
Miss Gerdys house although she has at least five dogs A mangy lot They
took everything they could lay their hands on and she slept right through

it Never heard a thing she said the next morning Im going to put up the burglar bars after all My dear remember the ten commandments and keep good and strong Kiss your hubby for me and tell your mother God bless Same Grand Ma Scottie

Notes on Authors

LOUISE (SIMONE) BENNETT was born in 1919 in Jamaica. She is identified with the folk culture and with years of struggle attempting to make 'dialect' acceptable to proponents of 'mainstream' culture. She is an accomplished performer, who trained at RADA from 1945 to 1947. She worked in English rep as well as in the USA on stage and radio. But, since 1955, much of her teaching and performances have been in Jamaica, resulting in many books of dialect verse (and stories), and long-playing records. The records include *The Honourable Miss Lou* (1980) and *Yes M'Dear* (1983). Louise Bennett now lives in Canada.

JAMES BERRY was born in 1924 in Jamaica, and was one of the early migrants to England (1948), having already spent some time in the USA. His interest in multi-cultural education has given him a pivotal role in Britain in reconciling Caribbean and 'black British' literary tendencies. Among the volumes of verse that he has edited are *Bluefoot Traveller* (1976; rev. ed. 1981) and *News For Babylon* (1984). His own collections of poetry include *Fractured Circles* (1979), *Lucy's Letter and Loving* (1982), *Chain of Days* (1985) and *Hot Earth, Cold Earth* (Selected Poems, 1995). Berry has won awards for his books of children's stories – the GLC/ Mary Seacole (1985) and the Smarties (1989). His *Anancy-Spiderman* was published in 1988. Berry received the OBE in 1990.

NEIL BISSOONDATH was born in 1955 in Trinidad. He read French at York University, Canada, and now lives and works in Toronto. His publications include two collections of short stories, *Digging Up the Mountains* (Toronto, Macmillan, 1985; Penguin, 1987) and *On the Eve of Uncertain Tomorrows* (Bloomsbury, 1990). His novel *A Casual Brutality* was published in 1988 by Bloomsbury.

KAMAU BRATHWAITE, born in 1930, is a distinguished poet, essayist and cultural historian from Barbados. In his two ground-breaking poetic trilogies starting with *The Arrivants* and ending with *X/Self*, he has redefined the Caribbean relationship with Africa. He coined the term 'nation language' to get rid of the pejorative connotations associated with 'dialect' and 'patois'. In *Dream Stories*, Kamau Brathwaite 'creates fiction from personal trauma and, in so doing, adds to the long tradition of dream journeying that stretches from Dante to Joseph Conrad'.

ERNA BRODBER was born in 1940 at Woodside, St Mary, Jamaica. She read history at the University of the West Indies and did graduate work in sociology in the USA, Canada and Jamaica. She is a freelance sociologist. She lives and works in Jamaica. Her publications include three novels, *Jane and Louisa Will Soon Come* (1980), *Myal* (1989) and *Louisiana* (1995), all published by New Beacon (London).

WAYNE BROWN, born in 1944 in Trinidad, is a poet and short-story writer. Educated at UWI, Mona, and at the University of Toronto, where he wrote a thesis on Sam Selvon, he has been a journalist (*Trinidad Guardian*), literary biographer (of Edna Manley) and editor (Derek Walcott). His volume of verse, *On The Coast*, came out in 1972. A second collection of poems, *Voyages*, and a collection of stories, *The Child of the Sea*, came out in 1990.

HAZEL D. CAMPBELL was born in 1940. She studied at the University of the West Indies in Jamaica. She has been employed at the Jamaica Information Service and has done freelance work in the media. She has published three short story collections, *The Rag Doll and Other Stories* (Kingston, Savacou, 1978), *Women's Tongue* (Kingston, Savacou, 1985) and *Singerman* (Leeds, Peepal Tree, 1992).

WILLI CHEN. His parents, John and Iris, came to Trinidad from the village of Tien Tsien in the Guandang Province of China. A businessman running a successful bakery and his own printing and packaging plant near San Fernando, Willi Chen is a painter who has also worked in ceramics and metal enamelling. Largely self-taught, Chen has won national drama, poetry and short story competitions. 'Moro' is taken from *King of the Carnival* (London, Hansib Printing Ltd, 1988).

AUSTIN CLARKE was born in 1934 in Barbados. He studied economics at the University of Toronto, and has taught in various universities in the USA. He has worked as a broadcaster, and has lived in Toronto since 1955. He is the author of six novels, including *The Meeting Point* (Heinemann, 1967), *Storm of Fortune* (Boston, Little, Brown, 1973) and *The Bigger Light* (Boston, Little, Brown, 1977), and an autobiographical memoir, *Growing Up Stupid under the Union Jack* (Toronto, Mclelland & Stewart, 1980). He has had three collections of short stories published: *When He was Free and Young and He Used to Wear Silks* (Toronto, Anansi, 1971), *When Women Rule* (Toronto, McClelland & Stewart, 1985) and *Nine Men Who Laughed* (Penguin Books Canada, 1986).

FRANK (APPLETON) COLLYMORE (1893 – 1980), from Barbados, was a short-story writer and poet alongside his other roles of teacher, actor and editor. He edited *Bim* for fifty-eight numbers from 1942 (no. 3) to 1975 – his eighty-second year. That George Lamming dedicated his seminal novel, *In the Castle of My Skin*, to his mother and to Frank Collymore reflects the influence Collymore had on the younger generation, most of whom he first published in *Bim*. His own books included *Notes for a Glossary of Words and Phrases of Barbadian Dialect* (1955), six volumes of poetry and a book of short stories, *The Man Who Loved Attending Funerals* (1993). Collymore was awarded the OBE in 1958.

LORNA GOODISON was born in 1947 in Kingston, Jamaica. She is a poet and painter. Her books of poems are *Tamarind Season* (Institute of Jamaica, 1980), *I am Becoming My Mother* (1986), which won the Americas Section of the British Airways Commonwealth Poetry Prize in 1986, and *Heartsease* (both New Beacon Books). *Baby Mother and the King of Swords* (Longman, 1990) is her first book of stories.

WILSON HARRIS was born in 1921 in British Guiana (Guyana). As a young man he led surveying and engineering expeditions into the heart of the Guiana rainforest and savannah. He came to England in 1959 and has published about twenty novels of singular distinction, including *Palace of the Peacock*, *The Guyana Quartet* and *The Carnival Trilogy*. He has reinterpreted many Amerindian myths and published volumes of criticism and numerous essays which have been a great influence on post-colonial theory and criticism.

CLYDE HOSEIN was born in 1940 in Trinidad. He has been employed in advertising, print journalism and the electronic media. He lived in London for a while, returned to Trinidad and now lives and works in Toronto. His publications include a collection of short stories, *The Killing of Nelson John* (London, London Magazine Editions, 1980).

C. L. R. JAMES (1901–89) was a Trinidadian writer, journalist, historian and political theorist. He was involved with Alfred Mendes and Albert Gomes in producing *Trinidad* and *The Beacon*. He worked in England as a cricket correspondent (1932–8) and then in the USA was active in the emergence of black politics. He published a novel, *Minty Alley* (1936), wrote a play, *Toussaint L'Ouverture* (1936), which is still staged, a memorable book on cricket, *Beyond a Boundary* (1963), and a seminal historical work, *The Black Jacobins* (1938). His numerous other works on literature, Marxism, the politics of Africa and the Caribbean have made him a central figure in Caribbean literary and political thought and in the extended east–west and north–south debates.

JAMAICA KINCAID was born in 1949 in St John's, Antigua, and spent her early years there. Her mother came originally from Dominica. She went to the United States in her teens to continue her education, and worked initially as a freelance writer, publishing articles in the *New Yorker*, *Ms*, *Rolling Stone* and *The Paris Review*. A staff writer for the *New Yorker* since 1976, she is the author of *At the Bottom of the River* (Picador, 1983), a collection of prose fiction which won the Morton Dawwen Zabel Award of the American Academy and Institute of Arts and Letters, the novels *Annie John* (Picador, 1985) and *Lucy* (1988). *A Small Place* (NY, Farrar, Straus & Giroux, 1988) is a witty, provocative, critique of her birthplace. She lives in New York.

EARL LOVELACE was born in 1935 in Toco, Trinidad, and grew up in Tobago and Port of Spain. He has studied and taught in the USA, and for some years taught at the University of the West Indies in Trinidad. His publications include *Jestina's Calypso and Other Plays* (Heinemann, 1984), a collection of short stories entitled *A Brief Conversion* (Heinemann,

1988) and four novels, *While Gods Are Falling* (Collins, 1965; Longman, 1984), *The Schoolmaster* (Heinemann, 1979; Collins, 1988), *The Dragon Can't Dance* (André Deutsch, 1979; Longman, 1981) and *The Wine of Astonishment* (André Deutsch, 1982; Heinemann, 1984).

CLAUDE McKAY (1889–1948), poet and novelist, was born in Jamaica and emigrated to the US in 1912. He travelled extensively in Europe and Africa. He published volumes of poetry, *Songs of Jamaica* and *Harlem Shadows* (both 1922). His first novel, *Home to Harlem* (1928), was a best-seller. Other novels and autobiographical writings followed, as well as a collection of short stories, *Gingertown* (1932). McKay was a leading figure of the Harlem renaissance of the 1920s, and is said to be the first West Indian writer, writing in English, to gain an international reputation.

ALECIA McKENZIE was born in Jamaica and educated at Alpha Academy in Kingston. She also studied at Troy State University in Alabama, and at Columbia University in New York. McKenzie has worked for various international news organizations, including The Wall Street Journal/Europe and InterPress Service. Her book of short stories, *Satellite City*, won the regional Commonwealth Writers Prize for Best First Book, Canada and the Caribbean. She currently teaches in Belgium at the Vrige Universiteit Brussel, Vesalius College.

ROGER MAIS (1905–55) was a Jamaican novelist whose book of short stories, *Listen, the Wind and Other Stories* (1986), was published posthumously. But it was as a journalist that Mais first attracted attention, earning a short jail sentence, in 1944, for publishing an article 'Now We Know' in the PNP journal *Public Opinion*. Involved in the nationalist movement, he wrote with passion and anger about people living in stressful circumstances in Kingston. His novels are *The Hills Were Joyful Together* (1953), *Brother Man* (1954) and *Black Lightning* (1955). He wrote many plays, and a collection of his unpublished work is held at the UWI library, Mona.

E. A. MARKHAM was born in 1939 in Montserrat. Since the mid-fifties he has lived mainly in Britain and Europe. He read English and philosophy at university. He has published several books of poetry, most recently *Misapprehensions* (Anvil, 1995), edited *Hinterland* (the Bloodaxe Book of

West Indian Verse) and published three collections of short stories, *Something Unusual* (London, Ambit Books, 1986), *Ten Stories* (Sheffield, PAVIC, 1994) and *Taking the Drawing-room through Customs* (Peepal Tree, 1996). Markham, who coordinates the Creative Writing Programme at Sheffield Hallam University, organizes the annual *Sheffield Thursday* poetry and short story competitions. He has edited several literary magazines including, at present, *Sheffield Thursday*. His travel book *A Papua New Guinea Sojourn: More Pleasures of Exile* is forthcoming (Carcanet).

PAULE MARSHALL, born in 1929, grew up in Brooklyn, New York, but both her parents were Barbadian and she has lived for long periods in the Caribbean. Many of her stories are about characters who are West Indian and who have West Indian connections. She has written three novels, *Brown Girl, Brownstones,* originally published in 1959 and reissued in 1981 by the Feminist Press, *The Chosen Place, The Timeless People* (NY, Harcourt, Brace & World, 1969) and *Praise Song for the Widow* (NY, Putnams, 1983). She has also produced a collection of stories, *Reena and Other Stories* (NY, Feminist Press, 1983), and a collection of novellas, *Soul Clap Hands and Sing* (1961). Paule Marshall has taught creative writing at Yale, Columbia, the University of Massachusetts (Boston) and at the Iowa Writers' Workshop. She lives in New York.

PAULINE MELVILLE, whose ancestry is Guyanese and Scottish, is a well-known actress of stage and film. Her poems have been published in anthologies, and 'You Left the Door Open' and 'Eat Labba and Drink Creek Water' are taken from her collection *Shape-shifter* (London, The Women's Press, 1990). *Shape-shifter* won both the Guardian Fiction Prize and the Macmillan Silver Pen Award, 1991.

SEEPERSAD NAIPAUL (or Nypal, in earlier transliterations from the Hindi) was a journalist on the *Trinidad Guardian*. He published a collection of stories, *Gurudeva and Other Indian Tales* (Trinidad, Guardian Commercial Printery, 1943) when he was thirty-six. Some of his stories were broadcast on Henry Swanzy's 'Caribbean Voices'. He was the first Caribbean writer of Indian descent who could be called professional in his attitudes, as attested by his redrafting. He died in 1953. (Seepersad is the father of V. S. and Shiva Naipaul and the great-uncle of Neil Bissoondath.)

V. S. NAIPAUL was born in 1932 in Chaguanas, Trinidad. He read English at Oxford and is the author of nine non-fiction books and twelve books of fiction, among them *Miguel Street* (André Deutsch, 1959), *A Flag on the Island* (André Deutsch, 1967) and *In A Free State* (André Deutsch, 1971) which includes short stories. He has won numerous awards for his work, including the David Cohen British Literature Prize in 1993. In 1990 he was knighted. He lives in the United Kingdom.

KENNETH VIDIA PARMASAD was born in Mayaro, Trinidad. He is a graduate of Mausica Teachers College at the University of the West Indies, St Augustine, where he obtained an MA in history. He is the author of a series of children's stories entitled *The Adventures of Ramu in Riverland*. The first in the series, 'The Broken Flute', was published in 1983. His *Salt and Roti: Indian Folk Tales of the Caribbean* (Trinidad, Sankh Productions, 1984) is an important contribution to the Caribbean folk tradition.

JEAN RHYS was born in 1894 in Dominica and came to England in her teens. After attending drama school, she drifted into a series of jobs – chorus girl, mannequin, artist's model – and lived in various European capitals. Jonathan Cape published *The Left Bank* (short stories) in 1927. Her work includes the novels *After Leaving Mr Mackenzie* (Cape, 1930), *Voyage in the Dark* (Constable, 1934), *Good Morning, Midnight* (Constable, 1939), and *Wide Sargasso Sea* (André Deutsch, 1966), which won the Royal Society Award and the W. H. Smith Award. In 1978 she received the CBE. Two collections of her short stories, *Tigers are Better-Looking* and *Sleep It Off, Lady*, were published by Deutsch in 1968 and 1976. A third, *Tales of the Wide Caribbean* (Heinemann), came out in 1985. She died in 1979.

GARTH ST OMER was born in 1931 in St Lucia, and was educated at UWI in Jamaica and also in France. He taught in Ghana for some time before going to the US in the early 1970s, where he is a professor at the University of California. His novels include *A Room on the Hill* (1968), *Shades of Grey* (1968), *Nor Any Country* (1969) and *J-, Black Bam and the Masqueraders* (1972).

ANDREW SALKEY (1928–95) was a Jamaican poet, novelist and children's writer. He is the author of five novels, at least nine books for children, three poetry collections and a collection of short stories, *Anancy's Score* (London, Bogle L'Ouverture Press, 1973). He also edited many anthologies of Caribbean writing including *Stories from the Caribbean* (Elek Books, 1965). From 1976 to 1995 he was Professor of Writing in the School of Humanities and Arts at Hampshire College, Amherst, Massachusetts. His awards include: Thomas Helmore Poetry Prize, John Simon Guggenheim Fellowship, Sri Chimnoy United Nations Poetry Award, Casa de las Americas Poetry Prize and Deutscher Kinderbuchpreis.

LAWRENCE SCOTT, born in 1943, is from Trinidad and Tobago, a Caribbean Creole. He came to England to be a Benedictine monk, but after studying philosophy and theology chose to leave the monastery and study for a London degree in English. He has taught English, drama and creative writing in schools and colleges in London and Trinidad. He has worked in the theatre in Trinidad. His novel, *Witchbroom*, was shortlisted for the 1993 Commonwealth Writers Prize. His story 'The House of Funerals' (included here), taken from *Ballad for the New World and Other Stories* (Heinemann, 1994), won the 1986 Tom Gallon Award. He lives in London and divides his working time between teaching English at the Islington Federal College and writing.

SAMUEL SELVON (1923–94) was born in south Trinidad. He is author of a short story collection, *Ways of Sunlight* (MacGibbon & Kee, 1957; Longman, 1973), and ten novels, including *A Brighter Sun* (London, Wingate, 1952; Longman, 1971), *The Lonely Londoners* (Wingate, 1956; Longman, 1972) and *Moses Ascending* (London, Davis Poynter, 1975; Heinemann, 1984). He was based in London from 1950 until 1978, and spent the last fifteen years of his life in Canada.

OLIVE SENIOR was born in 1941 in Jamaica. She studied journalism at Carleton University, Ottawa, and in the United Kingdom. Until recently she was editor of *Jamaica Journal* and managing director of the Institute of Jamaica Publications Ltd. Her books include *A–Z of Jamaican Heritage* (Kingston, Heinemann Caribbean & Gleaner Company, 1983), *Talking of Trees* (Kingston, Calabash, 1985, poems), *Summer Lightning and Other*

Stories (Longman, 1986), *Arrival of the Snake Woman and Other Stories* (Longman, 1989) and *Discerner of Hearts* (forthcoming). Olive Senior is a recipient of the Institute of Jamaica Centenary Medal for Creative Writing. She now lives in Canada.

MAKEDA SILVERA was born in Kingston, Jamaica, and spent her early years there before emigrating to Canada in 1967. Now living in Toronto, she is co-founder of Sister Vision: Black Women and Women of Colour Press, where she is the managing editor. Her previous publications include *Silenced*, an acclaimed collection of oral histories of Caribbean domestic workers in Canada; *Growing Up Black*, a resource guide for youth, and *Remembering G and Other Stories*, her first book of fiction. She is also the editor of *Piece of My Heart*, an anthology of writings by lesbians of colour. Her collection of stories *Her Head a Village, and Other Stories* was published by Press Gang Publishers, Vancouver, 1994.

SISTREN. A theatre collective, started in 1977; the names of the members are Vivette Lewis, Cerene Stephenson, Joan French, Lana Finikin, Lorna Haslam, Jennifer Williams, Pauline Crawford, Honor Ford Smith, Beverley Hanson, Beverley Elliot, Jerline Todd, Lillian Foster, May Thompson, Rebecca Knowles and Jasmin Smith.

ERIC WALROND (1898–1966) was born in Guyana and grew up in Barbados and Panama, and was educated in English and Spanish. Before going to New York in 1918 to study (literature and writing) at City College and Columbia University, he had worked as a reporter on the *Panama Star and Herald*. He worked on Marcus Garvey's newspaper *The Negro World*, but also circulated in the non-black literary world of Harlem. His collection of stories, *Tropic Death* (1926), was hailed as a significant event of the Harlem renaissance. Though supplied with funds and support to produce other work, he went to England, where he lived in obscurity and without publishing further.

N. D. WILLIAMS was born in 1942 in Guyana. He won the prestigious Casa de las Americas Prize for his first novel, *Ikael Torass*, in 1976. His collection of stories, *The Crying of Rainbirds*, appeared in 1992, and a novel *The Silence of Islands* in 1994. He lives in Canada.

WILFRED WOOD, born in 1936 in Barbados, is the Anglican Bishop of

Croydon. He was on the Archbishop of Canterbury's committee which produced the report *Faith in the City*, critical of government policies. 'God's Special Mark' is taken from *Keep the Faith, Baby* (Oxford, The Bible Reading Fellowship, 1994).

Acknowledgements

The editor and publishers wish to thank the following for permission to reprint copyright material:

Louise Bennett: to Bogle L'Ouverture Press for 'Anancy and Commonsense' from *Caribbean Folk Tales and Legends*, ed. Andrew Salkey (1980).

Kamau Brathwaite: to Longman Group Ltd for 'Dream Chad: A Story' from *Dream Stories*.

Erna Brodber: to Dangeroo Press for 'One Bubby Susan' from *Into the Nineties: Post Colonial Women's Writing*, eds. Rutherford, Jensen and Chew.

Hazel D. Campbell: to Peepal Tree Books for 'I-Calypso' from *Singerman* (1992).

Willi Chen: to Hansib Printing Ltd for 'Moro' from *King of the Carnival and Other Stories* (1988).

Frank Collymore: to The Hon. J. S. B. Dear, Attorney-at-Law, for 'The Man Who Loved Attending Funerals' from *The Man Who Loved Attending Funerals*.

Lorna Goodison: to Longman Group Ltd for 'Moon' from *Baby Mother and the King of Swords* (1990).

Wilson Harris: to Faber & Faber Ltd for 'The Laughter of the Wapishanas' from *The Age of the Rainmakers* (1971).

Clyde Hosein: to the author and Alan Ross for 'Crow' from *The Killing of Nelson John* (London Magazine Editions, 1980).

Claude McKay: to Carl Cowl, Administrator of The Archives of Claude

ACKNOWLEDGEMENTS

McKay, for 'Mattie and Her Sweetman' from *Gingertown* (Harper & Brothers, 1932).

Alecia McKenzie: to Longman Group Ltd for 'Full Stop' from *Satellite City and Other Stories* (1992).

Roger Mais: to Longman Group Ltd for 'Look Out' from *Listen, the Wind and Other Stories* (1986).

E. A. Markham: to the author for 'Miss Joyce and Bobcat' from *Ten Stories* (PAVIC, 1994).

Pauline Melville: to Aitken, Stone & Wylie Ltd for 'You Left the Door Open' and 'Eat Labba and Drink Creek Water' from *Shape-shifter*. First published by The Women's Press, 1990.

Seepersad Naipaul: to André Deutsch Ltd for 'My Uncle Dalloo' from *Adventures of Gurudeva and Other Stories* (1976).

V. S. Naipaul: to Aitken, Stone & Wylie Ltd for 'The Baker's Story' from *A Flag on the Island* (André Deutsch, 1967).

Jean Rhys: to Reed Books Ltd for 'Fishy Waters' from *Tales of the Wide Caribbean* (Heinemann, 1985).

Andrew Salkey: to Pat Salkey for stories from *Sketchbook Narratives Island* and for 'Anancy and Jeffrey Amherst'.

Lawrence Scott: to Heinemann Publishers (Oxford) Ltd for 'The House of Funerals' from *Ballad for the New World and Other Stories* (1994).

Sam Selvon: to Susheila Nasta, Literary Representative for Sam Selvon, for 'Song of Sixpence' and 'My Girl and the City'.

Olive Senior: to Longman Group Ltd for 'Country of the One Eye God' from *Summer Lightning and Other Stories* (1986); and to Canadian Publishers, McClelland & Stewart, Toronto, for 'You Think I Mad, Miss?' from *Discerner of Hearts*.

Makeda Silvera: to Press Gang Publishers for 'Baby' from *Her Head a Village and Other Stories*.

Eric Walrond: to Liveright Publishing Corporation for 'The Wharf Rats' from *Tropic Death*. Copyright 1926 by Boni & Liveright, Inc., renewed 1954 by Eric Walrond.

N. D. Williams: to Peepal Tree Books for 'Cats in the Eyes of the Pig' from *The Crying of Rainbirds* (1992).

Dr Wilfred Wood: to the author and the Bible Reading Fellowship for 'God's Special Mark'.

Every effort has been made to trace or contact all copyright holders, and the publishers will be pleased to correct any omissions brought to their notice at the earliest opportunity.